## DEMON'S LAW

'What are you afraid of?' the bard suddenly demanded. 'Why do you hide in a closed city, behind walls, and bars and water? What is it the great God of Death fears?'

Mannam turned away and strode rustling across the floor to stand before the window. The shadows danced as Paedur chased after him, but the Dark Lord cast no shadow.

'Tell me,' he demanded, reaching out to grip the god's arm.

The dry, faintly musty air of the room was suddenly charged with a sharp, acrid, faintly metallic odour. A mite of blue-white fire sparked from beneath Mannam's cowl and raced along the bard's hook, sizzling up his arm, twisting him around in soundless agony and flinging him across the room.

'Never touch me, mortal,' Mannam crackled.

# Demon's Law

## Tales of the Bard
### Volume Two

**Michael Scott**

SPHERE BOOKS LIMITED

**SPHERE BOOKS LIMITED**

Published by the Penguin Group
27 Wrights Lane, London W8 5TZ, England
Viking Penguin Inc., 40 West 23rd Street, New York, New York 10010, USA
Penguin Books Australia Ltd, Ringwood, Victoria, Australia
Penguin Books Canada Ltd, 2801 John Street, Markham, Ontario, Canada L3R 1B4
Penguin Books (NZ) Ltd, 182–190 Wairau Road, Auckland 10, New Zealand

Penguin Books Ltd, Registered Offices: Harmondsworth, Middlesex, England

First published in Great Britain by Sphere Books Ltd 1988

Printed and bound in Great Britain by
Richard Clay Ltd, Bungay, Suffolk
Filmset in 10½/11½ Monophoto Times

**For
the One that is All**

## List of the Gods

PANTHEON OF THE OLD FAITH

**Lady Adur**   Goddess of Nature; sister of Quilida
**Alile**   the Judge Impartial; Judger of Souls
**Bainte**   Winged messengers of Death, servants of Mannam
**Baistigh**   Lord of Thunder
**Buiva**   God of War and Warriors, the Warrior
**Cam**   God of Bridges
**C'lte, Qua'lte and Sa'lte**   The Triad of Life
**Coulide Dream-Maker**   God of Dreams
**Lady Dannu**   Prime female deity
**Ectoraige**   God of Learning and Knowledge
**Faurm**   Sea God; brother of Faurug
**Faurug**   The Nightwind
**Feitigh**   The Windlord, father of Faurm and Faurug
**Fiarle**   The Little God of Icy Spaces
**Hanor and Hara**   The First Great Gods
**Huide**   The Little God of Summer Rain
**Luid**   Fire Sprite
**Lady Lussa**   Goddess of the Moon
**Maker and User**   The Early Gods
**Mannam of the Silent World**   The Lord of the Dead
**Maurug**   The Destroyer
**Nameless God**   God of Madness and Delusion
**Nusas**   The Sun God
**Ochrann**   God of Medicine and Healing
**Oigne and Uide**   Gods of Cities
**Quilida**   Goddess of Growth
**Shoan**   The Smith
**Sleed**   The Maker of Mountains
**Snaitle**   The Cold God
**The Stormlord**   Unnamed God of Storms
**Taisce**   The Dewspreader

**Tatocci**   God of Fools
**Uimfe**   The Lord of Night
**Visslea**   The Spirit of the Mists


## GODS OF THE NEW RELIGION

**Aiaida**   Lord of the Sea Wind
**Hercosis**   The Dreamlord; one of the twelve Trialdone
**Hirwas**   God of Far Seeing; one of the twelve Trialdone
**Kloor**   God of War
**Libellius**   God of Death
**Quatatal**   Bronze Sun God
**Tixs**   Bat God; a minor godling
**Trialos**   The New God


## OTHER GODS

**Aonteketi**
   Six great birds that were once Gods of the Pantheon
   1 Scmall: The Spirit of the Clouds
   2 Kloca: Lord of Stone and Rock
   3 Aistigh: Lord of Subtle Harmonies; brother of Danta
   4 Danta: Lord of Verse
   5 Dore: Lord of Smiths (silver and goldsmiths)
   6 Fifhe: Lady of Beasts; daughter of Lady Adur
**Bor**   The Man God
**Chriocht the Carpenter**   Halfling carpenter of the Gods of the Pantheon; brother of Toriocht
**Lutann**   Demon God
**Quisleedor**   Life Child of Sleed, the Maker of Mountains (*see* Pantheon of the Old Faith)
**Sinn**   Mist Demon, Sun God
**Toriocht the Smith**   Halfling smith to the Gods of the Pantheon

## PRIMAL SPIRITS

**Chrystallis**   The wind that blew through the soul of the One; the Soulwind
**The One**   The First Being
**The Three Cords**   Disruption, Annihilation and Chaos

**Duaite**   Collective name for evil spirits; Duaiteoiri (singular)
**Auithe**   Collective name for good spirits; Auitheoiri (singular)

# Demon's Law

## Tales of the Bard

# Prologue

There are gaps in the life of Paedur the Bard, many gaps, and later bards and storytellers have made much of these, creating the most fantastical adventures for the Champion of the Old Faith.

The first major absence takes place almost at the beginning of his career, shortly after he returned from the Culai Isle. There are accounts of him in Maante, the seacoast town, and without exception they speak of this terrifying, awesome man, whose eyes were like polished mirrors and who radiated crackling power. And then one day he simply vanished.

It is important to remember that this was the Time of Cataclysm. The Chronicles speak of it as a time '. . . when the seas boiled and rose; lowlands were lost beneath the waves, islands sank without trace and others rose where none had been before. Mountains fell and rose again in new configurations and open-mouthed cones spewed forth burning filth while the northern and southern ice-caps shifted, crashing into the warming seas, melting, beginning the Flood.

'It was a time of Heroes, of Gods and Demons, when creatures out of myth, out of time, walked the world once again. It was a time when the world changed, a time of war and revolution, when Empires crumbled and were reborn, a time of death, disease and famine. .

'History has left us some of the names of those who lived and died in those evil times, of those who helped sculpt the shaken world. Some were mortal men, others more than human . . .'

The first of the legends surrounding him began then, tales of demons and devils, of assassins and murder, but in truth no-one really knew what had happened to the bard. Until now.

*Life of Paedur, the Bard*

# 1  The Silent Wood

Tradition tells us that the forest is now stone, but it has not always been so. In the days when the world was young it had once been a great forest, covering the land for leagues in every direction. But in that time when the Gods fought for control of the Planes of Existence, the trees had been warped and deformed by their magics and powers into grotesque and hideous shapes, and then the Gods and Goddesses of Life had abandoned them, revolted by their appearance, leaving them frozen. The place had become an abomination, and in an act of awesome destruction the ground had split and the frozen forest had been forever sundered from the world of Men by a Gorge of immeasurable depth. The forest was divided, the frozen trees marching to the very edge of the cliff, the last trees actually clinging to the lip, overlooking the Gorge, while on the far side, what remained unsullied and untouched grew normally.

No-one knows the extent of the forest of stone, nor the length nor width of the Gorge, although there are stories which measure the length by several days' journey, but no man ever tells of having completed it. For the Gorge defines the limits of the Silent Wood, the abode of Death, and its dread denizens walk its borders.

No-one has ever been foolish enough to attempt to build a bridge between the two worlds, that of Life and Death, for who knows what might walk from its grey domain to feed on the living. But there is a bridge of sorts – and perhaps it was the gods themselves that uprooted one of the great trees of stone and flung it across the Gorge, bridging the gap.

It was a temptation, and a temptation that proved too strong for many. They have walked the bridge of granite wood into Death's Domain – and never returned . . .

*Lilis' Geographica*

A figure crouched in the fringe of forest on the edge of the Gorge, still and silent, watching. The man touched one of the trees, the bark rough beneath his calloused hands, feeling the life coursing through the wood and swirling in eddies and circles around him as the forest hissed and whispered in the breeze. He drew a little of the life to himself, feeding on the sensation, the part of him that was still human taking a small pleasure from the richness of the air, and the myriad odours of the forest.

He allowed his senses to expand, taking in the sights and sounds, scents and hidden pulses of the living forest, becoming part of them, and then he deliberately closed his mind to the sounds of life and the creatures that swarmed in the earth and moved along the ground and nestled in the trees. Without their noisy, colourful intrusion on his senses he looked across the Gorge towards the petrified forest – and saw a shifting grey wall of fog!

With his human eyes he could see the grey pillars of stone, but with his enhanced senses he was blind. Paedur the Bard smiled grimly; it seemed everyone entered Death's Domain on equal terms. Pulling his furred cloak higher on his shoulders, the tall, thin man stepped out from the concealment of the trees and took the two steps necessary to stand on the fallen stone tree that acted as a bridge between the worlds.

If he had expected something – a tingling of power, an aura of arcane forces – then he was disappointed. There was nothing; it was merely stone beneath his booted feet. And so, slowly, carefully, checking every step on the stone-smooth bark, he moved out from the safety of the living forest and over the Gorge. The wind plucked at him then, ice-cold and tainted with the unmistakable fetor of death and decay, whipping his cloak around his legs, pulling at his long fine hair, dragging it across his thin, sharp-boned face. With the hook that took the place of his left hand, he dragged it back and, although reason told him not to look down, he still retained the all-too human failing of curiosity.

The walls of the Gorge were glassy smooth, as if the earth and rock had been seared by some incredible heat, and they fell away below into an abyss that at first glance seemed bottomless. However, as his eyes adjusted to the gloom, Paedur spotted the fires – scores of huge, blazing bonfires on the floor of the pit. Although he knew it shouldn't be possible, he thought he saw movement around the flames, as if figures were dancing before the fires. The breeze wafting up from the pit was heavy with a thick, cloying, vaguely unpleasant odour, like rotting fruit, and carried on it a tremulous sighing, which might have been the wind, or the moaning of scores of souls in mortal torment. He had seen the damned.

He looked away, recognising the danger of staring too long or too deeply into the pit, and turned his attention to the petrified forest that lay ahead of him. It was only as he approached it that he realised that it was not, in the true sense of the word, a forest. A forest suggested trees with leaves and bushes, grasses, vines and weeds, while this place had none of that. Now only the stark columns of the trees remained, most without branches, all without leaves, and where there had once been grass and weeds there was now nothing more than grit and slates and a powdered grey dust that covered everything.

Paedur hesitated before stepping off the makeshift bridge, waiting, listening, watching. But there was no movement within the petrified forest, no sound.

And yet he knew that that appearance was a lie. For the Silent Wood was the abode of the dead, the Kingdom of Mannam, the Dark Lord, the Lord of the Dead, and it teemed with life – if it could be called life. But perhaps here, close to the edge of the world of Life, the dwellers of the Silent Wood didn't care to venture.

Before he took the final step off the bridge, Paedur stooped slightly and pulled a long-bladed knife from the sheath sewn into his high boot, but he kept it concealed beneath his cloak. Away from the Gorge, the gusting foul wind died and there was no sound now but the crunch of gravel beneath his booted feet. Now that his enhanced senses – the gifts of the god C'lte – had been numbed and he was once again relying on his purely human senses, he realised for the first time how much he had come to rely on and accept the advantages they gave him. Without them he felt naked. He knew again what it was like to be human, although he was still without a human's capacity for emotion – that had been the price of his god-touched arcane senses.

The frozen stone trees stretched without a break in every direction, distance turning them into a solid grey wall, menacing and formidable, with the knots and boles of the trees assuming vaguely human features when looked at quickly. The branches of most were gone, either lopped off for some unimaginable purpose by the forest dwellers or else fallen to the ground under their own weight. He looked at the mass of trees and realised that it would be all too easy for him to become disorientated and lost within the grey sameness of the wood – then it would be only a matter of time before he joined the dwellers in the wood in earnest. He reviewed what he knew of the Silent Wood, what his myth and legend-lore told him, and found it was precious little.

The Silent Wood was the place where the souls of the dead dwelt until they had been adjudged by Alile, the Judge Impartial, and sentenced, either to the Broken Mountain to dwell with the Triad of Life or cast down into damnation in the Gorge. But while they remained unjudged within the confines of the Silent Wood, they were under the command of Mannam, the Lord of the Dead, a seared and withered creature who had assumed all the characteristics of his dead trees.

Legend spoke of peoples of all races and times still carrying on a semblance of life within the Silent Wood, kings and peasants, warriors and priests, all living out an eternal parody of their days in the World of Men, perhaps even unaware that they were dead, their kingdoms dust, their times long forgotten.

There was even a tale that Mannam deliberately kept the finest the World of Men had to offer, the wisest kings, the bravest warriors, the most powerful magicians, the most knowledgeable bards, and ruled them himself . . .

But no-one knew for certain, for no-one had ever returned from the Land of the Dead to speak of its wonders. And the bard wondered, would he too fail to return from Mannam's dead kingdom?

He spotted the track almost immediately; it was a mere discoloration, a slight curvature of the ground, but he knew a track when he saw one. He crossed to it, his feet crunching on the grit. It was broad enough for a man-track too; animals usually travelled single-file along an established run. Without hesitation he stepped on to it, and had taken barely two steps when the creature stepped out from behind a tree.

Paedur froze, dismayed that he hadn't sensed the presence of the creature. It was his height, standing on two legs and vaguely man-like, and covered in broad, shimmering, white scales that ran the length of its body but left its arms and legs free, and these were covered in a wrinkled pale hide. Its surprisingly slender feet ended in a single spike and its paws were two spiked pincers. Its head was huge and flat, with two sharply curving horns beginning alongside the eyes and almost meeting above its head. The eyes were tiny amber beads, deep-sunk into its skull, and the rest of the features were lost behind a mask of fine grizzled hair.

They stared at one another for perhaps a score of pounding heartbeats and then the creature deliberately stepped away from the man, paused, and then suddenly darted forward, two curved blades appearing in its misshapen paws. Paedur held his ground, both arms still concealed beneath his cloak, and something that resembled a smile touched his lips – this was something he could deal with. When the two curved blades had begun their whistling descent, the longer of the two cutting horizontally, the shorter, vertically, the bard moved. His deeply curved hook shot out, catching the long blade, snapping it down, while he pivoted on his heel, spinning in a half circle, smashing his back into the creature and allowing his attacker's arm to snap across his shoulder, the force of the blow knocking the sword from its paw. Paedur then rammed the knife in his right hand into the creature's underbelly. The blade scraped, screamed and snapped!

The creature grunted and smashed its head into the base of Paedur's skull, throwing him forward and on to the stony ground, and Paedur remembered what pain was. He hadn't experienced such pain in a long time and its very intensity shocked him motionless. He was dimly aware that the creature was moving closer. His body reacted automatically, rolling him to one side as the long blade hissed through the air where his neck had been. He scrambled to his feet, his head pounding, tiny spots of colour dancing before his eyes, his left arm held up across his body, the wickedly curved hook dull metal in the wan light.

The creature was now holding the sword in both hands weaving the blade to and fro in a move designed to draw the eye, cutting patterns on the air. It had lost its shortsword in their brief encounter but the very length of its longsword lent it a great advantage. The bard had broken his knife – he could see the scar across the creature's scales – and his only weapon now was the hook. The creature moved suddenly; emitting a terrifying scream it cut at the bard, the blade held high in both hands. Paedur immediately threw himself forward, rolling to his feet almost alongside the creature and inside the sword cut. His left arm punched up, catching the creature under the chin, the curved hook seeking a spot to sink into so as to rip and tear. The blade scraped and then caught. Paedur twisted his hand, securing the hold and then pulled. And ripped the creature's head off!

Even while he retained all his human characteristics, Paedur had long considered himself to have lost the capacity for surprise, and he looked now in astonishment as the head spun slowly through the air, the eyes empty, the neck bloodless . . .

Once again only his extraordinary reflexes saved him. He fell forward as the curved sword whistled over his head, so close he could feel the tug on his scalp as it cut through a lock of hair. He continued rolling, finally coming to his feet a score of paces away from the creature ... and then he received his second shock. He was looking at a cold-eyed, snow-haired woman. From the neck down she was still the scaled creature, but her head was that of a woman.

She spat something at him, the accent strange and sibilant but the words vaguely familiar, and then she snapped the sword up, the blade horizontal, level with her amber-coloured eyes, both hands wrapped round the long hilt.

And Paedur suddenly realised what she was. She was Katan, a warrior-maid, a member of the legendary Guard of Churon the Onelord. The legends spoke of their fabulous terrifying armour, the cast-off skin of the ice-serpents of Thusal. But the last of the Katan had died defending their lord on the Sand Plain in the battle with the Shemmatae several hundred years previously.

The woman took a step forward, her eyes never leaving his face, the sword in her hand rigid and unwavering. Paedur desperately sorted through his lore, sifting the various tongues and variants he knew, trying to establish a language she would have been familar with when she had lived.

'I mean you no harm,' he attempted, watching her eyes for a flicker of comprehension, and then repeated the sentence again and again in a score of languages. Finally he tried it in the Shemmat tongue, the language of the invaders she had died defending the land from. Her reaction was immediate. She attacked furiously, the blade coming in fast and low, the move designed to disembowel. Again, Paedur caught the sword on his hook, sparks shivering along the blade, but the force of the blow almost tore the hook from the bone of his arm. She cut again, high this time, and then changed the move as the weapon darted in, dropping the blade, slashing across his chest. It struck his furred cloak – with the sound of metal on metal, the force of the blow ripping the weapon from her numbed hands. And then Paedur was behind her, his hook completely encircling her slender throat, the point resting coolly beneath her ear.

'Move,' he hissed in Shemmat, 'and I will rip your head off.' He felt her stiffen, but she remained still and unmoving. 'Now, I am not of the Shemmatae,' he continued evenly. 'I merely chose their tongue because I thought you would understand it. If you give me your race, I may know that language.'

She remained silent so long that Paedur had actually opened his mouth to speak again when the woman spat one word. 'Lostrice!' Lostrice was the southernmost of the Seven Nations.

Her sibilant accent suddenly became comprehensible and Paedur was familiar enough with the three huge volumes of myths from the southern lands that had been collected by previous generations of wandering bards to know enough of the tongue to communicate.

'I am Paedur, a bard,' he said in that language.

'A bard?' she said after another silence.

'A bard.'

He carefully lifted away his hook and then quickly stepped away from the woman. When she turned to look at him, he lifted his cloak, revealing the triangular bardic sigil high on his left shoulder. He had no doubts but that the woman would be familiar with it; the sigil had remained unchanged for nearly two thousand years.

'Why did you attack me?' he asked finally.

'I guard the Way,' she said simply.

Paedur hooked the toe of his scuffed boot under the woman's shortsword, which was by his feet, and flipped it towards her. She deftly caught it and then pulled out a short length of white linen, which she used to wipe the blade clean before smoothly sliding it back into its scabbard. Still facing the bard she looked around for her longsword.

Paedur smiled, the movement transforming his face. 'Will you attack me again?'

'I guard the Way,' she repeated.

'From what?' he asked.

'From the humankind of the World of Life,' she said.

'I am from the World of Life,' Paedur said with a wry smile, 'but I am not wholly human.'

The Katan stared at him for a few moments and then she turned and went to where her sword had fallen. She sank on to the ground beside it, her legs folding gracefully beneath her, her oiled, supple armour settling noiselessly around her, and she began to wipe the blade. When she looked up at the bard again, there was something like humour in her amber eyes. 'No, I suppose you're not. No single human would have been able to defeat me.'

Paedur sat on the hard ground, not even feeling the grit and stones beneath him, well used to the rigours of the road by now. 'You haven't told me your name,' he said finally.

'What use are names in the Land of the Dead?' she said fiercely, and then lowered her gaze and continued polishing her sword.

'You realise you are dead, then?' Paedur asked.

'Of course,' she said in surprise. 'Whatever made you think I didn't?'

Paedur shrugged. 'I thought you might still be carrying out the role you pursued in the World of Men, unaware of your death.'

The warrior-maid slid her longsword home with a click. 'No. There are some who cannot accept that they have passed into another world, but they are very few.'

'You still haven't told me your name,' Paedur reminded her.

The woman smiled. 'I have told you that names are unimportant.'

'But you had a name?' he persisted.

'Once.'

He continued looking at her.

'You may call me Katani.'

'I thought that was the title of your warrior-caste.'

'It was, but I am all that is left now. The rest of my sisters accepted their judgement at Alile's hands and went their various ways. Only I remain.'

'Why?' he wondered.

'Because when I have been judged by Alile, the Judge Impartial, then I will be truly dead. This way I still have a chance.'

'A chance for what?' he asked.

'Why, for battle,' she said, her amber eyes opening wide in surprise. 'I was raised and trained for combat, I died in one of the most glorious battles the World of Men has ever known, and now I guard the borders of the Dead from intruders from the Living.' She looked quickly at the bard again. 'You are a fine warrior, and fast. I don't think I have ever seen anyone as fast.'

'I have some advantages.'

'I noticed. I should have opened you from shoulder to shoulder but for your cloak. Wearing it, you have no need to fight.'

'I wasn't sure if it would work,' he confessed. 'I thought that all the forces, properties and laws of the gods were negated in the Silent Wood.'

Katani frowned slightly. 'That I have heard also, but your cloak is obviously an exception.'

'Perhaps because it was a gift from Mannam himself,' Paedur said softly, watching her expression, wondering how she would react.

Her face remained expressionless, her eyes hard and cold, but the bard caught the tightening of the muscles and cords of her neck. 'You have met the Dark Lord?' It was a question, rather than a statement.

'I performed a small service for him once,' he said. 'And not entirely through choice either,' he added. 'He gifted me with the cloak when it seemed as if I might fall prey to the elements before I had completed my mission.' He ran his hook down the fine hair of the cloak, the rune-etched metal hissing slightly. 'I have found that it has certain properties.'

Katani relaxed again, the tautness leaving her face, and while she was not beautiful – her jaw was too strong, her nose too sharp, her eyes too cold – she was not unpretty.

'Why do you stare?'

Paedur shrugged apologetically. 'Forgive me. I was unaware that I was staring. I find it difficult to accept that you have been dead for some hundreds of years.'

Katani grinned, showing her small white teeth with the incisors filed to points, which had been customary with the Katan warriors. 'Why do you find it so strange? You would accept the concept of journeying between the various Planes of Existence?'

'Yes. I have done so.'

'That is all death is – another plane of existence. A different sort of existence, certainly, where the body is at last unfettered from the base needs of humankind, like food and drink and the desire to procreate.'

'Can you die?'

Katani came fluidly to her feet and the bard rose with her. 'We can be killed, but we will wake again. But if we have been injured in a battle here in the Silent Wood and have sustained a wound or lost a limb, then that loss will remain with us when we awaken, although the wound will be healed . . .'

They both heard the sound at the same time, a scraping,

rasping of stone on stone. Katani's swords slid noiselessly from their sheaths and she moved out into the centre of the clearing. Paedur took up a position behind her, his left arm raised defensively across his body.

'What is it?'

She shook her head. 'I'm not sure. It could be a score of different creatures, Mannam's pets. They won't be able to eat you, but they can inflict terrible wounds which will remain when you awaken.'

A single pebble rattled on to the track and then the bard actually saw one of the petrified trees shake. They both turned to the sound, and a huge head rose up over the trees and stared down at them.

'Peist!' Katani hissed, fear thickening her accent. She immediately began to back away from the wavering head.

Paedur looked up at the creature, recognising it as something from the very earliest legends of man. When the Culai had first walked the world, they had done battle with the Fomori, demonkind created and then outcast by the gods, who had ridden upon the backs of the peist, primeval horned serpents. The tales told of a score of Formori riding upon a single creature.

'Move, bard,' Katani murmured.

Paedur moved his left foot backwards and pulled away from the creature, his eyes never leaving it. The peist was huge, the width of its head easily the height of a tall man, its eyes wide-set and lambent yellow, its scales close-set and fine, looking as if they had been merely drawn on to its cream-coloured flesh. Two slightly curved and needle-pointed horns began above its eyes and there was a flat bar of hide above its broad mouth giving it a curiously comical appearance. The enormous mouth, which was easily the width of the head, was open, revealing that it was surprisingly toothless. Abruptly, the mouth closed in a firm straight line.

'Bard!' Katani screamed.

Paedur threw himself to one side as the creature's huge head lunged over the columns of stone and darted forward, striking hard into the ground where the bard had stood barely a heartbeat before. There was a solid jarring thump and when the head twisted away there was a slight depression in the hard-packed grit.

The bard rolled to his feet as the creature's head snapped

around again. He fell away as the broad, blunt head smashed into one of the petrified trees, pulverising the stone, cracking it in half.

'Bard!'

Paedur rolled towards the sound of Katani's voice, realising that the only way to avoid the creature was to delve deeper and deeper into the forest, weaving through the trees. He caught sight of Katani's extravagant armour and headed for it, not even daring to look back. He followed the woman, abstractedly admiring the skill with which she wove through the trees in the obviously heavy and bulky armour without even scraping the stone trunks. Behind them they could hear stone cracking and the grinding, tearing sounds of trees being uprooted.

They stopped running only when the petrified forest opened out on to a broad, gently sloping plain that led down to what the bard first took to be a black ribbon of road.

Katani stopped at the edge of the forest. She was breathing heavily and strands of her ice-white hair were plastered across her eyes. Behind them, but distantly, they could still hear the peist crashing through the forest.

'I have known them to track a person for days,' she gasped.

'Why, if they cannot feed?' Paedur demanded, hauling himself up by his hook on to one of the granite limbs of a gnarled oak to try and locate the creature. In the distance he could see the tops of the trees wavering slightly, marking the peist's approach.

'Do the Hounds of Maurug still roam the World of Man?' Katani asked.

Paedur nodded. 'Some, but the beasts are nearly extinct.'

'The peist kills, as they do, for sport, not to feed. They too are Maurug's creatures.'

The bard stared back into the forest. 'I've faced the dogs,' he murmured.

Another tree fell, the stone exploding with a roar. It was many years since the bard had stood against one of the huge slavering dogs; he had been a young man recently graduated from Baddalaur, the Bardic College. Only his razor-sharp hook had saved him, and only then because the creature had been so intent on killing him that it had sprung straight for his throat. He had instinctively raised his arm to protect himself and the dog had bitten down on the curved blade, completely severing its own jaw. But even though it had been mortally wounded, the hound had still worried at the man until it simply bled to death in the snow. The ferocious dogs had been named after the god Maurug, the Destroyer, and Paedur had reflected then that they had been well named.

Katani continued into the lengthening silence. 'I saw a man once who had fallen to the peist. His body had been pulped, for the creature kills by constriction, but the man still was aware. Every bone in his body had been broken, parts of him were unrecognisable, he couldn't walk or speak or move, but he was still aware.'

'What did you do?' Paedur asked, looking at her, his trained ear catching a subtle intonation in her voice.

'I killed him; a true death by the only means possible in this place – I burned his body, reducing it to ashes. He would not have suffered much.'

'You knew him?'

Katani pointed to the distant black line that cut across the plain. 'That is the River Naman, we'll be safe on the other side,' she said, quickly checking the buckles and ties of her armour. And then she added, 'He was a friend.'

The bard nodded but said nothing. He had already guessed.

If the stone forest had once been wood, then the plain would have been grass, Paedur reasoned, but now it was grit and sand and small rounded pebbles that looked as if they belonged on a seashore. It was flat and featureless, with no stone bigger than a small rock and the only colours those of slate and shale. Against the monotones, Paedur realised that his purple-black cloak and Katani's ice-serpent armour would have stood out even if they weren't the only beings moving on the blighted landscape. He also knew that when the peist finally worked its way free of the stone forest, then it would quickly gain on them, the slope of the gradient lending it speed.

Later he realised that the odour must have been present for a long time, and again he was dismayed by the loss of his especially acute senses. The stench was primarily of blood, the thick, cloying, bitter-sweet, copper-tart stench of blood. He glanced sidelong at Katani, but she seemed unaware of it.

Stone exploded and then every stone and pebble on the plain actually trembled. Paedur glanced back over his shoulder to find that the peist had finally broken free of the Silent Wood and that its horned head was now wavering above the tops of the petrified trees. The rumbling noise he had heard were two shattered tree-trunks rolling down the slight incline. As he watched the huge creature began to undulate down the incline, Katani started to run.

'Will it cross the river?' he shouted.

The woman didn't even look back. 'I don't know. I don't think so. I hope not.'

They had almost reached the river now and the stench had become unbearable. Paedur gagged.

'It is the Naman, the Black River,' Katani said.

The bard remembered his lore then, and recalled that he had seen its twin, the Aman, the milk-white river that flowed through the Fields of Eternal Life. It was Life and purity, while the Naman washed away all the blood that was spilt in the myriad worlds of men.

They stopped a few paces from the banks. The stench was unbearable, and even Katani, who was well used to the odours of Death, was pale, taking care to breath only through her mouth. The river flowed sluggishly, dark lumps of reeking matter moving within it, and whereas from the distance it had looked black, close-to it was a deep reddish purple, streaked with thicker, darker lines of ichor.

'It's not wide,' Paedur suggested.

'But if you fell in,' Katani said slowly.

'You cannot drown,' Paedur reminded her.

The woman shook her head. 'No. You can drown, you can die. But you will awaken again in the morning . . . and I'm not sure I want to know where that river ends.'

Paedur touched her arm with his hook. 'I don't think we have any choice.' The peist was undulating rapidly across the plain, dust and grit rising in its wake. 'Come!' The bard pounded down towards the river, took a deep breath, and then he leapt at the last possible moment. It wasn't a long jump and he landed well clear on the far bank.

Katani hesitated a moment longer and then she followed his example. She was loath to approach the edge of the lapping river and she jumped just a fraction too early, miscalculating, failing to allow for the weight of her armour and weapons. She hit the edge of the opposite bank with a thump, her legs sinking into the river of flowing blood. She scrambled for fingerholds as the force of the water began to pull her away, but she could barely see what she was doing with the eye-watering stench. The river was warm and clinging; it gripped like a gentle hand and pulled.

And then iron-hard fingers wrapped themselves around her wrist, pulling her up and out of the water easily, and set her down on her feet. She began to thank him when he suddenly raised his hook and brought it flashing down against her arm ... and sliced through a thin snake-like creature that had attached itself to the shoulder-plate of her armour. She looked down her body and discovered that there were scores of the eel-like creatures attached to her legs, sucking hungrily on her lacquered armour. Almost abstractedly she wondered what would have happened if one of them had managed to sink its teeth into her flesh.

The peist had stopped about a man's length from the river, its horned head twisting to and fro, its huge mouth opening and closing rapidly, pulsating ripples running the length of its armoured body.

'It seems reluctant to approach the river,' Paedur said, storing the information away, adding it to his already vast store of knowledge. 'Perhaps it is sensitive to the smell.'

'Bard,' Katani hissed through clenched teeth, 'there is no creature living – or dead – that wouldn't be sensitive to this smell!'

Paedur grinned. 'Of course.' They both watched in silence as the peist curled up on the opposite back, its horned head resting flat on the ground, and then it began to change colour, pulses rippling through its many segments, gradually assuming the stone and slate colours of the plain. Soon, except for the two curved horns and the glowing eyes, it was almost invisible.

'I didn't know they could change colour,' the woman-warrior said quietly, 'but it would explain how they can stalk and kill with such apparent ease.'

'It is waiting for us,' Paedur remarked.

'There's no way back,' Katani nodded, 'not at this place certainly. Further down the river widens, while upriver there is only the Mire, and that is infinitely more dangerous, where the outcasts – both human and otherwise – from Death's Kingdom congregate.'

'That is of no account. I had no intention of going back – not just yet at any rate.'

16

'Tell me, bard. Just why did you come to the Silent Wood?'

Paedur turned away and began to march across the plain. 'I am looking for something.'

'Something – or someone?' Katani asked shrewdly.

The bard glanced at her and smiled. 'You're right. I'm looking for two people, companions, friends – dead now, but they died before their time, died needlessly.' His voice changed slightly, becoming almost formal. 'And I took an oath to look for them, return them to Life to allow them to live out their allotted span of years.'

'I have never heard of Mannam giving up one of his subjects,' Katani said slowly.

'Oh, he'll give them to me,' Paedur promised, with a smile that had nothing of humour in it.

## 2   The Fortress

Although the Bard now walked the Silent Wood, the seeds he had
planted in the World of Men were beginning to bear fruit . . .
                                                *Life of Paedur, the Bard*

And so the Weapon Master returned to the way of the Faith . . .
              from . . . *The Warrior, the Life of Owen, Weapon Master*

The mountain had reclaimed the fortress, absorbing the
massively hewn blocks, blanketing them beneath vines, creepers
and clinging grasses. Now, only a vague regularity in the
mountainside betrayed its presence, and the casual observer
would have missed it all too easily.

But the two men standing in the lee of a tumbled cairn of
stones hadn't missed the building; they had journeyed across
half a continent deliberately seeking out the abandoned Culai-
built fortresses. Their instructions and directions had been
vague: they were seeking a group of wasteland outlaws who
were heading into the west seeking a suitable base from which
to conduct a campaign against the Imperials, and the only firm
information they had was that the outlaws would settle for one
of the Culai fortresses.

'What do you think?' the smaller of the two, a sallow-skinned,
tilt-eyed Easterner, asked.

'No sign of life,' the second man murmured. He was taller
and broader than the Easterner and wore a warrior's light mail
over a thick leather hauberk. 'Tracks?'

'Nothing. But the recent rains would have seen to that.'

'It will be dark soon. We'll wait until then before approaching
the fortress.'

'I'm not so sure I want to after the last time,' the small man
said with a wry smile. The previous fortress had been occupied
by a score of starving wolves and both men had been lucky to
escape with nothing more than scratched armour and torn
cloaks.

18

Owen the Weapon Master and his servant-companion Tien tZo had been on the road for close on nearly four moons now, trekking further and further into the west, seeking out the abandoned Culai fortresses, searching for Kutor the Renegade and his followers. It was a foolish, foolhardy mission, with no thanks and almost certainly no coin in it, but Paedur the Bard had suggested it and the Weapon Master was in no state of mind to refuse him anything at that time. And although he had never stated it directly, he had more than hinted that it might be a suitable way for Owen to redeem himself in the eyes of the Gods of the Old Faith.

When they had set off into the west trailing the bandits – from what they had gathered from the bard – the group had no more than a single moon's headstart and two men travelling fast and light would easily make up that distance.

But then the Cataclysm struck. It lasted only a single day, but in that short day the entire eastern coastline of the Seven Nations changed forever. No coastal town or village escaped unscathed. Roads were swept away: bridges destroyed. Islands were swamped, some vanishing forever beneath the waves, while in other places new islands appeared, torn, raw and steaming, from the ocean floor.

It was impossible to estimate how many had died on that single day of Cataclysm, or how many more would die of famine and disease because of the destroyed crops and the rotting corpses of man and beast alike. Communications with Karfondal, the capital, were disrupted, but Geillard the Emperor had reacted swiftly: law and order were slowly but surely coming back to the outlying provinces, while cartographers and surveyors were charting the new coastline and bards and scribes were working on a census.

But the loss of roads and the new configuration of the land had caused inevitable delays, delays which had lengthened as Owen and Tien tZo found work for their mercenary talents, defending small towns and villages from marauders, both human and animal, although in some cases the distinction was not so easy to make.

They stopped briefly at Baddalaur, the Bardic College, and while Owen made a few discreet inquiries into Paedur's background, Tien tZo paid a Scholar for a complete listing of all the ruined Culai fortresses in the westlands. However, the Weapon

19

Master was unable to discover anything about the enigmatic figure of the bard, save that his name and the appellation 'Hook-hand' appeared on the Roll of Bards, with an index of all the tales he had contributed to the college library. And because most of the senior bards and scribes, who would have been of Paedur's generation, had been called to the capital to assist in the census, there was no-one there who actually knew the bard personally. Equally, Tien tZo's task, which would have taken a competent Scholar a single day, took the apprentice he had employed four days.

Most of the Culai fortresses were on the King Road or a side road, and so their task was not difficult, merely tedious and often frustrating. The first two fortresses they had gone in search of were missing entirely, having been torn down and the stones used by the locals. The third was completely desolate, and the atmosphere of dread and the menace that clung to it so palpable that both men had left hurriedly, not even bothering to check the interior to see if it was occupied, knowing that nothing of human-kind could live in that blighted place. The fourth had been occupied by a pack of plains' wolves. Before them now was the fifth, and after this one the fortresses became further apart, with the next a six-day march, and then a ten-day march after that to the one beyond.

Night fell with the same unaccustomed swiftness of the past few moons. Owen was of the opinion that the Gods were warring amongst themselves, hence the destruction and the sudden change in the seasons and weather. Tien tZo, whose education was far broader than his master's, decided that the sudden early nightfalls were due to an excess of dust in the atmosphere, but he wisely kept his opinions to himself. Since Owen's release from the Iron Band of Kloor, the normally superstitious warrior had become almost fanatically religious, sometimes frighteningly so, and would hear nothing ill spoken against the Old Faith, even in jest.

Tien tZo suddenly pointed, but Owen was already nodding, 'I see it.' A light had appeared briefly, high up on the cliff wall, a tiny eye of light. It vanished and then reappeared, only to vanish again just as quickly.

'A candle flame,' Tien said quietly, his soft accent almost lost on the night air, 'lighting a guard's way up turret stairs.'

Owen nodded. 'Aye, of course; and we're seeing it as he passes the arrow slots. Well, it proves there's someone there.'

'It could be brigands,' his servant suggested, loosening the two hand-axes that hung on either side of his belt.

'It's unlikely that they would post guards.'

'Unlikely, but not unknown.' Tien smiled.

'But a nervous renegade prince might . . .'

Tien nodded. 'He might. How do we go in?'

'Through the main gate,' Owen grinned.

Soan sleepily watched the spider busily encasing the struggling moth in thread, idly comtemplating if it was worth his while cutting a few threads of the intricate web to make the spider's job just a little more difficult. A short time ago he wouldn't have had a second thought about it, but now, with all this talk of gods and powers, demons and forces, he found himself remembering his religion and he had begun to murmur the prayers again – just in case. He looked at the spider and its struggling captive and wondered which of the Gods or Goddesses of the Pantheon had dominion over the creature: probably the Lady Adur, the Goddess of Nature, he decided.

The knife came slicing through the web and stopped, resting just below his nose on the top of his lip. 'Don't even think about it,' a cruel, emotionless voice hissed, and then the glittering edge of an axe touched the soft flesh under his jaw. Soan's wide eyes twitched, and looked into the leering face of a yellow-skinned, slant-eyed demon.

The dagger moved down, dropping off his top lip to rest on his fuller lower lip. 'I have come to see Kutor the Renegade. Now, you can take me to him or I can kill you and find him myself. What is it to be?'

'I . . . t-t-take . . .'

'Try anything,' the grinning demon hissed in Soan's ear, 'and I'll cut your leg off. I haven't eaten in days.'

Soan resisted the temptation to throw up.

The Culai fortresses had been built in the earliest Age of Man, but by a technology or magic that was beyond the finest builders or magicians in the Emperor's court today. This particular fortress had been carved out of the cliff face and then dug back into it. Whole floors of rooms had been cut into the mountainside and never saw the light of day, while the dungeons and cellars were far below ground. The front of the building, the battlements, turrets and main gate were overhung by a huge outcrop of rock that effectively protected the occupants from attack from above, and from some of the sleet and rain storms that scoured this part of the continent. However, it also ensured that the fortress was in perpetual gloom, since the sun never shone directly on to it at any time during the day except briefly at sunrise.

The years had been kind to the fortress, softening its harsh edges, smoothing away the skeletal gauntness and then coating the entire building beneath a carpet of grasses and vines. No part of it had escaped, nor had it been discouraged by the scores of clans, tribes and other groups that had lain claim to it down through the years. It helped disguise the building, and also provided a little insulation from the icy fingers of Snaitle, the Cold God, and Fiarle, the Little God of Icy Spaces. The thick covering also ensured that the entire fortress smelt of growth and damp.

A meal was in progress in the main hall when Owen stepped into the room followed a moment later by Tien tZo with his axe at Soan's throat. The small grey-haired man at the head of the table spotted the intruders first and stopped, shocked and wide-eyed, with his glass raised halfway to his lips. Silence ran down the table like fluid as heads turned towards the door. Metal and wood scraped simultaneously as swords and knives were hurriedly unsheathed and chairs were pushed back from the table, and the Weapon Master and his servant found themselves facing over twenty armed men. Tien tZo pushed Soan away from him, sending him sprawling across the table, and then unclipped his second battle-axe, allowing it to swing loosely at the end of its thong.

Owen broke the startled silence. 'I have come for Kutor,' he said evenly.

A short, stout man near the end of the table suddenly produced a cocked and loaded crossbow and levelled it at Owen's chest, while the men standing beside the table immediately moved clear, allowing him a clear shot, and then they began to spread out and encircle the two.

'I take it you have come here for a reason?' The accent was cultured, the speaker a small, slender man at the end of the table. He raised his glass to his lips and drank. 'What are you?' he asked.

'Killers, more than like,' someone murmured.

'Killers don't usually announce themselves,' the man said, lowering his glass, positioning it precisely on the scarred table.

'The very confident ones do,' the stout man with the crossbow said quietly, his eyes never leaving the Weapon Master.

Owen bowed slightly. 'You do me honour, sir.'

'What do you want?' the man demanded, moving the crossbow slightly, positioning the broad-headed bolt on Owen's throat.

'We are seeking Kutor the Renegade.'

'You've found him,' the stout man said quickly.

Owen smiled. 'No, I don't think so. But you, sir,' he looked directly at the man at the head of the table, 'you have more the mark of a leader about you.'

The man smiled slightly. 'I think now you do me honour. Yes, I am Kutor. Now, perhaps you would answer Keshian's question. Who are you? And perhaps if I could add one of my own, why are you here?'

'I am Owen, Weapon Master. This is Tien tZo, my slave-companion. We have come to join with Kutor the Renegade.'

An uneasy laugh ran around the room, but then Keshian, the man with the crossbow, spoke suddenly. 'I have heard of Owen, Weapon Master. He is a legend; everyone knows of his defence of Car'an'tual with less than a dozen men. I am curious, though, why one of the finest mercenary soldiers in the Seven Nations would want to join with us – and I become more curious and perhaps slightly suspicious when I remember that the same Owen swears fealty to Kloor, the God of War, and is a member of the select Iron Band.'

Owen pushed back his sleeve, revealing the pale rectangle of skin which the metal band had once covered. 'I left the Band and the Religion. I have returned to the Faith.'

'No-one leaves the Religion, and especially not the Band of Kloor,' Kutor said quietly.

'Perhaps you're not even the real Weapon Master,' Keshian said with a cold smile. 'Perhaps you are a spy . . .'

'Oh, I am what I say I am,' Owen whispered.

'We'll see.' Without warning, he fired.

No-one even saw Owen's sword leave its sheath. All they heard was the crack as it sliced through the crossbow bolt in mid-air, spinning the two pieces of wood away. One length fell into the fire and began to burn unheeded.

In the stunned silence that followed, Keshian dropped the crossbow on to the table and placed two additional bolts beside it. 'He's the Weapon Master,' he said simply.

Kutor took a deep shuddering breath. 'Well, we've proven your identity. Tell us now, why are you here?'

For an answer, Owen unsheathed his knife and sent it sliding down the length of the table. Kutor picked it up, examining the heavy blade carefully, and then he silently passed it to Keshian. The old man looked at it for a long time and then he casually spun it through the air back to the warrior. 'It bears the mark of the Hook,' he said to the room, 'the sign of the Bard.'

The room was small and held nothing more than a simple bed that was merely a straw pallet thrown on to a low, raised stone dais. There was a fireplace in the corner and the small, guttering fire there did little to dispel the stone chill of the place. Four chairs had been dragged into the room and Kutor and Keshian occupied two, while Owen sat astride a third, but with his back to the wall. Tien tZo remained standing by the door, his arms folded, fingertips touching the butts of his axes.

'The bard sent you to us?' Kutor began without preamble.

'He suggested that we might wish to fight in a worthy cause,' Owen said slowly, looking at the Pretender to the throne of the Seven Nations.

'I doubt if there will be any money in it for a long time,' Kutor added.

'You can pay me when you're on the throne.'

The prince grinned almost shyly. 'Whenever that may be.'

'The bard supports your cause. That is enough for me,' Owen said simply.

Keshian sat forward on the edge of the hard chair and looked from Owen to Tien tZo. 'How well do you know the bard?' he asked.

'We met him once, spent a night in his company,' the Weapon Master said slowly.

'He is not human,' Tien tZo said abruptly, startling everyone. 'Man yes, but not wholly of this world.'

'He has power,' Owen agreed.

Keshian lifted a wooden flagon and filled the four glasses that had been left on a wooden tray by his feet. He passed a glass to Tien tZo, who put it to his lips and then, after a moment's hesitation, passed it on to Owen. The Weapon Master saw the flash of anger behind the old warrior's eyes. 'He does it out of habit,' he said quickly, 'and means no insult by it.'

Prince Kutor laid his hand on Keshian's arm. 'The Weapon Master does not know us,' he said reasonably. He deliberately lifted his own glass and drank deeply.

Keshian passed a second glass to the stone-faced servant and then lifted his own, but Tien still waited until the stout man had drunk first before he put his own glass to his lips.

'We have been on the road for nearly twenty summers,' Owen explained, counting the years in summers in the manner of the southern peoples; the northern dwellers counted the winters. 'One of the reasons we've survived so long and in relative safety is on account of the precautions we've adopted. Some' – he lifted his glass slightly and nodded at his servant – 'have become second nature and we do them unthinking.' The Weapon Master drank deeply and then looked directly at the prince. 'And if you intend to rule, then I would suggest you should begin to take the same precautions.'

Kutor grinned. 'Why, there's hardly any need here in the Outlands . . .' he began.

'There is every need,' Owen insisted. 'When you take the throne you must be in a position to surround yourself with people you trust, and trust with your life. Begin the process now.'

'Begin to live like a prince,' Tien tZo hissed.

'Tien is right. At this moment you are nothing more than a bandit. You think of yourself as a bandit and your followers consider you to be a bandit. And the people coming to your banner will consider you nothing more than a bandit. Your enemies will consider you nothing more than a bandit, and they will begin with that great advantage over you.'

'Think like a prince, an emperor,' Tien added.

'I can see now why the bard sent you to us,' Kutor smiled. 'You will stay?'

'We haven't crossed half a continent to leave now.' Owen grinned, passing his glass back to Keshian to be filled again 'What numbers have you?'

'Keshian can best tell you that. He has become my sergeant-at-arms, captain of the guard, commander of my forces, armourer, quartermaster – everything, in fact, since he joined us. Amongst us, his military service is certainly the longest and without doubt the most distinguished.'

'The prince does me too much honour,' Keshian smiled. 'I was merely a battle captain in Count Karfondal's guard before I joined the prince's band, and again the bard had a hand in that too. Before then I had seen some little service in the Island Wars and had patrolled the Fire Hills of Nasgociba with a band of mercenaries in the employ of the Taourg.' He refilled Kutor's glass and then offered the jug to Tien; Tien shook his head – the glass in his hand was almost untouched.

'We have a little over forty men at present. We started out with nearly double that number, but the rest drifted away as we travelled into the west, or returned to look for families or loved ones when the Cataclysm struck. Forty men,' Keshian repeated, 'five of those are deserters, and so I suppose you could say that they had some military service. The rest are a mixture of farmers, servants, runaway slaves and escaped convicts.'

'Women?'

'Ten women. Two are married, the rest just camp followers, and tend to drift from man to man.'

'Children?'

'None; athough one of the women is pregnant.'

When Keshian finished, Kutor leaned forward and watched the Weapon Master. 'Well?' he asked.

Owen leaned back against the cold stone wall. 'Well, you don't need me to tell you that you need more men.'

'Professional soldiers?' the prince asked.

Owen shook his head. 'The professional fights for coin – you have none – and he feels no loyalty to his employer. That is one of the reasons your last attempt for the throne failed so miserably. No, you need to get the ordinary people on your side . . .'

'But we tried that the last time,' Kutor interrupted, 'and it didn't work.'

'They lacked a cause and they were untrained,' Tien tZo said softly.

'Aye, and their enthusiasm probably caused more harm than good. No, this time we'll train them properly. Now, while I'm sure the bard will send you more men, I think you should go out and actually recruit . . .' He suddenly stopped, and looked from Kutor to Keshian. 'I'm sorry. I didn't mean to dictate. I am only making suggestions, you understand; I've no wish to usurp Keshian's position.'

'I would be honoured to serve under you,' Keshian said immediately.

Kutor nodded. 'And that is why Paedur sent you here, isn't it?' he asked.

Owen nodded. 'Aye. Well then . . .' He drank quickly, finishing his wine and refusing Keshian's offer of more. 'There are two things which must be attended to first; the fortress must be secured because – and you may be assured of this – you will be attacked by Imperial forces before this affair is closed; and we must begin stockpiling and constructing weapons.' He glanced up at Tien. 'If you will attend to that.' The Shemmat nodded. 'And if you, Keshian, will build up our defences.' He nodded. 'Good, then on the morrow, you and I, prince, will ride out in search of an army. Why do you smile?' he asked suddenly.

'From the moment the bard suggested that I might one day rule, everything seemed like a dream, everything seemed to happen so fast. And then we wound up here, and it was as if I had come back to reality: I was in a cold, dead fortress on the edge of civilisation, surrounded by a few dispirited men. And now you're here, and the dream is beginning again.'

Owen smiled and rose smoothly to his feet. 'This will be no dream, prince, this will be a nightmare!'

# 3  The Road to Manach

And he was god-like in the Worlds of Man, but human in Death's Realm . . .

*Life of Paedur, the Bard*

A warrior, whose race was not of the human kind, guarded the path.

'One of the frai-forde,' Katani hissed, 'the Star Lorn.'

They had spotted it earlier, a solitary figure standing still in the centre of the thin band of road that ran arrow-straight across the plain. Caution had taken them off the track, and they had used what little natural cover the plain possessed to approach as close as possible to the figure. They had finally taken shelter in a shallow dip in the ground not twenty paces from the figure. Paedur peered over the lip of the depression and looked closely at the creature. His first impression was of height; it stood half again his own height and he was accounted a tall man. The frai-forde was also completely devoid of hair and this only served to emphasise the rigid lines of corded muscle. The head was almost completely round and sat directly on the broad shoulders. Its only discernable features were two small, round eyes and a round mouth. As it breathed, the mouth opened and closed, disclosing that it was ringed by a series of tiny needle-pointed teeth, like those of certain species of fish the bard had seen in some of the warmer climes. Its only garment was a long kirtle of banded metal plates that began low on its chest and ended just below the knees. It was unarmed.

'It seems to be asleep,' Paedur said quietly, watching the rise and fall of the massively corded chest.

'They always do,' Katani remarked wryly, 'until you attempt to pass them.'

'Is there any way to go around it?'

The woman-warrior shook her head slightly. 'No, and even if you could, you're wasting your time. Just beyond the Star Lorn the road crests a rise and then it is downhill to Manach, the

City of the Dead. The city is completely surrounded by three circular rings of a river which are only bridged at one particular point, and at the three bridges you will encounter more of the frai-forde.'

'Perhaps it could be slain . . .' Paedur mused, almost to himself.

'When I was in the World of Men, the Katan fought one of these creatures – an assassin – who had been hired to slay the Lord Churon. We lost fourteen warriors before it was eventually slain. The Star Lorn are fast, bard. You have never seen a creature move so fast before. The Lord Churon formed the opinion that they lived according to a different timescale.'

Paedur looked at the huge creature again, examining the enormous body, searching for weaknesses. With its almost featureless face, it was impossible to make any judgement as to its expression, whether it was even awake or asleep.

'What would happen if we were merely to stand up and approach it?' he wondered.

'It would attack us both,' Katani said simply, 'without question, without reason, and tear us literally limb from limb. We, or rather I, would awaken again, and I'm not sure I want to regain consciousness without the use of my limbs.' Her eyes clouded. 'I don't know what will happen if you are slain here; because you are living in the Land of Death, would you then truly die, or would you reanimate again?' She shook her head. 'It is a paradox.'

'Have you ever visited the city of Manach?' Paedur asked suddenly, not looking at her, still watching the frai-forde.

'Bard, I think you should understand that I have always kept to the borders of Death's Realm. You are heading deeper and deeper into his kingdom, and this is a country I know nothing about, nor indeed want to know anything about for that matter. Manach, the City of the Dead, is a legend – even here, in the land of the Dead. No-one has ever come out of Manach to tell of its mysteries or wonders, and no-one has ever gone in, because no-one has ever managed to pass the guards.'

Paedur nodded glumly. He came away from the lip of the depression and moved down beside Katani. The woman was lying on her back staring up at the pale blue sky, her matched swords in their lacquered scabbards lying by her hands. 'What will you do?' she asked, without looking at him. 'Attack?'

The bard rested his chin on his clenched fist and stared blankly at the woman, wondering what he was going to do this time, evaluating the possibilities.

When he had been a younger man, before he had been visited by Mannam and set out on his quest, and before he had been gifted by the Lord of Life, Paedur the bard had been a shy, almost frightened man, living a quiet hermit's existence by himself after a brief, artistically successful but politically disastrous spell in the Imperial Court. He had always been too direct, lacking tact and discretion, and had managed to insult far too many of the Emperor's cronies with his historically truthful tales – truthful was not how they wanted to hear them. Eventually he even succeeded in enraging the Emperor himself when, at the feast following the Imperial Games, Geillard had suggested he tell the tale of his own ancestor Geillard the Great. The Emperor had expected to hear the accepted version of the tale, which told of a wise and benign sovereign freeing the land from the tyranny of the Court of Churon. Instead, Paedur told the story of a bloody courtier in the Onelord's court who had plotted and murdered his way into a position of authority, and then plunged the country into a bloody civil war which ravaged the countryside and laid waste enough fertile land to cause the Hunger, a twelve-season famine that had decimated the population of the nations and changed the political map forever.

Following that, the bard had wisely fled the court and retired to the solitude of the forests, where he had remained in obscurity until the Dark Lord, Mannam, had come to him.

But his stay at the Imperial Court had taught him many things. He had learned that men will listen only to what they want to hear, and that had taught him caution; and he had learned that there was no shame in subterfuge, and that a lie saved pain and hurt. And these were lessons which he considered to be as valuable as his training in Baddalaur.

And then he had been gifted by C'lte, the Lord of Life, and suddenly all the lessons he had learned were almost forgotten. His new-found power made him invulnerable, his knowledge, virtually omnipotent. He could now do what he wished without fear for his life, could say what he wanted, and tell his myths and tales whether men wanted to hear them or not. When he had fought the Three Cords on the Culai Isle, his powers had increased a hundredfold . . . and the cost had been the loss of whatever little humanity had remained in him.

And then he had entered Death's Kingdom – and found his god-gifted powers were negated. Paedur the Bard was a man once again, and now he had to re-learn the cautions of a frightened man. His only advantages once again were his knowledge and his lore.

'How did you kill the Star Lorn who attacked Churon?' he asked suddenly, looking at Katani.

Katani raised herself on her elbows, her face softening as she remembered. 'He was detected as he came in over the wall, and the alarm was sounded. In the pursuit he killed two of the Katan Sisterhood, but then he was trapped in a narrow corridor, so we could only come at him one at a time. He was unarmed and naked except for their customary long mail kirtle and a pair of metal gauntlets. But his speed was such that he would catch the sword blades and wrench them from my sisters' hands, and then throw them back like knives. Arrows were equally useless: he brushed them aside like insects or caught the shafts in mid-flight . . . He was an extraordinary opponent.'

'But you overcame him . . .'

'He was finally slain with a thrown talon.' Katani smiled as she remembered. 'Funny. He didn't even seem to see it coming.'

'What is a talon?' Paedur asked quietly.

'Ah . . . it is – was – one of the Katan warrior's secret weapons, and it was forbidden under pain of death to reveal it to one not of the sisterhood.' She smiled broadly. 'Under pain of death,' she repeated, 'but since I am dead, I suppose I can reveal it to you. A talon is a flat square of metal, the four edges sharpened to razor points. When thrown, the square naturally revolves at high speed and I've seen them actually cut through a piece of solid brukwood.'

'How many of these talons were thrown at the creature?'

'Three. The first two just missed its head, the third ripped out its throat.'

'And it didn't react when the first two talons missed?'

'Not at all.'

The bard traced an arcane pattern in the soil with the tip of his hook. He glanced up at Katani. 'I don't suppose you would have any of these talons?' She shook her head ruefully. 'No, I suppose not,' he answered his own question. 'So we'll have to make do. Now tell me, how big are these talons?'

*

31

The stone, no bigger than a man's eyeball, struck the frai-forde right between the eyes with a solid crunch that was clearly audible to the bard and the woman crouching by the side of the road. The Star Lorn fell without a sound.

'How?' Katani asked.

Paedur folded the sling he had fashioned from a strip of cloth and tucked it into his belt. 'I think their perception of movement is different to ours. You said it was fast, that it could pluck arrows out of the air, and yet it didn't even react to the talons. Perhaps simply because it couldn't see it, perhaps because it was too small.'

'Like the stone.'

'Just so. Hopefully, the same method will take us past the three guards on the bridges.'

They climbed up on to the road and walked to the fallen creature. The front of the skull was crushed with the force of the blow, the black stone protruding like a third eye.

'Let us hope his brothers are not expecting us,' Katani said quietly, nudging the creature with her foot.

'What do you mean?'

'I have heard that no-one sleeps – dies, if you will – in the Land of the Dead without the Dark Lord's consent.' She nodded to the frai-forde. 'He knows we're coming now.'

Paedur nodded seriously. 'I would imagine that there are scores of deaths occurring both here and on the various Planes of Existence where Mannam reigns as Death at the same time, and while he may be aware of their occurrence, he cannot know the details of each and every one.' He grinned. 'Anyway, I think if he knew I was here, he would have made some move against me by now.'

'What about me, the peist and now the frai-forde?' Katani demanded. 'Surely we all moved against you?'

'I prefer to think of you and them as part of the natural hazards of the Kingdom of the Dead.' He smiled. 'It will make a fine tale when I return to the World of Men. My journey through the Land of Death will admirably complement my stay in the Lands of Life Eternal.' He sobered and then looked at Katani. 'I think you should think very seriously about whether you want to remain with me or not. The nearer we come to the City of the Dead, the more dangerous it will become.'

'And what is the worst that can happen to me?' the woman asked with a sly smile.

'You could be kill . . .' The bard suddenly laughed, realising what he had been about to say. 'Have you ever died here?' he asked.

'Not here,' Katani said, something shifting behind her eyes. 'I have only died once, and that was enough.'

Paedur, sensitive to the emotion he now recognised as pain and loss, bent and heaved the incredibly heavy corpse of the frai-forde off the road and down the incline into the hollow. He slid down after it and kicked grit and pebbles over it, hiding it from a casual observer. When he was finished he straightened and looked up at Katani, who had remained standing on the road.

'How does it look?'

Her head snapped up. 'What?'

'I asked how it looked from up there.'

'Oh. It looks like a body covered by grit,' she said, smiling wanly.

Paedur clambered up the incline, using the point of his hook to pull himself up. He straightened beside the woman and looked into her deep amber-coloured eyes. 'Something is troubling you.'

'There is nothing.'

'A bard is trained to be sensitive to the mood of his audience. Tell me.'

She shook her head and turned away, settling her armour around her shoulders and adjusting her swords. When she looked back at Paedur, her face was completely devoid of expression. 'I would suggest we hurry. There's no telling how long the Star Lorn will stay dead, and I don't want to be around when he awakes.'

Paedur strode after her and the pair walked in silence for awhile. Finally the bard said softly, 'Something about your own death is troubling you. There are memories which are painful, that is obvious.'

Katani began to shake her head, but abruptly changed her mind and nodded.

'Do you want to tell me about it?'

'What good would that do?' she demanded, her voice sounding surprisingly bitter even to her own ears.

'It is said that naming something gives one power over it, and similarly, knowing the name of something or someone evil

33

lessens their power to harm. Perhaps by naming your hurt, you will lessen its power to distress.'

'I doubt that. You don't know what happened that day.'

'I am a bard; I know all the tales of the Battle of the Sand Plain with the Shemmatae, and the gallant defence of Churon the Onelord and his Katan warriors, and their victory over the invaders from the Land of the Sun even though it cost them all their lives.'

'You don't know the whole story, bard,' Katani said, derision in her voice.

'I am a bard,' Paedur said simply. 'I tell what I have learned. If you know more, then teach me.'

The road dipped, taking them down into a hollow where the walls on either side were a handspan and more taller than the bard. Their footsteps echoed in the defile, and they both instinctively fell silent, eyes and ears alert, aware that it was the perfect place for a trap. But they came up out of the long defile without incident and found the road now stretched away arrow-straight, sloping gently downhill to the horizon. Nothing moved on the flat expanse of grey stone and grit.

'Manach, the City of the Dead, lies just beyond the horizon,' Katani said quietly.

'A day's march,' Paedur estimated.

'There is no time here, bard, no day, no night. You will not tire, nor feel the need to sleep, but it would be best if you rest, lest your fatigued muscles suddenly betray you.'

Paedur nodded obediently, unwilling to tell the woman that it had been a long time since he had slept the true sleep of the humankind.

'Tell me your tale of the Battle of the Sand Plain, bard,' Katani said suddenly. 'I'm curious to hear how history has treated us.'

'It's a long story . . .' Paedur began.

'Just the battle will do. And then when you have done, I will tell you how that day went.'

The bard nodded. 'That would be interesting.' He adjusted his cloak around his shoulders, pulling up the hood, allowing it to fall forward across his face, cutting himself off from his surroundings, and then he began . . .

They came in crafts of metal, impossible constructions that had no right to ride the sea, ships that were an affront to the Lord of the Sea, and yet they remained afloat. The invaders beached their metal crafts on the Sand Plain, turning the sea-going fortresses into land castles, and from there conducted their reign of terror across the Seven Nations.

Armies rode against the savage yellow-skinned invaders, who fought back on the small sturdy ponies they had brought with them in the bellies of their huge metal crafts. And the armies, for all their armour and weapons, numbers and supplies, perished. The invaders – the Shemmatae – were warriors for whom death was a state to be embraced, a joy, and they threw themselves willingly on the spears of the mainlanders to allow their brothers to triumph. And soon, while they did not completely rule the coast, a major portion of it was under their influence, and by controlling the ports, they controlled the movements of supplies of food and fuel. And the Seven Nations began to hunger.

But finally a man appeared, a slave who had fought his way up from the slave-market at Londre to freedom. To overthrow a monarch in those troubled times was a simple matter for a man who had appeared out of the wilderness with the most feared warriors in the known world at his back, the Katan. Once he was secure on the throne, he immediately set about organising the defence of the Nations. Realising that there was safety only in strength, he set about extracting an oath of fealty from the Brothers, the six kings of the neighbouring nations. But the kings were proud, haughty men who had no time for freed slaves, and so the man – by name Churon – had to trick the kings into giving him their oath before witnesses ... and how he accomplished that would take a tale to itself.

And when he had their word and they had declared him the Onelord, he warred on the invaders. Over the next few moons, there were skirmishes and many died on both sides, but when Churon realised that the real victims were the common people, who were suffering not only the depredations of the Shemmatae but also from hunger and disease, the Onelord decided that there would be one last battle, a final effort to crush the invaders completely.

The battle on the Sand Plain lasted a day and a night, and when it was finally done and the dead counted and the wounded numbered, twenty thousand men had gone to their gods that day, and three times that number had suffered wounds. Over the next two days another six thousand men went into the Land of Death. The Shemmatae were completely crushed and the Onelord and his warriors took over fourteen thousand

Shemmatae men, women and children as slaves, and so even now it is possible to find pure-blooded Shemmatae still serving as slaves . . .

Paedur finished and looked at Katani. 'That is the shortened version,' he said carefully.

She looked at him in amazement. 'But it tells nothing, where is the detail? What about the Shemmatae's secret weapon of cold fire? What about the Magician's War before the battle took place, when our mages fought theirs? And the attack by the Chopt-like creatures they kept as pets, when Kutor the strong killed one with a single blow of his mailed fist? What about the death of the Katan?' she asked finally.

'We know nothing about such things,' Paedur lied. The events surrounding the Battle of the Sand Plain were documented in great detail, but he wished to draw the woman out to discover what was troubling her. 'Tell me,' he said suddenly, 'tell me about that day . . .'

Katani walked on slowly, her head bent, the knuckles of her left hand wrapped whitely around the hilt of her longsword. 'In truth the battle began just before dawn,' she said suddenly, 'when their sorcerers attacked our camp with a plague of tiny flying creatures completely alien to the Nations.' She shuddered, remembering. 'They were similar in shape and form to a sewing needle, no bigger than one, and blood red in colour. They attacked the face, flying straight into the eyes, the open mouth, up nostrils, into ears . . . and then they fed. We lost many fine men to that disgusting death. It was an evil death conceived by an evil man.

'And our sorcerers retaliated. Praetens was Churon's magician then; he was of the Susuru . . .' Katani broke off and glanced at the bard. 'You are familar with the Susuru? I am not sure if they still survive in the World of Men; they were a dying race even in my own time.'

'Their race became extinct only recently,' Paedur said with an enigmatic smile, recalling the half-human creature that had controlled the Quisleedor.

'Praetens wove a spell which sent the creatures back on the Shemmatae, and soon the screams of their maimed mingled with ours. Praetens and his fellow magicians then retaliated by sending a wall of freezing fog down on the invaders. The wall was no thicker than a sword's length and no taller than a man, and it moved in a straight line down across the Sand Plain and on to the beach. Everything it touched was coated in a layer of hoar frost. The Shemmatae invaders were terrified, such intense cold being completley unknown in their own land, and some broke ranks, turned and fled back towards their ships, but these were calmly shot down by their own officers.' Katani smiled. 'Some of us even believed that the battle had been won then, but we were wrong. The invaders' magicians brought fire down from the heavens in the form of a cold rain, like sleet, that burned, eating through raw flesh like acid. Praetens called up a wind and blew the sleet down on to the invaders; the Shemmatae turned it back. Praetens sent scores of tiny bouncing balls of fire into the invader's camp; their magicians called them all together and sent a huge fireball screaming back. The Susuru stopped it in mid-air, holding it floating just above his head like a second sun. He seemed to fold it in on to itself, and then encased it in something black and hard. When it was the size of a man's head he held out his talon-like hand and the ball dropped into it. And then he threw it at the Shemmatae ... at the same moment that they fired what looked like a tiny silver arrow at him.

'The black ball fell amongst the Shemmatae magicians – and exploded in a massive fireball that reduced everything around it to cinders, completely destroying the invaders' magical forces and a sizeable portion of their supplies and foodstuffs. But the tiny arrow they had fired had grown and grown until it was a shaft as thick as a man's body. It pierced Praetens, pinning him to the ground – and the shock of his death killed his fellow magicians, blasting their minds, leaving their bodies nothing but empty husks. One was standing quite close to me when he died and it was as if ... as if a candle had been snuffed out. One moment he was a man and his eyes were alive, and the next there was nothing there but a body devoid of all intelligence. That was the beginning of the attack proper.'

'When did the Katan enter the fighting?' Paedur asked, not wishing to hear a full blow-by-blow account of the battle.

'As the day wore on into evening,' Katani said slowly, 'the Shemmatae, perhaps sensing that they had lost, made one last desperate attempt. They concentrated everything on an assault on Churon's position on the hill overlooking the plain. Our forces were initially taken by surprise and forced back, and the Shemmatae drove a wedge straight through the heart of our lines to the foot of the hill. And there they encountered the Katan.' Her voice changed, becoming proud. 'They had saved their finest warriors, their elite Dragon Guard, for the attack, knowing that if they killed Churon, the alliance would fall apart – perhaps not immediately, but eventually – and even if they weren't victorious on the Sand Plain, then when the Brothers had gone their separate ways they could return.

'So the Katan fought the Dragon Guard, while the rest of our forces gradually forced the Shemmatae army back down to the shore, leaving the two elite forces fighting together. The Dragon Guard outnumbered the Katan by almost two to one, but we were the better warriors . . .'

The pause was so long that Paedur turned to look at her. Her face was pale and drawn and her eyes were distant. Her grip on the hilt of her sword was rigid, her knuckles white.

'What happened,' he asked eventually.

'We died defending our lord,' she said softly.

'All of you?'

'All of us.'

'Do you want to tell me how you died?' he asked, wondering how she would react.

Katani shook her head defiantly. 'I died defending my lord.'

'There is a tale – a legend, surely – of a single Katan warrior who betrayed her lord and attacked him, and was very nearly responsible for killing Churon the Onelord. Did you ever hear that tale?'

Her sword made no sound leaving its scabbard – and the point of the bard's hook touched her throat. The woman was shivering with rage and spittle flecked her lips. 'The sword . . .' Paedur said softly. Katani watched him, and for a single instant Paedur thought she might actually complete her move, draw the sword and attempt to disembowel him. He pressed the point of his hook against the soft flesh of her throat. 'I'll kill you,' he promised, 'and by the time you wake up, I'll be long gone.'

'You would?'

He nodded.

'I don't suppose your legend tells why the Katan attacked Churon?'

'I once read that she was in the pay of the Shemmatae,' he said quietly.

'I can believe that.' She pressed the blade back into its sheath and adjusted the catch that kept the blade locked in place.

'Tell me the real reason,' he suggested, removing his hook from her throat and stepping away from her.

'Churon was not a sane man,' Katani said slowly, watching him, gauging his reaction. 'He was arrogant, suspicious, petty in many ways, fearful of everyone. But he had vision, a vision of a united land, the Seven Nations, with him as emperor. He ruthlessly removed every obstacle in his path; the Shemmatae were merely another obstacle and he disposed of them as he had disposed of kings, lords, barons and beggars.

'When the Katan fought the Dragon Guard and died in doing so, he was, I think, secretly delighted. The Katan obeyed one basic tenet: loyalty to a cause of justice. Not loyalty to a man, but to an ideal, and in the beginning Churon upheld that ideal. But as he moved more and more away from it, so too did he lose the respect and loyalty of the Katan Sisterhood. Before the battle with the Shemmatae, the Katan had sent a request to the Onelord for an urgent meeting to discuss their future in his service. It is likely that we would have left, and more than likely that we would have been forced to do battle with his forces at some later date.

'But the Katan fought the Dragon Guard and died, but killed all the Guard in doing so. Only one Katan, mortally wounded, survived the carnage long enough to hear the Onelord say, "This saves me the trouble of poisoning them". I was enraged and attacked him – and his archers cut me down,' she finished simply.

They walked in silence for a while, and then the road began to slope upwards.

'And have you ever encountered him here?' Paedur asked.

'Not yet,' Katani said ominously.

They crested the slight rise and before them stood Manach, the City of the Dead.

'Not yet?' the bard asked, 'I would have thought you would have gone looking for him.'

'Oh, I know where he is,' she whispered.

'Where?'

Katani pointed. 'He is Mannam's closest adviser, protected

by him, surrounded by the frai-frode and Mannam's other pets. But this time . . .' she said, her voice trailing off.

'This time?'

'This time I'll do it properly,' she whispered, her voice a promise. 'I owe it to my sisters and myself.'

## 4    The Warning

If a cause is worthy, then it is worth dying for . . .
<br>          from . . . *The Warrior, the Life of Owen, Weapon Master*

The village was called Bridgetown, for no apparent reason since it possessed no bridge and the nearest river was half a day's ride away. It huddled in a valley around a freshwater spring, a miserable collection of stone and thatched huts, encircled only by a palisade of sharpened stakes.

Owen reined in his mount and let his eyes wander over the village, reading the signs of smoke, the dust of movement, the discoloration of the earth, looking for the flash of metal.

'What do you see?' Kutor asked, standing in the stirrups and shading his eyes with his hand from the early morning sun.

'I see a village of fifteen recognisable houses, an elder's house, a forge, what might be a place of worship or perhaps a woman's house and a well-house. I see it is surrounded by a flimsy wooden palisade, which is there obviously as a deterrent for animals, but no trench, and that tells me the village is too poor for bandits to bother with.'

'They could be paying the bandits to leave them in peace,' Kutor suggested.

'Did you do that often in the Wastelands?' Owen demanded abruptly, glancing sidelong at him.

Kutor looked away. 'We had to live . . .' he said defensively.

'And what of the villagers who were paying you? Did they not have a right to live as well?' he snapped.

'That is in the past.' Kutor mumbled.

Owen glared at him, and then he suddenly nodded and turned away. 'I'm sorry . . . I had no right. We have all done . . . well, we have done things which time has coloured and tinted.' He looked away. 'When I was a boy, my village was forced to pay tribute to a band of outlaws. It was a fierce winter and we lost many of the old, the children and the sick because we had less food and fuel. It has always been something that can raise me

41

to anger.' He finished suddenly, regretting his outburst, and urged his mount down the gritty track that led towards the village.

'Was that why you decided to defend Car'an'tual?' Kutor asked, coming up alongside.

The Weapon Master thought about it for a moment and then he grinned with rare good humour. 'Partially. The Brugh were attempting to extract tribute from the city fathers. And if they weren't paid, the Brugh were going to sack the city, level it to the ground, kill everyone and sell all the children into slavery at Londre.' He shrugged. 'I had very little choice in the matter.'

'And you stopped the Brugh on the city walls?' Kutor said in wonder. 'It is the stuff of legend.'

The Weapon Master smiled in something like embarrassment. 'Get the bard to tell you the tale. If we ever see him again,' he added.

'Oh, I'm sure we will.'

A small party was waiting for the two riders at the gate: two old men, obviously village elders, three large men behind them, farmers or shepherds more likely, and a little to one side a small, sharp-faced, barrel-chested man wearing a blacksmith's full-length leather apron.

Kutor reined in his mount and immediately dismounted, careful to show no discourtesy to these people. He bowed cautiously to the two older men, noting the wariness in their eyes and the open defiance and anger in the faces of the others. These people were afraid.

'A blessing on your hearths and families,' he said gravely, deciding on the standard Northland greeting.

'A blessing received and returned.' One of the old men bowed slightly. 'You are not Cormac's men?' he asked immediately.

'We know of no Cormac,' Kutor answered, glancing up at Owen, who had remained mounted and shook his head slightly.

'You are newly come to the Outlands, then?' the second man asked.

'Recently. Should we know of this Cormac?' Kutor asked quickly.

'He calls himself the King of the Outlands.' The old man almost spat the name.

'Hush now. These could be in Cormac's employ,' his companion advised.

'I care not. I've had enough of them,' the old man continued.

He stepped up to Owen's mount and glared up into his face, and then he tapped a long swollen-jointed finger against the warrior's high boot. 'Tell your master that. Tell him that Alun of Bridgetown has had enough . . .'

The second elder touched his arm and almost dragged him away. He looked up at Owen's impassive face. 'He does not know what he says. He is old and his wits are addled.'

Owen raised his hand, silencing him. 'I don't know this Cormac, and I am not in his service. I am Owen, a Weapon Master, currently in the employ of Prince Kutor.' To the villagers' obvious surprise, he indicated the small man standing before them. While their attention was on him, Kutor said, 'I take it this Cormac is extracting tribute from you?'

Alun, the old man, shook off the restraining hand. 'Aye, and every month his demands grow more extravagant. We're a poor village, a few shepherds, some quarrying, a little iron work. We have nothing . . . certainly nothing to spare.'

'I can see that,' Owen murmured.

Kutor stepped up to the old man and stared deep into his tired faded eyes. 'Would you be free of this Cormac, self-styled king of the Outlands?' he asked quietly.

'How?' The voice was a rasp, the accent thick and guttural.

Kutor turned towards the voice, and found himself facing the dwarf, the blacksmith. He was tall for one of the Stone Folk, standing just a little shorter than the prince, although his barrel chest and overdeveloped arms lent him an almost animal-like appearance, which was emphasised by his broad, flat face and thick unruly mop of hair.

'How?' he demanded again.

'I am Prince Kutor, half-brother to Geillard, the Emperor.'

'You are the Renegade,' the blacksmith stated flatly.

'So called,' Kutor admitted, 'but only by my enemies. My forces have recently invested the old Culai fortress just beyond the ridge under the mountains. I will have them wipe out this Cormac for you.'

'And the price?' the dwarf demanded.

'Join me.'

'Then we only exchange one slavery for another,' Alun said simply.

Owen said quickly, 'The prince was merely suggesting that if we defeat Cormac's forces some of you might wish to join us.'

'Another assault on the throne?' the dwarf sneered.

'Just so,' Kutor agreed, smiling pleasantly.

'And if we do not wish to join forces with you,' Alun asked, 'what will you do to us then?'

'Nothing!' Kutor sounded surprised. 'We are not bandits to force our will on others.' He was aware of Owen's impassive stare on his back. 'Tell us where this Cormac may be found and when we have dealt with him, then make your decision.'

'Prince,' the dwarf growled, 'how many men have you?'

'Enough.'

'Experience has shown me that enough usually means too few.' He grinned, showing his solid horse-like teeth. 'Cormac controls a legion of men.' He saw Kutor and Owen's look of disbelief and continued maliciously. 'Yes, a legion, a hundred decades, all armed, all armoured and half of them mounted.'

'And where can we find this Cormac?' Kutor asked.

The blacksmith shrugged his massive shoulders. 'Don't even look. He'll find you.'

'We had a visitor,' Keshian said, hurrying down the cracked steps to meet the horsemen. Behind them the two huge gates boomed closed and Owen nodded in approval as a newly trimmed tree-trunk slid home, barring it.

'One of the King Cormac's men?' Kutor asked, dismounting.

Keshian stopped in amazement. 'You met him?' he asked finally.

'We were told about him,' Owen said. 'Where's Tien?'

'Here.' The Shemmat appeared alongside Keshian, a double-recurved horn bow around his shoulder, a quiver of broad-headed arrows on his belt.

As the four men strode down the musty corridor, Owen and the prince listened intently to Keshian's and Tien tZo's account of what had occurred earlier that afternoon.

'There were three men,' Keshian began, 'mounted and armed.'

'Professional warriors,' Tien added, 'carrying weapons of choice rather than issue.'

'Experienced too, and although only three came forward, I'll wager there were more watching us.'

Tien nodded agreement.

'I've never seen warriors like them before. Tall men, dark,

weathered skins – but not black – oiled and curled beards, divided in the middle . . .'

'Gallowglas,' Owen said decisively. 'They carried swords almost as tall as themselves?'

Keshian and Tien both nodded.

'Gallowglas,' Owen repeated, nodding. 'Professional soldiers from the tribe of Gallowglas, which borders the Northlands. They have more than a touch of Chopt blood in them. They were said to be cannibal, like their savage cousins, but now they only eat human flesh on special ceremonial occasions. What did they say?'

'Very little,' Keshian continued. 'They demanded to speak to the lord of the fortress. When they learned he was not here, they said they were the men of Cormac, King of the Outlands, and would return to speak with you at dawn on the morrow.'

They had reached the rooms that had been set aside for the prince, but when Kutor would have strode straight in, Owen laid a hand on his arm and Tien moved ahead, an axe in his left hand. When he reappeared moments later, the Weapon Master allowed the prince to enter. 'Get used to it,' he said, smiling.

The prince's suite was a series of three interconnecting rooms – caves – cut into the heart of the stone. Each room was separated by a snugly fitting solid brukwood door and Kutor had, at Owen's insistence, chosen the last as his bedchamber. Owen had also insisted that later, when they had enough men to spare, they would position guards at each of the doors. They passed through the first room and into the second, which was almost identical except that it had a large, rough wooden table and a score of chairs of various types scattered around the room. The room itself, like most of the others in the fortress, was almost completely bare except for a series of fading pictures that had once been painted directly on to the wall and which Kutor thought might have been there to give the impression of windows.

The four men arranged themselves around the table and then, briefly and succinctly, Owen related what they had learned from the villagers.

'A legion,' Keshian whispered, 'one thousand . . .' He stopped as a sudden thought struck him. 'Surely not one thousand of the Gallowglas!'

Owen smiled and shook his head. 'No. I'm afraid there just aren't that many to go round. You saw three this morning . . .'

'There were more,' Tien interrupted.

'Even so, assuming there were another two in hiding, that gives us five ...' He paused. 'I would guess this king had a decade at his command. But remember, each Gallowglas is worth ... four, five ordinary warriors.'

'What do we do?' Kutor whispered. 'They'll be here in the morning.'

'Pay, fight or run,' Tien tZo said firmly.

Owen nodded. 'Aye, it's a simple enough choice: pay, fight or run.' He looked at the prince. 'Do you want to pay?'

Kutor shook his head. 'And we've nowhere to run to,' he added.

'So we fight.' The Weapon Master looked at Keshian. 'Can we defend the fortress?'

'Yes ... and no.' He spread his short, stubby fingers and began touching off points. 'We are not enough to man the walls, so we will lose the battlements, the courtyards, the well there, the provisions for the animals, and possibly the animals themselves. However, the fortress itself is accessible only through one reasonably solid door. Four men standing abreast could hold that door. But I discovered a mechanism earlier which allows an iron grill to fall from the ceiling into slots in the flagstones; it effectively seals the opening while allowing arrows or spears to be fired through. Should that gate fall, there is the door to the fortress itself, and that too has the iron grill behind it; but even without the grill, a single man could hold the door for days. There is also another lever just beyond the last gate which I think precipitates some sort of rock fall to seal off that entire corridor, but it also traps the defenders inside the fortress. There is food enough for all of us for just under a moon in here, and with the two freshwater wells, water presents no problem.'

'But we would be trapped?' Kutor asked.

'I have not yet found a way out, although I imagine there must be one.'

The Weapon Master nodded his thanks and turned to Tien. 'What weapons do we have?'

The sallow-skinned man pulled a disgusted face. 'Swords mostly, of every race and shape, and with hardly an edge on any of them. Some spears, axes, maces, morningstars, a few bows, not enough arrows, three crossbows, none of which are working properly, and we've few enough bolts for them in any case.'

'Well, we're not going to hold off an army with that,' Owen sighed. He looked from Keshian to Tien. 'We'll need arrows for the bows, and we'll need them soon. If you can get the crossbows working then so much the better.'

'That may be possible,' Tien agreed.

'We'll want broad-headed arrows and bolts – flesh-shredders – and also some armour-piercing . . .' He stopped as Tien shook his head.

'That may not be possible. I have neither the facilities nor the materials for forging armour-piercing heads here.'

'We'll need something to punch through the Gallowglas armour,' Owen said, looking at Kutor and Keshian for suggestions.

'Darts,' Keshian said slowly, raising his eyebrows.

Owen's face broke into a rare grin. 'Darts!' He looked at his servant. 'Darts and pipes?'

Tien smiled slightly. 'It is possible. I saw some suitable reeds beyond the fortress walls. You would want them poisoned?'

'Yes.'

'No!'

Everyone turned to look at the prince. 'I will not, cannot, allow my campaign to be tainted by the use of such things. It is hardly chivalrous.'

'Prince,' Owen said very softly, 'I came here to win you a throne. Now, if I am to do so, I must be given a free and full hand to wage this war in whatever way I see fit. You talk to me of chivalry now . . . now, after years of banditry in the wastelands, when you robbed and killed, raped and ransomed.' Kutor opened his mouth to protest, but the look on the Weapon Master's face quelled him. 'Do you think your enemies will fight by a code of chivalry? Do you? Did they fight by any such code in the past? Did you?' he asked savagely. 'Now, we will shortly be going up against one of the most feared clans of warriors in the Nations since the Katan. We need, desperately, to reduce their numbers, and I will do that by any and every means at my disposal.'

To break the growing silence Keshian said finally, 'Owen is right.'

Kutor sighed and nodded. 'I know. I just wish it were otherwise.' He looked at Owen. 'You are the Weapon Master. Do as you feel necessary.' He smiled hesitantly. 'I suppose when I am Emperor you will want to become the commander of my armies?'

Owen shook his head and laughed humourlessly. 'I am merely an adviser. Keshian is your commander, not I. And when you become Emperor, Kutor, you will not want to know me, or else will probably arrange to have me killed. Oh, don't look so shocked. It is a practice that has been hallowed by history.' He stood up suddenly. 'Come Tien, we'll look over the fortress's defences.' He nodded to the prince and Keshian. 'We will see you shortly before dawn.'

When the door closed and the footsteps had disappeared down the corridor, Keshian looked at the prince and poured him another drink. 'Was there any truth in what he said?' he asked softly.

'In what?'

'That you might order his death when you have gained the crown.'

Kutor lifted the glass and downed the fiery liquid in one swallow. 'Probably,' he gasped.

Owen and Tien walked the battlements, their greatcloaks wrapped around them against the chill of the night. They had made a cursory round of the fortress, only confirming what they already knew: in its present state the fortress was indefensible against a concentrated attack. It needed several moons work on the walls and complete refurbishment by skilled craftsmen to make it even halfway habitable. They stopped just above the main gate and leaned on the chill gritty stone, looking over the dimly visible plain, their eyes and ears alert for anything untoward. Experience taught them that the fortress was being watched and they both knew there was a possibility, albeit a slim one, that there would be a night attack.

'We could leave,' Tien suggested quietly, his soft voice almost lost on the wind. 'We could be far away by dawn. Our gear is still packed.'

'I have never run from a fight before, Tien,' Owen said coldly.

'No,' the Shemmat agreed, 'but you have made strategic retreats before, and returned to do battle when the odds were more in your favour. Even you cannot do battle with a decade of Gallowglas warriors.'

'But I cannot just leave.'

'Why not?' Tien asked in surprise.

'Because ... because the bard sent me to them. And I owe him, old friend, I owe him more than you can ever comprehend.'

'We spent but a single night with the bard,' Tien reminded him.

'It changed my life!' He unconsciously rubbed the wrist that had been recently covered by the Iron Band of Kloor. 'We may have spent just a single night with him, but I felt it was longer. I feel I've known him all my life.'

'And where is he now?' Tien demanded.

'I don't know,' the Weapon Master said feelingly, 'but I wish he was here!'

# 5   Manach

The city thrived and yet no life walked its cobbled streets . . .
*Life of Paedur, the Bard*

From the distance they could see that the tree bridges that led into Manach, the City of the Dead, were unguarded.

'Where are the frai-forde?' Paedur asked quietly.

Katani shook her head slightly. 'I don't know, but I have heard that they never leave their posts. In the way that I chose to guard the way from the World of Men, the Star Lorn are doomed to guard the bridges into the city.'

'And yet you left your post,' Paedur reminded her softly.

'Because of you,' she said with a smile, 'you broke the spell.'

Paedur turned back to the blasted landscape, looking for signs of movement, unable to shake off the feeling that they were under observation by someone or something just out of sight. 'Were you in fact under a spell – a proper spell, that is – that kept you at the entrance to this place or was it more like a vague compulsion to remain there?' he asked suddenly.

Katani thought about the question and then shook her head. 'I'm not sure. I wandered through the Silent Wood for a long time before I came to that place,  and when I reached it, I felt no desire to leave. It seemed only natural that I should stay and guard the way.'

'A *geasa* – compulsion,' Paedur grunted without looking at her. The feeling of being watched had grown and he had to resist the temptation to look over his shoulder once again. And once again he longed for his enhanced senses, realising how much he had come to depend on them.

'What do we do?' Katani asked.

'We've come this far . . .' Paedur said softly. He adjusted his cloak and strode off down the track.

They walked up to the first bridge – the Bridge of Wood – and then stopped, looking across its broad width. The bridge had been constructed of broad lengths of black wood which had been worn to a soft greyness in the centre with the passing of generations of the dead. There was no rail on either side.

Paedur walked on to the bridge, his boot-heels echoing thunderously, and strode into the middle before moving to the edge to stare down into the black water below. The river was surprisingly close to the underside of the bridge, less than one manlength – but because it was completely black, it was impossible to gauge any impression of its depth.

Katani joined him, looking in disgust at the sluggish, foulseeming liquid. 'It is part of the Naman,' she spat, 'the Black River.'

Paedur nodded. 'I know. Did I tell you I saw its counterpart, the Aman, in the Yellow God's kingdom?'

'You told me.' She nodded towards the river. 'It's not water. Have you any idea what it is?' she asked, tossing a stone into the liquid; it disappeared without a sound, without leaving a ripple in the tar-like surface.

'It is the River of Death,' the bard said, glancing at her, 'supposedly the tears of the One, from whose essence the Planes of Existence and the very first gods were created. When the One awoke from his slumber and saw what the Great Gods Hanor and Hara had wrought, he supposedly wept, tears of joy and tears of sorrow at the creation. And C'lte, the Lord of Life, gathered up the milk-white pearls of his tears of joy and set them in a river in his kingdom, and Mannam gathered the inky jewels of his tears of sorrow and caused them to flow around the city he was only then building for himself, Manach, the City of the Dead, protecting it.'

'And that brings us back to the Star Lorn,' Katani said. 'Where are the three guards? The first should be here, guarding the Bridge of Wood; the next, just beyond, standing before the Bridge of Stone; and the third, off over there, holding the Bridge of Crystal.'

'Wood for his body, stone for his heart, crystal for his eyes,' Paedur said softly, and then added, 'an ancient description of the Lord of the Dead. 'No,' he continued, 'I think it's obvious. The guards have been removed as an invitation.'

'I think there are some invitations best left unanswered.'

'Ah, but this is an invitation from Death,' Paedur smiled delightedly, 'and some invitations you just don't ignore.'

'So you're just going to march in?'

'Through the main gate,' Paedur stated, and crossed the bridge.

From the distance Manach, the City of the Dead, had looked white – startlingly so against the stone-greyness of the landscape and the leaden sky – but as the bard and warrior-maid neared it, the colour altered subtly, turning from cold white to a soft yellow and then to a faded ivory, the colour of old bones. The second bridge was of stone, each block incised with lines from the Book of the Dead, and, crossing that, they began to gain an impression of the actual monumental size of the city. The third and final bridge was of crystal which was so pure and clear that although it had been visible from the distance, close-up it was little more than a vague outline, only the lines of script in the ancient language of the Culai that had been cut into the crystal stones and which now hung solid and unmoving on the air giving it solidity. But it was firm and solid under their feet. They stepped off the final bridge and stopped to stare in wonder at Manach. It appeared to have been constructed of a single stone: there were no seams in the blocks of stone, no trace of the mortar that held them together. The only opening in the ivory walls was the main gate, a huge arch that was without doors. A dozen towers rose up over the battlements, regularly spaced and so thin and narrow that they couldn't possibly be habitable, with the exception of one that was larger and broader than the rest.

When they walked into the shadow of the walls, the temperature plummeted, and even Katani, whose senses had been blunted by the process of death, shivered. Katani settled her horned helmet on her head and adjusted the mail coif and neckscarf with a practised shake of her head. She pulled her heavy leathern gloves sewn with metal plates from her belt and dragged them on. Paedur pulled up his hood and settled his arms into his wide sleeves. He heard a curious hissing sound and it took him a moment or two to realise that the woman was laughing.

'What's so amusing?'

'I had forgotten what it like to be cold,' she said. 'It almost makes me feel alive again.'

There was a wide metal grid set into the ground at the entrance to the city and they both stopped before stepping on to it. About a single man-length below the grid they heard the slow gurgling movement of a river.

Katani leaned over and then just as suddenly recoiled, gagging. 'The Naman. But what's it doing here, and what is the purpose of this grid?' She looked at the bard.

Paedur shrugged, the movement dislodging his hood. 'I don't know,' he admitted.

'It is to ensure that you bring nothing from the Silent Woods into the city!'

Katani fell into a fighting crouch, both swords sliding free of their scabbards with a venomous hiss. Paedur remained unmoving, staring towards the slight figure that had stepped out into the shadows beneath the archway but who still remained shadowed. 'Who are you?' the bard asked calmly.

The figure shrugged, a movement that lifted its shoulders unnaturally high. 'A name is something left in the world of Men; in Manach all are known to one another and our Lord, and there is no need of names.'

'I am . . .' Paedur began.

'You, and your companion, are known,' the figure continued.

Katani described a circle with both swords, bringing them around until they touched, the metal singing, the sound taken up beneath the archway and magnified, leaving it shivering on the air long after she had sheathed her weapons. 'What do we call you, then? What are you?' she demanded, her accent turning the question into a growl.

'You may call me what I am, and I am but a servant.'

'A servant?' Paedur said, the question implicit.

'A servant of Mannam.' The figure moved towards them with a stiff-legged, unnatural gait. And it was only when it stepped into the light that they saw the wings.

'Bainte,' Paedur breathed. 'Mannam's winged messengers of death,' he explained to Katani, who was still staring curiously at the creature. The bainte was naked and about the size of a child on the threshold of adulthood, thin and gangling, and possessing the characteristics of both sexes. Its skin was completely hairless and milk white, and its large red-rimmed eyes and round open mouth gave it a skull-like appearance. Its arms were thin and straight with no elbow joints and hung loosely by its sides. Beginning just above the shoulder joints were the wings. They were folded now and it was impossible to gauge their size, but they were taller than the bainte and judging from the wedges and knots of muscle, they were incredibly powerful.

'Scrape the dirt from your boots and follow me,' the creature commanded, its voice clear and unaccented.

Paedur strode straight across the grill without stopping. The creature hunched and suddenly unfolded one of its wings, and a talon that was as long as the bard's arm and just as thick touched the centre of his chest. 'Your boots,' the bainte said emotionlessly, 'clean them.'

'Why?' Paedur demanded, unmoving.

'Because it is the law of this place. Nothing from the Silent Wood may come into the City of the Dead.'

'Why?' Paedur persisted.

'Ask Mannam,' the bainte said reasonably.

The bard stared at the creature, unsure if it was playing with him but unable to form any decision from its bland wide-eyed expression. He scraped his boots on the grill, knocking off the grit and stones clinging to the soles down into the glutinous water.

Katani joined him on the grill. 'Why the ritual?' she asked softly, tapping her boots together, watching the grit tumble into the water below.

With his eyes still on the bainte, he shook his head. 'I don't know. I have an idea, though.'

The bainte suddenly turned away and headed down the broad statue-lined avenue that led away from the gate. Paedur and Katani hurried after it, looking in wonder at the statues that lined the broad cobbled street. There were hundreds of them, all completely life-like, of men and women from a score of lands and from all ages on tall plinths which usually bore a single line legend. Some, history had awarded some recognition – kings, priests, leaders, warriors – but in the main they were of unknowns, or at least unknown to the bard's vast lore. There were non-humans scattered amongst them – Star Lorn, Susuru and Chopts – and some that looked close cousins to the Culai. Paedur attempted to read the script, but the language was strange and even he, for all his learning, couldn't decipher it.

'They're too real to be statues,' Katani murmured, looking at one particularly vivid representation of a Katan which was complete even down to the nicks in the scales of the lacquered armour.

'I thought that too, but what need would Mannam have for this type of sorcery?'

'Mannam is a vain creature,' Katani reminded him. 'It might please him to have these beings immobile here – living statues, as it were.'

'Living?' Paedur asked, smiling at her use of the word. 'But I agree, it is curious.'

'Something else we must ask Death,' the woman murmured to herself.

The avenue ran arrow-straight for a thousand paces and then it dipped gently down into a huge hollow and opened out, and here the first buildings began.

'It looks like any other city,' Katani said softly, looking from side to side, her left hand still resting on the cloth-wrapped hilt of her sword.

'Except for the people,' Paedur murmured.

'What people?'

The bard glanced at her and smiled enigmatically. There were no people.

'Did you ever visit Bannoche?' she remarked a little later, when they had walked deeper into the city and the buildings had become taller.

Paedur shook his head. 'In my time it had long vanished, the creeping sands having finally claimed it.'

'That was already happening in my day,' Katani said softly. 'And this place reminds me of it.'

'Because it is so empty?'

Surprisingly the warrior shook her head. 'Bannoche was already called the City of Ghosts in my time; it was dead during the day, but at night it came alive with the shades of a score of centuries, all going about their tasks as if they were still in the World of Men.'

'There is no night here,' Paedur said reasonably, but aware of what Katani was suggesting, recalling what he knew of the legends of the City of Ghosts. 'I wonder if the houses are really empty?' he murmured.

'Why don't you look?'

'No look! No stray from the path!' The bainte's words were clipped and harsh, and although it didn't turn around, its round head swivelled through a complete half-circle to stare back at them.

'Extraordinary hearing,' Paedur remarked with a grin. He turned back to Katani. 'Tell me about Bannoche. I think I would have liked to visit it.'

'My experience of the place is limited,' she said, 'and from what I now know, I am inclined to believe that it may be an outpost of Mannam's kingdom, a place where the fabrics of the various Planes of Existence meet.'

'What were you doing there?'

Katani smiled, remembering. 'We were chasing bandits, three of my sisters and I, and their trail led to the City of Ghosts. Of course, we had heard rumours about the city, but we thought them nothing more than the usual legends that always grow up around deserted villages or cities, and we chose to ignore them. What we didn't know then was that Bannoche was used as a bandit camp during the day, although they always left as the sun was setting and spent the night in a series of fortified caves close to the walls. And so we four rode unsuspecting into the city and promptly found ourselves in the midst of a bandit camp. We contemplated a struggle, but they had archers and crossbowmen and we knew it would only be suicide, so we surrendered.'

'I thought the Katan warriors never surrendered,' Paedur said.

'Being a warrior means not only acknowledging victory but accepting defeat,' Katani quoted.

'Fand,' Paedur said, 'the foundress of the Katan Sisterhood.'

'How do you know that?' she asked, surprised.

'I am familiar with her monumental work on the Path of the Warrior. Surprisingly, it is required reading for those studying to be a bard, and I know some of the warrior schools still use it as a textbook. But I interrupted you; please continue.'

'There's little enough to tell. The bandits captured us and abused us somewhat, in the way of such creatures, although they didn't manage to take our virginity, which was their aim. They stopped because night was drawing on and their fear of the place was far greater than their lust. They promptly gathered up their belongings and rode out of the city to huddle in their caves like beasts. But they left us behind,' she said slowly, her voice falling to a whisper. Her eyes closed briefly, and when they opened again, they were clear, the grief and pain hidden once again. 'I am dead now, bard, dead these many years, and I am familiar enough with the ways of the Silent Wood and its occupants to know that we have little interest with the living, and even less interest in interfering with them. Oh, there are some, of course, who spend more time in the World of Men than is proper, and their motives may not always be good, but in the main, fear is their only weapon. However, at that time I didn't know that, and you can imagine how terrifying it was for the four of us to be suddenly confronted with the shades of the dead.

'We had been tied to a pillar in the centre of a square, and before our eyes the city slowly came alive – if that is the right word – and a market was set up around us. In the early twilight the shades were tenuous and from Bannoche's recent past, but as the night drew on we found ourselves able to distinguish the different ages and cultures of the city, until towards dawn we were looking at the earliest age of Bannoche.

'It would have been bad enough if the dead had merely walked around us, but some seemed to be able to see us, and examined us curiously like specimens in a glass phial.' She shrugged. 'Again, I understand that now, but at the time . . .'

'It must have been terrifying,' Paedur said absently, not looking at her, watching the buildings on either side. He had the impression that they were not as empty as they seemed.

'It was,' she whispered.

'It says much for you that you survived with your sanity intact,' Paedur continued.

'We retreated into the lore of our Order, repeating the lessons again and again, meditating on Fand's teachings.'

'And the bandits?'

'They never returned to Bannoche,' Katani smiled. 'They were ambushed by a party of our sisters as they rode back towards the city the following morning. None of them survived, especially when they admitted what they had done to the four of us . . .'

Paedur suddenly reached over and touched her arm. He said nothing but his eyes moved towards an open doorway ahead of them. Katani continued to chatter, but nodded almost imperceptibly, following his gaze. She nodded briefly again; she too had seen the movement in the darkened doorway.

The bainte had now led them into what was obviously a fairly prosperous part of the city. The buildings were tall and imposing, and temples, fine houses, merchants' stores and brothels lined both sides of the streets, the frescoes above each doorway proclaiming the trade or occupation. The street itself narrowed and then narrowed again, until it was little more than a broad alleyway, and the only thing that distinguished it from a street in any city or town in the World of Men was the absence of awnings or stalls lining the walls. And people.

Paedur started suddenly, something of his old awareness making him turn, but there was nothing behind him.

'You need not fear, bard,' the bainte said abruptly, without turning around. 'Nothing will harm you here in the Drear God's Kingdom.'

'Oh, I know that,' Paedur said with a grim smile. 'I was merely wondering where the inhabitants of this city were.'

'Dead,' the bainte remarked.

Mannam's palace was set on a low knoll in the middle of an artificial lake in the centre of the city. The only access to it was by a single drawbridge, which was raised. The palace itself was long and low and sprawling, primitive and ugly in appearance – but on second glance, artificially so. Its style was blocky and massive, in the manner of the Culai builders, but unlike their work, the huge square stones had been polished to a mirror brightness and some had been gilded. The windows, which were set high into the wall just beneath the sloping, polished roof, were surprisingly barred and the portcullis was down across the low double gates.

A double line of trees ran around the edge of the island – the first sign of vegetation the bard had seen since he had crossed into the Silent Wood. But when he looked closely at the trees, he realised that they were artificial; they had been cast from stone and then painted in superbly realistic colours.

The bainte walked to the edge of the black waters of the lake and hunched over. It then raised its two huge wings and brought them together in a thunderous clap that rolled across the water, setting its blood-black surface vibrating. There was movement on the walls and more bainte appeared, and then slowly and ponderously the portcullis was lifted and a single span of wood was pushed across the lake, barely a hand-breadth above the surface of the water. It thumped on to the land and without hesitation the bainte walked out on to it and then its head described its unnatural half turn. 'The wood will only support one at a time.' It turned back and continued across the bridge.

'This . . . this is all wrong,' Paedur whispered. 'Something is amiss.'

'You are wondering about the bars on the windows,' Katani said.

Paedur nodded. 'Aye, and the other precautions. Hardly the signs of a secure monarch.'

'But surely nothing can threaten Death?' the warrior asked.

'Nothing,' Paedur said slowly, 'unless . . .'

'Unless?'

'Since you walked the World of Men, a new religion has grown up. It is a false belief, ruled by false, base gods with none of the qualities of godhood and all the vices of mankind. They constantly war with the Gods of the Old Faith, attempting to overthrow them, warring for control of all the Planes of Existence. There are times when the Gods of the Old Faith triumph, but the New Religion daily grows in strength and numbers and its gods grow arrogant. I wonder if the war has gone against the Old Faith?'

'Is that possible?'

'Mannam is afraid. He protects himself behind water, behind bars, in a closed city. Obviously he fears.'

'But what would frighten Death?' Katani wondered.

'That only thing that could threaten Death is death itself!'

# 6   The King of the Outlands

'Any man with an army at his back can call himself king, but only
the fool thinks he can rule.'

*Owen the Weapon Master*

The dawn sunlight was lancing low across the plain when the
first rider appeared on the crest of the rise, his shadow etched
long and sharp on to the stony ground. He was followed, a
moment later, by two more riders, but these were taller, broader
men, riding huge southern shire-mounts, their size dwarfing the
first rider between them.

'An emissary with his guards,' Keshian said, squinting against
the glare of the early morning sunlight.

'And the guards are for show,' Owen murmured.

'Are they Gallowglas?' Prince Kutor asked, shading his eyes
and staring at the guards. 'A handsome addition to any army,'
he murmured.

The Weapon Master passed Kutor a wooden seeing-tube.
'They are difficult to control and it is foolishness bringing two
or more together; when they are not fighting amongst themselves, they are plotting to overthrow their employer.'

Kutor turned the wooden tube slightly, attempting to sharpen
up the image, but the glass had been poorly blown and the
image of the warriors and the emissary remained indistinct and
fuzzy. 'Perhaps if we were to offer to employ them,' he suggested.

'With what?' Keshian snapped, fear sharpening his voice. 'We
have no coin and no comforts here, and even if we had, I'm not
sure I or the men would want these flesh-eaters amongst us.'

The two Gallowglas stopped and allowed the smaller, human
rider to continue forward a score of paces. The man reined in
his mount and plunged the spear with the black truce-ribbon
tied to it into the ground. Then he threw back his head, contemptuously scanning the battlements.

'I am Diarmon, emissary of King Cormac, and I ride under a

60

flag of truce.' The man's voice was strong, well-modulated and obviously cultured. He waited a few moments, and then added, 'Do I speak to stones?'

'You do not speak to stones.' Kutor climbed up and stood astride two of the merlons with his hands on his hips. 'I am Kutor, a prince of the blood, half-brother to the Emperor. And I know of no King Cormac in the rolls of nobility.'

The messenger grinned, revealing a smile that was all the more unusual for being perfect, and completely insincere. 'I do not recall reading the name of Prince Kutor there either.'

'Do not allow him to anger you,' Owen snapped.

'State your business.'

'My master, King Cormac, wishes to deal with you.'

'I have no business with your master.'

'But you have taken one of his castles. Tribute must be paid, a debt must be discharged.' The messenger's face was a study in surprised innocence.

'Don't argue with him,' Owen advised, his eyes on the two warriors sitting grim and impassive on their mounts behind the messenger, seemingly unconcerned with the proceedings.

'I have incurred no debt and there will be no tribute, no dealings,' Kutor said flatly and climbed down from the merlons.

'My master commands a legion,' Diarmon said proudly to the now invisible figure, 'and the Gallowglas honour us with their presence. Your paltry force cannot stand against us. Now, my master is a reasonable man and so he offers you the option of tribute rather than death.' He stopped. No movements were visible on the battlements and he glanced around at his guard in frustration. They looked at him as if he were an animal, beneath contempt. 'Then you will all die,' he screamed to the stone walls and wheeled his mount round and galloped away, followed at a more leisurely pace by the warriors.

Tien tZo returned a little after noon, when the shadows were beginning to stretch again. Kutor, with Keshian and Owen, was in the process of poring over a hugely intricate chart they had discovered in a small room off one of the main corridors. The room had been shelved and the shelves had been lined with books and scrolls. And while all of these turned out to be nothing more than the daily fortress history as recorded by a succession of bards, pinned to one wall had been a plan of the

*Demon's Law: Tales of the Bard*

fortress itself, laid out floor by floor and indicating in faded coloured inks the various hidden entrances, including one which ran for almost three thousand paces and came out on the far side of the mountain.

'Well, at least we cannot be trapped,' Keshian was saying when Tien tZo came into the room. He stopped when he noticed the Shemmat.

The three men looked at the small warior expectantly. 'Cormac is Gallowglas,' he said simply.

Owen nodded. 'I suspected as much. There was no other way for him to control so many Gallowglas.'

Tien tZo sat in one of the high-backed wooden chairs and slowly and carefully made his report. 'I followed the emissary to Cormac's camp, which lies in a guarded valley less than half a morning's ride from here. There is a town, but it has now been turned into an armed camp and fortifications are being built. I saw Cormac's legion, and they are conscripts to a man, with little training and in absolute fear of the Gallowglas. I saw a man being flogged and there was a body on a gallows beside the main gate.' The small man sipped the proffered wine, his sharp green eyes moving from face to face. 'The Gallowglas are everywhere and they treat the legion soldiers badly. Free the legion from the Gallowglas and you will have recruits,' he added shrewdly.

'And Cormac?' Keshian asked eagerly.

'I was coming to him. He is a big man, bigger than the Gallowglas riders who came with the emissary. There is much of the Chopt in him; he is beast-like and brutal. When I saw him he was devouring a lump of meat that looked suspiciously like a human arm.'

Kutor looked at Owen. 'I though you said the Gallowglas only ate human flesh on special ceremonial occasions.'

'Obviously this Cormac is not an ordinary Gallowglas – if there is such a creature as an ordinary Gallowglas,' the Weapon Master added wryly. He turned back to Tien tZo. 'You say the legion fears the warriors.'

'They are terrified.'

'Then why do they not rise up and attack these creatures?' Kutor demanded. 'Surely a thousand men are more than a match for . . . for how many Gallowglas?' he asked Tien tZo.

'It was impossible to estimate their numbers, but I counted two decades of shire-mounts.'

Keshian sat forward. 'I think you'll find the Gallowglas are holding hostages,' he said quietly. 'When I was a mercenary in Nasgociba, fifty of us once held a city of three thousand by simply taking as hostages the women and children of the likely troublemakers.'

Tien tZo bowed slightly. 'I saw few women and equally few children.'

Owen stood up suddenly. 'We need a map of this district,' he announced, 'there may be one in the library.'

'You have a plan?' Prince Kutor asked hopefully.

'Merely an idea.'


There was no moon and the sky was obscured with thick, roiling clouds that had blown up just as the light was beginning to fade. Thunder boomed in the distance and there was the ghostly promise of lightning on the horizon.

Beneath the overhang of rock the fortress was in total darkness and, on Keshian's orders, no lights or fires had been lit in those rooms which had a window opening out on to the rocky plain. Almost certainly the fortress was under observation, and while it was possible for the guards on the battlements to just about make out the vague shapes of larger boulders and stones on the plain, it was hoped that any watchers would find it extremely difficult to distinguish the fortress from the rock face.

In the blackness a small arched side gate opened on thickly oiled hinges and ten men crept out. Keshian watched them melt into the plain and become invisible although they were no more than a handful of paces in front of him. The last one stopped briefly beside him. 'We will be back,' Tien promised, and then moved on.

'I hope so,' Keshian murmured, locking the door and heading up the stairs for the battlements. It promised to be a long night.

Owen's idea had resolved into what Keshian had declared to be absolute folly: ten men, all volunteers, would be chosen to infiltrate Cormac's camp and kill as many of the Gallowglas as possible. If they could kill Cormac, then so much the better, but no-one seriously expected to slay the king on their first raid, no-one except Owen, that was.

There was no shortage of volunteers, and both Kutor and Keshian eventually ended up picking eight of the fiercest of their brigands. Tien tZo had then explained the mission to them and detailed the risks involved, and gave them the opportunity of stepping down with honour. Perhaps unsurprisingly, none of the men stepped down. Their clothing had been blackened with soot and their skins likewise covered in a mixture of soot and grease; even the blades of their weapons had been blackened with a mixture of candlewax and soot.

Shortly before the moment of departure, Kutor made his way to the Weapon Master's room. The door was locked and he had to knock before Tien finally opened it. The Shemmat smiled apologetically. 'Habit,' he said.

Owen was putting the finishing touches to the blacking on his sword; he was already completely black himself.

'You look like a shadow,' Kutor said nervously.

'That is the idea.'

Kutor nodded and moved around the room, stopping briefly at the door to watch Tien blackening his skin in the small side-room.

'What's wrong?' Owen asked suddenly.

'I want you to call off this mission,' Kutor said, turning to face him.

'Why?'

'You are the only one amongst us with the knowledge and experience to raise and train a fighting army. Without you, we have nothing; we are nothing but a band of outlaws.'

'We don't stand a chance against the Gallowglas on their own,' Owen stated flatly, 'never mind the legion forces. But if we should slay some of these "invincible warriors" then we gain a twofold advantage: we reduce the numbers of the warriors and we demoralise the legion. There is also the added possibility that the legion will realise that they can throw off the shackle of the Gallowglas.'

'And assume Keshian is correct and they have captives. They will do nothing while their wives or children are held as surety for their conduct,' Kutor protested.

'Well, we'll have to see if we can do something about that too.'

'And if you are killed . . .?'

'I'll try not to be,' Owen said wryly.

Against the rocky plain, the ten men were invisible. Owen led them, while Tien tZo ranged ahead to deal with any sentries. The Weapon Master was only too aware of the risk he was taking. Should they be captured, Prince Kutor's dream died with them. The eight men with him represented the best that Kutor had to offer and his own and Tien's experience was invaluable to the Renegade's cause. However, it was not in Owen's nature even to consider defeat . . .

Hesht dug the heels of both palms into his eyes, watching the coloured lights explode against his eyelids, and yawned hugely. In his opinion, there was nothing more useless or soul-destroying than sentry duty. Who in their right mind would even consider attacking one Gallowglas, never mind two decades of the animals?

He never even saw the figure that rose up out of the ground and noiselessly opened his throat . . .

Dyfa raised the wooden tube to his eye and looked out across the plain, smiling a little self-consciously, knowing the device was almost useless during the day and more so on a cloudy night. But when the nights were clear and the Lady Lussa rode the heavens, then the far-seeing tube showed him the wonders of her unearthly chariot. Now all he could see was a vague circle of dull grey on black . . . with a tiny spot of silver in it.

Dyfa removed the tube from his eye and was wondering vaguely if he had seen a star when the arrow ripped into his eye, piercing his skull, killing him instantly . . .

The click of the bone dice was barely audible on the outspread cloak and the tiny stub of candle cast just enough light to read the cubes by. 'Two horns! Mine!' The voice was young and excited. He had just won the equivalent of a night's pay with one roll of the dice.

'We're only starting,' the second voice replied. He was older, more mature, and not unduly worried about losing; he had two loaded dice in the top of his boot and in this light he had no doubts but that he could substitute them when the young recruit grew greedy.

'Whose turn?' the youngster asked.

'Mine!' a third voice hissed, twin hand-axes whistling in the night air, striking flesh . . .

When Owen and the rest of the group joined Tien tZo moments later they found him carefully positioning the two dead men in such a way that to the casual observer they would seem to be still alert and on duty.

'How many?' the Weapon Master asked softly.

'Four.'

'I thought there might be more,' Owen remarked.

'I was expecting less. These are arrogant people with nothing to fear,' Tien tZo said. 'They have the Gallowglas.'

There was a low ridge ahead of them, and while Kutor's eight warriors couched in the small hollow, Owen and Tien tZo crawled to the lip and looked down. Cormac's camp lay spread out before them but, more importantly, directly below was the corral and, off to one side, a separate corral for the huge shire-mounts.

'Fire or poison?' Tien tZo asked, looking at the mounts.

'Fire,' Owen said without hesitation. 'We'll drive them into the camp. That will create even more confusion.'

'When? Now, or . . .'

'After we kill as many of the Gallowglas as we possibly can,' Owen murmured.

'I'll fetch the men,' the Shemmat said, moving silently back down the incline, rejoining the waiting men.

From Tien tZo's earlier reconnaissance of the camp they knew, albeit roughly, the placement of the Gallowglas' tents and the king's 'palace', which was in reality nothing more than a rather crude wooden hut that had been daubed with a yellow paint and the thatch roof replaced with one of slate and sods of black turf. The plan called for Owen himself to attend to the king, while Tien tZo led the rest in an attack on the tents. The element of surprise was essential, and Owen had ordered no actual contact with the enemy unless it was completely unavoidable. All the men had been issued with hollow tubes and Tien tZo had brewed a foul-smelling black tar-like substance which had been painted on to the overlong darts.

Three of the Gallowglas were standing outside the king's house, heads bent in conversation, when the lone man approached, weaving drunkenly down the main street that was little better than an open sewer. Their large dark eyes immediately fixed on him and, with a mercenary's true instinct, their hands found weapons. The man stopped and peered uncertainly at the three huge creatures, then he lifted a stone crock and swallowed long and hard. And then he wandered over to the three guards. A sword the length of a tall man tapped against his chest, stopping him. Smiling widely, he extended the stone jug. 'Drink?' he slurred.

The guard with the sword shifted the ungainly weapon, resting the flat of the blade on his shoulder. He stepped forward and took the jug, sloshing it around, breathing in the fumes of raw rofion.

The drunken man swayed on his feet and then sank to his knees in the muck, hiccupping loudly.

The Gallowglas grinned broadly, showing his yellowed, pointed teeth and then he threw back his head and tilted the jar back, noisily swallowing the fiery liquor . . . only to end up gagging on his own blood. He reached for his throat, aware of the chill and the bitter taste and then the pain. He touched the bone handle of the knife embedded in his throat and died as he attempted to pull it out. Owen's second knife took the second guard through the eye as he ambled forward to see what was amiss, and he had another knife in his hand and his arm back ready to throw when the third guard went down without a sound. He darted forward and rolled the man over; in the little light that came seeping through the ill-fitting door the Weapon Master saw the tufted dart that protruded from the man's jugular. He raised his hand to the shadows, silently acknowledging Tien tZo's handiwork. He eased the door open, calling on the Gods of the Pantheon that it wouldn't creak, and as he made his way through the palace, Owen wondered how his men were faring . . .

The Gallowglas were dying.

Two had been slain in their tents as they slept, the poison darts ensuring that they would never wake again. Another had died as he stood by the cesspit relieving himself; he had toppled forwards into the filth and had been immediately swallowed up by the seething muck. Two of the foul creatures had been taking their pleasure together when the darts had struck, joining them together in the final ultimate union. One of the Gallowglas had been in the process of slowly and methodically whipping a man who had been bound to the frame of a door. The man's back was now merely raw flesh and it was obvious that the Gallowglas had been at his work for some time; he had stripped to the waist, exposing his corded, muscled back that was covered with a bristling reddish-black hair. Every now and then he stopped and stretched out, rubbing his coarse hands on the man's raw flesh and then licking his fingers with great enjoyment. He drew back his arm for another swing with the metal-tipped whip, and then he froze, feeling the insect nick on his broad bare back. There was a second and then a third sting and the huge mercenary turned – and there was another pinprick in the centre of his chest. He looked down to find a long feathered sliver of wood protruding from his flesh and as he opened his mouth to cry out, he died.

Owen padded noiselessly down the length of the wooden corridor, his short sword in his left hand, held reversed, the blade flat against his sleeve, a throwing knife in his right hand. The hut – he could never think of it as a palace – was silent, unusually so, and it was only when he cracked open one of the doors that lined the corridor that he discovered that the floors, walls and even the ceilings had been covered with scores of rugs and carpets, which completely sealed the room and deadened all sound.

He stopped at the juncture of another corridor and, pressed flat against the warm wood, risked a quick peek around the corner. He spotted the two guards standing outside one of the doors – Cormac's room, or was it? He knew of several kings who posted guards outside empty or trapped rooms, while they themselves slept securely in small, unguarded bedchambers. He smiled tiredly. He had been in cities too long – here he was up against a primitive, barbarian Gallowglas tribesman, an arrogant braggart, unsuspecting and therefore vulnerable.

Owen pulled a blowpipe from his belt and slipped two darts out from the pouch sewn on to his sleeve. It was going to be a difficult shot; both guards would have to be taken out almost simultaneously. The furthest guard first, then, while the guard nearest to him was hopefully looking at his companion as he crumpled to the ground, Owen would be able to dart him. He forced a dart into the tube, took a deep breath and blew!

And missed.

The Gallowglas looked dumbly at the feathered sliver of sharpened wood that protruded from the door-frame beside his face. He had been drinking heavily earlier that evening and his reactions were slow. He opened his mouth to say something when a second dart took him through the mouth, and he died with a look of absolute amazement frozen on to his face.

The second guard was reaching for his huge sword when the thrown knife ripped out his throat. He reeled backwards, crashing against the door, partially tearing it off its leathern hinges. There was an almost animal-like roar in the darkened room and Owen saw a huge, pale shape moving in the darkness. He quickly spat two of the poisoned darts into the room, hoping for a lucky hit and then turned and ran . . .

Tien tZo waited until the eighth man had passed him and then he sank back into the shadows to await Owen. He reached into his pouch and touched the two remaining balls of Shemmat-fire he had prepared earlier. They were small earthen bottles filled with a mixture of powder and acid that were kept separate by a thin wafer of soft metal; when the acid ate through the metal, it mixed with the powder to produce a brief and fiery explosion. Usually he placed the bottles in puddles of lamp oil, but this night he had to content himself with tossing them on to the tents and into the animals' straw. While he was waiting for the first to explode – and they were unstable and temperamental – he strewed the beaten track with caltrops – spiked balls that lacerated the feet of men and animals alike.

The Weapon Master moved slowly and confidently through the men that were spilling out from the tents alerted by the sudden commotion from the palace. The huge, bellowing, roaring sound was like that of a bear in heat, Owen mused. And then there were other shouts as the dead Gallowglas were discovered. Somewhere a gong began booming as a general alarm went up.

And then the first tiny bomb exploded. It had been placed under a fold in a tent and even when it burst it went completely unnoticed, even though two men were standing directly in front of it. The intense heat quickly melted through the heavy woollen fabric and it smouldered for a score of heartbeats before the entire side of the tent exploded into flames. And suddenly all across the camp the tents were beginning to burn.

The fires in the corrals terrified the animals, shire-mounts and horses alike, and as the stalls themselves began to burn, hissing sparks and stinging cinders, the animals surged away from them lunging against the stout palisade, which immediately buckled beneath the weight of the enormous shire-mounts. Free, the animals raced down the track, straight on to the caltrops. Their screams were almost human-like. Completely maddened now, the crippled beasts thundered through the camp, flattening everything in their path, destroying the tents and the flimsy wooden shelters. Two of the shire-mounts blundered against Cormac's palace and actually managed to knock it from the support poles that lifted it up off the muck. One end of the building crashed to the ground, caving in the roof, leaving a jagged rent that almost split the building in two.

Owen stood back in the shadows and smiled triumphantly at the chaos and destruction. It was good to be working again.

King Cormac lost nearly two hundred of his legionaries that night, as well as fourteen of his Gallowglas mercenaries. Ten of them had been slain by the intruders and four had died beneath the flailing metal-shod hooves of the panicked horses. Of his twenty shire-mounts, all but one had to be slain, and over fifty of the horses had to be butchered also. The town was a shambles: not one building remained standing, everything had been trampled into the dust, and all their food and supplies for the coming Cold Months had been destroyed. But more dangerously, there was now a definite air of mutiny about the men. The Gallowglas had brought down the attack; they were to blame for it. And the men had learned a very valuable lesson: they had been taught that the feared mercenary warriors were not invincible.

Around noon a single rider approached the camp. He was challenged only when he reached the spiked palisade, which the men had worked all morning at re-erecting.

'What do you want?'

'I want to see this self-styled King of the Outlands.'

The guard fitted an arrow to his bow. 'The king will see no-one today,' he called.

'He will see me,' the stranger said mildly, sitting easily on his mount, not even looking at the guard, watching the men working on a section of the palisade.

The guard contemplated loosing an arrow into the smug stranger. 'Why should he see you?' he asked contemptuously.

The stranger looked up and favoured him with a chilling smile. 'Why, because I caused all this!'

# 7   *The Lord of the Dead*

Mannam is the God of the Dead, and his guise is that of a withered
and blasted tree . . .

*Pantheon of the Old Faith*

'You are impudent, bard, and your impudence will have you . . .'

'Slain?' Paedur suggested, stepping into the room. The bainte
had left them in a corridor of the palace, standing before a tall
golden-wood door that was worked with a design of leafless branches and twigs. Paedur had touched the knot-like handle with
his hook and the door had swung open, and then the voice had
spoken from within.

As the bard turned to look at the creature, there was a sound
of snapping, crackling branches – a noise the bard had come
to recognise as the sound of Death's laughter. 'I think I recall
now why you were chosen.' The figure turned away from the
low, arched window, a shadow in black, shapeless and menacing.
'The Gods of the Pantheon met in conclave – a rare event, I
assure you – and tried to decide upon a mortal man to carry
our battle for us, a Champion. Some called for bravery, others
for intelligence, others for cowardice and cunning. I called for
stupidity, maintaining that the line between a hero and a fool is
very slender indeed.' The voice was sibilant, hissing like the wind
through bare branches. 'And now here you are, boldly marching
into the very heart of my kingdom, and that, I think, proves my
point.'

Mannam glided silently across the room, his cloak of seared
and withered leaves noiseless now, although the bard could remember occasions when it had hissed like a nest of serpents.
Katani had encountered Death on only one previous occasion and
then their meeting had been brief; she had been but one of many
dead that day. He was taller than the bard, thin, and covered
from head to foot in the long leafed cloak. A deep hood covered
his head and the warrior wasn't sure if she wanted to see what
it hid.

*Demon's Law: Tales of the Bard*

In the centre of the room was a large triangular table of a black and slightly leprous-looking wood, with three chairs around it, one large and grotesquely ornate, the others simple and plain. Mannam settled into the largest chair, his cloak rustling now like a leaf fall. 'Sit,' he said, extending an arm, although no hand appeared. 'Sit, and tell me what you want.'

Paedur glanced at Katani and then he crossed the duncoloured marbled floor and sat in one of the chairs. Katani remained standing, taking up a position behind and to his left, her left hand resting on the hilt of her longsword, the fingers of her right hand touching the slender throwing dagger that was strapped under her armour.

Paedur rested his hook on the coal-black table and then placed his hand over it; almost automatically, the index finger began tracing the runes cut into the metal. 'Why do you assume I want something?' he asked, looking directly at the Dark Lord, remembering the fleeting glimpse he had once had of the creature's face, vaguely relieved that without his enhanced senses there was no chance that he would be able to see it again.

Mannam gave what the bard assumed was a sign. 'Paedur Hookhand, do you know how many from the World of Men come into my kingdom daily?'

The bard shook his head.

'And do you know how many come here willingly?'

Again he shook his head.

The Dark Lord leaned forward. 'And do you know how many of those who come here are alive?'

Paedur smiled.

Mannam hissed. 'So, you want something, something which only I can give, and that means someone dead.'

The bard nodded seriously. 'I want you to return two people to me, two who died in the World of Men, but two whom I had come to love and who had come to love one another. They died in defence of the Old Faith. Their deaths were untimely,' he added.

'No death is ever untimely, no matter how it looks at the time,' Mannam hissed. His cowled head moved from side to side, and then he suddenly stopped and looked at the bard. Paedur shivered, feeling two dead, knowing eyes watching him, the sensation one of a crawling, prickling insect, and he experienced a sudden moment of ice-cold dread.

72

'What you are asking is impossible,' Mannam said simply.

'No! You accepted their deaths then. You can refuse them now.'

'I cannot.'

Paedur brought his hook crashing down on the black table, the metal ringing through the huge room, but the table was unmarked. 'You can do it. There is a precedent in the myths and legends of the Nations. The Gods have returned the dead to the World of Men.'

'The circumstances were exceptional,' Mannam said very slowly.

'These circumstances are exceptional. These people gave their lives for you and your kind. Refuse to help them now and you become nothing more than the Religion's petty godlets, cruel, blustering and powerless.'

Wood snapped. In the almost physical silence of the room, Katani eased her sword a finger-length free of its scabbard, ready to move, to bring the long razor-edged blade around in a sweeping decapitating half-circle. By his very precautions, Death had shown himself to be vulnerable.

'You go too far, bard,' Mannam hissed.

'They were my friends,' Paedur said simply. 'I owe it to them. Why won't you help them?'

'I will not . . .' Mannam began.

'Will not or cannot?' Paedur said coldly.

'You try my patience,' Mannam said, and rose in a rustle of autumnal leaves plainly signifying that the audience was at an end.

'What are you afraid of?' the bard suddenly demanded. 'Why do you hide in a closed city, behind walls, and bars and water? What is it the great God of Death fears?'

Mannam turned away and strode rustling across the floor to stand before the window. The shadows danced as Paedur chased after him, but the Dark Lord cast no shadow.

'Tell me,' he demanded, reaching out to grip the god's arm.

The dry, faintly musty air of the room was suddenly charged with a sharp, acrid, faintly metallic odour. A mite of blue-white fire sparked from beneath Mannam's cowl and raced along the bard's hook, sizzling up his arm, twisting him around in sound-less agony and flinging him across the room.

'Never touch me, mortal,' Mannam crackled.

73

*Demon's Law: Tales of the Bard*

Katani's swords hissed as she slid them free of their oiled scabbards. She brought both swords around and touched them gently together and assumed a fighting stance.

Mannam's left arm began to rise; a bony, stick-like finger and then a gnarled, knotted tree stump of a hand appeared. The finger pointed . . .

'No!'

Paedur pushed himself into a sitting position, his left arm pressed tightly against his pounding ribs. 'No . . . no more. You forget we are on your side, god,' he spat.

The Dark Lord turned slowly. 'I do not know what side you are on, bard.'

'I fought for you,' Paedur said, coming to his feet, feeling the sting as he breathed in, knowing he had cracked one or more ribs. 'Surely that entitles me to some trust?'

The silence between the two began to lengthen uncomfortably, but neither seemed inclined to break it. Finally, Katani brought both swords around in a complete circle and slid them home into their sheaths, the collars clicking solidly. The sound broke the tableau.

'I will tell you,' Mannam said, and then immediately turned away and rustled across the floor towards a staircase.

Katani stretched out her hand and the bard grasped it. She hauled him to his feet with surprising ease, her eyes on the Dark Lord's retreating back. She turned back to Paedur, her eyes questioning. He shrugged and shook his head slightly; there was little they could do but follow him.

The Dark Lord led them up a steep, winding staircase that quickly had the bard gasping as his cracked and bruised ribs throbbed. After a score or more steps, what vestiges of light that had been seeping up the stairs from the long room disappeared and they were ascending in complete darkness. Once again Paedur was reminded of what he had lost when he had entered the Silent Wood. In the World of Men, his enhanced senses allowed him to see clearly in the dark; now he was like an ordinary man, sweating with pain and exertion and yet shivering with fear as he felt the ever-growing distance between himself and the floor far below, and no rail to keep him from plummeting down into the room below. It had been a long time since he had feared heights.

He stumbled once, clattering on to the worn stone steps. In

the darkness Katani reached for him, touching his cloak, and then he felt her iron-hard fingers dig deep into the muscles of his arm, hauling him up. 'I will carry you,' she said seriously.

But the bard shook his head stubbornly. 'No, no. I can manage,' he gasped weakly, resisting the urge to vomit.

'Is it much further?' Katani demanded into the darkness ahead of them. 'Where are you taking us?'

'To the tower,' Mannam said shortly, his voice sounding surprisingly close.

Katani was half-carrying Paedur by the time they reached the top of the seemingly interminable staircase. Like the Dark Lord, the climb had no ill-effects on her in any way, but the bard was close to collapse. The bard cried out in pain as he stepped through a tall arched doorway and on to the roof of the tower. After the absolute darkness, the grey diffused twilight of the Silent Wood was painfully blinding and he sank to his knees and buried his head in his cloak, allowing his sensitive eyes to adjust. When he could see again, he found that Mannam had led them out on to a broad flat roof that overlooked his palace, the lake and the town beyond. In the distance they could see the wall that surrounded the city, and beyond that the greyness of the Silent Wood, and the snaking black line of the Naman as it wound its way through the heart of the Land of the Dead.

'This is the Tower of Time,' Mannam said suddenly, startling them, walking over to an ancient sundial and resting his stick-like hands on it.

Paedur limped over to the stone plinth and looked at the obviously Culai-wrought relic. It was marred by a jagged gash that split it in two. He traced the crack with the point of his hook. 'I thought the sun never shone on the Silent Wood,' he whispered.

'It doesn't.'

Paedur touched the dial again and looked quizzically at the Dark Lord.

'There is no time in the Land of the Dead,' Mannam said with one of his branch-snapping laughs.

'Why is the dial here, then?'

The edge of Mannam's cloak brushed across the crack. 'It shows that here even Time is dead.'

'Why have you brought us here?' Paedur was suddenly weary of the god's strange humour.

'Here we are assured that there are no listening ears,' Mannam said. He turned and looked quickly at Katani. 'And can you trust this warrior-maid?'

'I think I can. I think I already have.'

'Can you trust her with your life, your soul?'

'There is no life in this place and the Pantheon holds my soul.' He nodded. 'I trust her.'

Mannam nodded reluctantly. 'On your head be it then, bard. You must know that there is something greater than the gods themselves,' he said softly, almost to himself, the words whispered like rain on leaves, 'and that is Fate. Even the gods must bow to their Fate. Perhaps Fate has brought you here,' he said with sudden animation. 'Yes, yes. Fate.' He touched the blocky script of the Culai that was set into the outer ring of the sundial and the runes glowed briefly. 'You asked what I feared, bard.' He turned to look at Paedur and the man had the fleeting glimpse of a face beneath the cowl – a human face – but it was immediately replaced by the sickening image of the wormy skull. 'I fear death, bard,' he hissed.

'You are Death,' Paedur said slowly.

'I am of the Old Faith. The Deathgod of the New Religion threatens me.'

'Libellius? How?' Paedur demanded incredulously. 'And here in your own kingdom? Surely it is not possible.'

'What does Libellius promise to his followers in the World of Men?' Mannam asked harshly.

'A life after death.'

'And what is my promise?'

'Just death.'

'So you see that his promise is more attractive than mine. The people flock to him and why? Why? Because he refuses to accept the death of some of his followers – returns them to life, if you will. Rumours and stories of these miracles spread, and grow, and so do his followers, and as their numbers increase, so too does his power, and so mine weakens.'

Paedur nodded. 'Aye, I can appreciate that, and I will see what I can do about it when I return to the World of Men. But I still cannot see how this godlet can possibly threaten you in your own kingdom.'

'Because he has had help.'

Katani moved forward. 'Help? What sort of help?'

'One of my captains made a pact with Libellius, and this man has been operating on his behalf within my domain.'

'Someone close to you?' Paedur asked.

Mannam turned away and stared out over the city. 'Close to me,' he agreed reluctantly.

'Who?' Katani asked, and the bard turned to look at her, catching the undercurrent of excitement in her voice.

'A creature called Churon. In the World of Men he was called the . . .'

'Onelord,' Katani hissed triumphantly.

Paedur settled himself against the cracked and useless sundial and looked at the tall, stooped figure of Death standing against the twilight sky. 'I think you should tell us,' he said simply.

'He came to me when he died, as all men do, but unlike some, he was not confused, nor was he troubled, nor fearful that he was now dead and in the Silent Wood. My bainte brought his essence here, and when he had taken the shape of man again, he was as a lord, tall and proud and vain, unbowed by his bloody demise.

'I watched him as he woke from the Sleep of the Dead. He woke not as some men, slowly and brokenly, but came alert and awake as if he had but closed his eyes a moment before. When he come to his feet, he checked his weapons and then touched his armour where he had taken his mortal wound, but the armour was whole again, and then he ran his gauntleted hands through his blond hair, brushing it away from his forehead, and then he threw back his head and laughed.

'And in the Land of the Dead, laughter is a strange and frightening thing.

'My bainte appeared as they always do with the new-dead, and he looked on them, not as some men do, as duaite – as demons – but rather curiously, much as you looked on them earlier, bard, merely as strange creatures. And then he spoke to them. "Tell your master Churon the Onelord is here; he is expecting me."

'So came Churon to my kingdom.

'Death did not bother him; he had no regrets for the life he had left behind, no sadness at leaving his new bride, nor his children by his previous marriages, nor the huge treasure he had amassed in his lifetime.

'And let me say this to you now. Every man and woman who has ever lived in the World of Men and worshipped the Old

Faith has, with few – very few – exceptions, passed through my domain. Emperors and kings, warriors, princes, murderers, bandits, thieves, artists, peasants – an endless list – they have all come here. But none of them ever interested me. Some I took, yes, keeping them here, but only as a collector amasses varieties of types to complete his collection, but Churon ... ahhh, the Onelord was different.

'And now I must tell you something which no mortal has ever known, bard, and I tell you this so that your understanding of my tale will be clearer, but you must never repeat it. You see, bard, the task of Death is unlike the tasks of the other Gods of the Pantheon. From the earliest time, when the gods first ascended to their position as gods or godlets, spirits or sprites, they have remained unchanged to this day. But this is not true of the post of Death. The Lord of the Dead is set apart. Unlike the others, he alone is not dealing with the living, be they human or animal, vegetable or mineral or spirit; he alone deals with the dead, those who have left the World of Men and are now but dust and rotting flesh and bone.

'And had I a soul, I would say it was soul-destroying. You smile bard, but you lack understanding. It takes a special man, someone cold and unhuman, someone more than a little mad, to hold this post. Someone like you, Paedur Hookhand.

'I am the third to hold this post. I do not know where my predecessors went. The last merely cursed me with this shape and walked out of the Silent Wood, and even the gods do not know where he went.

'And now I am weary, so weary. I know how he must have felt. So when I saw Churon, saw him as a man apart, a special man, cold and unhuman and more than a little mad, I knew he would be my successor.

'So I took him and made him a captain in my army – and you have not seen my army, but it is huge – and I ensured that he wanted for nothing. He accepted it all – indeed, he almost expected it as a right. He was a wealthier, mightier, more powerful man here in the Silent Wood than he ever was in the World of Men.

'But he was greedy.

'As much as he had, he wanted more. He wanted it all. He wanted to rule the Silent Wood, to command the Host of the Dead. He wanted to be a god. He could have had it all with my blessing, but perhaps he did not believe me when I told him that it could be his, perhaps he was just not prepared to wait.

'He must have learned of the New Religion from one of the dead. I don't know, but he always questioned those newly come to this place. Nor do I know how he made contact with Libellius, except that he often disappeared for long stretches, "riding the marches", he would say on his return. But I suspect – in fact, I know now – that he was meeting with Libellius in one of the Shadowlands which border my kingdom.

'About this time too my power began to weaken, not dramatically so, not by much, and perhaps not even enough for me to notice. But then a plague swept through one of the southern towns in the World of Men. They are a common enough occurrence there and kill perhaps three-quarters of the population, but this time less than half arrived here. Libellius had claimed the rest. I took it as a measure of his growing power.

'And so it went on, with Libellius claiming more and more of the dead and in turn my power becoming weaker and weaker. And then finally, I was attacked. Attacked, here in the Silent Wood, my own domain!

'Very little can harm me, you know that, but because of the corporeal form I was cursed with, fire is one of the few things which can.

'I do not sleep ... but you know that, bard. I think it has been a long time since the sleep of Man claimed you, and so it is with the gods. There is no night in this place, but on a whim I sometimes allow a darkness to fall over the land; the reactions of my subjects always afford me some innocent amusement. But as I walked the battlements, listening to the howling of the dead and the wailing of the damned – for their voices are always clearer at night – I saw something that had no right to exist in this place. A light, a star, a meteor ... a fire!

'It lay out beyond the furthest reaches of the Naman in the Mire, which is a place not rightly of my kingdom nor truly of one of the myriad Worlds of Men but it partakes something of each. It is not a Shadowland, because a Shadowland is a separate place, something apart, while the Mire is of two or more worlds and exists completely in all of them. What I was looking at was a fire, a huge blazing conflagration, sparks spiralling like stars to the starless heavens, and the stench of smoke was as foul to me as that of offal is to you.

'And then the arrow came. It was more than an arrow; it was a spear, a huge blazing spear, streaking through the night sky like a thunderbolt. It screamed across the Mire and over the Naman and sped towards me . . .

'I was frozen, shocked, amazed, aye, and terrified if the truth were known. I watched it coming and there was nothing I could do. But it was low and shattered against the wall below me, exploding in a shower of metal and wood, pitch and sparks. I felt the cinders sting, and I realised then that the unthinkable was happening. Someone – or something – was attempting to destroy me, to destroy Death.

'There was a second spear of fire and then a third, but my attackers had lost the advantage of surprise and those I deflected easily enough, throwing up a shield of power over the city. There have been three other attacks, and there was a recent attempt when a creature from the Silent Wood calmly walked into the palace and attempted to set fire to my cloak. Hence my precautions.

'And Churon? Churon disappeared after the first attack. I knew it was him and he in turn knew I would be aware of his treachery. But I think he momentarily forgot that I am a god and although I may not always be aware of what is happening in my kingdom, I am capable of finding out, even though it happened in time past.

'So Churon betrayed me. The plan was simple: he was to slay me and take my place as Lord of the Dead, and then he would lead an army of the dead back into the World of Men! Aye, Churon wished to be Onelord again, but lord not only of the World of Men but of the Silent Wood also, and who knows – for even the gods know not the future – perhaps he would even scale the Broken Mountain and attack C'lte, one of the Gods of Life, in his kingdom.

'And he must be stopped!

'Stop him for me, bard, and in return you will have what you came for in as much as I can grant it to you. You must become the Champion of the Faith again, and you must stop the Onelord before it is too late, for this world and for yours!'

# 8   The Blood Price

'Always believe you can win, never doubt it in your own mind. If you believe strongly enough, you have already won.'

*Owen, the Weapon Master*

'YOU!' King Cormac leaned over the edge of the palisade fence and glared at the man who had remained still and unperturbed on his coal-black gelding. 'You caused all this? You attacked my palace, killed my men, crippled my animals?' He was almost incoherent with rage. The huge head disappeared and then the double gates were thrown back and the giant strode out, the long-spiked battle-hammer in his hands looking like nothing more than a child's toy. Cormac was a huge man, his face level with Owen's – and he was still mounted – and he was broad in proportion. He was naked except for a long, blood-stained leather apron; he had been slaying the crippled horses and there was blood on his arms and across his furred belly. Matted, filthy, flame-red hair framed a flat, broad face which was more beast-like than human and his lips were drawn back exposing his cruelly pointed teeth.

He stopped in the shadow of the gates and looked at the mounted warrior, his small dark eyes assessing him, his mount and weapons. 'You did all that?' he suddenly bellowed and ran towards the seated man.

'Stop!' A crossbow had appeared in the warrior's hand and a hollow-headed bolt screamed through the air to embed itself in the wooden haft of Cormac's battle-hammer. 'No further,' the warrior warned.

The king reluctantly stopped. 'I'll have the head off your shoulders while you're reloading that toy.'

'Move towards me and my companion in the trees behind me will put an arrow through your head.'

'And I am supposed to believe that you have more men in the trees?' Cormac sneered.

'Believe what you want,' the rider said dismissively.

But to punctuate his reply a broad-headed hunting arrow

whistled out of the bushes and hammered into the soft earth between Cormac's feet. The king didn't even flinch, nor did he take his eyes off the rider. 'Who are you?' he snarled.

'I am Owen, a Weapon Master.'

'I don't know you.'

'Your emissary visited my employer yesterday.'

'Your employer?' The king frowned. 'Your employer? The Renegade, Kutor?'

Owen nodded. 'The same.'

'And so you killed, destroyed, maimed and mutilated because of my request for rent on the fort your employer stole from me!' From Cormac's tone, it was obvious that he thought himself to be dealing with a madman.

'No-one had ownership of the Culai fortresses.'

'This is my land,' Cormac snapped.

'This is the Emperor's land – my employer's half-brother, you'll remember.'

'This is my land by right of conquest.'

'And you conquered it from farmers and herders?' Owen sneered.

'Push me and I'll kill you,' Cormac warned.

'Threaten me again and I will come back and finish the job I started last night.'

Cormac ran his fingers through his flame-red hair, unable to believe the audacity of the man. 'Do you know how many of my men you slew last night? Do you know how many animals had to be slaughtered because of you?' Recognising that the questions were rhetorical, Owen remained silent. 'There is a blood debt between us, Weapon Master, and this must be cleared.'

'That is why I am here,' Owen said mildly.

Startled, Cormac said, 'You are familiar with the Gallowglas custom. You must pay coin or blood.'

'We will pay blood.'

'Single or multiple combat?' Cormac demanded eagerly, eyes flashing.

'Single.'

'Weapons?'

'Of choice, with the exclusion of spears, bows or slings.'

'Agreed.' Cormac rubbed his hands together briskly. 'And the stakes?'

'What remains of your legion!'

The king looked at him as if he hadn't heard him correctly.

'Your legion,' Owen insisted.

'And what will you wager?' Cormac asked eventually.

'You can have Prince Kutor and what remains of his rebel band. The reward on them is high.'

The king nodded slowly. 'Your champion against mine?' he asked, his small eyes narrowing, calculating.

'Just so.'

'Agreed!'

'When?' the Weapon Master asked, gathering up his reins, already turning his mount's head.

'On the morrow at noon.'

'Where?'

'On the flat ground before the Culai fort.'

'Agreed,' Owen said, and then turned his back on the king and allowed his mount to canter away.

Cormac watched him go and then he began to shake. He drove the battle-hammer spike first into the earth and placed both hands on his hips and began to rock to and fro with uncontrollable laughter.

In the bushes Tien tZo pulled his recurved bow over his shoulder and found he could only agree with the king's sentiments. This was absolute folly of the worst kind. This was suicide.

'I think you'll be up against the king himself,' Keshian said quietly, glancing sidelong at the Weapon Master.

Owen nodded non-committally. He was walking the battlements with the old soldier, inspecting the repairs and changes that had been made to the defences.

'I've had new mortar poured into the cracks along here,' Keshian pointed, 'and the men will be setting sharpened slivers of wood and nails into the tops of the merlons – which should surprise any climbers.'

Owen nodded again, his eyes distant.

'This outer wall is indefensible, so I intend to booby-trap it,' Keshian continued. 'I'm going to saw through all the support struts on the walkways with the exception of one or two, which I'll keep intact. I'll attach a length of rope to these and we should be able to pull the walkways down from the windows opposite.' He jerked his head in the direction of the building proper, but Owen didn't even look.

They continued walking in silence while the evening drew quickly on for night, the shadows already thickening in the mountain-wrapped fortress. 'It will be the king,' Keshian said then.

And the Weapon Master nodded. 'I know. His honour demands it.'

'He'll use a Gallowglas sword or a battle-axe,' Keshian continued.

Owen leaned on one of the merlons and looked out across the flat stony plain in the direction of King Cormac's camp. There was a storm hanging low and purple on the horizon, whipping up distant dust clouds. 'Would the sword not be too long and unwieldly in a confined place?' he wondered.

'Have you ever seen a Gallowglas use one of the longswords?' Keshian asked.

Owen shook his head.

'I did once. When I was a mercenary many years ago, one of them rode with us. In the beginning we all laughed at his sword, which was nearly as tall as himself and so heavy that even the strongest amongst us could barely lift it. But let me tell you, Weapon Master, the Gallowglas can wield them one-handed, using them as if they weighed nothing more than a knife. And I needn't tell you that a weapon that is as long as a tall man, with all the weight and strength of a powerful Gallowglas arm behind it, will cut a man clean in two. I've seen it happen,' he added hoarsely, the suddenly lurid image flashing behind his eyes, and he saw again the explosion of flesh and blood and bone and matter against the searing golden sands of the Fire Hills of Nasgociba.

'I've heard tell that the blades are magically bonded to just one man at the moment of their construction and that only he can lift and wield it,' Owen said, almost absently.

'I've heard that also,' Keshian agreed. He nodded at the growing clouds. 'Storm coming.'

Owen ran his hands across his greying hair, which Tien had recently cropped close to his skull. 'What weapon would you suggest I use?'

'I'm honoured you should ask me,' Keshian began, 'but surely you are the Weapon Master, surely that decision is best left to you.'

'I am asking the advice of a fellow-warrior,' Owen said with a smile, and in that moment whatever reservations the battle-captain may have had about the infamous mercenary vanished.

'I would suggest something like a mace. You can use a mace?' He caught Owen's disgusted look and hurried on. 'Use a mace with an especially heavy head.'

'Why the extra weight?'

'To batter aside or even trap the longsword, while you strike with a sword or thrown knife.'

'Can I break the blade?' Owen asked.

'Impossible. You are talking about a bar of metal as tall as a man, which is a hand-span broad and as thick as two fingers from the guard almost to the tip. It is double-edged and sharp – but not unusually so – for most of its length, but at its tip, which is pointed, it is sharp enough to shave with. There is no possible way you can break a blade like that.'

'Armour?'

The wind shifted, smelling of salt and spices and carrying dust and sand. Keshian spat grit over the battlements. 'I would advise against it. You're going to need all the speed and agility you can get. If you're wearing armour, it'll just slow you down and even if one of the Gallowglas' blows strikes you, it will crush your bones to powder despite the protection.'

Owen nodded. 'Thank you, you've cleared my own thoughts on the subject.'

'Have you made any decision as to how you're going to fight him?'

'Not yet. I'll speak to Tien tZo later when he returns.'

'I didn't know he had gone out,' Keshian said, surprised, automatically scanning the plain below, even though he realised the chances of seeing the Shemmat were almost nil.

'He had a little . . . job . . . to do,' Owen smiled.

The Weapon Master sat in the small room he had taken close to Kutor's quarters and carefully cleaned and sorted his weapons. Usually, Tien tZo took care of this, but the small Shemmat warrior still hadn't returned. With his warrior's sense of time, he knew that full night had fallen outside, and even through the solid stone he could hear the distant hissing of the storm against the exterior walls. Tien tZo's absence had made him apprehensive, although he knew that the Shemmat was an extra-ordinary warrior in his own right, and the two men had been in each other's company now for so long that each had absorbed much of the other's fighting skills.

Owen glanced at the pale yellow candle sitting before a polished rectangle of metal in a niche high on the wall; it had perhaps half a finger's span left to burn. When it had guttered out he would go in search of his slave-companion.

The Weapon Master looked at the weapons laid out on the cot and once again realised that these were his only possessions, these tools of death, together with a few clothes, and they too were connected with death. It was little enough to show after over twenty years on the mercenary trail. He reached into his belt and spilled the contents of his pouch on to the cloth: a dozen copper coins, barely enough for a night's drinking in a reasonably clean inn. But then, he had never had a great head for money. A trained sword never lacked for hire, and he had been able to command a good wage, but that money was just as easily spent: there was always fine food and drink, and women . . . always the women. It was the mercenary's disease; when the next day might be the last, every day had to be lived to the full. And when the money ran out, there were always more wars to replenish the coin, and after a while it became a wretched cycle from which there was no escape.

He had tried, though. He had moved out of the cities and practised his art in the provinces before moving on to the Outlands and then finally the Wastelands, training petty lordlings how to hold a sword or pull a bow. But these were men with little respect for the title of Weapon Master, and these were the people who attempted more often than not to cheat him.

He had been fleeing one such stupid lord when he had met up with the bard, and from that single meeting everything had undoubtedly changed. Suddenly he had his Faith again, and he had a course to follow. When the bard had suggested he join the Renegade's group, he had been more than a little doubtful, but recently he had begun to see Kutor's cause as a chance to change the direction of his own life, to earn a little wealth and settle down, perhaps even open that warrior's school he had dreamed about so often and begin training his successor. Throwing in his lot with the renegade prince was a chance – a desperate gamble – but if it paid off he would be able to realise that dream.

And that was one of the reasons why he was prepared to challenge one of the fearsome Gallowglas in single combat.

The candle in the niche guttered out and Owen stood up, reaching for his sword belt ... and the door opened and Tien tZo stepped into the room, something like a smile playing about his lips. 'It's done.'

'You killed my men!' Cormac screamed as soon as Owen appeared on the battlements.

'I thought our contest was at noon,' the Weapon Master shouted down, squinting against the glare of the early morning sun.

'You killed my tribesmen last night!' the king repeated, 'all of them.' He was wearing full armour and the square plates took the early morning sun and blazed, lending the huge Gallowglas an almost godlike appearance.

'Your men were slain?' Owen asked innocently.

'What happened?' Prince Kutor asked quietly, coming up behind the Weapon Master, a bow in his hands.

'My men were murdered last night!' Cormac raged, spittle flecking his chin.

'It seems his nine remaining Gallowglas brothers were killed last night,' Owen smiled.

'And you had nothing to do with it?' the prince asked.

'I did not go out last night.'

'Did I see Tien tZo coming back late?' Kutor wondered aloud.

'I think you might have.' Owen smiled.

'We will fight now!' Cormac roared.

'I am not ready,' Owen said mildly, spreading his arms wide.

'Then ready yourself!' Cormac screamed, the cords in his neck standing out, the veins writhing along his bare arms and temples.

Tien tZo touched Owen lightly on the arm. 'Anger lends strength,' he said softly, his eyes on the king.

'And angry men make mistakes,' Owen replied.

'He is not like other men,' Tien tZo said patiently. 'He only needs to hit you once – just once, that's all.'

The Weapon Master nodded. He leaned over the edge of the battlements, studying the king's armour. He was wearing a leather jerkin and kirtle, which had been sewn with crude overlapping squares and rectangles of metal. His head was uncovered and his arms and legs were bare although he wore thick, studded wristbands on either arm.

'Fight me now, man!'

'Wait, Gallowglas. Let me arm myself.'

In the stillness of his room, he dressed himself for what might very well be the final battle. Jerkin and leggings of supple black leather, with the jerkin woven through with strands of wire, designed to turn a knife blade or arrowhead, while its high collar was stiffened and plated with metal to protect the back of his neck and head. High metal-toed and heeled boots, with a flat-bladed throwing knife in each. He wore fighting gauntlets which had been banded around the knuckles with stiffened wire, and there were plates running along each finger, and disc-shaped metal plates on the back of the hands. He strapped his scabbard across his back with the hilt of his longsword projecting above his left shoulder, and there was a broad-bladed Chopt knife in his belt. He had followed Keshian's advice and had opted for the mace, but where he would have fought with mace and short-sword, Tien tZo had suggested two maces and had spent most of the night demonstrating the effectiveness of the unconventional weapons.

Owen slipped the leathern thongs around his wrists, loosely held the short leather-wrapped handles and allowed the spiked balls to dangle at the end of their chains, scraping the floor. He glanced at Tien tZo. 'Well . . .?'

The Shemmat nodded. 'It is how I imagine your god of war would look.'

Owen nodded, pleased. 'I know he often used the mace as his weapon of choice.'

'But two of them?' Tien tZo asked.

Owen laughed and went out to face the Gallowglas.

'I am going to kill you, little man,' Cormac snarled, his face turning into an animal's mask.

'You're going to try,' the Weapon Master corrected him mildly.

'Before there is any killing done here,' Keshian interrupted, 'we must finalise the stakes and rules.'

His opposite number, one of the captains of Cormac's legion, nodded in agreement.

Cormac spat between Owen's feet. 'There are no rules.'

The Weapon Master nodded.

'I will wager the loyalty of my legion to the victor,' Cormac snapped, lifting his enormous sword with one hand and allowing it to drop into the palm of his other hand, his eyes on Owen's face.

'If you are defeated, the legion will swear loyalty to Prince Kutor,' Keshian persisted.

'That is what I have said!'

The legion captain cleared his throat. 'And you will wager the renegade prince and his followers?'

Keshian nodded. 'Agreed. If our champion is defeated, they will surrender to you.'

The legion captain nodded and then both men backed away, leaving Owen and Cormac standing alone on the rocky ground before the ruined Culai fortress.

Both men stared at each other for a score of pounding heartbeats and then they attacked simultaneously.

Cormac brought up his sword, which was actually taller than Owen, as easily as if it were a rapier and brought it down in a fast scything blow that would have cut the Weapon Master in two had it connected. Owen threw himself forward and down, beneath the cut, and slashed at Cormac's legs with the mace in his right hand, but the range was too great and his blow fell short. Continuing to move, he rolled away just as the king brought the sword around and down, gouging deep into the ground where Owen had lain. The Weapon Master came to his feet, facing the Gallowglas, and began the complicated movement Tien tZo had taught him, working both hands together, the balls on the maces spinning in two lethal, humming circles.

Cormac slashed again, leaning back away from the spiked balls, using his great reach and the full length of the sword, and this time its tip ripped through Owen's jerkin, slicing the leather and exposing the silver wire beneath. The force of the glancing blow sent Owen sprawling back, just as he released the mace in his left hand. The solid ball struck the Gallowglas square in the chest, instead of the throat, punching him backwards, staggering the giant. Owen, from a prone position, spun the second mace in a tight arc and released it, but Cormac saw it coming and brought his sword up, and the chain wrapped itself harmlessly around the blade. The king roared triumphantly – he had the Weapon Master now – and the first knife took him through the throat, while the second merely glanced off his skull.

Mortally wounded, the Gallowglas raised his sword above the fallen warrior, determined to take him into the Silent Wood, when the broad blade of a Chopt knife almost tore the head off his shoulders. He was dead before he hit the ground.

In the confusion and uproar that followed a hand reached down and hauled the Weapon Master to his feet. Owen found himself looking into Kutor's eyes and the look on his face was one of extraordinary surprise.

'Now tell me why. And the truth this time,' the prince murmured.

'Reasons . . .'

'Reasons?' Kutor persisted.

'It was a ready-made army,' Owen said in a hoarse whisper.

# 9  The Onelord

And he was always the Champion of the Gods of the Pantheon . . .
*Life of Paedur, the Bard*


'There has been another attack on Mannam!'

Paedur looked up as Katani strode down the length of the library. 'What happened?'

'I thought you would have heard the uproar above. I thought you would have been there.'

Paedur shrugged. 'I heard nothing.'

'I should have known I would find you here,' the warrior grumbled.

Mannam had lodged his visitors in rooms in the cellars close to the library. The bard's incredulity that there should even be a library in Manach had turned to absolute amazement when he saw it.

The library was enormous – bigger even than the fabulous library of Baddalaur, the Bardic College, which was reputed to contain all the knowledge in the known world. It was said that if the planes of Existence were to be destroyed, it would be possible to rebuild them from the records in the library at Baddalaur. But Mannam's library dwarfed it.

The shelves ran the entire length of the cellars, which the bard paced out at a thousand paces from end to end, and were four times the height of a tall man. And they were crammed from end to end with books, scrolls, manuscripts, folios and charts. There was no order, no systematic collection of authors or subjects, and Paedur knew that it was a lifetime's task – no, two or more – just to prepare a catalogue of the enormous collection.

Mannam's library was unique in one other way: none of the books in it had ever been published; they were all posthumous works and they were all original. It had intrigued and delighted the bard, and Mannam had laughed his crackling laugh and said that every writer died with at least one work unfinished. His stick-like fingers had then indicated the shelves. 'These are the finished works.'

From that moment on, Paedur was lost, and it was all Katani or indeed Mannam could do to drag him away from the library.

Katani nervously strode around the book stacks and shelves. She had left off her horned helmet and her ice-white hair hung down her back whispering off her lacquered armour like oiled silk. Her weapons were noiseless.

'One of the newly dead attacked him,' she said abruptly. 'Mannam had gone to inspect a batch of those newly come to his kingdom when a blacksmith from one of the border villages launched a vicious attack on him. I was directly behind the Dark Lord and could do nothing; I couldn't even reach him, the man was so fast, so beserk.'

'And Death?' Paedur asked urgently.

'Unharmed, but frightened. The blacksmith's huge hammer shattered against Mannam's cloak, and by that time the bainte were on him and had removed the spark of his soul, leaving him "dead" again. He was chained and the spark returned to him, and then I . . . questioned him. And I know many ways to loosen a man's tongue.'

Paedur laughed without humour. 'I am sure you do. And what did you discover?'

Katani grinned savagely. 'The man had been a follower of the New Religion in the World of Men, and had been a special devotee of Libellius' Cult of the Dead. It seems the leader of this cult had received a message from their god asking for a volunteer to go into the Silent Wood to assassinate Mannam; if he succeeded, then Libellius would come to power and the man would be returned to life with great glory and honour.'

'I wonder how many men would have volunteered for such a mission,' Paedur remarked sourly. 'Surely they knew it had no hope of succeeding.'

'Obviously something must have encouraged them to think that there was a hope, because there were so many volunteers that the winner had to be chosen by lottery – and the blacksmith won.'

'Well, he won little enough. Not one, but two quick deaths, followed by torture by a Katan.'

'There will be more attempts,' she said seriously. 'If we're going to do something, we'll have to do it soon, before an attempt succeeds!'

Paedur nodded. 'I know.' He turned away and walked down

along the untidy shelves, his fingers brushing the backs of the polished leather and vellum bindings. The warrior fell into step beside him. 'Tell me about Churon,' he asked suddenly.

Katani grinned humourlessly. 'I would have thought that you as a bard would know more about him than any man.'

'My knowledge is taken from my lore and the myths and legends of the Nations, but you met with him, spoke with him. I can tell you about the historical man; you can tell about the real person.'

Katani turned and swept clean a section of shelving, tumbling the books and manuscripts on to the floor, and then she heaved herself up on to it. 'What do you want to know about him?' she asked, watching the bard carefully.

'Anything. Everything,' he amended quickly, stooping down and beginning to gather the books Katani had tossed on to the floor. He quickly stacked them and straightened, leaning back against the shelves, facing the woman and folding his arms. 'Describe him to me.'

Katani closed her eyes, remembering. 'He was tall – taller than you – and broad, and although the colour of his skin was black, his hair was white and his eyes were blue, so there was mixed blood in him.' Her amber eyes flickered open and she smiled, almost shyly. 'He was a handsome man, and he exuded an aura of absolute authority.'

'And what were your impressions of him?'

'My first impressions were of a man of great strength and power, a man of vision. His virtues seemed to me – and not just to me – to be similar to those of the Katan Sisterhood: he was a warrior with honour, a man of courage and charity. But as I grew to know him, I formed a clearer impression of the man behind the mask, for believe me, it was a mask. It was an image he projected like some cheap fairground magician.' Katani shook her head, smiling sadly. 'The title Onelord was of his own choosing. And that was what he wanted to be – a Onelord, an Emperor – the ruler not only of the Seven Nations but of all the known lands. And I have a vague memory of hearing him say once that he would climb the Broken Mountain and trek the Silent Wood if he could free his homeland.'

'And where was his homeland?' Paedur asked.

Katani shrugged. 'No-one knows. His colouring suggests the southern lands, but he had been sold off the slave-block at

Londre when he was around twelve. He ended up in Thusal. But I never heard him call any one place home, unless it was Shansalow, his capital . . .'

'Was the city really built entirely from silver?'

Katani looked at him in disgust. 'The palace roof was sheathed in silver. The city itself was of white brick – and it was a shabby, smelly, foul and dangerous place. It was no fit place to live.'

The bard nodded. He had walked the tumbled ruins of the Silver City and spent some time with the prospectors who dug in its ruined streets searching for the hoard of silver bricks that was reputed to lie buried in some cellar. 'And what do you know of his family, his advisers?' he asked.

Katani shrugged. 'He had no close advisers, except perhaps Praetens, his magician, and he was slain on the Sand Plain. Kutor the Strong would, I suppose, have been closest to him, but Churon grew mistrustful of his popularity and banished him to the west, to Gallowan, where he died mad and almost forgotten.'

'I know,' the bard said softly, remembering the legends. 'And Churon's family?'

'There was Deslirda, his queen, and one legitimate son, Chural. There were stories, of course, of his many mistresses and catamites – for Churon was a man of large appetites in every respect – and he was reputed to have sired several bastards.'

'Tell me about Deslirda,' Paedur said. Before he went in search of the Onelord he needed to have as much information about the man as possible.

Katani surprisingly shook her head. 'I know very little about her. She was a strange, shy woman, quite small, almost childlike, who rarely appeared in public and was surprisingly plain – not ugly, you understand, but just plain.' She paused and added, in a tone almost of wonder. 'And I really think he loved her.'

Paedur looked up quickly. 'Truly?'

Katani nodded. 'Truly.'

The bard tapped the wooden shelving gently with the flat of his hook, the delicate ringing hanging on the soft, musty air. 'That might be a place to start. But first, tell me about Chural, the son.'

The woman warrior smiled again, warmly this time. 'He was

his mother's son in every respect, quiet and gentle, not a fighter, but with enough knowledge of strategy and weaponcraft for him to gain his father's respect. I don't know what happened to him. Did he succeed Churon?'

Paedur shook his head. 'It has always been accepted that Churon had him murdered for those very qualities you mentioned . . .and also because he became an extraordinarily powerful magician when he reached his maturity, with special control over the elements. It was when the common people began calling him the Stormlord that Churon turned against him and had him killed.'

Katani hissed through gritted teeth. 'When I kill him, bard, I'll make sure it will be impossible for him to return to any semblence of a life.'

'If I don't do it before you, or Mannam doesn't do it before either of us,' Paedur smiled.

'If I don't do what?' The Dark Lord glided silently into the room, his cloak of seared and withered leaves making no sound on the polished wooden floor.

'I was merely saying that you would ensure that the Onelord never returned to any semblance of life – in this world or the next.'

Mannam laughed, the sound snapping on the air. 'I have Churon's future mapped out,' he whispered, the sound ominous and shrill. 'I can destroy his body, but I cannot destroy his soul. However, I can place it in the body of an animal, something suitable . . . some crawling, slithering thing.'

'Something edible,' Katani suggested. 'An inoffensive cuine that will be slain and eaten.'

'Something foul,' Mannam continued, almost gleefully, 'something loathed and feared, something that will be hunted and slain by man.'

'Or what about something defenceless? Katani added, with a broad grin. 'One of the creatures that is hunted by just about every predator . . .'

'If you can both contain yourselves,' Paedur said quietly, 'let us remember that we are dealing here with one of the most dangerous men ever to have walked the World of Men; a man of great strength of will, a man of vision and imagination, and with enough daring to carry his plans through. We are talking about a man who has not let death stand in the way of his plans of conquest. I do not think it will be too easy to kill this man, if indeed we can kill him.' He turned to Mannam. 'Is it going to be possible to knock him down, cut his throat, disembowel him, something – anything – and ensure that he stays that way for some time?'

'For how long?'

'As long as it takes to bring the corpse back here to you. Can that be arranged?'

Mannam shook his head rustlingly. 'Not easily, no.'

'Why not?' the bard demanded.

The Dark Lord shook his head impatiently, the movement curiously human, and Paedur once again had the fleeting impression of the face beneath the cowl. 'When a human dies, bard, his essence leaves his body and is taken by one of my bainte and carried here, and here we replace it in a replica of the body. When someone in the Silent Wood is slain the essence, the soul, remains within the body and therefore the body regenerates within a short period.'

Paedur shook his head, brushing his fine hair back off his forehead. 'You have not made yourself clear.'

'If – when – you kill Churon, I or one of my bainte would have to be on hand to rip the essence from his body, and that can only happen at the traumatic moment of death. If that moment is missed, even by so much as an instant, then the body will regenerate. The timing is essential. To have even a slim hope of success, I would have to accompany you, and that, as you know, is impossible.'

'If I totally destroyed Churon's body . . .'

'Have you ever tried to completely destroy a human body, bard?' Mannam hissed. 'Obviously not! All the bones have to be reduced to powder and the dust scattered, the tissues, organs and muscles have to be completely shredded, the hair and nails similarly disposed of. And even if you do that, then we cannot be certain that Churon's essence will not end up in another body . . .'

Paedur raised his hook, the runes sparkling slightly in the wan light. 'Wait. You are saying that this man cannot be killed, and even if he could be killed then there is no point because he will return to life again. And even if we totally destroy his body, we cannot be sure that his essence will not regenerate in another body? Well then, god, with all due respects to you, you are asking me to do the impossible.'

'Not impossible . . .'

Paedur suddenly smashed his hook into the shelving, the razor edge cutting deep into the hard wood. 'Well then, help me!' he demanded. 'Suggest something!'

Katani slid off the shelving and crossed to rest her gloved hand gently on Paedur's arm. She looked at Mannam. 'He is right. You are not helping us in any way. You must suggest something.'

The Dark Lord glared at them both for a moment and then he suddenly turned away and swept down the length of the library, his cloak rustling loudly like leaves in a storm-shaken tree. When he reached the far end of the cellar, he abruptly turned and shouted, 'I don't know what to do!' His anger and anguish sent something like forked lightning running along the floor, buzzing and crackling, sparking on the polished wood.

Paedur raised his left arm, holding his hook straight out from his body, the point downwards. The lightening hissed like serpents and then raced along the floor and leapt upwards towards the hook, where it spun and crackled, bringing the runes to sparkling life before disappearing into the dark metal.

Paedur looked at the Spirit of the Dead and shook his head. 'You must not fear him,' he said softly.

'He will kill me,' Mannam whispered sibilantly, his voice echoing along the length of the room.

'If you allow him to.'

'I don't see how I can stop him.'

'You are Death,' Paedur reminded him.

'Bard, in the World of Men, you are as a god, while here you are nothing more than a man. In the World of Men I am a god, but here in my own kingdom, my powers are limited.'

'What about the other gods?' Katani asked softly, looking from Paedur to Mannam.

A smile touched the bard's thin lips and he looked up at the Dark Lord, now hunched still and silent like a blasted tree at the far end of the cellar. 'Yes, what about them?' he asked, 'surely they would help?'

Mannam remained silent for a long time, and when he finally spoke his voice was slow and cautious, 'Few of my bretheren in the Pantheon can enter my kingdom. They deal with life, I with death.'

'But surely some of them can . . .' Paedur began.

'Yes, yes,' Mannam said impatiently, 'some can, some can.' He glided back to the pair, his movements now silent again, the leaves on his cloak quivering slightly. 'Whom would you suggest?' He looked at Paedur.

'Buiva, the War God,' the bard said immediately, and Katani nodded with a smile.

'And what of the Nameless God of Madness,' the warrior suggested.

Mannam nodded, then there was the sound of a branch snapped in half, and then he spoke one word, 'Maurug'.

'Maurug?' Katani asked, frowning, trying to recall the Pantheon of the Old Faith.

'The Destroyer,' Paedur smiled. 'Maurug the Destroyer.'

Mannam reached out to touch Paedur but drew his stick-like hand back when a spark shot from the bard's hook to coil around the twig-like fingers. 'I am confident again,' he said. 'I will call them to us.'

'I want you to call upon one other, if you can,' Paedur said quickly, as the Dark Lord began to turn away.

'Name them?'

'I want you to call on Deslirda, Churon's lady!'

Paedur and Katani walked the streets of Manach and looked at the people. The bard had to keep reminding himself that he was looking at the dead, men and women who had left the World of Men, tens, hundreds and in some cases thousands of years ago. As in Bannoche, the City of Ghosts, the people from all ages existed now side by side, and none seemed to think the differing styles of dress, the customs or mannerisms to be strange or unnatural.

At one point, Paedur turned to Katani and asked, 'Do you think they know they are dead.'

'Oh, they know, but like humankind – and I know because I did this myself – they forget, or at least prefer not to think on it. I think you will find that they have come to terms with their present existence.'

They turned into a small, quietly beautiful plaza and stopped beside a fountain. A creature from one of the southern mythologies, a beast with curling tusks, carved from the same dirty grey stone as the city, spouted water from its tusks.

'How did you find your own acceptance?' Paedur asked, touching the surface of the water with the point of his hook and snagging up a long tendril of weed.

Katani sat on the low fountain wall and looked across the square at the merchants tending their stalls; no-one bought anything, no-one sold, but people still came to browse. And there was no food of any description, no fruit or meats, no eggs or fish for sale. She nodded and the bard followed her gaze. 'I returned to my old profession, like them. They have nothing to sell, no-one buys, but they still go through the ritual of setting up their striped and colourful awnings and spreading the tables, setting out their wares. I returned to what I had been trained to do almost from my birth – I killed.'

'Why?' Paedur asked very quietly, his voice a murmur.

'In the beginning I think I was a little mad. Any man that stood before me I slew. And when I realised that they would rise again, I maimed them, so that they would never walk again, or speak, or perform the act of a man with a woman.' Her voice had become hoarse with the memory and she shook her head and fell silent.

'And?' he prompted.

'And then I suppose I realised what I had become.'

'And what was that?'

'A beserk – a killing-machine without soul . . .' She smiled at that. 'Without soul. But with that realisation came a form of acceptance, and it was as if the madness had been burned from me. I set about exploring my surroundings, learning more about where I was, going to the Fairs.'

'The Fairs?'

'Yes, the Fairs. They are huge gatherings of the newly dead and those recently come to the Silent Wood. It is a place of meeting, where friends and relatives can be reunited, where the last barrier – death – no longer exists. There are bainte there; they explain what has happened and where you are and how to go to the Place of Judgement if you desire to be judged by Alile, the Judge Impartial. But they always add the warning that while we could walk the Silent Woods unjudged for all eternity, once we went to the Place of Judgement and Alile had passed judgement, then we would be bound to accept his decision, which was final.'

'And what sort of decisions does he hand down?' Paedur wondered.

'No-one knows. No-one has ever returned.' She pushed herself off the wall and walked away quickly, heading out of the plaza. Paedur followed more slowly.

'Is that why you have never gone for judgement?' he called after her.

Katani stopped and looked back over her shoulder. 'What do you mean?'

'Is it because you are afraid?'

'I am of the Katan; I fear nothing. Not even death, not any more,' she added.

'Then tell me why have you not gone to stand before Alile, the Judge Impartial?'

'Why do you ask?' Katani turned around to face him, her left hand resting on the wrapped hilt of her longsword. There was a chill edge to her voice.

Paedur walked across the cobbled stones to stand directly in front of her. And then he placed his right hand on her shoulder and looked deep into her hard amber eyes. 'Because when I face Churon the Onelord, I will need to know, I will need to trust, the person standing by my side. Surely you can comprehend that?'

Katani nodded silently.

'I need to know why you have refused to face the last great mystery of this place: the Judgement of Alile.'

Katani looked into his deep dark eyes and saw only sympathy there, no mockery. 'Because I don't want to return to the World of Men,' she said very softly.

The bard stared blankly at her.

'Don't you see? When you have been adjudged by Alile, you are returned to the World of Men in another life, another guise, to start again!'

'But you've just said no-one knows what those judgements are?' Paedur protested.

'Bard, the finest necromancers, magicians and sorcerers have passed through this place. And I have always put the same question to all those I've met: what is Alile's judgement? And their reply is always the same. He passes judgement on one's life and then sends one back into the World of Men for another span of life.'

'For how many spans?' Paedur asked, suddenly terrified by the very thought of it. In the World of Men he was virtually immortal. What would happen when he died and was adjudged? Was he to return as an ordinary man, ungifted and untalented?

'No-one knows,' Katani answered him, 'except Alile, the Judge Impartial. And no-one has ever been able to discover the truth.'

'Oh, I will,' Paedur promised, 'I will.'

# 10   A Cause

'A just cause does not automatically guarantee victory, but if a man
believes his cause is just, then he will defend it all the more fiercely.'

*Owen, the Weapon Master*

Sunlight the colour of smoke slanted in through the stained-glass
windows and ran like coloured inks down the faces of the four
people sitting around the ornately carved brukwood table. The
warm light lent the room a slightly mysterious atmosphere,
softening all the edges, and the delicately cut crystal goblets on
the table had taken on an insubstantial, ethereal air, as if a
reaching hand might pass right through them.

Conversation had lulled, the routine business of the day
having been conducted, and by unspoken consent they took a
few moments respite before moving on to more pressing matters.
By their clothing and studied mannerisms they could have been
taken for merchants or bankers, and they had that unmistakable
air of those who were used to commanding rather than being
commanded.

However, this small, dimly lit room was part of the Emperor's
personal chambers and these four people represented the ultimate power in the Seven Nations.

Geillard XII sat with his back to the window. He was a tall,
rather thin man, his features sharp and severe, his eyes deep-sunk
behind prominent cheekbones, giving him a permanently morose
expression. His hair, which had faded to a pale nondescript colour,
was thinning and his bare scalp burned redly in the reflected light.
His hands, which were unusually long-fingered, rested easily on
the table, the tips barely touching his goblet of wine.

To his left sat Salier, his chief counseller, magician and personal attendant. There were rumours that Salier was more than
just a servant to the Emperor, and it was widely recognised that
he exerted a more than natural influence on the throne. He was
a small, dark man, soft-spoken, quiet and evasive, with the man-
ners of a cleric and the morals of an assassin.

Directly facing Salier sat Fodla, Geillard's Captain of the Guard. By tradition the Emperor's bodyguard was always female, a tradition that had begun when Churon ruled and kept the Katan as his personal guard. Her bravery and weaponcraft were legendary and it was considered a great honour for a young girl to be chosen to be trained under her command. She was a huge woman, tall and bulky, her green eyes perpetually wide, giving her an innocent and slightly lost expression, and the splash of freckles across her face lent her an almost girlish appearance. Her ancestry was shrouded in mystery, but rumours abounded which ranged from the fanciful to the outrageous. She had served with Geillard now for twelve years, and she was one of the few people he actually trusted and listened to. Her contempt for Salier was matched only by her respect for the man, whom she considered to be absolutely evil.

Facing the Emperor sat Barthus, the Hierophant, newly elected pope of the New Religion, which the Emperor recently had taken up and pronounced as the official religion of his empire. The Hierophant was a slender ascetic whose features were so indeterminate that he might easily have been taken for either sex. He seemed to deliberately accentuate his hermaphroditic appearance by his choice of extravagant clothing and his movements and gestures were studied and precise. Of them all, he was the one the Emperor trusted the least, and he was equally loathed by both Salier and Fodla, but they were all forced to recognise the immense power he had at his command.

The Emperor touched his goblet with the tip of his finger and the crystal rang like a bell. 'I will have your reports now, if you please,' Geillard said softly, studying his hands.

In keeping with the tradition, Salier began. 'Precise and verifiable information is difficult to obtain since the Cataclysm. All that is certain is that the New Religion has been dealt a serious blow, and that the Pantheon has consolidated its position. The Planes of Existence are in turmoil and the Void is wracked with spasms of such power that several of our magicians and sorcerers have been destroyed as they travelled in search of information.'

'Does anyone know what brought on the Cataclysm?' The Emperor looked from Salier to Barthus.

The magician grimaced. 'We have nothing definite at the moment, but my lord Barthus has suggested that it is in some way connected to this so-called Champion of the Old Faith.'

103

'And have you discovered anything about this person or being?'

Salier nodded. 'As far as we can determine, it is a bard, by name Paedur . . .'

Geillard started. 'Was there not a bard at court by that name?'

The magician nodded again. 'We believe it is the same man. This champion is described as a bard with a hook in place of his left hand.'

The Emperor nodded. 'The same,' he breathed.

'He is also inciting revolution!' Fodla said abruptly, her deep masculine voice startling them all. The Captain of the Guard leaned forward and began tapping out her points on the table with a stubby finger. 'Although hard information is difficult at this time, my spies have reported that Kutor the Renegade and his outlaws have vanished!' She saw the Emperor's startled expression and continued more slowly, her eyes now on his face alone. 'A hook-handed man spent a single night with his band before their departure. I have further reports of them heading into the west.' She paused and then added more slowly, 'I also have reports of a Weapon Master accompanied by a Shemmat slave travelling into the west . . .'

'Owen,' Salier whispered, and Fodla nodded in agreement. 'It can only be him.'

The magician turned to Geillard. 'You will recall him, Majesty. We hired him on two previous occasions through intermediaries, and his defence of Car'an'tual has made him a legend.'

'I remember him,' Geillard said, suddenly looking at Barthus. 'He is one of the Iron Band of Kloor?'

Surprisingly, the Hierophant shook his head. 'No more. The link was severed, the band shattered.'

'That is impossible,' Salier snapped.

'I have always believed so, but it has happened.' He coughed delicately. 'Our last Sighted image of Owen is of a silver hook striking the Iron Band and destroying it.'

'The bard again,' Fodla grunted. 'I should have killed him when I had the chance. I would have, if it hadn't been for your meddling,' she snapped, looking at Salier.

'The man was a genius, and useful too. It would have been such a waste.'

The Captain snorted and opened her mouth to reply, but the Emperor raised a hand, the rings on his fingers taking the light, red reflecting from a large ruby darting across their faces like new scars. 'What else do you have?'

'Cormac, the Gallowglas King, is dead!' she said simply, and allowed the sentence to hang on the still air.

'How?' Barthus whispered.

'When?' Salier demanded.

'Tell us what you know without dramatics,' Geillard said tiredly.

'I know very little,' Fodla confessed. 'Cormac is dead, killed in a fair fight – if you can believe that – and his Gallowglas warriors slain to a man.'

'And his legion?' Salier asked, his agile mind desperately working out all the possible implications.

'I don't know.'

'Is it perhaps too much of a coincidence that both Kutor and Owen have headed into the west, and now Cormac, one of our creatures, is slain?' Barthus asked, forgetting for once his lisping, derisive tone.

'Barthus is right,' Geillard said decisively. 'Fodla, send your people into the west and have them seek news of Kutor and his people, the Weapon Master and the fate of Cormac's legion.'

'It's my guess that we'll find them all together,' Fodla said grimly.

'That's what I'm afraid of,' Geillard admitted, reaching for his glass and draining it in one swallow.


Prince Kutor turned as someone noisily mounted the steps behind him. 'I'm getting too old for this,' Keshian moaned, leaning on the battlements to catch his breath.

Kutor smiled. 'Strange. I thought I saw a man who looked just like you spend most of yesterday morning showing men the safest and quickest way to run up and down a ladder wearing full armour.'

'That was yesterday,' Keshian growled, 'and some days are easier than others.'

The prince nodded down into the courtyard below, where their new-found army was training. 'How are they working out?'

His captain shrugged. 'There's very little to do with them.

When we got them a moon ago, they were a well-trained legion and now – well, now they're the finest fighting force I've ever worked with. Owen and Tien tZo have worked them hard – very hard – but somehow the men don't seem to resent it.'

Kutor nodded. 'I know. I think it's a matter of pride with them now, they feel honoured to be trained by the finest Weapon Master in the Nations, the man who defeated Cormac in single combat. How go the defences?'

'Almost complete. But that's what one thousand men can do. The outer walls have been completely repaired and the moat has been cleared and reset with spikes and stakes. We are re-directing the stream which once fed it back into its original course. The two wells we discovered within the fortress have been cleared and the escape tunnels have also been cleared of debris and shored up.'

Kutor nodded. One thing he resented about the present state of affairs was that he was not as involved as he wanted to be, or felt he should be. 'Has there been any more trouble?'

'None. Owen has seen to that.'

Although the legion had been properly oath-bound to Kutor once the Weapon Master had slain the Gallowglas, he gave them the choice of joining him or moving on into the west if they desired. Some chose to move on, taking their chances in the westlands, but the majority of the legionaries, knowing no other life, accepted his invitation to join with him in his attempt on the throne. Naturally, there had been a certain amount of fric-tion between the new arrivals and Kutor's men, and there had been several incidents, the last of which had ended in a vicious fight which had left two men dead and a dozen injured. Owen's justice had been swift and merciless; the two ringleaders, one from each side, had been taken out and challenged to a duel by the Weapon Master. And he had killed them, swiftly, easily and with no apparent effort. There had been no trouble since.

'Where is the Weapon Master now?'

'When I last saw him, he was setting out to check on the sentries. He's convinced the Empire will be sending a force here very soon now.'

Kutor turned to look at the distant hills, wondering whether he would one day see them alive with the blue and black of the Imperial troops. 'And what do you think?'

Keshian shrugged. 'Even allowing for the breakdown in communications because of the Cataclysm, I'm sure some sort of rumour has reached them of Cormac's death. It's not every day a Gallowglas is slain in single combat.'

'What will happen?'

The captain shrugged again. 'I would imagine they'll send a raiding party rather than an army, looking for information, troop deployments, fortifications, leadership. Perhaps they'll even try to capture one of our leaders.'

'Are the men ready to fight?'

'They're ready to fight; all they need is a cause.'

The prince smiled. 'I thought they were fighting for my cause?'

'They're grateful to you, or rather to the Weapon Master, for freeing them from Cormac's tyranny and returning their wives and children, but remember that most have joined you merely because you offer them security of a sort in this wild land. They need, they expect, to see some gain at the end of all this. You need to make them think that they're fighting for their freedom and faith and, more importantly, for their families.'

'They need a cause,' Kutor smiled.

'They need a cause.'

The Weapon Master lay flat on the ground and watched the line of horsemen wind their way slowly up along the treacherous defile below. The afternoon had turned towards evening and the shadows were already beginning to thicken at the foot of the gully, and he knew if he was going to act, he would have to do it soon.

He watched the shadow of a tall silver-white tree grow along the ground, timing it, and he was actually rising to his feet when he heard the long, slow, grumbling rumble of falling rock off down at the far end of the defile. Tien's timing was as precise as usual. He immediately applied his weight to the long lever he had wedged beneath a boulder on the lip of the gully and pushed. The rock groaned and then moved – fractionally at first and then with a sudden give that almost precipitated him out over the edge. It thundered down the rockface, ripping smaller rocks and boulders from the cliffs and pulling them down with it. By the time it reached the canyon floor it was carrying enough debris to effectively block the mouth of the defile.

Owen almost reluctantly picked up one of his servant's recurved bows and prepared to do the methodical work of butchery. Away at the other end of the defile he heard an unholy agonised scream echoing off the rock walls and knew that Tien's first arrow had sent one of the Emperor's men to the Silent Wood.

Owen and Tien rode back into the fortress as dusk was drifting in like fog. They were both silent, but while Tien tZo's silence was one of exhaustion, the Weapon Master seemed almost angry. Kutor strode out to meet them, followed now by the guards Owen had picked and trained himself. Kutor had resented them at first, but gradually realised that they helped promote his image in the eyes of his men – and he was thinking of them as his men now – as a prince and future ruler. He watched the two men wearily dismount and then noted that although both men were carrying bows, their quivers were empty.

Owen stopped in front of him, his face tight, his eyes hooded. 'We will speak later,' he said, his voice cold and distant.

Kutor opened his mouth to protest, but caught Tien tZo's tiny shake of the head. The prince nodded. 'Of course, later.'

Owen nodded and then brushed past the prince, heading in the direction of his quarters, Kutor's guards and the guards on the door coming alert and saluting him as he passed. Uncharacteristically, he didn't return the salute. 'What's wrong?' Kutor asked the Shemmat.

'He's tired. He has had a hard day.'

'Doing what?'

'Killing,' Tien smiled uneasily, and then hurried after his master.

Owen flung open the door and stormed into the room. The feelings that had been boiling up within him since the first killing earlier that afternoon now threatened to explode and he had to make a conscious effort to lower himself into a seat and clasp his hands together, interlacing the fingers, lest he suddenly grab a weapon and begin laying about him.

Behind him the door closed with a barely audible click, and although Tien tZo's footsteps were noiseless, Owen felt him approaching and then his practised fingers began loosening his belts and ties.

'What's wrong with me, Tien?' Owen asked, his voice a harsh whisper.

'The killing bothers you?' the Shemmat asked.

'No – yes! I know it shouldn't have, but it did.'

'We've slain in that fashion before,' Tien remarked, removing Owen's broad leather belt with his scabbard and knife sheaths and laying them on the smooth stone floor. 'You once killed two squads of conscripted youths without a qualm of . . .'

'Conscience,' Owen finished. 'That is what is bothering me about the killings today. They were all innocent men and women . . .'

Tien moved around the table and sat down opposite the Weapon Master. His eyes caught and held Owen's troubled gaze. 'Can you honestly say that all those you killed were deserving of death?'

'No,' Owen whispered.

'These were Imperial troops. Why are they different?'

'I don't know. I don't know!'

'The Gallowglas were evil, killers and murderers to a man. There was never any doubt but that they would be – must be – killed. That was a judgement you made; you judged them and found them guilty. Today you made a similar judgement and found the Emperor's men innocent, but still you killed them.'

'What is the point?' Owen snapped.

'In the past,' Tien tZo continued patiently, 'you would have killed them all – good and bad alike – with no hesitation, no second thoughts.'

'In the past?' Owen asked.

'Before you met the bard.'

'While I was in the Iron Band you mean?'

'Just so.'

Owen remained silent for a long time, and when he finally raised his head, the Shemmat was horrified to find moisture around his eyes. Instinctively he reached out, his long-fingered killer's hands gentle as they touched his master's face.

'What is happening to me?' Owen moaned.

'You are becoming human again,' Tien said very softly, his voice awed. 'It seems the bard gave you a far greater gift than you imagined.'

'We killed forty warriors today,' Owen said, looking at Kutor and Keshian. 'They were the Emperor's people,' he added, watching their reactions.

'Did you have to kill them?' the prince asked quietly.

109

## Demon's Law: Tales of the Bard

'I felt it was necessary,' Owen said quickly, surprised at his own defensiveness.

'Of course, and I abide by your decision. I was merely wondering why they had to be killed.'

'We knew we would attract interest sooner or later. In fact we're lucky to have survived this long, but we've had the Cataclysm to thank for that. Undoubtedly word has trickled through to the capital that something is amiss here in the Wastelands, and they have decided to investigate. I would imagine we have a moon – certainly no more – to consolidate our defences here, or to attack.'

'Attack!' Kutor started. 'You mean begin ... carry the fight to them? But surely it's too soon? We need men ... weapons ... food ...' He felt suddenly breathless with the thought of it.

'The Cold Months will soon be here,' Owen said reasonably, 'and they are harsh in the Wastelands. We will undoubtedly be sealed within the fortress and almost certainly lose some men as desertion and boredom eats away at them. By the time the season changes, news of our strengths and numbers will have reached the Emperor.'

'It seems so sudden,' Kutor breathed.

Tien grinned. 'Not so sudden. Even if we start tomorrow, it will be fully a moon or more before we are ready to move out.'

Owen nodded. 'Tien is right. But I think this is a decision which should be made now.'

'We're not ready,' the prince protested.

'We are,' Owen said calmly.

Kutor looked to his captain for support, but surprisingly Keshian also nodded. 'The men need to fight.'

'A victory would be good for their morale,' Tien agreed.

Kutor smiled tiredly. 'I have a feeling this is not really my decision, is it?' He shook his head and folded his hands. 'Fine, arrange my future between you. I will go along with whatever decision you make.'

'Without you there are no reasons for decisions,' Tien said quietly.

'Our decisions will make you an Emperor!' Owen grinned.

The Emperor Geillard awoke suddenly from a terrifying nightmare in which a vaguely humanlike creature loomed over him, drooling jaws wide and dripping scalding acid. His eyes snapped

110

open to find Salier leaning over his bed, a long blood-coloured candle in his hand, hot wax dripping on to his bare chest. For a single instant, the dream creature and Salier's face superimposed and the Emperor resisted the impulse to scream and strike out at the were-beast.

'What . . . what is it?' he mumbled.

Salier suddenly threw back the covers, revealing one of the Emperor's concubines lying crouched in a bundle by Geillard's side. The woman's eyes were wide and terrified as she looked up at the magician.

'Begone,' he hissed, and with a squeal like a trapped animal she rolled out of bed and darted for the door. Salier watched her naked form for a moment longer than necessary, letting her know that he was watching her.

'What is it?' the Emperor demanded.

'The patrol we sent into the Wastelands is no more, but never mind; their mission was successful,' Salier said, a barely disguised note of triumph in his voice.

'What do you mean "no more"?'

'They have been slain,' Sailer hissed.

'How do you know this?'

'One of them was my creature. Although its body went into the Wastelands, its essence remained with me. I won't bore you with the process, but when a body dies or is slain that essence is released into the Void, where, according to whatever belief you follow, it is seized by Mannam's bainte or floats on Libellius' river to its ultimate destination. To shorten the tale, a bainte came for the essence I still held, but I managed to trap it within a Circle of Power, where I was able to question it at length about the situation in the Wastelands.'

'And?'

'You must prepare for war, Emperor. Your bastard half-brother is coming for your throne!'

## 11    The Gods

Maurug is the Destroyer, and his guise is that of a small and stunted
man, but his power is awesome . . .
    Buiva is the God of War, an old and grizzled man, wise in the
ways of war and of Man, but weary . . .
    The Nameless God of Madness, the Fool, the Innocent, a
hermaphrodite, whose touch can drive men mad . . .

*Pantheon of the Old Faith*

Buiva arrived first, a tired-looking old man in a simple suit of
rusted chainmail. His face was gaunt, pinched and lined, and
there was a three-day growth of stubbly beard on his chin. Only
his eyes were alive; they were bright, alert and darting, and a
deep luxurious brown in his weatherbeaten face. Indeed, it could
have been the face of any nameless mercenary who had fought
across the Seven Nations. There was a sword strapped to his
shoulders and a long-bladed dagger and mace and chain on his
belt.

He appeared on the top of the Tower of Time silently, and
then, with a warrior's ingrained caution, paused in the darkened
doorway before stepping out into the light. When he moved, he
made no sound. His mail, though rusted on the surface, had
obviously been kept oiled, and he had wrapped his huge gloved
fist around the haft of the mace and chain to ensure its silence.

He stepped out on to the roof and immediately approached
Paedur and Katani, ignoring Mannam. The bard was wrapped
in his long dark-furred cloak but with the hood thrown back
and the ties undone, allowing it to flap open, revealing the
wicked hook in place of his left hand and the bardic sigil on his
left shoulder. Katani was in her full grotesque armour but with
the mask-helmet lying by her feet. War looked them both up
and down and then stepped over to Mannam, who was standing
by the cracked sundial.

'I trust you have a reason for all this, Death?' Buiva rasped,
his voice raw and hoarse and inexpressibly weary.

'I would not have asked you here if I had not,' Mannam snapped.

Buiva nodded at the man and woman. 'These?'

The Dark Lord raised his stick hand. 'Allow me a moment, War. Two of our kind have yet to arrive. I will make the introductions then.'

Buiva nodded grumpily and then stamped over to stand before the woman. 'Katan warrior,' he growled.

Katani nodded slowly, unsure whether it had been a question or a simple statement.

'What weapon?' Buiva asked suddenly.

'All,' she said quietly, with just a touch of pride in her voice. Advancement in the Katan Sisterhood was measured by proficiency with weapons; the greater the warrior, the more weapons she had. There were few who could have said all.

'No weaknesses?'

Katani smiled at the fierce-seeming old man. 'I'm sure there must be now; it has been long since I practised with more than sword, spear, knife and bow.'

Buiva was about to say more when he suddenly turned, moments before a second figure appeared in the doorway.

'Maurug,' Mannam and Buiva said simultaneously.

The Destroyer was a small, stunted man, squat and with a potbelly. His face was round and fringed with a few remaining strands of snow-white hair that mingled with the similarly ragged threads of a beard. His eyes were cold, black, hard, piercing and completely without compassion. He was wearing a courtier's robe of crimson silk that had been fashionable several centuries previously, high-necked, puff-sleeved and ground length; the sleeves were wide and flowing and the small man's hands were lost in them.

He looked slowly from face to face, his eyes lingering on Paedur and Katani, his lip curling in something like disgust. 'I smell intrigue.' His voice was a whine. 'Death and War together, an interesting and apt alliance.'

'And now Destruction,' Buiva added slowly. 'The trinity is complete.'

'Not quite,' Mannam said, his rasping, cracked voice sounding weary. 'There is one yet to come . . .'

'Who?' Maurug snapped.

'Me, perhaps?' The voice was high and lisping, sounding slightly breathless.

Paedur distinctly felt the atmosphere change and beside him Katani stiffened; whatever feelings the three gods of the Pantheon had for each other, they were at least tempered by something close to respect, but the bard, even without his enchanced senses, knew that this feeling did not extend to the Nameless God of Delusion and Madness.

The god was tall and thin, his build similar to the bard's, but fair where he was dark. His features were soft, almost gentle, with a definite effeminacy about them, until one looked at his eyes – and they were bronze and quite, quite mad. He was barefoot and wearing a simple peasant's garb of jerkin and breeches, which looked completely incongruous on such a soft-looking creature, for he seemed more suited to satins and silks than the rough woollens and worn leathers.

'Well, well, well,' he lisped. 'Death entertaining War and Destruction, how interesting. And two others also . . .' He turned, the movement deliberately exaggerated, and stared at Paedur and Katani, and his glittering bronze-coloured eyes narrowed, and suddenly he didn't look quite so crazed, only infinitely cunning and dangerous. 'What have we here, eh? A creature from the World of Men, but not wholly a man, and a woman of the Silent Wood, but not completely dead. What a truly interesting combination.' He put his large and surprisingly rough hands on his hips and turned to look at Mannam. 'You must explain.'

'These two,' Maurug growled, his thin voice querulous, turning his large head and glaring at the two silent figures. 'Who? Why?'

'The woman is a warrior of the Katan,' Mannam said slowly. 'She has been within my domain for some time now. Her presence here is perhaps fated; she chose to accompany the man, and she has his and my trust. The man . . . well the man is Paedur, the . . .'

'Bard!' the Nameless God hissed in delight. Maurug merely grunted but turned to look at Paedur more closely, while Buiva remained silently watchful. 'Why, this is becoming enthralling,' Madness enthused. 'You must know that I was entirely in your favour when we chose a champion,' he said to Paedur. 'I just knew you would be the most successful . . .'

Paedur raised his hook, the sudden movement silencing the god. 'We have much to do, much to decide upon,' he said quietly, using his trained voice to project a sense of urgency, 'and while I know time holds no sway here, our time – or rather your time – is being measured on different planes, and slipping away.'

Buiva shifted his grip on his mace and chain, the rattling sound shifting all attention on to him. 'You should explain,' the God of War said quietly. Madness opened his mouth to add something, but a glare from Maurug kept him silent.

Paedur went and sat on the edge of the low wall that surrounded the roof and looked down over the city. It was unnervingly quiet, Mannam having returned his subjects to their dwellings, where they stood in the shadows like statues, their senses active, their bodies immobile, and now the only movement was the turgid flowing of the Naman, the air bitter and foul with its stench. When the bard looked back, he found the gods had settled themselves in various attitudes of attentiveness; Madness was now leaning eagerly across the cracked sundial, Mannam had stepped back into the shadow of the doorway, while Buiva was sitting with his legs stretched out straight in front of him, his eyes closed, his back against the low wall. Maurug was crouched on his heels close to the God of War. Katani had taken up position beside the bard, her eyes alert, watching the city – and beyond – for any movement, any signs of an attack.

'I will speak,' Paedur began, 'and I must beg of you not to question me at this time; there will be time enough for questions later.

'Now, the situation is a simple one. Mannam is threatened with death. Aye, someone is attempting to kill the Dark Lord. But it is not just Death and the office of Death that is in danger here, but also all the Planes of Existence. We are facing an enemy who is not content with securing Death's somewhat dubious crown, but also seizing the various crowns of the differing kings of all the Planes of Life. And I would imagine he intends to do this with an army of dead.

'That man is Churon, who in the world of Men bore the title Onelord. Ah, you all smile. I see you know the name. Well, if you are familiar with the name then perhaps you will recall something of the man behind it. Yes, a man who secured the Nations from the Shemmatae and founded the Seven Nations as they are now, but also a man who butchered untold thousands because he felt that in one way or another they stood in his way or opposed him.

'History has made much of this man, has made him what he was not, and the myths and legends that surround his name only add to the glamour. But you all knew him, and knew what he truly was – a warmonger, a destroyer and quite, quite mad.' Paedur glanced at each god in turn and they all slowly nodded. 'And now this man wants Mannam's place!

'He has already made some attempts on Death, and waiting in the wings is Libellius, the Deathgod of the New Religion. Now, we cannot imagine what dealings these two have had together; perhaps Churon will take the crown for Libellius, and the New Religion will rule this place, or perhaps Churon will rule as Death ...' He shrugged. 'We cannot tell. Personally, I imagine the Deathgod of the Religion would be only a figurehead; the real power would be Churon. I think it is plain that he wants to be Onelord again, lord of this place and all the Planes of Life.' He stopped and then added slowly, looking at each face, noting their expressions. 'And he must be stopped, not just for my sake and the sake of all those in the World of Men, but for yours also. For if he triumphs here, how long do you think it will be before he sets his sights on your positions? We have to kill Churon,' he finished.

'Impossible,' Maurug snapped.

'Completely so,' Madness agreed.

Buiva remained silent, but he nodded his head, an almost private movement.

'Why?' Paedur suddenly thundered, startling them. 'You are Maurug, the Destroyer, a joyless creature whose only pleasure is destruction, and whom legends accuse of being almost entirely responsible for the fall of the Age of the Culai. Think of the challenge, think of the joy, it would be to destroy the greatest threat not only to this world but to all the worlds, a threat to the very gods themselves.

'And you, you are Madness, Delusion and Madness. Surely we have here one of your creatures, one of the god-touched. Tell me how difficult it would be for you to make further suggestions to this man, to drive him further over the brink into absolute raving insanity? If it is true that you feed on the essence of those whom you claim, think of the feast you would have on Churon's blighted essence.

'And what of War? What do you say? Churon has served your cause often and bloodily. With all your experience of the man, can you not tell me how I can defeat him?'

116

Buiva was the first to break the long silence that followed. 'I can tell you what will defeat him,' he said softly. 'It is true that I sat with him often enough while he planned his campaigns, and so I can tell you that he is a brilliant man, with that depth of vision that is found only in the greatest of warriors. Defeating him is relatively simple – after all, he is but a man – but I think your greatest problem will be getting close to him.' He sat forward, his rusted mail scraping off the stone. 'Do you know that he always wears a suit of leather next to his skin? It encases him from neck to groin and is woven through with strands of supple iron wire, designed to turn a knife or even a sword thrust.' He paused expectantly.

'A precaution for a man in his position. I know that there were several assassination attempts,' Paedur said slowly.

Buiva smiled mirthlessly. 'But that is not the reason. Do you know that Churon the Onelord has a fear, a simple dread?'

'I never knew him to fear anything,' Katani interrupted, turning slightly to look at the War God.

'He fears spiders,' the Nameless God lisped, 'small, harmless, unobtrusive things, but he has a dread of the creatures. But then, he is mad, I suppose,' he added with an innocent smile.

'I know of people who fear spiders,' Paedur said in surprise, 'and I would not have considered them mad.'

'But do you know of someone who feared spiders enough to kill one by plunging a burning torch down on to it ... when it was walking on his own leg!' the Nameless God lisped.

'Are you saying he fears them even to his own destruction?' Paedur asked, looking at the gods.

Buiva, Maurug and the Nameless God nodded in unison.

'Well then, surely here is a way to his destruction?' Paedur said slowly.

'I don't think the sight of a spider, no matter how big, will frighten him to death,' Buiva said gruffly.

'I know that, but it might distract him long enough to lower his guard, and then he is just as open to a sword or knife blade as any man.' He looked at Maurug. 'Let us say I manage to kill this man. Can you destroy his body so that he cannot return to any semblance of life?'

Maurug nodded sharply. 'Once Mannam or one of his creatures takes his essence, he could pass it to Madness, who will feed on it, and I can then feed on his body. Nothing will survive when we are done with him.'

'That still brings you back to how are you going to slay him in the first place? How are you going to get close to him?' Buiva asked.

Paedur smiled grimly. 'I intend to ask his lady those same questions.'

'I am Paedur, a bard, and this is Katani, a warrior of the Katan Sisterhood. You are Deslirda, wife of Churon the Onelord.'

'Once,' the woman whispered very softly. 'No more.'

'You are comfortable, my lady?' Katani asked, stepping out of the shadows that clustered about the edges of the long cellar library.

The woman nodded, the movement quick and shy, her sky-blue eyes darting from man to woman and then dropping back to her hands, which were resting on the simple table she had been seated behind. 'I am comfortable.'

She was a small, delicate-seeming woman, with pale, almost translucent skin, and bright blue eyes that seemed far too large for her face. Her hair, which was the colour of old ivory, had been crudely chopped in a ragged line across her forehead and hung in untidy clumps down her back. She was wearing a simple peasant-woman's gown of rough sacking tied around the waist with a belt and she was barefoot. Her long-fingered hands were raw and chapped and her nails were broken and ragged.

The bard had watched her from the shadows when she had arrived. His legends had constructed him an image of a completely different person, and he found it hard to think of this simple, frightened peasant-woman as the Lady Deslirda, the Light of the Nations. A bainte had brought her and Paedur watched it bend its round head and whisper something to the shivering woman before it stepped away and pulled the library door closed behind him.

Katani touched his arm lightly. 'What was that all about?' she murmured.

'Last minute instructions – what to tell us, or what to withhold. I cannot help feeling that Mannam is playing with us, using us to further some obscure end of his own.'

The warrior nodded.

Paedur stepped out of the shadows, visibly startling Deslirda.

He bowed deeply without speaking and escorted her to the far end of the library to where a small, ancient table and two chairs had been set up. He seated her and then sat down opposite the woman and introduced himself.

'My lady, I must apologise for bringing you here so abruptly and without so much as a by-your-leave . . .' Paedur began.

'Are you Death?' Deslirda asked suddenly.

'No, my lady,' Paedur smiled, 'I am not Death.'

'You remind me of him.' Her eyes drifted off his face and then slowly returned. 'You are somehow connected to him?'

'No, my lady,' the bard said softly, something in the woman's attitude and manner beginning to alarm him.

'I met him once,' she breathed, her large eyes darting.

'Who?'

'Why, Death. I met Death, when I died.' She smiled. 'One of his winged creatures brought me to him, the same one that brought me to you. Or at least I think it was the same one; they all seem alike.' Her eyes focussed briefly. 'You must have some influence with Death.'

'I think I might have a little,' Paedur smiled, his eyes never leaving her face. He was aware of Katani moving around behind the woman, knowing that she too was aware that something was desperately wrong with the woman.

'What did the bainte tell you before he left?' Paedur asked softly, projecting calmness and confidence, using his trained bardic voice to lull her suspicions.

'He brought me, as he once brought me to Death, and now he brings me to you, but he tells me not to speak to you of the Place of Judgement. Why is that, I wonder, if you are Death?'

'I am not Death,' Paedur repeated patiently. 'What is the Place of Judgement?'

'Where Alile sits,' Katani said very quietly, 'passing judgement on the dead. Obviously there is some *geasa* about speaking of the judgement.'

The bard nodded, his eyes never leaving Deslirda's face. 'I do not wish to speak to you about Death,' he continued, calmly, softly, 'nor do I wish to speak to you of the Place of Judgement. I want to speak to you about Churon.'

Something moved behind Deslirda's eyes at the mention of the name, something fearful. 'You are not from him, are you?'she asked, a thin, high note of desperation creeping into her voice.

'No,' Paedur said forcefully, 'we are not from your husband; we have no connection with the man, and we mean you no harm. Do you fear him?' he asked in the same tone of voice.

'No, not now. He can do nothing to me now; he is dead and I am not!'

'My lady,' Katani said very gently, 'you too are amongst the dead.'

'No, no, no,' Deslirda said quickly, 'I have been judged, I am dead no longer.' And then, suddenly realising she had said something she shouldn't, she clapped both hands to her mouth, her eyes wide and terrified. 'Oh, I didn't say that! You didn't hear me say that!' she said fiercely, pleadingly.

'We heard nothing,' Paedur said quickly, glancing at Katani.

'Nothing,' she agreed.

'Tell us about Churon,' Paedur said, watching her face closely, and once again he saw the reaction, saw the fear flicker in her eyes.

Abruptly the woman's shoulders slumped, and the tautness left her face. 'Why do you want to know?' she asked tiredly, and suddenly the slightly mad and terrifed woman was gone and in her place was a tired young woman in a shapeless, foul-smelling dress.

'We need to kill him,' he said evenly.

Deslirda stared at him for a moment, and then she began to laugh, the sound shocking and terrifying in the still silent place. When the laughter grew towards hysteria, Paedur slipped his hook from beneath his cloak and touched the back of her hand with the ice-cool metal. The shock brought her back to her senses. 'He is dead, bard, dead,' she gasped, 'and he cannot be slain now. You are too late, you and all the others who would, who should, have slain him during his life, cannot harm him now. Kill him and he will rise again and again . . .'

Paedur abruptly tapped the metal surface of the table with the point of his hook, scattering sparks, shocking her into silence.

'I intend to kill the man, my lady, and I intend to ensure that he does not rise again. When I am finished, Churon the Onelord will be no more.'

'No more,' Deslirda whispered. 'No more,' she nodded, liking the idea. 'And how will you do this?' she asked.

'That is to be determined, but I will need your help,' Paedur said cautiously.

'Freely and gladly given,' Deslirda said quickly, something like animation coming back into her face.

'I need to know about the man,' Paedur said, 'and I am drawing an image of him from various sources. But you knew him best of all. You lived with him for what, twenty summers?'

'Closer to twenty-five,' Deslirda said absently.

'How did you meet him?'

'I was sold to the Onelord when I was twelve summers old,' Deslirda closed her eyes, remembering. 'But I suppose the legends about him don't say that now, do they?' She opened her eyes and looked at the bard. He silently shook his head. In the myths, the fearless warrior Churon wooed and won the heart of the beautiful princess of Broar only after defeating several other claimants for her hand.

'I was twelve years old,' she murmured, shaking her head slightly. She looked at Paedur and smiled. 'Before I died I decided I would leave a record of my life with Churon telling how we met and how I came to be his wife – for, you see, even in my own lifetime the myths were already growing up. But I never committed it to paper; I was afraid Churon or one of the servants – and they were all his spies – would find it. But I have it all written down here.' A slender finger touched her head.

'Tell me,' the bard said quietly.

She nodded, her expression now calm and composed, her earlier fear and nervousness forgotten as she remembered. When she spoke, her voice took on a sing-song quality, almost as if she were reading from a page of script.

Churon began his career as a slave and then became a bandit, and he was ambitious even then. Unlike conventional bandits who contented themselves in the main with stealing from caravans and merchants, Churon and his gang would raid villages and, as they grew in numbers, towns and finally cities.

My father was King of Broar, with his capital in the city on the road to the west, when it was attacked by Churon and his army of brigands. However, this time, instead of sacking the city and enslaving the inhabitants, as he had lately been wont to do, he demanded just one thing: the hand in rightful and lawful marriage of the Princess of Broar – me. His reasoning was simple: by marrying a princess of the line, he would become heir to the throne of Broar, which, although a small and rather unimportant kingdom, was of some strategic importance; but more importantly, it would enable him to pursue his claims to the throne of the Emperor – or the Onelord as it was known then – with a certain amount of respectability.

And respectability was something Churon always desperately wanted.

He was born a slave, the son of a noble woman who indulged her appetites for coupling with animals by mounting a Chopt. When she had finished with the creature, she cut its throat, and then when she found she was with child, she kept it. Even Churon himself was unsure of the reasons; perhaps she was unsure just who the father was, for she had many lovers, but she was also a cruel woman, and perhaps the idea amused her. When she was delivered of a black-skinned, white-haired babe, her secret was out, and it is a measure of the widespread knowledge and acceptance of her licentious extravagances that no-one thought too much of it. The child was given to a servant to raise as her own, and he grew up thinking himself a slave.

But his mother was a strange and cruel woman, and when he was fourteen or fifteen winters, she seduced him. She slept with him a dozen times before she finally told him the truth. He said nothing to her then, but the next time they made love, he strangled her at the height of her passion with his bare hands.

So . . .

So, this man, this terrible, terrifying man, more beast than human, gave my father a choice: allow him to marry me or he would destroy Broar. And he was quite capable of doing it. So I was married to him.

He felt nothing for me, he knew nothing about me, didn't even know my name when he was demanding my hand in marriage from my father. All he knew at that time was that the King of Broar had one daughter and through her he might legitimately pursue a claim to the crown.

He took me with him into the countryside, but I was only so much extra baggage, and I felt that there were times when he thought about killing me – he would still retain the title to the city of Broar and the rights that went with it – but otherwise he ignored me. He killed and tortured, burned and pillaged and whored without any thought for me, and many a night I sat in the back of the tent and watched him take two or more women to his bed, some of whom were willing, others less so.

It was some two summers later before he consummated our marriage, and if the truth be told, he remained faithful to me for at least two moons after that, although we were making the beast with two backs every night for those two moons. And then he lost interest; there were other bodies to explore and he moved on. Oh, he still returned to me occasionally, much as a child will return to a favourite toy, or a storyteller will come back to a favourite tale, but it was always only briefly.

For Churon had one ambition: to rule. And he set about achieving that ambition with singleminded determination. Marrying me had been a step, deciding on a cause was the next. He wanted a cause which would unite the people behind him, something emotive. And he settled on the Shemmatae.

The Shemmatae had been in this land for a long time before Churon made them a cause. He accused them of being recent invaders, but in truth they had been trading with the Nations from the First Age of Man. They were never well liked but they were always respected. They were great traders and brought spices and rare herbs, furs, precious stones, fabulous armour and weapons and rare books from the Land of the Sun. They were wealthy – wealthy beyond belief in some cases; indeed, there was a story current then that the poorest of them was wealthier than the richest king.

To achieve his ends, Churon employed a group of wandering bards to campaign against the Shemmatae. He had them create myths and stories about them and their atrocities; if the truth were only known, some of the Shemmatae atrocities Churon had perpetrated himself, and then these bards took to the roads spreading the tales.

And you are only too aware of the power of the bard . . .

Public opinion turned against the Shemmatae – surprisingly quickly too. Indeed, it happened almost too quickly for Churon, and he was forced to act swiftly to put his army together to achieve his great victory. But when he tallied his troops and those who owed him allegiance, he was honest enough with himself to admit that there was no possible way he could win; he needed more men. So he set about extracting an oath of fealty from the Brothers, the Kings of the Nations. Some he tricked and some he threatened, but in the end they all gave him their armies, and with them . . . well, he won the Battle of the Sand Plain and defeated the Shemmatae. And he was the hero of the nations. In return there was nothing left for the Brothers to do but to acknowledge him the Onelord.

And although he had achieved what he desired, he remained unsatisfied.

He sat about building his dream, the Silver City of Shansalow. But that was something he never saw completed. From the very start it was a shambles, and he was still naïve enough to be cheated. The silver with which he had ordered the palace roof sheathed turned out to be nothing more than polished and painted tin. The diamond wall he ordered built in our bed-chamber – that was a whole wall inset with diamonds – turned out to be base also, the diamonds were nothing more than quartz.

And what a rage he flew into when he discovered that. He had the gem merchant flayed alive and then had the quartz stones ground into powder and rubbed into the man's raw flesh. That was before he boiled him in oil.

I would not say his reign was successful. He was a man of great ambition and vision, but he was a bloody barbarian at heart. He lacked tact and was unable to see – except for a crude instinct – that he was being plotted against. He quickly attracted a huge crowd of hangers-on, and most of these he foolishly appointed to posts way beyond their abilities to control or indeed even comprehend in some cases. The Empire he had come to rule quickly began to fall into disarray, although that was not immediately apparent on the surface. There were wars aplenty, and this kept the people and the merchants happy, and for the first time in many years the Nations knew prosperity.

But it was all a lie, a lie . . .

Deslirda abruptly fell silent and eventually Paedur leaned forward and touched the rough cloth of her sleeve. When she looked at him her eyes were wild and darting again.

'You see bard, he destroyed the Empire, destroyed it – because of his ego and stupidity. Churon the Onelord was a fool.'

'And you loved him!' Katani stated flatly.

Deslirda nodded briefly. 'And I loved him.'

'What did he fear?' Paedur asked quietly.

'He feared nothing.'

'Every man has a secret fear, something which brings him awake in the dead hours of night, heart pounding.'

Deslirda opened her eyes and stared at Paedur. 'When he died, bard, I heard he stood up and demanded that he be taken to Mannam. Even death held no fears for him.'

Paedur glanced quickly at Katani and then looked back to the woman. 'I have been told that he had a morbid fear of spiders . . .' he said slowly, watching her reaction.

'Spiders,' she whispered, a broad smile spreading over her wasted face, 'ah yes, how he feared them. And yet snakes and lizards held no fears for him. Is that not strange?' She looked at the bard, her eyes wide and staring.

'Strange indeed,' Paedur returned her smile. 'What were his

interests?' he asked gently, grasping for something, something which would give him an insight into the man.

'His only interest was himself – and his dream,' Deslirda said bitterly.

'He took no special joy in something: in good food, wine, art, jewellery, weapons?'

'He collected women, bard, briefly and with the sole intention of impregnating them!'

'Why?' Katani blurted.

Deslirda half turned to look back over her shoulder at the warrior-woman standing in the shadows. 'He had this idea of siring a child on a woman from every land, so that one day all the nations on this Plane of Existence would be ruled by his children.'

'Did he like children?' Katani asked.

'You forget, lady, this was the man who burned the monastery school of Moise, but only after ringing it with his troops to ensure that no-one – and they were his orders, no-one – escaped. I don't know how many children and monks died that day.'

'Half a thousand,' Paedur said sombrely.

Deslirda turned back to the bard. 'Now I have answered all your questions fairly, and I would have you answer just one of mine. Can you kill him – kill him so that he will never rise to walk again?'

'I intend to kill him,' Paedur said simply, 'I must!'

## 12   The First Battle

'I think perhaps it was the first cause he truly believed in.'
*Tien tZo, biographer of Owen, the Weapon Master*

The first sightings were made just before the grey lights of dawn brightened the east. By sunrise the sightings had been confirmed: an Imperial army of three legions was marching into the wastelands.

Although the number was a surprise, their coming was not unexpected. Recently, the numbers of refugees coming in from the devastated coastlands, fleeing the erratic tides and unnatural weather into the more stable interior had died to a trickle and for the previous few days none had come through the mountain passes which Kutor's men held.

On Keshian's instructions, spies had been sent out into every village and town on the borders of the wastelands, but none of them had returned, and similarly a small foraging party had also vanished without trace.

Curiously, Keshian had been inclined to treat this as a good sign. With his experience of the Imperial forces, he explained that it was common policy to completely seal off a suspect town or area, allowing nothing in or out, and then gradually pick off the raiding parties or individuals who ventured out. The purpose was twofold: it served to reduce the numbers of defenders and instil a degree of fear and uncertainty. However, he added, it was a policy they pursued only when they were unsure of the numbers they were facing.

Kutor found Owen in one of the towers with his eyeglass in his hands, slowly and methodically scanning the horizon. He didn't move as the prince entered the small chilly room. 'You've heard?' he asked quietly.

'How many?' Kutor asked, strangely feeling nothing now that the moment of truth was fast approaching. Up to this point he had been entertaining the vague fantasy of just leaving, of just mounting up and riding away with his own men, heading south into the forest lands and taking up his old trade as a simple bandit. The prince was quickly coming to the conclusion that he was not cut out to be a leader – certainly not on the scale that Owen and Keshian were suggesting. And by acknowledging that, he knew that he was also in some vague way acknowledging the fact that they were in control. Owen and his slave-companion were organising the men, had turned simple, badly-trained and crudely organised farmers and shepherds into dedicated warriors; Keshian had turned a tumbledown fort into a fortress the Culai themselves would have been proud of. What place was there for him? 'I'm sorry?' he said, realising that the Weapon Master was speaking to him.

'I said there are about three legions. I certainly counted three different standards, and that would confirm the earlier reports. I can see no siege weapons and certainly there are too few wagons for a sufficient quantity of either food or weapons.'

'And?' Kutor asked.

The Weapon Master looked at him. 'And what?'

'And what happens now?' the prince asked in exasperation.

'And now we wait for them to attack,' Owen grinned.

'How can you be so sure they'll attack?'

Owen pointed and handed the prince the eyeglass. 'Look. See there and there. You can see the cavalry spreading out for a charge, and there, close to the front and centre, the huddled figures, you can just about make out a battering ram.'

Kutor turned the wooden tube and a dim shape mistily resolved in the poor glass. 'A tree trunk?' he asked.

Owen nodded. 'A crude battering ram. They obviously brought no assault or siege weapons with them this time, but the next time they'll come prepared.' He saw the grimace move across the prince's lips. 'You don't approve?'

'Does it matter?' Kutor said, his voice sounding more bitter than he had anticipated, surprising him.

Owen took the glass from Kutor's hand and then turned the prince by the shoulders to face him. He looked deep into his dark eyes. 'What's wrong?' he asked easily, almost gently.

'There is nothing wrong.'

'There must be. Prince, we're on the eve of the first battle of your revolution. When we win this, the men will be a fighting force, confident and strong, able to face whatever the Imperials throw at us. This is important – vitally so. I would have expected

127

many reactions from you: fear possibly, eagerness, excitement ... but why the anger?'

'I've a feeling I'm not needed in this.'

'But you're the reason we're doing this!' Owen said, surprised.

'No!' Kutor suddenly shouted, 'No, I'm not the reason! I may be the excuse, but I'm not the reason. You all have your own reasons: for power or glory or coin or land. I don't know and I'm not sure I care. But I know I'm only a figurehead, like a piece on a gaming board which remains static while all the other pieces move around it.'

'I think you're making a mistake, prince,' Owen said coldly.

'I wish I was,' Kutor snapped. 'Tell me, why are you doing this, for what reason, for coin, land, favour, position?'

'But you can give me none of those,' Owen reminded him, 'not now and possibly never. No,' he shook his head, 'I'm doing this because the bard suggested that herein lay my destiny.'

'And you generally follow the advice of someone you've never met before?' Kutor sneered.

'Didn't you?' Owen asked mildly, turning back to the battlements and raising the glass again. 'They're coming,' he whispered, and suddenly Kutor's anger vanished to be replaced by something very close to fear.

'What do we do?'

'Do?' Owen turned to look at him, surprise on his face. 'Do, we do nothing. We let them come to us. This fortress will withstand many moons of siege from a fully supplied and properly armed siege-force. This force can do nothing against us. We'll let them come, let the traps take their toll, and then I'll lead the men out and they can finish off the rest.'

'Do you intend to kill them all?'

Owen dropped the eyeglass into the pouch on his belt and pressed the heels of both hands against his eyes. 'It would be nice to think we could, but that of course is impossible. What we must do, however, is to kill the leaders. They must die. It is vitally important that we ensure than no officer or experienced soldier lives to report back to camp.'

'Why?'

'An experienced man will be able to give fairly accurate details of the fortifications, our numbers, arms and skill,' Owen explained. 'However, an inexperienced, frightened soldier who has

128

just seen his comrades butchered will tell hugely exaggerated tales of an impregnable fort and thousands of heavily armed and ferocious warriors.'

'Surely that just means that the next time they will send a huge army against us?'

Owen grinned delightedly like a small child. 'But we won't be here, prince. We will be knocking at Geillard's door while his army knocks on ours!'

The legion horsemen made their stately way down the incline towards the fortress, slow and confident in their numbers, expecting only a token resistance and a quick victory. According to their intelligence, the Culai fortress before them had lain empty for nearly a century and certainly from the distance it looked neglected and tumbledown. The company leaders drew their commands to a halt nearly three thousand paces from the open and rotted main gates of the fortress and on order spears were levelled with all the precision that was the hallmark of the Imperial forces. And then, without any visible instruction, the legions started moving again, a trot that gradually gave way to a canter and then finally, with the open gates looming large and inviting, a gallop.

Less than a hundred paces from the fortress they hit the first of the pits. Those lucky enough to avoid the pits galloped directly into the small holes in the ground which were just deep enough to trap and snap a horse's hoof. Beyond the holes were another series of pits. Tien tZo and Keshian had dug the pits, staggering them to trap the greatest number of men and beasts, causing the most disruption. The screams of men and horses mingled together in an abominable cacophony. Those who rode into the pits died instantly on the poisoned stakes, but those who fell in on top of them were not so lucky. The warriors whose mounts had broken legs and hocks but had survived themselves were ridden down by their comrades in their headlong gallop, or the horses crashed into fallen mounts, sending their riders tumbling.

In a score of heartbeats the orderly, precise formation of the Imperial legions had been reduced to chaos. And while men and beasts milled around, archers appeared on the fortress walls and began pouring scores of poisoned shafts into the ragged lines.

Crossbowmen suddenly appeared then behind the disordered lines of the legions. Working in groups of two – one firing, one loading – these had been carefully chosen by Owen for the task of slaying the legion officers. They wore legion armour and leathers, and worked slowly and methodically, relying on the confusion to cover their actions, picking out the captains, with their distinctive long straight-bladed swords, then the decade sergeants, with their shorter curved blades. The crossbowmen were using broad-headed, barbed quarrels, designed to punch through even the thickest metal-plate armour and inflict the greatest possible injury. And Tien tZo had coated the bolts with a virulent poison.

Ironically, the legion commander, whose weapon was traditionally a mace, had been killed in the first few moments of battle, his mount snapping its foreleg in a hole, sending its rider tumbling on to the ground and then crashing over on top of him, killing him instantly.

The three legion captains died in the first volley, and nearly two-thirds of the decade captains had fallen before someone realised that specific targets were being chosen. The remaining decade sergeants attempted to rally the men together, but the signallers were dead, and when a man picked up one of the long curling horns to sound a command he suddenly sprouted bolts.

And then, into all the confusion, Kutor's forces marched out from the fortress.

The battle was brief.

Owen and Kutor walked the battlefield as night was drawing in. The sky was clear and the heavens sparkled with the familiar constellations but also some of the new stars which had arrived with the Cataclysm and which were strangers to both men. The plain had been more or less cleared of all the usable arms and armour and the dead had been stripped of everything, and in the fading light, the naked bodies looked like strange fungoid growths. In the distance the first tentative howlings of the wolves began, the blood and dead meat calling to them. With first light, Keshian and his men would build a score of funeral pyres and burn the bodies of men and beasts together.

'It seems I owe you an apology . . .' Kutor began.

'For what?'

'For doubting that you could do it.'

'There was never any doubt of that,' the Weapon Master smiled slightly.

Kutor detoured around the bodies of two men and a horse. They all bore the neat puncture wounds of arrows or quarrels, but the shafts had been removed, to be cleaned, refletched if necessary and reused. 'I wasn't quite so sure,' he admitted. 'What happens now?'

Owen stopped by a corpse and turned the head slightly with the toe of his boot. 'I knew him once; he was a captain in the legion,' he remarked expressionlessly, and then continued on. 'What happens now? In the morning we go through the prisoners, removing those whom we consider to be intelligent enough to give a coherent and informative report of what they have seen here.'

'Remove?' the prince asked.

'Kill,' Owen said, glancing at him. 'Now is no time to be fainthearted,' he warned, watching the prince's face change.

'I wish it were otherwise.'

'You knew what you were getting into when this started,' Owen reminded him.

'I'm not so sure I did,' Kutor muttered. He pressed both hands to his throbbing temples and nodded. 'Continue, please.'

'We give the prisoners the opportunity to join us, and then we release those who wish to go.'

The prince avoided a pit which was reeking with the stench of horse and human meat and waste. 'Is that wise?' he asked.

'We want only those who want us. We need no conscripts. That was the mistake you made the last time you set your sights on the throne; your warriors either didn't want to fight in the first place or were simply paid to fight. I am giving you an army that want to fight for you. These men have a cause; they may not realise it yet, but they need to know that their cause is just, that when they die they can do so with honour. I wish to all the gods the bard was here; he could put it into words that would have them willing to die for you. But he is not and it's up to us, or rather to you, to do that.' He paused and stooped down, examining the line of tattoos on a warrior-maid's upper arm. 'Stone Clan from the Islands,' he murmured, dusting off his hands and standing up, looking at the young woman's blood-splotched face. 'What a waste.'

'How did we fare today?' the prince asked.

'Well,' Owen said, sounding almost pleased. 'We lost twenty men – only twenty – and there are another forty or so wounded, but none of them seriously, and Tien is attending to them with his salves and potions. We captured close on a thousand horses, good beasts too, strong, healthy and in excellent condition, and by my estimates there must be another thousand roaming the Wastelands by now, and I would be surprised if we didn't capture the vast majority of them within the next few days.

'The armoury has swelled to bursting, and I went through it earlier this evening with Keshian and Tien, sorting through the weapons, discarding those we considered unsuitable. As you know, we raided their camp late this afternoon and as a result we have usable plate and chain armour for over half the men now, and we took enough scraps and bits to kit out the rest in some sort of body armour. Added to that, we have a huge quantity of clothing, beddings, cutlery, jewellery of all types and coin. We also have the legion's supplies – mostly hard bread and dried meat, but it is just the fare we'll need when we march on the capital.'

'You're serious about that, aren't you?' Kutor asked. 'You seriously want to march on Karfondal?'

'Are you serious about ruling?' Owen snapped. He stopped and, taking Kutor's arm, turned him around, so that he was looking across the plain towards the dark bulk of the fortress and the plain was dotted with white corpses, like huge patches of moonflowers, their open faces turned towards the Lady Lussa. 'We did this for you, prince,' Owen hissed, 'no matter what you might think, we did this for you. All of these souls went either to Mannam or Libellius this day. If you quit now, or consider this as less than deadly serious, then you do their honour and the honour of our own dead a great disservice.'

Kutor nodded, looking across the battlefield, glad of the night and the enveloping darkness; he didn't want to know what creeping, crawling things were feeding now. He nodded abruptly. 'What now?' he asked, suddenly decisive.

'Now we consolidate our holdings here in the Wastelands, prepare camps and supply bases closer to the Nations, and set a series of guards on all the routes into this place.' He walked down the slight incline and waited for the prince to join him, and then they walked side by side back towards the fortress. 'And as soon as we have word of an approaching Imperial army, we head for the capital.'

'And let us assume we manage to take Karfondal, then all that leaves us with is an Imperial Army at our back.'

'Oh, I've a few surprises lined up for them,' Owen said with a wicked grin.

Salier sat before the leather-topped wooden table and slowly and deliberately spread the cards before him, reading aloud their meanings to his scribe, who sat out of sight behind a screen by the door where his presence wouldn't offend his master. Salier himself was in a mild trance-like state and was almost completely unconsious of what he was saying, and it would be only later, when the scribe's notes had been written up, that the magician would attempt to put some order to them.

He turned each card with exaggerated slowness, allowing its full implications to sink into his bemused brain before pronouncing on it. 'I see War . . . and Trickery, Knavery, a soldier trapped by knavery . . . no, an army destroyed by trickery. I see a man . . . a man of the blood, a Prince . . . and another, a Soldier . . . and another, a Hermit . . . a seeker of knowledge . . . these are all influencing the Wheel, but the wheel is still turning and the future remains mutable . . .

'I see death and the fall of cities . . . and death again. And I can see a dangeous hidden foe who brings death or who carries the taint of death on him. Avoid him at all costs . . .'

Salier was silent for a long time then, turning card after card, his lips moving noiselessly, his eyes tiny in his head, pupils lost in the shadows. 'I see the death of a king, the end of a cycle, and yet I can also see the beginning of the family's rule.' He shook his head angrily. 'It is unclear. Damn this means of divination,' he suddenly shouted, his frustration breaking his trance. 'Would that I could travel the Void again.' The small man stood and stretched and then strode over to his scribe, and snatched the notes from him. 'I hope you got it all,' he hissed.

'Every word, Lord Salier,' the scribe promised.

Moments later the magician was on his way to the Emperor to inform him that his army had been slaughtered.

# 13   The Mire

He was destined to rule, and his one great boast was that he would
continue his reign after his death . . .

*The Onelord: The Barbarian Saviour*

The Mire borders Death's Kingdom, but is not truly part of it, and
extrudes into several Planes of Existence . . .

*Lilis' Geographica*

The Silent Wood had an odour, a dry, desiccated odour of something long dead that had mouldered into dust; but the Mire
smelt of warm, fetid death and decay, overlain by the offal
stench of the Naman.

The Mire bordered Death's Kingdom, a huge area blighted
by seepage from a rupture in the fabric of the Ghost Worlds
that separated the various Planes of Existence. The dead walked
in the Mire, those who had come in from the Silent Wood, and
they mingled with the living from a dozen Planes of Life.

The Mire was a refuge on the fringes of Life and Death; there
was no law and while death was commonplace, resurrection of
those already dead was equally frequent. Consequently, the inhabitants of the Mire had refined torture to a very fine art. It
had become a game of sorts, a game played to certain obscure
rules, the principal one being to keep the victim alive for as long
as possible; death was a release.

Whole towns had grown up in the Mire and there was a city
of sorts, and because the Mire bordered the others Planes of
Existence, time touched it somewhat and it had a recognisable
night and day.

It was night when Paedur and Katani came to the Mire.

The atmosphere in the tavern was redolent of sweat, sour
wine, smoke from a score of filthy oil lamps, urine and the acrid
odour of fear. No-one even looked up as the tall, hooded figure
and the rag-wrapped woman entered the long room; the inhabitants of the Mire paid no notice to any of the strange creatures,

be they human or otherwise, that wandered through its crazy streets and twisted alleys.

The man pushed the woman into a rough wooden seat in a corner while he went to the bar, which was nothing more than a score of roughly planed planks on crudely shaped uprights. The barman glanced in his direction and the man tapped two fingers on the scarred wood; the barman immediately set up two small mugs of a bitter-smelling black liquid that obviously had too much of the River Naman in its making. The hooded man produced two of the flat bronze chips that were one of the accepted currencies in the Mire and then carried the mugs back his female companion. He set one down in front of her and raised his mug to his lips.

'I think you're taking your life in your hands drinking that stuff,' Katani murmured, raising her own mug to cover her lip movement.

'I've no intention of allowing even a single drop to pass my lips,' Paedur said earnestly.

'A nice place,' Katani said, looking around.

'I've been in worse,' Paedur said, pretending to concentrate on his drink whilst he took in his surroundings, noting the entrances and exits but more especially the tavern's extraordinary clientele.

Many were from the Silent Wood and were dead, their weapons and costumes dating them from nearly every age, with the exception of the First Age of Man. Others were Sons of Men from the various Planes of Existence that bordered the Mire, and then there were others that were only vaguely human – the Were-Folk, creatures with too much non-human blood in them. The group was almost evenly divided between males and females; however, the majority of them were warriors of some sort, the remainder thieves or harlots.

An uneasy truce prevailed in the bar, all the more extraordinary when there was such a mixture of races and clans, some of whom were inimical to the other and all of them heavily armed. It was only when Paedur looked up and discovered the score of hard-eyed crossbowmen standing on the first-floor balcony that he realised how the peace was kept.

Paedur and Katani had come to the Mire looking for Churon. Because of their lack of knowledge, it had proved almost impossible to formulate a plan of campaign except in the very vaguest terms, but their first priority was to get close to the Onelord, join his forces if possible. If, as Mannam claimed, Churon was operating out of the warren of the Mire, then it followed that he was recruiting his army principally from there also.

As the night wore on, the bar became even more crowded, and although tempers often flared, a warning from the bowmen above was usually enough to finish the argument. However, one dispute went beyond words and, amidst much wagering, the two warriors decided to settle the argument in the street outside. The tavern fell silent, the sounds of metal on metal, the grunts of the men and the final scream were all clearly audible to the silent listeners. All heads turned towards the door and money was already beginning to change hands when a soul-chilling howl ripped through the tavern. In the breathless silence that followed, the sounds of an animal feeding were clearly, disgustingly audible. Even the hardened warriors looked vaguely uneasy and Paedur noticed that the crossbowmen had transferred their attention to the heavily barred windows and the solid iron-studded door. And even in this place, where the gods had few believers, amulets and talismens were touched and rubbed, and lips began to move in quick, silent prayers.

The sounds of feeding continued – bones snapping and cloth or flesh ripping – for what seemed like a very long time, and then the creature moved on, something metallic scraping along the cobbles and against the alley walls to eventually fade on the warm night air. Eventually, when nothing further happened, the buzz of conversation began again, but it was muted now, the drinkers listening, hands never straying from sword or knife hilt.

The door abruptly burst open; an almost visible ripple of shock ran through the crowded room and the rasp of steel being drawn was plainly heard in the sudden silence. It remained open and empty for a few long moments and then an old man with thinning grey hair and a lined weary face, a cloak of broad dark-patterned tartan over rusted, stained mail, staggered into the inn pulling a length of chain.

'Brought your pet, eh, Grandad?' someone called.

A ripple of laughter ran around the room, and abruptly died as the old man hauled in the chain and they found it was attached to a long serpentine head easily as tall as anyone there present. Flat plates of overlapping scales covered the snout and two long curved tusks as large as a man's hand protruded from its snout. Its eyes were closed, or rather one of its eyes was closed; there was a gaping hole where the second had been.

The old man straightened up and pressed both hands to the small of his back. 'I found this piece of vermin down the alley. It looks like it had been feeding on some offal outside,' he said pleasantly, looking around the room.

'You . . . you killed it?' A huge warrior with skin the colour of saffron and eyes of coal said incredulously, looking down on him and his bloody burden.

'Butchered it more like,' the old man agreed.

'I don't believe it,' the warrior said.

'Nothing to it.'

'I don't believe it,' the warrior repeated, shaking his head. He nudged the creature's head with the point of his boot.

The old man's deep brown eyes hardened as he looked up at the warrior. 'Don't call me a liar again,' he said, the warning plain in his voice.

The saffron-skinned warrior grinned hugely, displaying his teeth, which had been filed to points. 'Why? Are you going to kill me, as you killed this?' he demanded, his hand going to a huge broadsword that stood propped against the bar beside him.

'Aye, I'll butcher you, as I butchered this,' the old man agreed without raising his voice, but everyone in the room heard it.

The warrior looked over his shoulder at the barman. 'Indulge me this one, let me fight him here. My honour is at stake.'

'Threatened by an old man?' the barman asked with a leer. Nevertheless he looked up at the bowmen and nodded his head. 'Let them fight.' And then he turned back to the room. 'I'm giving odds on Gutandard.'

In the general laughter that followed, a cold, curious voice cut through the hubbub. 'And what are the odds on the old man?'

All heads turned to the hooded man sitting in the corner. 'You've got money to waste, eh?' the barman asked, rubbing his hands on his broad, much-stained apron.

'I only bet on sure things,' the hooded man said with a laugh. 'All I've heard from this one is talk, while the old one is hauling a dead mireworm.'

The saffron-skinned warrior strode over to the table and

dropped his sheathed broadsword on to the wood. 'When I kill the old one, I'll kill you, but slowly . . . slowly.'

The seated man threw back his hood and looked contemptuously at the huge warrior, his face flat and hard, his eyes expressionless. 'And what will you do? Talk me to death?'

Gutandard snarled and reached for the hilt of his sword, and suddenly his hand was encircled by a gleaming half-circle of polished metal. He looked incredulously at the hook that took the place of the man's left hand.

'I can take your hand off as easily as plucking an apple,' the hard-eyed man said very quietly. 'Now, why don't you go and die at the hands of the old man.'

Something like doubt flickered behind the warrior's eyes as he carefully wriggled his hand free of the encircling hook. Abruptly, he grabbed his sword and strode into the centre of the room, pulling his sword free and tossing the stained leather sheath to one of his companions. 'Come, Grandad, it is time to die.'

The old man nodded wearily. 'Yes, time to die.' He dropped the chain he was holding and walked over to meet Gutandard, his hand closing around the haft of his mace and chain. He was within half a dozen paces of the bar when the huge warrior charged, his broadsword sweeping around in a high decapitating cut.

The old man ducked with a swiftness that belied his years and the spiked iron ball at the end of the arm-length of chain snapped towards the warrior. It struck low, hitting him squarely in the belt buckle, but with enough force to wind him. Gutandard staggered back, one hand going to his midriff, expecting it to come away sticky with his blood and almost shocked it didn't.

'Let us end this,' the old man said reasonably. 'I have no wish to kill you.'

Gutandard looked at the gouge marks in his thick leather belt and experienced an emotion he hadn't felt for a long time – that of fear. But he forced a sneer to his cruel lips. 'A lucky blow, old man. But you are dead now.'

He cut wide and low, the sword coming up in a move that should have split the old man from hip to shoulder, all of Gutandard's broad shoulders behind it. But the old man merely stepped back and the blow went wide, leaving the warrior slightly off balance.

138

The spiked ball of the mace ripped most of Gutandard's face off, splattering bloody matter all across the walls and the gaping onlookers. The warrior stood swaying for a moment and then he sank to his knees before finally collapsing full-length on the dirt floor. The old man nodded and then he lifted the corner of his tartan cloak and began to methodically clean the gore from his mace. 'Anyone else?' he asked very quietly. The occupants of the tavern turned to their drinks, the body on the floor unheeded and almost unnoticed when it was dragged away a few moments later.

The old man picked up Gutandard's drink at the bar and then sat down beside the bard and Katani, his back to the wall. He drank deeply and then wiped his sleeve across his mouth.

'I'm astonished,' Paedur said softly.

'For what,' Buiva asked in surprise. 'He was an amateur.'

Paedur shook his head and smiled. 'No, not for that – that's no more than I would have expected. I'm astonished you managed to drink that foul stuff.'

Buiva smiled tightly. 'Killing always makes me thirsty.' He drank again, as if to emphasise his point.

'How long will it take?' Katani asked softly, directing her question to no-one in particular.

'Not long, I expect,' Buiva answered. 'If Churon is as good as I believe him to be, then he will soon know what has happened here. I think he'll want to meet the man who slew a mireworm and then Gutandard, one of his captains.'

'He might decide to send you an invitation on the end of a sword,' Katani remarked.

Buiva shook his head. 'No, he needs good men badly. He'll be curious enough to send for us.'

'Or come here himself,' Paedur said, stiffening as the sound of a horse-drawn cart rattled over the cobbles.

'Unlikely,' Buiva said quietly.

The door of the tavern scraped open and a half dozen shabbily dressed men entered, rough peasant's clothing knotted around their waists with lengths of rope. They made their way to the bar and were immediately served by the tavernkeeper, who set up six cups of the dark foul-smelling drink that seemed to be the only beverage the tavern posessed.

'Warriors,' Katani said decisively, watching them closely.

'Are you sure?' the bard asked.

'I'm sure.'

'How do you know?' he asked, dropping his head to his drink but continuing to watch the group.

Katani shrugged. 'The way they walk, the way they hold themselves.'

'A weaponed man walks and holds himself differently to an unarmed man,' Buiva said without turning around. 'Beneath the rough tunics, I'll wager they're wearing leathers and carrying knives or shortswords, and almost certainly one will possess a crossbow.'

'There is one stooped over almost double, like a hunchback,' Paedur said.

'That's the one.'

'One is coming over,' Katan hissed, loosing her dagger in its sheath.

The man was tall and broad and his face would have been handsome except for the scar that began just above the bridge of his nose and then traced its way through his eyebrow and disappeared into the thick, curling hair just above his ear. 'You'll pardon me?' he asked, indicating the space beside Buiva.

The old man nodded. 'Please.'

'All the talk is about you,' the newcomer said, bringing the chipped cup to his lips but not actually drinking.

'And what do they say?' Buiva asked with a smile.

'They say you killed a mireworm and then killed Gutandard because he laughed at you.'

'They talk too much.'

'Is it true?' the stranger asked with a smile that curled his lips but didn't reach his eyes.

Buiva turned to look at him. 'I killed the last man because he doubted my word,' he said very quietly.

'It's true,' Paedur said from across the table. 'Now, why don't you tell us what you want?'

The man spread both hands wide. 'I'm just a simple peasant . . .'

Paedur's hook shot out, wrapping itself around his wrist, and then with his right hand he pushed up the rough woollen sleeve, exposing a broad metal-studded leather band. 'Not many peasants wear a warrior's wristband,' the bard smiled.

The man pulled his hand free, scraping the flesh of the back of his hand on the inside of the hook. 'Just who are you?' he demanded, the voice now hard and arrogant, the tone one of command.

'Travellers,' Buiva said slowly.

The man's five companions had now surrounded the table and the tavern had fallen ominously silent. Katani looked up and nudged Paedur's foot with hers. He followed the direction of her eyes and found that all the crossbowmen on the floor above had their weapons trained on them.

The seated man pulled open the ties of his tunic exposing the metal-plated leathern tunic beneath. On his chest was an emblem, a single white circle on a black field. 'We are Churon's men.'

'Then it is you we want to see, or rather your master,' Buiva said quietly.

'I'm not sure I understand.'

'The mireworm and the warrior were both slain to attract your attention,' Buiva said without expression.

'But why not come directly into our camp. We are recruiting warriors every day.'

'I am not just another warrior!' Buiva said coldly, turning his curiously soft, gentle-seeming brown eyes on the man.

'So what was the point?' the seated man demanded.

Paedur smiled tightly. 'This was an example.'

The warrior shifted his attention from the old man to the hookhand. 'And just who are you?'

'I am Paedur, a bard, newly come into the Silent Wood in search of the greatest myth in the Seven Nations.'

'A myth?'

'Churon the Onelord.'

The soldier smiled, nodding his head. 'A myth, aye. A myth-made man, a man-made myth.' He glanced quickly at Katani. 'And this?'

'My woman,' both Paedur and Buiva said together.

The warrior looked from man to man and smiled knowingly, and then he turned back to Buiva. 'And you, grey-hair. Who are you?'

'I am Bove, mercenary warrior in the World of Men, until I came into the Silent Wood.'

'I'd like to meet the man who dispatched you,' the soldier grinned.

'Eight of them came with me into Mannam's Kingdom, the other twelve even I couldn't account for.'

'If any other man had told me that I'd say he was lying.'

'But you won't say that about me, eh?' Buiva asked.

The warrior shook his head. 'I won't.' He stood up and pulled off his peasant's garb. His squad likewise stripped themselves of their guise. Both Buiva's and Katani's estimation had been correct: the stooped man had been holding a cocked and loaded crossbow.

'I am Rade, captain of Churon's personal guard,' the man finally introduced himself. He looked at Buiva. 'If the Onelord finds you acceptable, I'll take pains to have you placed in this unit. We could do with a man of your experience.' He glanced at Paedur, obviously dismissing him. 'I haven't seen you fight.'

'Pray you never have to,' the bard said with a smile.

Rade glared at him, attempting to size up the enigmatic man. He was not a warrior, but he didn't look like any bard he had ever seen. 'I'm sure the Onelord will find some use for you,' he said finally. 'We are always in need of jesters.'

'I am quick to avenge my friends' honour,' Buiva said softly, looking at the man.

Rade ducked his head, his eyes avoiding Paedur's. 'Come then, and I will take you to Churon the Onelord.'

# 14  Tien tZo's Tale*

Like most great men he saw things in stark shades, black or white,
good or bad, right or wrong – there were no half-way measures for
the Weapon Master . . .

from . . . *The Warrior, the Life of Owen, Weapon Master*

It was, if the truth were told, an easy victory, and not truly
ours. The men were jubilant and naturally so; for most of them
it was their first battle of any scale. But there were a few amongst
us who recognised that the Imperials had been defeated by the
use of the pits, and so our victory couldn't be taken as an indication of our strength.

I watched the Master walk the battlefield with Kutor the
Prince in the aftermath of the battle and I knew by both their
expressions when they returned that their discussion had not
gone well. They parted company without words at the gate, the
prince following the sounds of revelry towards the main hall,
while the Master headed in the direction of his rooms. I finished
up with Keshian – we were in the process of sorting the weapons
– and hurried after the Master.

'The man is afraid,' Owen snapped as I fell into step beside
him. 'He wants and yet he does not want the crown. He would
like someone to give it to him painlessly and bloodlessly; I dare
say he'd like Geillard to abdicate and pass the crown on to
him.' He shook his head savagely. 'I cannot understand him!'

'Is he frightened of winning the crown?' I asked, 'or is it that
he fears your way of achieving it?'

The Master sighed and shook his head, running his hands
through his thinning hair. 'I don't know, Tien. Truly, I don't.
He had a reputation as a ruthless brigand, and yet here he is
now and I find myself fighting for a man I'm beginning to think
of as a coward.'

'But he fears for the lives of others,' I pointed out.

* from . . . *The Warrior, the Life of Owen, Weapon Master*

143

The Master grunted and said nothing further until we had reached the door of our cavern-room. He paused with his hand on the latch. 'I wonder where the bard is now. We need him.' He looked at me, his eyes wide and troubled. 'We need a bard, someone to fire the men with ancient battles, someone to remind Kutor that the price of most kingships is paid in blood.'

'Finding a bard may well be difficult,' I reminded him, following him into the room, 'you recall the trouble we had in Baddalaur. All the bards and scribes seem to be in Karfondal restoring the records.'

Owen pulled off his sword-belt and flung it on to his sleeping pallet. 'Not a trained and recognised bard then, but a storyteller or reasonably literate historian.' He pressed the palms of his hands deep into his eyes, wiping away the fatigue. 'Oh, I don't mean now, not immediately. But you might bear it in mind when we go on the road.'

'And when will that be?' I asked.

'The sooner the better,' Owen sighed, sinking down into a chair, resting his elbows on the table. 'If Kutor is left to brood for too long, I think we might lose him.'

I sat down facing the Weapon Master, watching him, clearly sensing his concern and the underlying fear that everything might indeed come to naught. For as long as I knew him – and I knew him for most of my life – I think I truly began to understand him more in those few minutes than I had at any other time in our association. 'This campaign means more to you than it does to him,' I suggested softly, watching his face. 'He is right, isn't he? He is only a figurehead.'

Owen stared at me for a few moments without replying and then he said very slowly and deliberately. 'He will make a fine Emperor.'

'That is not what I asked.'

'I know.'

'Why are you doing this? What makes this war so special? And don't tell me you owe the bard a debt,' I snapped, my voice louder than I intended it to be.

'You forget yourself!'

'I apologise.' I immediately stood up and stepped back away from the table and bowed.

Owen suddenly sighed and buried his head in his hands, covering his face. 'Sit, sit . . . please.' When he looked up his eyes were red-veined and looked bruised, and in that moment he looked all his years.

'How long have we been on the road, Tien?' It was a rhetorical question and I didn't even attempt to answer it. 'For too long,' Owen said. 'And what have we achieved, what have we gained? Lesser Weapon Masters are now wealthy men, whilst we have nothing except what we can carry on our backs.'

'We have our honour and our reputations,' I said quickly.

The Master nodded. 'And there is a place for both, but we cannot live on honour and reputation; we cannot eat honour and our reputations will not keep us warm in the Cold Months.' His voice fell to an awed whisper. 'We are getting old, Tien my friend, old.'

'And you think this great campaign will make up for everything you've missed, give us everything we need?' I asked, conscious of the bitterness in my voice.

'It might,' he said defensively. 'It should mean we will not spend our last years in misery, as guards on some borderland fort.'

'Have you forgotten that it was you who said that Kutor might have you assassinated when you had achieved his aim?'

Owen smiled, but there was no humour in it. 'I said he would try. But I intend to have our position secured by that time, making our removal impossible.'

'How often have you said to me that if someone wants you dead badly enough . . .' I reminded him. 'We have killed kings and princes who thought themselves secure.'

He nodded, leaning back and sighing. 'It's a risk,' he agreed. He suddenly sat forward in the chair and clasped both hands together on the table before him – a gesture of rare trust, since one of his hands was usually on a weapon. 'Now, your estimation of today?' he asked, the decisive warrior again.

'We were lucky,' I said shortly.

'I know. But your estimation of the men in general.'

I shook my head. 'It will be very hard to make any decision about them until we have actually gone on the road. You're sure to lose a few then.'

'And Keshian?' he persisted.

'A fine soldier. A little staid and predictable perhaps, but solid and dependable.'

'Do you think he could control this army alone?'

'Without us?' I asked, surprised.

Owen nodded silently.

I looked at his face, but he had schooled it into that impassive mask he usually wore when he was planning something audacious. I thought about it and then finally nodded. 'Yes, I see no reason why he could not. He has both the will and the experience, and his natural caution will be no hindrance in this campaign. A minor problem perhaps is that you will have to ensure that the men respect him. Perhaps a ploy?'

Owen nodded impatiently. 'Of course, make him a hero in their eyes. But you are agreed that he can do it.'

'I've no doubt of it.'

'Good,' he hissed in satisfaction, my conclusion obviously agreeing with his. He closed his eyes and relaxed, and I could almost see the tension draining out of his body.

'Do you want to tell me why it will be necessary for him to command the army?' I asked eventually when he continued to remain silent.

Owen stood up and strode around the room, slowly and methodically removing his weapons and piling them on his sleeping pallet. 'You agree we won today by the will of the Old Gods . . .' he began, but I interrupted him.

'I didn't say that,' I protested.

'By chance then?'

'I'll agreed to that.'

'Well, whatever,' he said impatiently, 'we are agreed that something worked in our favour and the traps worked to perfection.'

'Granted,' I nodded, wondering where all this was leading. It was not unusual for the Weapon Master to ask my advice on matters of warcraft, and we were friends and battle-companions in many ways, but there was always the constant, albeit unspoken, reminder in our dealings that we were Master and slave.

'I think you'll also agree that taking out the legion captains and decade sergeants worked to our advantage.'

'It was a master stroke. It left the legion like a serpent without a head, coiling to and fro without direction.'

Owen nodded triumphantly. 'It is a ploy I intend to pursue!'

I shook my head. 'I'm not sure I comprehend . . .'

His eyes blazing, Owen sank into the chair opposite me and began to talk in a low intense whisper, using a version of one of the Shemmat dialects he had picked up from me. The chances of anyone understanding the obscure language was very small indeed.

'We are both agreed that Keshian can command this army and so there is little need for us here. But we must carry on the fight, we must carry it to the capital. You and I, Tien, are heading back east to Karfondal!'

'What!'

Owen nodded, pleased.

'Our names and descriptions are known all across the Nations,' I said, a little breathlessly. 'I'm sure every mercenary knows you by sight, every bounty-hunter knows the price on our heads – and these are people who would burn down a house full of people just to ensure that we died.'

'You exaggerate,' Owen said mildly. I shook my head and opened my mouth to reply, but he held up both hands for silence and continued. 'I don't intend to walk straight into Karfondal with you trailing alongside carrying an armload of weapons. We will have certain advantages, including the fact that by now we will have been placed with the rebel forces. The Imperials know that the rebels are many days away and so we will not be expected – and man does not see what he is not expecting to see.'

I nodded, accepting his argument. 'What are we doing in the Karfondal?'

Owen smiled, showing his teeth in a feral grin. 'We are going to kill Salier and Barthus, Fodla and, if possible, Geillard himself!'

Ignoring my appalled silence, he calmly went on. 'Salier is the Emperor's magician, counsellor, friend and some say his catamite. Remove him and Geillard immediately loses someone he depends on a great deal, as well as one of his principal sources of occult power. Barthus is the Hierophant, the temporal representative and spiritual leader of the New Religion. He backs Geillard fully by word and deed and he has an army of warrior priests at his command. He is a powerful force behind the throne but if he is slain, then the priests of the Religion will be caught up fighting amongst themselves for control of the Religion, and the Emperor will lose what little control he has over the holy warriors. We could gain much by that confusion. Fodla is Geillard's Captain of the Guard . . .'

'I have heard of her.' I interrupted.

'Kill her and the Imperial legions fall apart.' Owen persisted.

'Did you ever hear of a Battle-Captain called Loust?' I asked him suddenly.

He stopped, confused, wondering at the abrupt, seemingly irrelevant question. 'No . . .' he said slowly.

'He was a warrior,' I said, carefully keeping my tone neutral, 'one of the finest natural killers I have ever seen. As good as – and I say this most respectfully – perhaps even better than you. He took a commission to assassinate Fodla. By dint of bribery and trickery, he managed to evade her guards and reach her bed-chamber, but instinct or chance saved her and Fodla awoke as he was poised to strike and rolled from her bed as he cut. The man was armed with shortsword and knife and wore leathers, while she was naked and defenseless except for a small metal hand-mirror and a solid silver comb, which she snatched from a bedside table. She could have cried out and her guards would have cut Loust to pieces, but she didn't; she attacked him! The noise eventually brought the guards running and when they burst into the room, they found the huge woman standing over the broken body of the assassin. She had beaten him to death, using nothing more than the metal mirror and comb to defend herself.'

'You're telling me this as a warning?' Owen asked.

'An illumination,' I smiled.

'Assuming I can kill this mountain of a woman, the next will be Geillard himself.'

'I would advise against it,' I said quickly.

'He too has beaten someone to death with a comb?' Owen said derisively.

I shook my head. 'For Kutor's claim to the throne to have any real validity, it would be better if Geillard retained the throne. He must then lose it to Kutor, and more importantly, be seen to lose it.'

Owen considered for a moment and nodded. 'Agreed. It seems to be a relatively simple matter.' He rubbed his hands together and laughed aloud. 'Why, we're practically giving Kutor the throne.'

'You still have to take it from Geillard,' I reminded him.

I went in search of Keshian later that night; I wanted his opinion of Owen's scheme. I had come to like the small, rotund grey-haired battle-captain, and he in turn had, I think, formed a certain measure of respect for me.

I had encountered his like before in many lands; men grown old in the service of war. They were never brave men – brave men die young – but they were always competent, and age and experience had taught them the skill of killing with the least effort. Their lives always seemed to be ones of missed opportunities, of backing the wrong side, not running when they should have or perhaps even running too early and quitting an ultimately winning side. And now, as ageing warriors, perhaps with a commission in an Outlands or provincial lord's force, they had little to show for all their years of war and battle. They were invariably unmarried and their friends were few. But they were rarely discontented: they lived, when so many of their companions over the years were dead or maimed.

I found Keshian in one of the well-rooms, deep in the bowels of the mountain. When we had first discovered it, the room had been filthy, the well almost completely hidden beneath piles of debris, but it had been scoured, washed with a mixture of lime grit and brightly lit. The well itself had been cleaned of the filth and muck of ages, the slime scraped from the walls, the ropes replaced and large waterproof buckets fitted. In times of siege a room such as this was life or death to the occupants. The battle-captain was sitting on the step that surrounded the well, holding up a crystal glass of well-water to the light and watching a thin, green thread slowly twist and weave through the water.

I joined him and stared into the glass. What I had first taken to be a solid thread, turned out to be a darting spark of fire. I looked through the glass at Keshian.

The old man smiled almost shyly. 'The only magic I know,' he said softly, lifting the glass slightly, 'is a small spell my father taught me when I was a child and used to creep into his forge to watch the sparks fly as he shaped white-hot metal. It's a spell of water purification and calls upon the Lady Adur, the Goddess of all natural things, to cleanse and purify.' He smiled as the darting green light winked out. 'I was just making sure.' He lifted the glass and drank half of it in one swallow. 'Aaah, cold, cold, from the very heart of the mountain, and tart too. I once knew a man who could tell what land the water flowed through just by drinking it. And my father could tell what water was good for ironwork just by touching it to his lips.' He handed the glass to me. 'Drink?'

I hesitated before touching it, attempting to interpret his gesture. Amongst my people to share a glass is to create a bond, but I did not think this man would be aware of it. I nodded my thanks and accepted the glass. The water was as he had said, ice-cold and slightly bitter, tasting of copper and mineral salts.

'Will your water purification spell work on the whole well, or just on small amounts of water?' I asked.

Keshian shrugged. 'I don't know. I've only ever used it on small amounts, usually only my own personal drinking water, but I could certainly try it on a suspected poisoned well or water-hole.' He paused and then said, 'But we would need volunteers to drink the water.'

'Volunteers?' I scoffed. 'Have we no prisoners?'

'I thought there were to be no atrocities,' the battle-captain said warily.

'I hardly think giving the prisoners water would be considered to be an atrocity.'

'But poisoned water?'

'No-one would know,' I pointed out.

'I would.'

I looked at him again, this short, grey man with his too-soft eyes and his quick concern. 'A battle-captain with scruples.'

He smiled easily. 'That's why I'm still a battle-captain and not a commander.'

I drank again and then to change the subject, explained Owen's plan.

'It is madness, absolute madness!'

I nodded silently.

'Has he no idea of what he is up against?' Keshian demanded. 'It is suicide! Surely these are not the actions of a Weapon Master?'

I shook my head. 'That too has troubled me. And I will admit he has been acting strangely since we encountered that cursed hook-handed bard.'

One of the sconces guttered in the draught coming up from the well, plunging one corner of the room into shadow. The battle captain got up stiffly and crossed to the bundles of rushes, pulling one from its rusted holder and holding its pitch-daubed head against a lighted one. When it was burning again, he reset it but remained standing, with his back against the smooth white wall, his arms folded across his chest.

'The bard is the key to this,' he said slowly, 'he has influenced us all in one way or another, drawn us all here, and has done more than his share to precipitate this coming conflict. And where is he now?' He suddenly shivered and rubbed his hands quickly against his arms. 'I sometimes wonder if he is indeed the Champion of the Old Gods, as people are claiming, or just another Duaite in disguise.'

'A Duaite?'

'An evil one, a dark one.'

'There was nothing comforting about his appearance,' I offered.

Keshian smiled mirthlessly. 'Though I should not talk about him so. He did save my life.'

'It appears he saved all our lives, and what greater debt can a man owe than his own life?'

'A ploy to trap us perhaps?'

I nodded. 'Perhaps.'

'And now we have the Weapon Master, our prime hope, preparing to go off on a wild, misconceived, hasty plan to Karfondal.'

I held up a hand, stopping him. 'It may be wild, but I doubt if it has been hastily conceived. I've known the Weapon Master for many years and when he finally sets out a plan of this kind before me, he has usually been considering it for quite some time. However,' I added slowly, 'in this case I am forced to agree that it does seem particularly ill-considered. But his mind is set; he passes command to you and we set out for Karfondal.' I shrugged.

Keshian crouched until his eyes were level with mine. 'But we need you both,' he said softly, and there was a note of genuine concern in his voice that truly touched me. 'Both of you are keeping this legion together, not Kutor and the promise of kingship, not the vague promises of payment and position someday, but the honour of being trained and fighting alongside Owen the Weapon Master. That is what they want, that is what keeps them here. They will not fight for me. I don't command enough respect in their eyes.'

'But if Geillard's advisers could be slain . . .' I persisted.

'We would win,' he said simply.

'That is the conclusion the Master has reached. And he feels strongly enough in this cause to risk everything to achieve it.'

'But it still comes back to the simple fact that the legion will follow neither Kutor nor me.'

'If Owen tells them?'

Keshian shook his head. 'Would you follow second best?' he asked.

I was forced to agree. 'Well then,' I said, 'we will have to give the legion a reason to follow you!'

## 15   Churon

He was the Onelord, a man who knew it was his god-given right to
rule, and the obstacles in his way were merely trifles to be disposed
of.

*The Onelord: the Barbarian Saviour*

One Faith, One Land, One People . . . and One Ruler.

*motto of Churon, the Onelord*

'You bring me from my bed to show me a grey-hair, a one-
handed cripple and a woman! Have you taken leave of your
senses?' The voice echoed down the cold stone corridors, booming off the chill sweating stones. The shouts were clearly audible
to the three companions, who had been left to wait in a small
chamber in what had obviously once been a monastery but was
now being used by Churon as his headquarters.

Rade had led Buiva, Paedur and Katani to the monastery on
foot by a long and winding route that doubled back on itself
more than once. The ploy was to meant to confuse, but the bard
knew that with his trained and  near-perfect memory he would
be able to retrace their steps back to the tavern and thence to
the monastery again if need be.

Katani started at the harsh voice. 'Churon,' she whispered.

'You're sure?' Paedur asked.

'Some voices you never forget, especially when it's the last
voice you heard before you died.'

Paedur nodded and was about to speak when Buiva raised a
hand. 'They're coming.'

There was movement in the hallway outside and then Rade
stepped into the doorway. He was white-faced and there was a
sheen of sweat on his face. Before he could  speak, he was
roughly thrust aside and Churon the Onelord strode into the
chamber.

Partially from Katani's description and partially because he
had been expecting more, Paedur was disappointed with the Onelord. He had formed an image of a tall, broad, perhaps even a

153

Chopt-like man but what he saw was a man no taller than himself, broad-shouldered but not excessively muscled, and it was only his ebon skin that contrasted sharply with his snow-white hair and eyebrows and startlingly blue eyes that lent him a slightly unnatural appearance. He was naked except for a heavy wollen cloak thrown across his shoulders, and he carried a thick-bladed hunting knife. He stood in the doorway and looked at each in turn, beginning with Buiva and finishing with the woman. He turned to look at the bard again and then walked up to him. It was only when Churon stepped up close and fixed his ice-blue eyes on him that Paedur realised that here indeed was a man of great power. Even without his senses he could sense the aura that surrounded the man.

Churon looked at the bardic sigil on Paedur's shoulder and then turned his attention to the hook, his eyes narrowing. He looked up suddenly. 'Rade tells me you are a bard?' His voice was deep, slightly harsh, as if his throat had been damaged at some time, and his accent was that of the Northlands.

'I am Paedur, a bard.' He bowed slightly.

'Why have you come to me?'

Paedur heard the note of eagerness in his voice and hid a smile. This would be easier than he thought. 'I am but newly come to the Silent Wood, lord, and when I heard of your existence here in the Mire, I knew I could not let the opportunity pass to see the great Onelord. In my time, lord, you are a legend.'

'A legend,' Churon said softly. He pulled his heavy woollen cloak tighter around his shoulders, for the night was chill and damp. 'So, they still remember me.'

'There is no greater hero in the mythology of the Seven Nations,' the bard replied truthfully.

'You must speak to me of these legends, bard,' Churon said slowly, a thin smile touching his lips. He turned away from the bard and looked into Buiva's deep, brown eyes. 'I am told you killed a mireworm and then one of my warriors – and all just to attract my attention.'

'The mireworm was to attract your attention; the man called me a liar.'

'And you killed him for that?'

'He besmirched my honour, and a man without honour is not a man,' Buiva said with a smile.

Churon grinned. 'I believe I said that.'

'I believe you did. I am Bove, a mercenary in the World of Men.'

'And now?'

'Still a mercenary.'

Churon half turned to Rade. 'Perhaps you did not do so badly after all.' He turned back and looked at Katani, staring into her eyes, the only part of her face that was visible. 'And you, what are you?'

'She is nothing, she travels with us,' Paedur said quickly. There was always the possibility, however distant, that the One-lord would recognise Katani, or that her hatred for the man would betray her.

Churon looked at the bard and then at Buiva. 'If she stays with you, she is your responsibility. Women are few enough in this camp and my men are . . . well, men.'

'I can take care of her,' Buiva said quietly.

'I'm sure you can,' Churon said easily. 'Rade will find you quarters and we will speak again in the morning. I can best decide then what to do with you.' He nodded briefly and then left the room, followed by Rade.

The three companions remained in the chamber until Rade returned. There was a smile on his broad face and his scar stood out white against his tanned flesh. 'Welcome to the Onelord's army. The pay is lousy, the food inedible, but the prospects are excellent.'

'What are the prospects?' Paedur asked lightly.

'Life for those who have died.' He laughed at their obvious surprise and hurried on. 'And we're going to rule the world – and not just this world, but every world, every Plane of Existence.' His voice fell to a whisper and he leaned forward, as if imparting a secret. 'Perhaps even the Realm of the Gods themselves.'

Katani stood with her back to the door of the turret room, one side of her face pressed against the wood, the fingers of her left hand brushing the handle, her shortsword in her right hand. Paedur leaned against the room's only window, a tall, arched opening that had once held glass but now only the rotted remains of a wooden frame remained. He was watching movement in the courtyard far below but his attention was in the room behind him. Only Buiva was resting, lying full-length on one of the room's two straw pallets. The only other furniture in the circular room were two bowls: one held water, the other was stained and foul-smelling.

Rade had apologised when giving them the room, explaining that there were no others available as the earlier arrivals had claimed them but suggesting that if they saw something they liked he would have no objections if they were to claim it for themselves.

'We could have killed him,' Katani said softly, almost accusingly. 'He was there in front of us, naked, unguarded. We could have gutted him, should have.'

'I know. However, I must admit to a certain curiosity,' Buiva said, lacing both hands behind his head and staring up at the filthy beams that supported the conical ceiling. 'I want to know how they are going to go about attacking not only the Worlds of Men but also the Realm of the Gods.'

'There is a sizeable army camped here,' Paedur said, nodding down into the courtyard. 'And I can see what looks like hundreds of campfires burning in the surrounding countryside.'

'Campfires are no indication of an army's size,' Buiva remarked absently. 'But you miss my point, bard. No army, no matter how big, how well equipped and trained, could hope to stand against the Gods of the Pantheon. Your friend Mannam would reap as he has never reaped before. Men can stand against men, but men cannot stand against the gods.' He shook his head, 'No, there is something more here.'

'Unless he intends to unleash his army of dead and undead on to the planes of existence and slay the followers of the Old Faith. Without their faith, the gods would be sufficiently weakened to enable the Gods of the New Religion to successfully attack,' Paedur suggested very quietly.

'I know. I had considered that.'

Paedur turned from the window and looked at the god. 'Then surely by killing Churon . . .'

'But we don't know his plan, and without it there is little point in killing him.' The god settled himself on the mouldy straw. 'But there is little point in speculation now. Try to rest. We will see what the morrow brings and plan our campaign then.'

\*

156

'Churon stumbled across the monastery when he first came to the Mire,' Rade said, answering the bard's question as he led the trio down the spiralling stairs. 'It was a ruin then, and almost exactly as you see it. We've fixed up the gates, repaired the rents in the walls and cleaned out the cellars, but that's all.'

'And you found no artifacts, no inscriptions?' Paedur persisted.

'Nothing. And I know Praetens has conducted several ceremonies in an attempt to discover the identity of the religious order that worshipped here.'

'Praetens is here?' Paedur asked, surprised, 'I thought Churon's magician had been destroyed in the battle of the Sand Plain?'

Rade laughed, 'Aye, so did Churon. You should have seen the look on his face when the mage wandered into the council chamber one morning.'

Alarmed, Paedur glanced back over his shoulder at Buiva. The god nodded, silently. If Praetens was as powerful a magician as legend made him, then he would immediately recognise the god.

'I would like to meet Praetens,' Paedur said to Rade, his voice echoing off the walls. 'I have never met one of the Susuru folk.'

'An ugly devil,' Rade admitted, lowering his voice, 'but I'm afraid you'll have to contain yourself for a while longer. He left some days ago. I heard he had gone deep into the Mire, almost to the edge of the Shadowlands, on a mission for Churon.'

Paedur looked back at Buiva and the god smiled. Praetens would be the perfect intermediary between Churon and Libellius. 'I look forward to meeting him,' he said.

'I don't know when he'll return,' the captain confessed.

The captain led them out into a broad courtyard that had once been paved with countless tiny mosaic tiles. Many were missing now, grasses and clumps of bushes and in some places just patches of bare earth breaking up what must have been a hugely complicated pattern. Paedur promised himself that if he got the opportunity he would walk the battlements and attempt to make sense of the pattern.

The courtyard was still and silent at this early hour. Twisting wreaths of yellow mist coiled around the remains of a score of camp fires and the huddled bodies of warriors from a dozen races and times as they slept, wrapped in blankets and hides.

'If these are Churon's personal guard then they leave a lot to be desired,' Buiva remarked.

'They are not part of the Onelord's guard,' Rade replied without turning round. 'The Onelord needs no guard here in the Mire: he has no enemies in this place.'

'What about all the Shemmatae he dispatched in the World of Men?' Paedur asked with a smile. 'Churon was the most powerful man in the known world in his day, and a man like that does not come to the throne without making some enemies.'

Rade looked back over his shoulder, his face expressionless. 'But there are none in this place.' He led them into what had obviously once been the chapel of the monastery, but only its shape and the remains of a huge slab of stone that had once served as an altar betrayed its previous purpose. The tall arched windows that were set deep into the thick walls had all been boarded up and hung with moth-eaten tapestries on the inside to cut down on the draughts. The floor had been cleared of pews and there had obviously been tiles set on to the floor; now only broken chips remained. The walls and the high, vaulted ceiling were flaking, and there were gangrenous stains creeping up the walls in the darker corners. An odour of decay, of rot and damp and hidden foulness pervaded the building.

The Onelord was alone in the monastery, sitting on a simple wooden stool and using the altar stone as his table. He was clad in silver-blue body armour with a white snowbeast fur cloak thrown across his shoulders, and their opulence and colour only served to emphasise the desolation of the place. A naked flame-edged dagger lay on the altar beside him.

Rade turned away at the door without a word and without announcing them, and then he turned and hurried back across the courtyard, finally disappearing into the shifting mists.

Buiva and Paedur strode down the length of what had once been the aisle leaving Katani behind them standing just inside the door in the shadows.

'Ah, you slept well, I trust?' Churon half turned and lifted a delicate bottle of green-tinged liquid, shaking it slightly. 'Drink? No? Pity, you don't know what you're missing.' He tilted his head back and drank deeply, a trickle of liquid finding its way down his chin and settling on to the breastplate of his armour. Paedur noted that the fine silver metal was already stained a deep emerald and seemed to be blistered.

'I take it you want to fight with me?' Churon said suddenly, looking at both in turn.

'I will fight if the price is right,' Buiva said slowly. 'I do not know about the bard. We met on the road and only later discovered that we shared a destination.'

The Onelord nodded. 'Ah. I wondered how two such odd characters should come to be keeping company. And the girl?' He looked up searching the shadows for her. 'She is?'

'A camp-follower in the World of Men who carried her profession with her into the Silent Wood,' Paedur said with a smile.

Churon grinned hugely. 'Of course. Old habits die hard.' He turned his attention to the bard. 'And why have you come here, bard?'

'I told you last night, lord. To meet with a legend.'

'Is that the only reason?'

'I am a bard,' Paedur said slowly, 'I did wonder if it would be possible for me to create a new version, the true version, of the Tale of Churon the Onelord.'

'Tell me, man. What do they call me in the World of Men now?'

'The Barbarian Saviour.'

Churon threw back his head and howled with laughter, slapping his hands down on to the hard altar stone. 'The Barbarian Saviour, eh? And what of my city, is that still remembered?'

'Shansalow, the Silver City?' Paedur shrugged. 'Like most other cities of its type, it is assumed that it was a legend, a myth – like the Culai Isle,' he added, with a slight smile.

'What! Shansalow was real. It was eighteen years in the building, and even when I left the World of Men it was still expanding. It was the finest city in the world. Why, the bards of my day compared it to ... to ...' He shook his head in exasperation, searching for the word, 'the Culai capital,' he said eventually.

'Ui Tyrin,' Paedur supplied.

Churon nodded. 'That was the place.' He grinned fondly, remembering. 'I will speak to you of Shansalow sometime. It so happens,' he continued slowly, 'that I think I am in need of a bard. The legend of Churon did not end when I left the Planes of Existence. I have been labouring long and hard both in the Silent Wood and in this place. I should imagine I have enough material for you to fashion a score of ballads.'

'I am a bard, lord. My material is not set to music,' Paedur interrupted him.

'I think my lord Churon knows that, bard; I imagine he has

159

been subtly testing you, determining if you are indeed a bard,' Buiva said with a grin.

Churon stood up and came down the steps to stand in front of Paedur and Buiva. He was holding the long flame-edged dagger in his left hand, tapping it absently against the rings of his silver-blue body armour. 'You are a clever man . . . eh?'

'Bove.'

'Aye, Bove. But I am satisfied he is what he says he is. But you, tell me how I may test you. When I walked the World of Men, I never met a mercenary as old as you.'

'Do not let my looks deceive you, lord,' Buiva smiled.

'For a mercenary, you are remarkably unscarred. How sure am I that you were indeed a hireling blade in the World of Men?'

'A scarred man is usually unlucky or just slow; I like to think I am neither of those things. I was a mercenary on the Planes of Existence, just that. A professional soldier, my sword and skills for hire to the highest bidder. I have fought in every land and for more causes than I even remember. In the last few years, however, because of my experience, I've commanded others, and before I entered Mannam's kingdom it was enough for me to sell only my advice and not my weapon skill.'

'You are that good?' Churon asked, the disbelief clearly audible in his voice.

'He is known as the Master Warrior in the World of Men,' Paedur said. 'His fame is widespread.'

The Onelord walked back up the steps and sank down on to his simple wooden stool, one elbow resting on the altar stone, his head on his hand. 'I have an enemy,' he said slowly, 'a powerful man commanding a very powerful army. I want control of that army. How do I go about it?'

'Are they loyal to the man or the office?' Buiva asked.

'The office, I believe.'

The war god shrugged. 'Replace or buy the man.'

'He cannot be bought.'

'Replace him.'

'How?'

'Assassination, of course.'

'No stranger can get close to him. He is protected by . . . by an elite force, and he is also a magus of some strength and surrounds himself with spells and wards.'

'Attack from within. If you cannot get close to the man, work on someone close to him, perhaps even use his elite force against him. Either have one of them kill him or turn them against him.'

'And when he is out of the way,' Churon persisted, 'what then?'

'Replace him with a man of your own. Someone you either trust or control. Preferably the latter.'

The Onelord nodded. 'Your judgement is sound.'

'Was that a test case or a real situation?' Buiva asked.

'Why?'

He shrugged. 'Just curious. But if it was a real case I might volunteer to dispose of this enemy for you.'

'Just to prove yourself?'

'Something like that.'

'I doubt if even you could dispose of this enemy,' Churon laughed.

'And why not? I've slain magicians before. Counter their spells, negate their power and you'll find they bleed like other men.'

'Not this one. I see the disbelief in your eyes.' Churon smiled humourlessly. 'My enemy is Death, old man, the Lord of the Silent Wood, Mannam.'

Buiva nodded wordlessly.

'A powerful enemy,' Paedur said. 'I know of no other man who has earned Death's personal enmity.'

'I am not as other men,' Churon said coldly.

'Death must have a foe. There must be someone or something inimical to him,' Buiva said slowly, almost as if he were thinking aloud. He looked at Paedur. 'With your bardic knowledge, can you tell me what Death fears?'

'Death has no enemies,' Paedur said, lifting his hook and beginning to clean it on the end of his furred cloak. 'C'lte, one of the Lords of Life, might be considered a natural foe, but their enmity is more in the way of a game than anything else. The only person – being – inimical to Mannam would be Libellius, the Deathlord of the New Religion . . .'

Buiva nodded decisively. 'Then that's it. You must enlist this Libellius and use him against Mannam.'

'Hah!' Churon crowed triumphantly. 'I am ahead of you, way ahead of you.' He saw the puzzled looks and came down the steps to place a hand on both their shoulders. 'Libellius is in my employ, and had been for some little time now. We are already plotting to overthrow Death. My magician meets with him and his cohorts this very day to plan the final assault on the Lord of the Silent Wood.'

'And Libellius will take Mannam's place?' Paedur asked.

'Aye.'

'And you can control this Libellius?' Buiva asked.

'This Death God of the New Religion was a man before he became a god, but he has taken his vices and habits of one life into another. He can be controlled.' The Onelord threw back his head and the flaking monastery walls echoed with his laughter. 'Nothing can stand in my way. First I will take Death's Domain, then the World of Man and finally the Realm of the Gods. I will be the Onelord!'

Two thin needles of steel touched the Onelord's throat. 'I think not!'

## 16  Plans

'Men believe only what they want to believe, even when all the evidence points to the contrary.'

*Tien tZo*

Details emerged only later.

The assassins had come in over the cliff face that jutted out over the fortress's walls, dropping down on to the battlements on hempen ropes woven around wire. The men, six of them, had killed the guard and then made their way down through the main body of the building, seemingly finding their way by trial and error to Kutor's guarded room. What happened then was unclear, but it seemed that one or more of them had returned to the supply room, which they would have had to pass, and started a small fire there. It was obvious that the intention was to create a diversion which would draw the guards, leaving Kutor alone and unprotected. However, as the will of the Gods would have it, Keshian, on his way to his own chambers, spotted the fire and the masked assassin and, although he was unarmed, tackled and killed the assassin. Grabbing the dead man's weapons he had raced down the corridor to Kutor's room and had reached it just as the five remaining assassins were preparing to attack. Without hesitation he attacked them and although they were bigger, well-armed and more comfortable with their weapons, he killed them in the time it took for Kutor's guards to race down the corridor to join him. The two guards had stopped in amazement, looking at the five dead bodies with the small stout man standing in their midst, bleeding from a score of small cuts.

The realisation of what might have happened, combined with shock, brought a rictus that might have passed for a grin to one of the guards lips 'Is that all?' he had asked hoarsely.

'There's another in the storeroom,' Keshian had said without expression.

*

'I feel sullied.'

'There was nothing else we could do,' Owen said quietly, patiently, but he avoided Keshian's accusing eyes.

'It was wrong,' the warrior protested.

'It was necessary!' Owen insisted.

Kutor tapped the base of his goblet on the polished wooden table. 'And it was successful. I've heard the tale a score of times today and each time it grows in the telling.' He looked across at his captain with a smile. 'Do you know you slew a dozen Gallowglas?'

Even Keshian grinned, and then sobered. 'But if they ever find out?'

'They won't,' Owen said, 'and as the prince said, it has achieved our aim, the men are now looking on you as a hero.'

'But I'm not a hero!'

'Have you never done an heroic deed?' Tien tZo asked quietly. He was standing with his back to the door, his hands behind his back, the fingers of both hands resting lightly on the rough wood. If there was movement in the corridor outside, he would feel the vibrations through the wood.

Keshian looked at him and shrugged in embarrassment. 'I don't know.'

'You are too modest,' the Shemmat said quickly. 'If the honour the men pay you now sits uneasily with you, then consider it as nothing more than payment for your past deeds of honour.'

'Tien is right,' Owen said, his voice weary, 'and now let us end it. Keshian is a hero, the men will accept him as their leader – and that is enough,' he added warningly, seeing Keshian about to protest again. 'Now let us turn to the real business of this meeting.' He looked at both Kutor and Keshian and glanced across at Tien, and then turned back to the prince and his captain. 'It is necessary to add one thing further to the plan. No-one must know where Tien and I have gone, no-one must know the reason. Put out whatever story you wish, even that we just upped and left because there was no possibility of pay. That should be believed. After all, I am a professional mercenary soldier . . .'

'Was,' Tien corrected with a slight smile.

The Weapon Master nodded, acknowledging the jibe. He too has been coming to the realisation that his days as a professional mercenary were nearing an end; he was now a soldier in Kutor's army. 'Whatever story you decide upon regarding our disappearance must be kept up. In the next few days and in the moons leading up to action, there will be desertions and volunteers. Treat all newcomers as possible spies, for you c̵ ̵ be certain some of them will be Geillard's people, and I wou̵_ suggest you deal with caught deserters with the utmost severity to discourage others.'

'I will not agree to barbarity,' Kutor said imm̵

Owen looked at him in astonishment. 'Is ̵̵̵̵̵̵̵̵̵̵̵̵ ̵̵̵̵̵̵̵̵̵̵̵n who regularly cut off merchan̵̵̵̵̵̵̵̵̵̵̵ ̵̵̵̵̵̵̵̵̵̵̵̵̵̵̵̵̵̵ ̵̵̵̵̵turning them to his family until a ransome wa̵̵̵ ̵̵̵̵̵̵ ̵̵ ̵̵̵̵̵̵̵ ̵ the same man who removed a distinctive birthmark from̵̵ ̵̵oman's thigh by the simple expedient of removing the skin ̵̵̵ ̵̵r leg which was then sent back to her family to encourage them to pay up quickly? Is this not the man who paid the Chopts a bounty on the travellers' trains they frightened off the main trade-routes and into his traps? Don't talk to me about barbarity!' he spat.

'What's past is past,' Kutor said smugly. 'and cannot be undone. But my reign must not be achieved by excessive methods.'

Owen's fist crashed on to the table. 'W̵̵'ve just slaughtered the best part of three legions and you speak to me of excessive methods? How do you want us to win this throne of yours? By soft words and diplomacy, no doubt?' He made them sound like obscene acts. 'Well, it is too late, princeling. You are committed, like it or not. Let's just say it's your destiny,' he added with a chill smile. 'The Gods themselves are now directing you.'

Keshian cleared his throat into the long silence that followed. 'When will I start moving men back into the Nations?'

'Give us a moon's start. It will enable us to make our way into the city and establish a base there. Tien has also suggested organising the disaffected parties within Karfondal and inciting them to revolt, and that may indeed be possible, although I think it will probably happen of its own accord in any case once the city is attacked.'

'Will a warrior and a Shemmat entering the city together not be noted?' Keshian asked.

Tien tZo answered. 'We will be entering by different gates on different days at different times; ideally, close to the end of the shifts when the guards are tired and careless. The Master will adopt the guise of a wandering soldier, down on his luck – there will be many such on the road – and I will be one of the Andam Brotherhood.'

'When will we strike?' Kutor asked suddenly, his voice low and subdued.

'I would suggest you merely continue to press forward, bringing the battle to them, forcing them to fight you on your terms. As you approach the capital, you will be up against the pick of the Imper████████ and by then all the odds will be in their favour. They ██████████nting on their own ground and they will have the added impetus of desperation spurring them on. However, by that time you should have a sizeable army at your back and the men you have now will be well trained in the art of war. Also, the sight of Karfondal's walls should spur them on. Listen to Keshian,' he urged. 'I know we set him up as a hero, but he has a wealth of knowledge; he knows the ground, he knows Imperial tactics and troops dispositions – and he has survived.'

'But when should we strike?' the prince persisted.

'We will time our action to aid you; you are not there to aid us,' Tien said softly, his gaze distant. 'In every war there is a decisive battle, usually just one, which swings the balance of the whole course of the war. The Sand Plain was the one which destroyed my people . . .' His eyes re-focussed and he looked at Kutor and Keshian again. 'And so we will strike when we see your army preparing to march on Karfondal.'

'Should I attempt to send men into the city beforehand?' Kutor asked.

Suddenly all three men were shaking their heads. Finally, both Owen and Tien looked at Keshian. The battle-captain turned to the prince. 'Once news of our approach has been confirmed, the gate guards will be doubled and then re-doubled and their vigilance will be such that no-one unknown to them or to someone within the city walls will be able to get past them.' He paused as a sudden thought struck him and he looked across at the Weapon Master. 'And that of course means that you will be trapped in the city. If your attempt fails, you will not be able to flee.'

'If our attempt fails there will be no need to,' Owen said very softly, his voice no more than a whisper.

Barthus the Hierophant glared down at the shaven head bowed

low before him. 'Is this all?' He contemptuously tossed the rice-paper scroll into the low smouldering fire.

'Yes, Holiness. Salier has re-doubled the guards around the Emperor, and Fodla herself inspects them at irregular intervals. She personally strangled a guard she caught drinking on duty.'

Barthus glared at the terrified priest for a few moments longer and then abruptly dismissed him. 'Continue with your work.'

'Yes, Holiness. Thank you.' The man scrabbled to touch the hem of the Hierophant's gown, but Barthus impatiently twitched it from his grasp and turned away. The man backed from the room and the door clicked shut behind him, and then Barthus heard the clink and jangle of metal as the warrior-priests outside his door settled themselves. Alone at last, the slender young man relaxed and allowed the haughty, arrogant pretence to fall away, revealing the fear beneath. He sat back into a high-backed, winged chair, massaging the tight skin around his eyes with his long, fine fingers and stared deep into the fire, watching the edges of the intelligence report begin to twist and curl with flame. He rested his head against the polished brukwood and allowed his mind to wander, letting it find and settle into the soothing rhythms of his beliefs, taking comfort from their familiarity. And while on one level he was praying to the Gods of the New Religion, on another deeper level, his mind was sorting through the various threads of information which he had in his grasp at the moment.

From what he could gather, the situation in the Outlands was worsening at a terrifying rate. What had started as an outlaw band had turned into an army, and an army on the move, and the small, independent townships each with their own tiny militia forces were flocking to the Renegade's banner, swelling his numbers. The Emperor's expeditionary force had been decimated and there had been another equally brief and even more bloody struggle at the Line Bridge, the traditional place of demarcation between the Outlands and the Provinces. Two legions had attempted to stop Kutor's army by holding the bridge and the approach routes. The Renegades had simply hung back and laid down a devastating fire of poisoned arrows and crossbow bolts which massacred the Imperial forces as they camped on the open ground and bridge. That night what was left of the Imperial troops had been attacked by a raiding party from Kutor's army. From an estimated force of nearly two legions, less than two decades had survived. The way was now open for the rebel army to march directly into the western provinces.

There would be a decisive battle without any doubt, but where? How close to the capital would Geillard allow his bastard half-brother to come before he destroyed him? But, and more importantly, could this present situation be used to further Barthus' ambitions, and that of the New Religion too, of course?

He knew the Emperor was somewhat in awe of him, and that was something he wished to encourage, but he also knew that both Fodla and Salier distrusted him, hated what he represented. For what he represented was power, the like of which had not been seen in the Nations since the Gods and Culai had last walked the World of Men.

Barthus was no magician, no necromancer, no magus, he had neither sorcerous nor shapeshifting powers, but he could call on the Gods and they visibly and tangibly answered his call. He was Hierophant of the New Religion and that entitled him to the respect and adulation of a vast number of people – including, in theory, the Emperor himself. If Barthus called on the followers of the Religion to rise up and fight, then they would do so; for example, if he called upon them to support the Renegade, Kutor, then they would do that . . .

The Hierophant sat up suddenly, an idea flitting around the edges of his consciousness. A piece of coal cracked and sparks fell in the large grate, and the idea crystallised. The followers of the Religion must follow the Hierophant's dictates, that was part of the accepted creed of the Religion, and if he ordered them – no, if he informed them that he was convinced of Kutor's right to the throne – then they were bound by their Religion to follow his command. Now, Barthus wondered, how much bargaining power did that lend him, not only with Geillard but also with his half-brother? Barthus would deal with either.

He sat back into the chair, his long fingers steepled before his face, working out the ramifications of his plan, the gains and possible losses. One of the advantages of dealing with Kutor, for example, would be that there was no Salier, no Fodla to interfere with his plans. Something cold and inhuman settled down behind his eyes and then Barthus began to quiver with suppressed humour; whatever happened in this coming war, he would ensure that neither the mage nor the warrior-maid would survive.

But first, Kutor must be acquainted with his plans. Barthus leaned forward and stared at the dancing flames and curling smoke of the fire. And then he called upon his Gods . . .

Fodla was entertaining Salier in her chambers, which was something she would rather not have been doing, and she had the vague idea that the very presence of the magus in her rather spartan chambers sullied them.

Salier had looked around in frank interest when he entered the rooms – this was his first, and for all he knew, his last invitation, and the magician was of the opinion that it was possible to learn more about a character from their rooms than from the person themselves. Look at the person and you saw an image; look at the room and you saw the personality. Fodla was the perfect example. Her image was of cold ruthlessness, a killer without conscience or care, and at times she accentuated her feminine characteristics almost as if to make her actions seem even more incomprehensible. She was called the Weapons-Maid, not only on account of her skills with the tools of death but also because of the huge number of weapons which she carried about herself; two matched swords rode on her back, there were knife sheaths sewn on to the sleeves of her uniform just above the wrists, which allowed the handles of the knives to fall easily into her hands, and there was another set of sheaths sewn into her boots. There was occasionally another longer sword on her belt, and she sometimes carried a small hand-axe or a mace.

So, Salier would have almost expected to find the walls hung with weapons, shields and banners, perhaps captured colours, but instead they were bare, painted a dull oatmeal colour which matched the off-white cuine-skin rugs scattered across the chill stone floor. There was a long ironwood table beneath the window, glowing in the late afternoon light, and two matching chairs were placed at either end. A broad metal-bound travelling chest was tucked into a corner and a low, two-shelf bookcase completed the room's furnishings. However, he knew there was another, smaller room leading off this one – Fodla's bedchamber, where her armour, clothing and weapons would be kept no doubt.

The huge woman crossed to the ironwood table and took one of the chairs, plainly indicating that Salier should occupy the other, facing her down the length of the table. The mage sat easily, his hands folded on the polished grey wood table before him, looking at the woman and realising for the first time that she was actually quite lovely. Without the enveloping armour and the shapeless mail, her figure, although full, was firm, her skin smooth and unwrinkled and her red hair had been swept back off her face leaving her bright green eyes staring out of a broad oval face.

'You're staring,' she said coldly.

Salier attempted a short bow. 'I apologise, my lady, but this is the first time I have seen you without your armour.'

'And you have discovered I am a woman?' Fodla asked, the bitterness in her voice surprising even herself.

'I have discovered that you are a very beautiful woman,' he said, a smile touching his thin lips.

Fodla grimaced. 'You and I are too old for these games,' she snapped.

The mage nodded. 'Too old to play them, and that means my compliments are truthful observations and have no other intent.'

The woman nodded stiffly. Compliments had been rare in her life and she had never learned to accept them easily.

'You asked me to come here?' Salier said, breaking the growing silence, settling into the high-backed chair.

Fodla nodded gratefully, glad to be back on safe ground. 'We need to talk, you and I, and this is the only place within the palace where I know we will not be spied upon.'

'There could be listeners, secret passages, listening tubes,' Salier suggested with a wicked grin.

'There is nothing. I checked the room myself, and to ensure our privacy, I've invoked a small spell I know which should work.'

'And what spell is that?' Salier asked, taking a professional interest, more than a little surprised that the captain knew any spellcraft.

She dismissed it with a wave of her hand. 'It is nothing, a trifle I learned from my mother.' Her tone indicated that the subject was at an end. 'We need to talk about Geillard and Barthus and this situation in the western provinces.'

Salier nodded. He was about to speak when the door opened and a young woman entered, carrying a plain wooden tray holding two glasses and a crystal goblet worked in the blue glass of Lostrice. The woman was wearing the armour of Fodla's own regiment, the Emperor Legion, the dagger crest indicating that she held the rank of captain. She put the tray down in front of Salier, her eyes on the mage, and then she went to the far end of the table and spoke briefly to her commander in a soft whisper before she left, moving almost noiselessly despite the heavy armour and weapons.

Fodla looked at Salier and smiled, and the magician, for all his powers, felt the skin at the back of his neck tingle and something cold move down his spine. For a single instant, the moment when her lips had curled in a smile, Fodla had ceased to be a woman and he had glimpsed something else behind the mask, something cold and merciless, bestial and slavering, and he wondered briefly if she had any beast blood in her. 'It seems you disobeyed my command to bring no weapons with you,' she said, her voice silk and ice-cold. She reached in under the table as she spoke and brought out a cocked and loaded hand-crossbow and pointed it squarely at Salier's chest.

'I brought no weapons,' Salier protested, staring at the weapon held unwaveringly in the woman's large hands. The crossbow was a perfect miniature of the larger model and the broad-headed triangular bolt was perfectly capable of punching clean through him and into the chair he was sitting on at this short range.

'There is a knife in your sleeve and another in your boot,' Fodla said, grinning mirthlessly.

Salier silently produced both weapons and placed them on the polished grey wood of the table. 'I've carried them for so long now, I don't really consider them . . .' he began to explain, but Fodla waved his explanation aside.

'Business,' she snapped. She placed the crossbow on the table by her left hand, but left it cocked and loaded and still pointing at Salier. 'Let us begin with this Prince Kutor,' she said. 'His threat this time is much more serious than the last and his men are disciplined and trained. And what's more, they seem dedicated to their cause. This is no rabble helped along with a few score hired mercenaries, and I think we must both consider the very real possibility that Kutor will march to Karfondal's walls to enforce his claim to the throne.'

'He is certainly showing unusual determination,' Salier agreed.

'I need to know if he has any legitimate claim to the throne.'

Surprisingly, the magician nodded. 'He has. He is the present Emperor's half-brother, born on the wrong side of the blanket, it is true, but his claim is legitimate nonetheless. He is actually next in line to the throne after Geillard; he is the nearest living relative.'

The woman grimaced. 'I've seen men put on the throne with even less claim. It's a pity; I had rather hoped he was just another imposter.'

'Does it matter?' Salier asked, surprised.

'It does. I could have convinced my people that we were fighting a renegade imposter, a commoner with ideas above his station, as it were. But if Kutor has a legitimate claim. . . .'

He nodded. 'It makes it a little more difficult,' he agreed.

'My spies can tell me nothing about who is training this army. The Weapon Master, Owen, has been mentioned, but his name turns up everywhere these days.'

'His name is mentioned in my reports,' Salier interrupted.

'Then do you think there is any truth in these stories?'

He shook his head. 'The Weapon Master always travels with a Shemmat, and they are a distinctive enough race in the Nations, but none of my reports mentions him.'

Fodla nodded. 'As I thought. The man is a legend amongst the common people, so it is almost natural that his name should come up. The only other name which appears is a Keshian or Kesian, but I know of no-one of any calibre called Keshian or Kesian. Has his name appeared in your reports?'

'No.'

Fodla ran a blunt nail down the polished wood of the hand-crossbow. 'So we may assume he is an Outlander, with little or no experience, and therefore only a limited threat.' She moved the crossbow again, shifting it slightly, so the bolt now tilted upwards, pointing at Salier's throat. Seeing his startled expression, it was only with some difficulty that she managed to keep her face straight. 'And we must also consider the reports that King Cormac and his Gallowglas army have been slaughtered.'

'I have a similar report, but can you see anyone killing Cormac or indeed even one of his Gallowglas, let alone an army of them?' Salier asked derisively.

'The Gallowglas are mainly reputation,' Fodla remarked. 'I once killed one of them.'

'But you are an exceptional woman!'

The warrior smiled and hurried on. 'They would have been difficult to kill by fair means,' she admitted, 'but treachery might account for it.'

'One or two perhaps, but all of them?' Salier shook his head. 'I don't think so.'

'When was the last time you received a report from the King of the Outlands?'

The mage stared at the warrior for a few long moments without replying.

Fodla grinned mirthlessly. 'Come, come now, magus, don't be so shy. I've known you were supporting the Gallowglas for a long time.'

'And you're not interested in a reason?'

'Whatever opinions I hold about you, I've never considered you to be a traitor,' she said with a tight smile, 'and I can only assume that what you were doing was in the best interest of the Emperor.'

Salier bowed, his estimation of the woman soaring. 'I've heard nothing from Cormac,' he said shortly.

'Then we must assume he is either dead or captured.'

'Dead, I would think.'

'And the Gallowglas?'

He shook his head. 'Dead or scattered. I know it seems inconceivable, but I am left with no alternative.'

'But where is the remainder of his army, his legion?' Fodla asked eagerly.

Salier nodded in understanding. 'The core of Kutor's army?'

'Precisely.'

'But what would have encouraged them to fight for Kutor, especially if he had killed Cormac.'

'I don't imagine the Gallowglas was a benign ruler,' she shrugged. 'Perhaps it was simply a better cause.' She looked directly at Salier, noting with some surprise the worried frown on his face. Perhaps there was still something human in him after all.

'And we may have another problem,' Salier said slowly, with the air of a man imparting something he would rather have kept to himself.

Fodla continued to watch him in silence.

'It is my belief,' Salier continued, carefully picking his words, 'that Barthus is not to be trusted. He will place his precious Religion above everything else, and if he thinks he will get a better deal from Kutor, then I have no doubts but that he will try. And if he does, then he will have no use for either of us.'

Fodla nodded. 'We should dispose of him,' she agreed.

'Now!' Salier snapped.

'It is not an immediate worry and would cause more confusion while the church bickered amongst themselves. Right now we have to decide where and when to attack Kutor's forces.'

The wind changed, scattering the flames, sending long shadows dancing up along the walls of the shallow cave Kutor had settled down in for the night. On the plain down and around him the hundreds of camp fires of his army and followers winked like fallen stars. The wind gusted again and he lifted his face to it, smelling it, tasting it, realising that the wind was from the sea and that there was rain or possibly sleet to follow. Shivering, he leaned forward and dropped some long slivers of dried dung on to the flames. The fire hissed and crackled and thousands of tiny points of light spiralled heavenwards.

Kutor lay back against the rough stone wall, ironically aware that although the cave was cold, chill and smelt of something long dead, he felt comfortable here. Owen's six hand-picked and trained guards were dotted around him – even he didn't know where – and he was surrounded on all sides by men. Some of whom were devoted to his cause while others were honour-bound to follow him. There had been assassination attempts, both of them brief, botched affairs but they had brought home to him the need for guards. But here, in the middle of a wind-swept plain, he was safe; here there was no possibility of anyone attacking him. Here he could rest.

'*K-K-Kutor-r-r.*'

The prince sat bolt upright, his knife coming to his hand. But there was no movement in the gritty darkness, no one around. Even his guards had remained invisible and they were usually on hand if he so much as turned over in his sleep.

'*K-K-Kutor-r-r.*'

The sound was directly in front of him, coming from just beyond the fire in the mouth of the cave. Dragging his short-sword free, he crept towards it.

'*K-K-Kutor-r-r.*'

174

The voice was sharp, brittle almost, the accent unnatural, as if the speaker was articulating with great difficulty. But he had indentified its position now; it was coming from a point directly beyond and to the left of the fire.

Kutor crept up to the mouth of the shallow cave, gripped his sword tightly in both hands and then rolled through the opening, coming to his feet with his back to the wall, his sword extended – and found himself facing nothing more than a shadow.

But it was not his own.

The shadow on the wall was tall and thin, vaguely manshape with the edges decidedly indistinct. Even when the outline of the shadowshape was still, the image on the wall seemed to be writhing within itself.

'Who ... what are you?' Kutor demanded, pleased at the steadiness of his voice.

'*I am Tinis, Firelord of the Gods of the New Religion and servant of Barthus, Hierophant of the True Belief.*' The voice was cracked and clicking, like burning wood, and came from the heart of the fire.

Kutor knelt and looked into the fire, but all he could see were the tiny dancing flames, nothing even remotely manlike about them.

'What do you want?' he demanded.

'*My master Barthus sends me to convey his greetings and to place his terms before you.*'

'What terms?' Kutor asked, intrigued although his heart was hammering.

The dancing shadow leaped into a paroxysm of activity. '*His full support and the support of all the followers of the New Religion.*'

'In return for what?' Kutor asked, immediately suspicious.

'*In return for your loyalty,*' the shadow crackled, '*in return for your support in turn for the cause of the New Religion.*' Another gust scattered the creature's shadow momentarily and Kutor had the impression of a man-shape flying apart, arms and legs all disappearing in different directions. '*Come, I need your answer. Barthus will support you, make you Emperor in effect, if you will support him. What say you?*'

Kutor took a moment to consider and then he said slowly and distinctly. 'I have never had much in my life, but whatever else I lacked, I've always had my faith. It may have drifted sometimes, but it was always there, and the bard reminded me what I owed it and what it could do for me.' He suddenly threw a handful of dust on to the flames, dousing many of them, destroying the creature. 'I owe the Old Faith too much, and that is my answer!'

# 17   The God's Tale

All men die, few can kill.

*Katan proverb*

'Don't kill him!' Paedur hissed desperately, as blood began to trickle from the soft flesh just beneath Churon's ears.

'Why not?' Katani demanded. 'He killed me.'

'You can kill him, but not now,' Buiva said reasonably.

'You're mad, all of you,' Churon said tightly, his head rigid, unmoving with the two spikes against his flesh. 'What do you hope to gain? You cannot kill me, not permanently in any case.'

Katani moved one of the spikes up Churon's face, leaving a glistening red trail against his coal-black skin, stopping when it was touching the corner of his eye. 'I can maim you, Onelord. I can ensure that when you walk again, it will be blind and deaf, dumb even, with severed tendons and mutilated nerves. How would you like that, Onelord?' she spat.

'There are those in the Mire to whom torture is an art, a fine delicate art, and each body a tapestry to be worked upon. I will ensure that you will be their masterpiece,' Churon said coldly. He shifted the flame-edged dagger which he still held in his right hand, but Paedur leaned forward and knocked it from his grasp with his hook.

'I am of the Katan. Ah, I see you recall the name. Well then, you'll know your threats mean nothing to me. By killing you, I avenge my sisters and the honour of the Katan warriors.'

With a scream of wood on stone, the chapel door scraped open, but only Paedur turned towards the sound; both Katani and Buiva kept watching their prisoner. Rade, Churon's captain, strode into the chapel carrying a tray holding a bottle and four crystal goblets. The bard was actually moving towards him before the man realised what was happening.

'Hey! Guards! Guards to Churon!'

Rade flung aside the tray and ran down the aisle, his sword in his hand, while behind him the doorway immediately began to fill with the Onelord's mercenary guards. Paedur met the captain's downward swing on his hook, catching and then snapping the blade in one smooth move, while his right hand shot up, the stiffened fingers catching the man in the throat, crushing his larynx, leaving him choking and dying.

Buiva raced to the bard's side and found himself facing two pikemen whose height, colouring and weapons suggested they came from the Whale Coast. The Whale warriors were fisher-folk and their preferred and traditional weapon was the long, barbed and hooked fishing gaff. But while they had the reach on the war god, they lacked his speed. One jabbed, while the second brought his pike around in a long, low sweep. Buiva almost casually batted aside the first weapon and then hopped up as the pike came around and then dropped on to it. His weight slammed the weapon from the warrior's hands, and while he fumbled for it, Buiva's mace and chain ripped off the top of his head. His companion jabbed again and Buiva grabbed the weapon behind the barbed head and jerked forward, pulling the man off his feet. As he went down, Buiva drove the spiked haft of his mace into the base of his skull.

The bard meanwhile had dispatched another guard, opening the man from neck to groin through his thin leathers. 'Let's go,' he called, heading back towards the altar stone. 'There's another door.' He pulled a long, slim stiletto from his boot and placed it in the hollow of Churon's throat. Katani gratefully pulled off her peasant's dress, revealing her Katan armour beneath, and pulled both swords free with a blood-curdling shriek. And while a guard looked at her in astonishment, she took off his head with a single sweep of her longsword.

Paedur looked into the Onelord's wide blue eyes. 'Now, I can kill you, Onelord, and carry your lifeless body until it revives, or you can run with me,' he said simply. 'The choice is yours.'

'I'll run.'

'A wise choice.' He urged Churon around the altar and back towards the small wooden door he had noticed earlier. Katani and Buiva covered their rear, dissuading the Onelord's warriors from becoming too courageous. He sheathed his knife and gripped the ornate metal handle in his right hand and turned, or attempted to turn it, but the lock wouldn't move. 'Open it,' he commanded, pressing his hook to Churon's neck.

'It will not open,' Churon said calmly. 'The lock has rusted solid and the door has warped into its frame.'

Paedur hit the door with his hook, the razor sharp metal biting deep into the wood above the lock. He struck again and a sliver of wood jumped out. He was about to cut again, when there was a sudden hiss of air and the spiked ball of Buiva's mace shattered the lock, almost ripping the stout door from its huge hinges, snapping it open. The bard pushed the Onelord through, his hook never leaving his back; Buiva followed while Katani lingered in the doorway, the entrance small enough for one person to defend.

They were in a long, low chamber lined with cross-shaped pieces of wood; long, filthy tatters of coloured cloth were hanging from the crosses. 'A vestment chamber,' Paedur said, looking around.

Buiva pushed past him seeking an exit.

'Can we kill him now?' Katani called back over her shoulder.

'No,' Buiva snapped, 'not here, not now.' He reached the end of the chamber and swore loudly, slapping his gauntleted hand against the blank stone wall. There was no exit. He returned to Churon and, grasping the Onelord by the throat, lifted him off the ground. 'Is there any way out of here?'

Churon choked and gagged but managed to shake his head. Buiva dropped him to the ground and then allowed the ball of his mace to dangle before his eyes. 'Is there?' he demanded.

'I don't think he knows,' Paedur said softly. 'This room has not been used for a long time ...' He broke off as there was a sudden flurry of activity at the doorway and Katani's swords sang their whistling death song, accompanied by the warrior-maid's keening death psalm. The guard retreated, leaving two more of their number behind them. When they had moved back, the Katan warrior busied herself hamstringing the corpses, ensuring that even if they rose again, they would never walk properly.

Buiva turned back to the bard. 'Use your bardic lore, find us a way out of this place.'

'If this monastery follows the pattern of all the others I've been in, then yes, there should be. The priests or monks come in here, robe themselves and then make their way out on to the altar to perform their ceremony. They would usually then return here, divest themselves of their robes and then leave by the same door they entered by.'

'Then there is a door. Find it!' Buiva commanded. He glared at Churon. 'I'll take care of this.'

Paedur made his way down the chamber, tapping his metal hook on the stones, listening for a change of sound, straining to hear a different tone above the clash of swords at the door. He finally thought he had detected a change, an echo, when he was near to the back of the room. He pushed aside two tall wooden crosses with their ragged remnants still on them and tapped the stonework again. The sound rang hollowly. He tapped on the wall again, moving to one side and then back again, judging the extent of the opening, and then he began to probe with the fingers of his right hand, seeking the lever, looking for an indentation, a crack, an irregularity in the stonework.

'Well?' Buiva demanded.

'It's here, behind a false wall. I just cannot find the mechanism for opening it.'

'Try the corners.'

'I've tried,' Paedur said desperately, vainly wishing for his enchanced senses once again.

'They're bringing up archers!' Katani suddenly shouted.

'Bard!'

Paedur hissed in exasperation and then he felt something give. Abruptly the back section of the wall moved inwards – and something leaped forward on to the bard!

He shouted aloud, his left hand snapping up, catching the creature under the chin, slicing through bones, ripping the head clean off the body, shattering it against the stonework. The body fell to the ground, and when the bard looked down he found there was nothing more than the tumbled bones of a skeleton around his feet. The bones had been bleached by time to a pale ivory whiteness and were wearing the remnants of hideously ornate ceremonial robes. Still clutched in one hand was a small leather-bound book. Paedur stooped to lift the book, but the skeletal fingers were wrapped so tightly around it that he had to snap them off. Without even opening it he slipped the book into his inside pocket.

He heard the whistling scream of a hollow-headed crossbow bolt and then one shattered into the stonework over his head. He looked up and saw a second, large triangular-headed bolt glance off Katani's ornate armour to clatter harmlessly on to the floor, but the force of the blow was enough to stagger her. A huge, bearded guard leaped into the doorway, a broad-headed axe that looked far too small in his hand raised over the Katan's head. The bard's thrown knife took him through the eye and he swayed on his feet before finally falling into the doorway, partially blocking it.

Katani scrambled to her feet and pulled the bard's knife from the dead man's face and raced back to Buiva, who was pushing Churon down the room towards the opening. Katani was first through the opening, followed by Churon, Buiva and finally Paedur. As the bard was desperately looking for the lever which would swing the section of wall back into place, a score of guards finally managed to clear the door and pushed into the room, two archers in the lead. One fired blindly into the dark circle he could see at the far end of the room. The arrow hissed past the bard to shatter on the wall, while the second man, spotting the glint of Paedur's hook, loosed an arrow towards the shape. The bard desperately threw himself to one side as the bolt screamed towards him and it struck sparks from the ground not a hand-span from his face. Then suddenly the slab of wood began to grind closed. As he climbed slowly to his feet, he realised the palm of his hand was resting on a smoothly rounded lump in the otherwise rough-hewn corridor.

The tunnel was high and surprisingly dry, although the throat-catching odour of dust and powder made him gag and there was the ever-present damp reek of the Mire about it. It wasn't completely lightless either; at some stage in its history the walls had been painted with a series of religious frescoes in what the ancients had called winterlight, a natural pigment that glowed in the dark, and enough remained on the walls to emit a dim, green-tinged glow.

He had taken no more than a score of paces when the smoothly curved wall of the tunnel was broken by an oblong opening which might have once held a door but which was now barred across with four wrist-thick metal bars. The bard glanced out, and was surprised to find that the opening was high off the ground and concealed behind a trailing screen of greenery. He found he was looking down on to the courtyard they had crossed earlier, which was now alive with confusion, and he suddenly found himself wondering how, in the name of all the Gods of the Pantheon, he had come to find himself in such a hopeless situation. Well, he had no one to blame but himself, and the same Gods of the Pantheon, for that. Shrugging his thin shoulders, he hurried on. He found Buiva and Katani further down the corridor standing before another barred opening; Churon was sitting with his back against the wall. Paedur silently joined them and peered through the bars. It seemed as if they were now around at the rear of the monastery and about one man-height up from the ground; if there had ever been steps or a rope, they were long gone now.

Buiva hit the bars with his mace, but they merely vibrated, the sound thrumming through the stones, and a shower of rust flaked away.

Behind them, something solid and metallic began a steady hammering on stone, the sound vibrating through the corridor, sending dust-motes shimmering. Patches of winterlight flaked off the walls, deepening the shadows.

Churon smiled broadly. 'My men will be here soon and then this charade can end.'

Katani moved her sword so that the tip rested on the Onelord's cheek. 'Shut up,' she advised.

Buiva hit the bars again with his mace, but with as little result.

'Let me try.' The bard knelt before the opening and wrapped his hook around the centre of the three bars close to the floor. Then, holding his left wrist with his right hand, he pulled. There was a moment's resistance and then the hook slid silently through the rusted metal bar. He stood up, rubbing flakes of rust from the inner curve of his hook. 'Hold the middle of the bar,' he said to Buiva, and then he repeated the procedure, cutting into the bar at a little above eye level. Once again his hook slid through with ease. Buiva pulled the bar back out of the way and examined the cuts; they were clean and smooth.

Katani squeezed through the opening and dropped down, landing noiselessly on the soft boggy ground, moving quickly into the shade of a stunted, sickly-coloured tree. She scanned the monastery walls above them, but there was no movement. When she nodded, Buiva merely pushed Churon through the opening and when he hit the ground, Katani's swords immediately crossed against his throat. Buiva followed; he sank up to his ankles into the soggy mulch, his mail pulling him down. He swore softly and dragged his feet free, glaring at Churon as if it was all his fault. The bard was the last down, his black cloak flapping out behind him like wings. He landed lightly on his feet and darted into the bushes.

'Let's go,' Buiva said.

Paedur grabbed the god by the arm. 'Wait a moment, if you will. What is stopping us from killing Churon now?'

'We still do not have the information we need,' Buiva explained patiently.

'And?' the bard persisted, something in the god's manner not quite ringing true.

'And the Gods of the Pantheon hold no sway here. Neither Mannam, Maurug nor Madness would be able to come to this place,' Buiva said, his voice weary. 'I'm afraid we must take Churon out of the Mire and back into the Silent Wood for the gods to exact their vengeance on him.'

'Mannam forgot to mention that,' Paedur said grimly.

'Aye, well he would,' Buiva smiled.

'You will never cross the Mire,' Churon said with a smile. 'My men control all the access routes to this place from all the Planes of Existence and including the road from the Silent Wood.'

'Even you have not enough men to watch all the roads,' Buiva said evenly.

'I have enough,' he boasted.

'Well, if we cannot go around them, we'll just have to go through them,' Katani said almost eagerly.

'Could we perhaps discuss this later?' Paedur asked. 'Somewhere not so close to the Onelord's warriors.'

Buiva grinned broadly, but when he turned to Churon the smile faded. 'You have the choice again: you can walk or we can kill you and carry you with us. We'll still have you when you revive.'

'I'll walk,' Churon said, his eyes narrowing.

'Try to escape and I'll cut off your legs,' Katani warned.

'I've no need to escape. My people will rescue me.'

'Don't count on it,' Paedur smiled, hauling him to his feet and pushing him through the bushes.

The ground was soft and boggy underfoot, low stunted trees and twisted scrub growing in patches on the little islands of dry soil in the marsh, and they made slow headway until before noon when they struck a rough hard-packed track. Without discussion or hesitation they struck to the east, heading back in the general direction of the Silent Wood. The track was deserted and there was no evidence that it had been used recently, with neither spoor nor droppings to indicate an animal run. Indeed, this part of the Mire, so close to the Silent Wood, was completely devoid of all animal, bird and insect life, although the remainder of the Mire was inhabited not only by peoples and races from countless lands and times but also by the flora and fauna from those places.

They marched for the most part in silence, the atmosphere oppressive and the heat stultifying. Around noon the pale disc of the sun burned through the ever-present clouds that blanketed the Mire, and the marshlands began to bake, steaming in the abrupt heat, but the thick, foul-smelling fog only served to slow them down. Paedur shaded his eyes with his hand and stared at the orange disc and then shook his head, deciding it was not the sun he was familiar with.

They stopped only once and that was to allow a score of Churon's warriors to gallop past on animals that had too much deer in them to be truly called horses. Katani ensured Churon's silence by placing a knife in his mouth: any sound would have ripped his tongue in two.

The misty, fog-bound forenoon slipped quickly into a deeply shadowed afternoon and then night fell with its usual swiftness. And even though the fog lifted, there were no stars and no moon visible. With the onset of night, they were forced to make camp. Although Paedur found that he could just about make out the shapes of his companions and prisoner and Buiva moved with perfect ease, both Churon and Katani were almost completely blind. Buiva took the lead and struck off the track they had been following, heading for one of the tiny dry islands in the marsh; if they were discovered, their attackers would have to come at them through the marshy ground. The island was no more than an outcrop of dry land barely a score of lengths across and almost smothered beneath a thick covering of flourishing vegetation. Close to the centre of the island, they found a dry hollow almost completely surrounded by trees and bushes. Large chunks of polished and worked stone were scattered around the hollow and Paedur was just about able to make out the outline of a circular building on the hard-packed ground. Fire was impossible under the circumstances: even if the light remained invisible, the odour of smoke and fire would have been a beacon amidst the rancid odours of the Mire, and so they broke their day-long fast on strips of dried meat and stone-hard bread washed down by tepid water. Churon's legs were then staked to the ground and his arms and torso lashed to the bole of a tree. He was neither gagged nor blindfolded, but Katani positioned herself behind and to his right, her shortsword in her hand, the tip resting on the Onelord's shoulderblades.

Buiva and Paedur walked around their makeshift camp, closing off the openings, tying branches of trees and bushes together and lacing vines across the paths, ensuring that a noiseless entrance to the dry hollow would be impossible.

'I wonder what stood here,' Paedur said, rubbing his hook over one of the large flat stones, scraping off the moss.

Buiva shook his head, his mail tinkling softly. 'Too small for a house, the walls are not thick enough for either defence or a tower . . .'

'A shrine?' Paedur suggested.

'Possibly, but not to any god I know.'

The two men sat down in the lee of the highest remaining wall. Against the stones which were shadowed from above by a twisted march-tree, they were invisible, but they had a clear view of the only large entrance to their camp. Across and to their right they could make out the shapes of Churon and Katani; the Onelord was slumped against his bonds, his head on his chest as if asleep.

'He doesn't sleep yet,' Buiva remarked.

'I know. His breathing has not yet changed.'

Buiva smiled, his teeth white against the shadows. 'You are a remarkable man, bard. Here you are wandering through the Mire, the Borderlands, in the company of a murdered warrior, a dead tyrant and a god, and you accept it so casually.'

'What else can I do? Besides, I've grown used to gods. I spent time in the Kingdom of Life, remember. I walked the Culai Isle. I watched the destruction of the Cords. I saw the last of the First Race die. And after that . . . well, little surprises me now.'

'I was not in favour of you, bard, when we were choosing a Champion. I thought a military man would be more suited, a man of action, and yet on reflection a man of action would perhaps have been too hidebound in his ways and thinking to accept all this.'

'Show me a warrior who does not fear what he cannot kill.'

Buiva nodded. 'Aye, there's the rub.' He turned to look at the bard, his eyes glittering slightly. 'Why are you doing this? The gods wanted a Champion in the World of Men; they gifted him for the Planes of Existence. Here, you are a man again, and surely you knew that you would lose your powers once you entered Death's Kingdom?'

'I guessed.'

'So, why did you throw it all away? What brought you into the Silent Wood in the first place?'

Paedur laughed. 'I thought you would know that.'

'I am War, a powerful but not a very intelligent god. There are others, the Weavers of Fate, the Judgers of Souls, aye, Death too, and even the mis-named God of Fools and Madness, who are far cleverer than I. It takes very little to bring men to War,' he added ruefully.

'Have you always been War?' Paedur asked.

'I have been War since . . . since the time of the First Race of Man, when the Gods of the Pantheon were fully established.'

'I thought all the gods were created by Hanor and Hara, the First Great Gods, who were in turn created by the One,' Paedur murmured, attempting to keep the edge of excitement out of his voice.

Buiva nodded. 'The major gods and forces, aye, they were, and they in turn created the others, the world gods, the plane-gods, the gods of bridges and winds, of night and the mists and all the lesser gods, spirits and sprites.'

'And War?'

'The creature Man had a hand in the fashioning of more than one god, but perhaps his greatest creation is War.'

'You were created by Man?' Paedur whispered aghast.

Buiva nodded slightly. 'In his own image.'

'Were you human once?'

Buiva laughed shortly. 'I suppose if I don't tell you, you will worry at me like a dog at a bone until you have your answer. But since you are our Champion . . . well, I will tell you, but only on condition that you never repeat it, never!' The warning was clear in his voice.

'You have my oath,' Paedur said immediately.

'And how do you swear?' Buiva asked with a wry smile.

'Why, by the Pantheon, of course.'

The god shook with silent laughter. 'I think you and I will become friends,' he said eventually when he caught his breath.

'Well then, listen, bard, and I will tell you a tale no other man knows, nor has ever heard. Now remember that I speak of the time in the shadow of the Culai race, when Culai and Men walked the worlds and mingled with those Gods that were already in existence, a time when there was no such thing as legend for all the world was legend then . . .'

They had sat in council for a score of days, and when the High Chamber of the Culai ended, there was no announcement, and the First Race returned to their palaces and villas on the coast in covered carriages and with perhaps more haste than was seemly. And those who had waited at the foot of the white and gold marbled steps went away disappointed and vaguely troubled.

Rumours abounded in the City, for there was but one in this time of legend and with no need of a name, and the taverns were full that night and the stories told varied only in the vividness of the imagination of the tellers. One tale, however, was commonplace, and that was that the Culai race had come to the decision to subjugate the race of Man, as well as the Were-Folk, those with too much beast blood in them to be called fully human. Other tales suggested that the Culai folk had plans to enslave their fellow creatures, using them body and essence in their foul sorceries to prolong their already overlong lives.

But the truth was far simpler, but equally despicable: the Culai, who were the offspring of Man and God, had simply grown tired of its parent race of Man, with its petty squabbling, its arrogance and ignorance but more importantly, its independence and inventiveness, and had decided to destroy them.

And so while the more rational elements amongst the humanfolk attempted to quell the growing tide of fear and mistrust, the Culai set about annihilating the race of Man, the race they had sprung from. And paradoxically, they instructed the elite Storm Warriors to begin the genocide. But the Storm Warriors were all drawn from the ranks of humankind . . .

The Battle-Captain crumpled the fragile rice-paper and dropped it to the intricately tiled floor of the roof garden. Then, deliberately, he ground the heel of his boot on to the ball. 'That is what I think of your orders,' he said, looking into the blank, slightly hooded eyes of the Culai.

The Culai nodded, his finely boned head bobbing on a neck that seemed far too slender to support it. 'A predictable reaction and one which I was prepared for.' His speech was clipped, as if speech was not his natural mode of communication, and indeed, when in company together, the First Race were never known to speak. 'Those are your orders, Battle-Captain. I would suggest you obey them.'

'I will not slay my own kind!'

'They are human, Battle-Captain,' the Culai protested mildly, turning his face slightly to catch the warm breeze that was blowing in off the ocean.

'I am human! You were human once!' the warrior protested, his hands on his hips, the fingers of his right hand resting almost unconsciously against the haft of a mace and chain.

'I was never human!' the Culai snapped, a distinct glottal stop between each word.

'You had a human parent.'

'There was a woman once,' the creature acknowledged, 'but there was a god also.' The Culai paused, turning its head slightly from side to side, light reflecting off its bald head. 'You claim you are human too, but you spent many years in our service; there is nothing left for you in the World of Men, you have no ties, no relations . . . none of the Storm Warriors have. We own you.'

'And when we have killed the human folk, will you then have the were-creatures kill us?'

'Why would we do that?' the Culai asked, sounding genuinely puzzled.

'And what will you do when the Race of Man has been destroyed?' the warrior continued without answering. 'How will the First Race of Culai survive?'

The Culai's bland features creased in a puzzled frown. 'Why should I discuss this with a Battle-Captain? What gives him the right to even ask?'

'Because you asked this Battle-Captain to butcher his own race.'

'I asked a Battle-Captain to obey an order.'

'I will not do it,' the man said simply.

'Then I will have someone else do it, and you of course . . .'

The Culai never even saw the spiked ball of the mace which exploded against the side of his head, crushing the large skull. The force of the blow should have sent the creature reeling, but he remained standing, an expression of surprise etched on to his long face. The Battle-Captain brought his weapon around in a tight arc ready to strike again when the Culai merely toppled over. The Battle-Captain knelt beside the body and cleaned the spiked ball in the Culai's robes and then went to stand against the low wall that surrounded the flat roof, leaning both fists on the sun-warmed stone, his head bent, breathing deeply. When he finally looked up, he allowed his gaze to wander out over the City, past the carefully planned and flawlessly executed designs for houses, palaces and theatres of the Culai to the more random, tumbled, jumbled human constructions. Scattered through the City buildings were a score of temples, each inhabited by its own god. Beyond the City, the intense blue of the ocean was shimmering like molten metal in the morning light, the harbours bright with the sails of a hundred ships from half as many places, with the scarlet sails of the Were-Folk predominating. At this hour of morning, the odours of cooking were beginning to waft up the hill which held the majority of the Culai dwellings and the Battle-Captain breathed deeply, savouring the rich smells, mentally identifying the peoples and races by their food. It was all so peaceful, so natural.

And then the Battle-Captain turned and looked again at the body of the Culai, his head now completely swathed in a thick, glutinous pool of blood, and knew that with this simple act he had changed the face of the world. This was the first of the Culai folk to die by the hand of a human and the Man's name was Buiva.

A lesser man would have turned and run then, fled the City, taken ship to another place and prayed that he would not be found. But Buiva was not as other men. He retrieved the paper he had so contemptuously ground underfoot and returned to his barracks. There he had called his men together and calmly read out their orders to them, and then quelling the uproar that followed; he had equally calmly and with no expression told them how he had killed the Culai. The stunned silence lasted only long enough for someone to draw his breath and begin to cheer. And without exception the Storm Warriors defected from their Culai paymasters to the leadership of Buiva.

Before the day was out, the entire City knew of the Culai plan and the death of one of the self-styled First Race and Buiva's name. He was hailed as a hero, the saviour of Humankind, and by nightfall the leaders of the various races and peoples and factions had come to him in the Storm Warriors' fort, pledging their oath and support.

And so the man found himself trapped in the position as the leader of all Humankind.

The war with the Culai was long and bloody, with the technology of the First Race ranged against the numbers and determination of the human folk, but that is another tale in itself. It was principally fought in and around the streets of the City and many of the battles were planned and commanded by Buiva himself; his name became the war-cry of the humans, and soon the Culai grew to loathe the buzzing of 'BUIVA-BUIVA-BUIVA' as it came up from the City to their stark, white-walled houses.

The tide of war had swung in favour of the humankind when

their commander died, not by treachery and not by violence. He died simply and peacefully in his sleep on the eve of what everyone, both human and Culai, knew would be a decisive battle. News of his death rippled through the human army like wind across a field of wheat, but paradoxically, instead of disheartening them, it only served to urge the people on to greater efforts, and before the battle all of those present – and they numbered many, many thousands – bowed their heads and prayed for Buiva to aid and guide them.

And Faith lends substance.

And towards noon, when the battle seemed to be going against the human folk, a single warrior dropped on the battelfield, a thin sliver of metal buried in his chest, and called aloud for his old commander . . .

And Buiva returned.

In the midst of battle, a creature of fire and bronze, of death and destruction – of W A R – stalked, rallying the human kind, striking terror into the Culai. A new god had been born . . .

'So my advice to you is to be careful, Bard,' Buiva finished with a smile. 'I understand your name is already honoured and revered by the followers of the Old Faith. Be careful, lest you too might one day join the Pantheon's hallowed ranks. We have not had a new god for many, many years.'

Paedur shivered and pulled his cloak tighter around his shoulders. 'I prefer being a man,' he said sincerely.

'Bard, you ceased to be a man a long time ago,' Buiva said drily.

'Men kill for reasons, for coin or honour, for duty or pleasure. The Master killed for all these reasons, but often he killed simply because it was necessary.'

*Tien tZo*

They came into the city separately, using two different gates on successive days. The Weapon Master maintained his role as a warrior, merely adding some dirt to his clothing and allowing a rough growth of beard to cover the scars on his face and add to his disguise. Tien tZo adopted the loose, grey, ragged robes of an Andam, a holy man afflicted by the disease that touched many of the followers of the strange sect. Their temple was deep in the heart of the Southern Marshes and eight out of ten that went to study this early and primitive version of the Old Faith came back afflicted by the terrifying disease which wasted the flesh and drew the skin so taut on the bones that it eventually cracked and split, leaving long, open sores and weeping scars.

The Master had no problems entering the city: mercenary soldiers were arriving from all across the Nations, news of the coming conflict having spread like a summer fire, and he wandered in through the open gates surrounded by a score of his ill-assorted brothers in the mercenary trade.

Tien tZo, however, did not find entrance to Karfondal so easy. It was market day when he arrived and although it lacked some time to sunrise already a long line of farmers and merchants was filling the great road that led up to the city walls. The Shemmat hung back from the end of the line, his long robes of filthy grey cotton wrapped around him, completely obscuring his body and face, leaving only one eye showing. There was a simple wooden begging bowl in his right hand and his cloth-wrapped left clutched a long metal-shod walking pole.

A coin clinked into his bowl.

'Blessings on you,' he murmured, pitching his voice low, turning stiffly to look at his benefactor, and finding himself looking up at a man wearing the loose grey robes of the Andam. For a moment he thought he had been discovered and his grip tightened on the walking pole, preparing to bring it around in a crushing blow if the man seemed about to betray him.

'We must support our own,' the taller, older man said wearily. 'Give when we have a little to give.'

Tien bowed. 'Just so. And what is life, but giving of oneself to the creator?'

The Andam stopped, seemingly surprised, although like Tien most of his head was hidden within a deep hood and it was difficult to gauge his reactions. 'Yes,' he said finally, 'that is good. A refreshing viewpoint. Good. Yours?' he asked, gasping slightly, as if the effort of speaking exhausted him.

Tien shook his head. 'I have wandered far, brother, and spent many years in the Land of the Sun and have absorbed much of their culture. The saying is theirs, not mine.'

'But it holds true nonetheless,' the Andam priest said. He nodded towards the city. 'You are going there?'

Tien nodded.

'Permit me to walk awhile with you?'

'I would be honoured.'

'The honour is in the giving,' the older man said, and Tien could almost imagine the smile.

'There is also honour in a gracious receipt,' he said.

The two grey-robed men walked up past the line of carts and wagons, the stamping horses and the patient horned bothe with their cartloads of grains and fruit for the market. Those carrying slaughtered blood-meat were black with flies and the air around them fetid with the smells of offal and the metallic odour of blood.

The villagers and merchants signed themselves as the two figures walked slowly past. The Andam were both respected and feared, and in parts of the Nations they were considered almost as Duaite. The Andam belief in a single God or Being of creation ruling all things rather than in the Pantheon found little favour and much distrust with the common people, even though both the Andam and the Old Faith worshipped the One.

'Tell me about the Land of the Sun,' the older man said suddenly as they began to climb the long, wide road that led up to the city gates.

Tien, who had been frantically trying to remember what he

knew of the Andam and their beliefs, groaned inwardly. Although he was directly descended from the Shemmatae who had been defeated on the Sand Plain and knew of their lore and culture, he had never visited the Land of the Sun and his knowledge of it was very sketchy and composed mostly of hearsay and travellers' tales.

He coughed and drew the cloth even tighter across his mouth, hoping that at least a part of what he said would be muffled. 'It is a land of beauty, rich in history and pomp, but poor in good land and forests. Their Gods are those of the Old Faith,' he said, hurrying on to safer ground, 'but with some additions: local deities who have assumed a rank all their own in the eastern lands, and naturally they are the ones most frequently called upon.'

'Of course.' The Andam walked on in silence for a few steps and then, without turning, he said, 'And do our brothers hold much influence in the Land of the Sun?'

It was the question he had been waiting for, fearing. They were now too close to the gates for Tien to turn and run, and so he was forced to brazen it out. 'I worked mainly in the highlands to the north of the country and I can honestly say I saw none of our brothers there.'

The older man nodded, his breath coming in a long hissing sigh. 'Ah, I had heard it was not going well there. Perhaps I should go.'

'The journey is long and the way is hard.'

'The One will protect,' the Andam said quickly, ritually, almost in the form of a benediction.

'The One will protect,' Tien repeated.

They walked on in silence, the shadow of the gate looming over them. Tien could see the guards stopping and checking each cart, and not a quick, cursory glance either, which would have been usual, but a thorough and detailed search by two men of the Gate Squadron while what looked like at least a decade stood guard beyond them. 'There are more guards than usual,' he said slowly.

'It is the trouble in the west,' the Andam said quickly, glancing at him, his face barely visible behind the tattered grey cowl.

'Will they let us through?' Tien wondered aloud.

'They will not stop us,' the priest said, and then he corrected himself. 'Well, they will not stop me, but I am known to them.'

He paused and then stated very softly, his voice so low that Tien was unsure at first if he had heard the man correctly. 'You are not of the Brotherhood.'

Tien didn't have many alternatives, and of the few he had none of them seemed particularly attractive. 'What are you going to do?' he asked, determined that if the priest betrayed him, at least he would die first.

'My actions are, I would imagine, determined by yours. Why have you assumed the guise of an Andam to enter the city?'

'I intend to kill Salier and the Hierophant,' the Shemmat said simply, surprising himself with his answer.

The Andam nodded. 'And your companion?'

'What companion?'

'You have a companion. Who does he intend to kill?'

'Geillard and Fodla.' Again, the answer was completely involuntary.

'You are agents of the Prince Kutor?'

Tien nodded.

'And what faith does he profess now?' the Andam asked, his voice silk and ice.

'The Old Faith!' Tien gasped against his will, his eyes locked on the gate and its guards now barely steps away.

'And you are?'

'Tien tZo, slave-companion of Owen, the Weapon Master.' Tien was shivering now; he could feel the icy sweat trickle down the back of his neck beneath his robes. He knew what the Andam priest was doing, and yet there was no way he could fight it.

'I have heard of this Weapon Master,' the priest said softly, his voice becoming distant. 'He is of the Iron Band of Kloor, is he not?'

'He was, but no longer.'

The Andam looked at him and the early morning light shafting over the city walls illuminated the interior of the priest's cowl. Two metal-grey eyes burned in a face that was little more than raw meat, a mass of blood and scar tissue. 'I have never heard of a man leaving the Band of Kloor,' the Andam said slowly, his teeth surprisingly white and strong behind bloodied lips.

'He did!' Tien snapped involuntarily.

'Oh, I believe you,' the priest said. 'I was merely curious as to how he achieved the feat.'

'There was a bard.'

'A bard!' The Andam stopped and reached out, his cloth-wrapped fingers tightening around Tien's forearm. 'A bard with a single hand and a hook in place of his left?'

'The same.'

The Andam hissed softly. 'And all this is his doing?'

'He started it.'

'And where is he now?'

Tien shrugged. 'No-one knows. He has not been seen in a long time.' Realising the Andam was no longer exerting his insidious control over him, Tien managed to ask. 'You know of him?'

'I know the bard. All the followers of the Faith know the bard.' He reached out and took Tien's arm again, but gently this time. 'Come, let us enter this city together. You have work to do.'

Geillard XII, Emperor of the Seven Nations and the Island Kingdoms was sitting beneath the carefully pruned and shaped branches of one of the oldest trees in the palace, his eyes blank, the scrolls in his hands lying unopened and unread. There was no reason to read them; he knew their contents by heart, for they were his father's diaries.

Geillard XI, his father, should never have been a ruler. He was a scholar and a historian, a minor magician, a necromancer of some power, a mediocre alchemist, superb herbalist and healer, but he was not a leader. He had neither a ruler's temperament nor patience, and was easily led and swayed by his advisers. They, in effect, had ruled the court, corrupting it, weakening it, ultimately destroying it. And that was one of the reasons why when Geillard XII, the present ruler, had come to power, he had had them all slain in a single bloody night; he had seen how they had destroyed his father by allowing, even encouraging, him to indulge himself.

Geillard XI had one other failing, which in other men, other rulers, was dismissed as a mere right of office but in the Emperor's case became something much more. His appetite for women was extraordinary and as Emperor of the Seven Nations he was able to indulge his appetites. Before his legitimate son had come to power, there were at a conservative estimate at least forty children who could claim Geillard XI as their father, and in other courts and other times, they would have been brought to court and given a minor title and some land – and watched. But the old man had always ignored them and if they or their mothers became difficult or demanding, they were wont to disappear. When Geillard XII came to power, one of his first acts was to instruct his spies to seek out the remaining bastard sons of his father and slay them. More than thirty young men met mysterious and curious deaths. Some survived, naturally, and one of those was Kutor, self-styled Prince, the Renegade.

A shadow fell across him, breaking into his reverie.

Salier bowed stiffly. 'My lord, I did not mean to startle you.'

'I was dreaming,' the tall, gaunt man said, his dark eyes fixing on the darting colours of the fish in the extravagantly ornamental pond.

Salier's eyes glided across the rolled diary parchments and he concealed a smile. 'The bastard again?'

Geillard nodded. 'I have begun to fear him,' he confessed. 'He is beginning to haunt my dreams.'

'Then it is time to act. Do you wish me to arrange his death?' Salier asked smoothly.

'Is it possible?' the Emperor asked without much enthusiasm.

'Everything is possible.'

For a long time Geillard didn't react and his attention remained riveted on the darting splashes of colour in the pond. Salier was beginning to think he hadn't heard the question and was about to repeat it, when the Emperor suddenly nodded. 'It is necessary. He has become a positive danger. His progress across the Nations has been too swift. Soon people will begin to think that the Gods are on his side.'

'I have already heard that,' Salier lied.

'Well then, arrange his death, but make it look like an accident or the result of his own stupidity if possible. We don't need a martyr with a cult growing up around the name.'

Salier bowed.

'Don't use any of our own men. Hire mercenaries from the taverns. I've read the reports that hundreds are flocking in for the coming battle.'

'Oh, there are mercenaries aplenty in town. We should have no difficulty finding a man to suit our needs.'

*

The atmosphere in the tavern was thick with smoke and sweat, and something else – the tart odour of blood on the air. The tavern was called The Barracks and in the capital it was the unofficial hiring station for the mercenary troops that periodically wandered through the city. Men looking for a hired sword, for defence or attack, sought them out at The Barracks. It was run by a man whose name had once been legendary through the Nations, Thome the Iron Man. Age had tarnished the iron man's image somewhat, but even now, at eighty and more summers – an unheard of age for a mercenary – he was still tall and straight, his eyes sharp and knowing, and he still commanded much of the respect that he had enjoyed in his youth.

Thome leaned against the polished wooden bar, idly watched the two knife fighters in the sunken pit in the centre of the room. They were competent fighters, both using two knives, but their footwork was wrong and their balance off. Both had shallow cuts across their chests and arms and he was wagering that the taller of the two, a blond-haired youngster from Thusal or thereabouts, would tire first. His opponent, although a smaller, darker man of indeterminate origin, had conserved his energy and the cut to his chest had stopped bleeding remarkably quickly, indicating some formal body training or perhaps a minor spell. It was enough, though, to give him the advantage, and this time it would probably save his life.

The old warrior allowed his gaze to wander across the motley mixture in the tavern. Most he knew – the professional mercenary trade was a small and select one – but there were one or two newcomers, noticeable by their too bright eyes and nervous swagger. One of them was attempting to buy what he obviously thought was one of the tavern women for the night. Thome suppressed a grin as the tall, buxom woman almost casually struck the man in the groin with her mug of rofion. The blow doubled him up, smashing his face into the table, and then there was a knife at his throat and Thome saw the woman's lips move. He knew the woman and could guess what she was promising the man if he so much as came near her again. But the newcomer had learned a valuable lesson – neither judge quickly nor by appearance. And he had also been painfully reminded that the mercenary trade was staffed by as many female warriors as male.

The door opened and Thome, who was turning away from the bar, glanced up and then stopped. The old man had worn a weapon since the time he could walk; he was a warrior and the son of a warrior, and he could trace an unbroken lineage of freelance soldiers back through seven generations. And if there was one thing he knew, it was a warrior, a professional soldier. It showed in the way he stood, the way he moved, the way he wore his weapons, in the way his eyes took in the room, noting the exits first, and then fixing the principal groups and their leaders in his mind, and then the tavern guards.

Thome was already setting up two jugs of rofion when the man approached the bar. Without a word he pushed one across. The stranger looked at the grey-haired man and then silently nodded his thanks before taking it. Thome lifted the second jar and both men toasted one another.

'Life!'

'Death!'

It was the drinking toast of the mercenary.

'You are Thome.' It was more a statement than a question. 'I understand you could find employment for a man of skill.'

'There is always work for a skilled man. But the level of skill is important.'

'I have the skill.'

Thome nodded non-committally. 'And you are?'

'I am Owen, the Weapon Master.'

'The Defender of Car'an'tual?' Thome asked, keeping his expression neutral.

'The same.'

'There was a man in here recently claiming to be Owen, the Weapon Master, the same Defender.'

'And?'

'He was killed in the ring.'

'Hardly likely if he were the real Owen.'

'Accidents happen,' Thome remarked with a grin. He knew beyond any shadow of a doubt but that this was indeed the real Owen, the Weapon Master. When he looked at him, Thome saw himself as he must have looked when he was a younger man, a lifetime – ten lifetimes – ago. He wondered if his eyes had looked so tired then, so weary.

'You wish to test me in the ring?' Owen asked, finishing the last of the drink.

'I must be certain.'

'I understand.'

'And if you are indeed the Weapon Master, then there is employment, lucrative employment, when you have done.'

'Announce it then,' Owen said softly. He had been expecting the test and knew it was the only way Thome would believe him. He also knew that Thome supplied the mercenary instructors to the Imperial army and had the monopoly for supplying professionals on demand; he usually guaranteed his choice, and took his cut from both the employer and the employee.

In the ring, as Thome had predicted, the blond young man was being dragged out by two of his friends. He wasn't dead, not yet anyway.

'A trial!' Thome suddenly shouted, his deep, resonant voice booming throughout the tavern and instantly silencing it. 'This stranger challenges all comers.'

There was a quick murmur of excitement and a general movement towards the bar, and Owen suddenly found himself being scrutinised by a hundred and more iron-hard, ice-cold and pitiless eyes. Some recognised him for what he was, reading the same signs Thome had, and they turned away, but there were still some takers. 'What's the wager?' someone shouted.

'The Imperials are looking for a man, high risk, high pay. The winner will be that man.'

There was another surge towards the bar and Thome suddenly found himself facing a score of knife hilts. Closing his eyes he stretched out his right hand, running his calloused fingertips along the handles, and suddenly closing around one. The warrior whooped with pleasure and spun around to face Owen.

'I am Brega of the Isles and you are going to die!'

'It will take more than your wind to kill me,' Owen said quietly. 'Your weapons?' he asked.

'Knives,' the man announced gleefully. He was taller than Owen and broad, his skin dark and weathered, his eyes startlingly blue against the colour of his face. He turned away and headed towards the steps that led down into the ring, already pulling off his cloak and unbuckling his sword belt.

There was a general move away from the bar towards the ring and someone began shouting odds, and coin and script were produced and exchanged.

Owen turned back to Thome and pulled off his cloak and tossed it across the bar. 'Will you take care of these for me?' He unbuckled his shoulder straps and shrugged off his buckler, and passed the two matched fighting swords across the bar. He pulled a pair of gauntlets from his belt and pulled them on, and then stooped and pulled a knife from his right boot.

'May I?' Thome asked, nodding at the knife. Owen flipped it and silently passed it hilt first to him. The old mercenary lifted the knife, noting the balance, tilting it, allowing the light to run along the blade. The blade was not long but it was thick and broad, pointed and double-edged; the hilt had obviously been wrapped in soft resin, which had now assumed the shape of Owen's hand. Thome placed the weapon down on Owen's cloak. 'A fine weapon.'

Owen picked the knife up, rubbing the blade against his sleeve, polishing the blade to mirror brightness. 'Do you want this swift or slow?' he asked.

'Brega is a good fighter, that choice may not be yours to make.'

Brega of the Isles stood in the centre of the ring, confidently awaiting the stranger. He was wearing a hauberk of large-link mail over a cotton shirt, which left his muscular arms bare. He wore two studded wrist-bands and he was casually twirling two broad-bladed Chopt knives when Owen climbed down into the ring.

'Are you ready to die?' he asked, noting Owen's single knife, the leather jerkin and the gloves. He would have to assume the jerkin would turn all but the most forceful of blows, but the single weapon puzzled him. Most professionals fought with two knives – one to parry, one to thrust.

'No man is ever ready to die,' Owen said softly, watching the man move and the ease and dexterity with which he manipulated the heavy, ungainly knives. He might indeed be a dangerous opponent.

Brega went into a crouch, his right arm close to his body, his left outstretched, his wrist pointing down, the knife angled up.

Owen remained still, only his eyes moving.

Brega began moving the knife in his left hand to and fro, allowing it to reflect the light, the movement designed to catch and hold his opponent's attention, and then he began to spin the blade, turning it on his fingers with extraordinary skill until it was spinning at high speed. And then he suddenly thrust with his right hand!

The blow should have taken Owen low in the stomach, the angle of the knife would have brought it up, the heavy Chopt blade easily sundering through the leather jerkin, slashing across muscle and ribs, disemboweling him. But the knife never reached its destination.

Owen's gloved hand closed on to the broad spine of the blade just above the hilt, turning it – and Brega's arm with it. The knife in his right hand moved, slashing the exposed flesh, opening the flesh, sundering the veins along the full length of the arm. The blood loss was massive and immediate and dropped the warrior to his knees with the shock. Reaction set in and he began to vomit. Owen pushed the man away from him, shaking his head in disgust. He wiped the knife on his sleeve and slid it back into the sheath sewn inside his boot. 'Tend to his arm before he bleeds to death,' he said to no-one in particular and climbed up out of the pit and moved back to the bar. 'You mentioned something about a job,' he said to Thome.

## 19    *The Torc Allta*

He had enemies aplenty, and they were not always of humankind.
*Tales of the Bard*

Dawn came suddenly to the Mire and brought with it the unmistakable sounds of pursuit. The sudden crashing, although muted by the fog, brought Buiva and the bard to their feet, eyes and ears alert.

Paedur hopped up on to the tumbled stones of the wall and tilted his head to one side listening, sorting through the sounds. 'Ten men,' he said confidently, 'armed and wearing mail, and one other, older and wheezing.'

'How close?' Buiva asked, turning to awaken the woman warrior, but finding her wide-eyed and listening.

Paedur shook his head. 'I'm not sure. The boggy ground and this cursed fog distorts all sound. But close, else we would not have heard them.'

Paedur dropped down off the wall. 'I'm just wondering how they can follow our trail through this muck,' he said.

Buiva strode over and hauled Churon up. 'On your feet. We're moving.' He glanced at the bard as the sounds shifted, becoming more distinct. 'Well, they have our general direction, but either they have a very good tracker or else they're using sorcery.'

Paedur looked up sharply. 'But I thought few, if any, sorcerers could work here in the Mire, so close to the Planes of Existence, the Shadowland and the Silent Wood. If it is sorcery, it means a very powerful sorcerer indeed.'

Buiva nodded. He roughly spun Churon around and pulled a length of braided cord from his belt. Gripping the Onelord's hands above the wrists he began to tie them up, lacing the cord through the fingers, fashioning a noose around the thumbs. When he pulled the cord tight, Churon's hands were securely locked together, the fingers meshed. Spinning Churon around again, his gauntleted hands tightened into the soft flesh of his

202

cheeks, just below the jaw joint. 'Tell me, what sorcerer is powerful enough to work in the Mire?'

The Onelord's eyes remained mocking, and even when the god increased the pressure until the black skin turned purple and he felt the bones beginning to grate together, there was no change in Churon's defiant expression.

'Perhaps if we remove his eyes he'll talk,' Katani suggested with a pleasant smile.

Paedur strode cross the clearing. 'Look, we have no time for this.' He brought his hook up and rested it on the bridge of Churon's nose and then slowly allowed it to fall, the razor-cool metal leaving a burning trail down the Onelord's face and throat. The bard continued to move his hook downwards, until he stopped just below the man's midriff. His flat, dark eyes looked into Churon's, and for the first time in many years, the Onelord felt something like fear touch him with a chill. 'You, I think, prided yourself upon your manhood and your ability to sire children in the world of Men. Now, I know you intend to return to the Planes of Existence, and if you intend to keep your manhood you will tell the god what he wants to know.' His voice remained low and without inflection, but the Onelord had absolutely no doubt but that he meant it.

'The only magician working in the Mire at the moment is Praetens,' he said quickly.

'The Susuru warlock?' Paedur asked.

The Onelord nodded.

Paedur placed his hand in the centre of Churon's chest, and pushed. The man sat down with a thump. 'Stay there,' he commanded. He inclined his head and Buiva and Katani moved away with him, and the three stood talking quietly together, watching the man on the ground.

'I think I should stay behind and try to kill this Susuru warlock,' Paedur said quietly.

'If he isn't stopped, he will dog us every step of the way to the Silent Wood and there is no telling what his sorceries or powers are like, but he must be powerful indeed if he is able to operate within the Mire.'

'The Susuru are a dangerous race, bard,' Buiva said quietly, 'and I must say I've never heard of one being killed by any means other than sorcery.'

'I have slain one,' Paedur said.

'So what are you suggesting?' Buiva asked.

'You and Katani go ahead with the prisoner; I'll stay here and deal with some of the pursuers and the Susuru if possible.'

'And then?'

'I'll catch up with you.'

'One man against ten men and a Susuru?' Katani asked in disbelief.

'It's been a long time since I was a man,' Paedur said mockingly, glancing sidelong at the god.

The first two warriors cautiously approached the tumbled ruin of stones, nostrils flaring. There was beast blood in them and their features were the flat, broad, snouted masks of boars. Two tusks protruded up from their lower lips and these had been decorated in a twisting, curling caste-mark.

'Humankind,' the larger creature said, snouted nostrils wrinkling, 'and others, non-human, but not were-folk.'

'Two bodies,' his companion grunted, 'no, three, four?' he asked, looking confused.

The larger creature, wearing a captain's insignia on his helmet, pointed with his short-hafted jabbing spear. 'The Onelord here, another humankind here beside him, someone from the Silent Wood by the smell of death about them.' He raised his head, eyes and nostrils wide. 'There was another creature and something else, something unhuman here.' He turned, his spear pointing – and the bard's flashing hook tore into the soft flesh beneath his ear and ripped, neatly severing his throat.

The second creature turned at the rattling, gurgling sound, and a spear took him through the mouth, pinning him to the trunk of a twisted, blighted tree. He died without a sound.

Shortly afterwards a small group of the boar-creatures approached the ruins, led by a small, frail-seeming white-haired man. Even on the tainted air of the Mire they smelt the metallic odours of blood and death. They stopped in sight of the ruins, and even the bravest of the Torc Allta – the Boar Folk – felt something like fear touch them when they saw the crucified bodies of the two scouts on the walls.

'How many within the walls?' the small man demanded of the huge were-creature towering above him.

'I cannot tell, master. The blood overpowers all else. I cannot detect anyone, although I know it would have taken many men to do this.'

The old man frowned. The Torc Allta were truly terrifying creatures, bloody, merciless warriors without compassion and with one other useful attribute – they ate their victims, even if those victims were of the Torc Allta. He suddenly shivered, conscious only of the cold, the damp and interminable fatigue. This body was always tired, but when he had been forced to take it, he hadn't much choice at the time. He consoled himself with the thought that soon, soon he would be able to choose a body more suited to his station.

'Master?' the huge Torc Allta asked.

'Send two warriors in and then two more in directly behind them. I can feel nothing there, but just in case.'

The warrior nodded and silently pointed his spear at the two nearest creatures, then waved it towards the ruins. Without hesitation, they moved off towards it. The captain then pointed to a second pair and repeated the gesture, and again they responded without hesitation.

'Those we hunt,' the Torc Allta asked, 'they are from the Race of Man?'

'Does it matter?' the old man asked, tired, faded eyes looking at the warrior.

The creature shrugged, snout wrinkling. 'I am a connoisseur of flesh,' he said slowly, 'and much of the enjoyment is in the anticipation of the feast.'

'You are an animal,' the old man smiled.

'I am Torc Allta,' the warrior said proudly.

Shaking his head, the old man turned back to watch the four armoured figures moving in towards the tumbled ruins. 'We hunt three,' he said slowly. 'From the descriptions of those at the monastery and my own little magics, one is from the Silent Wood, another is a god and the third, the third is neither man nor beast, neither living nor dead, but something else, something else.' He glanced back over his shoulder at the were-creature. 'The Dead and the God are yours, the other is mine – briefly – until I determine what it is, and then its flesh is yours.'

Satisfied, the Torc Allta nodded, swallowing saliva. 'Dead flesh is interesting, spicy, savoury, but I have never tasted the flesh of a god.' He nodded. 'I look forward to the feast.' His head came up sharply and the short-red-bristled hairs on the backs of his hands rose.

'What is it?' the old man demanded.

'Blood,' the Torc Allta said simply. 'There has been a killing.'

Katani's sword whispered from its scabbard as the two beast-creatures rose in front of her; behind her she heard the rattle of Buiva's mace and she risked a quick glance over her shoulder to find two more of the creatures.

'Torc Allta,' she hissed.

Buiva nodded and sighed, glancing longingly at the black line of the River Naman which separated the Mire from the Silent Wood. He had wanted to cross and wait for the bard on the far side, but Katani had been insistent, and so they had sent away the boatman empty-handed and had camped on the filthy, bloody banks of the River of Death waiting for Paedur.

Behind them Churon began to laugh. 'You are mine now. They are the Torc Allta. I will have them eat your flesh.' The Onelord struggled uselessly against the chains that Buiva had used to bind him to a shattered remnant of a temple column that they had found on the rough beach.

'Where is the bard?' Katani hissed.

The god shook his head. 'It is not a good sign.' He stopped as the two creatures before him separated and a small white-haired man stepped out. He ran a speckled, trembling hand through the thinning wiry strands of his hair and smiled on them both. 'So we have finally found you.' He looked from the man to the woman. 'I recognise the armour of course, Katan.' A smile wrinkled his face. 'I thought they had all been slain on the Sand Plain.'

'They were,' Katani hissed venomously.

'And not a moment too soon,' the old man said simply. 'It should have been done much sooner, would have been if Churon had listened to my advice.' His eyes flickered in the Onelord's direction. 'But, of course, he could never listen to advice.'

'Who are you?' Katani whispered. 'I never saw you at court.' She was aware of the Torc Allta moving in.

'Oh, you saw me,' the old man smiled, 'but not in this corporeal form.'

'He is Praetens, the Susuru,' Buiva said quietly.

The old man bowed. 'And you are Buiva, God of War of the Pantheon of the Old Faith.' He looked back to Katani. 'At the precise moment when my body was destroyed during the Battle of the Sand Plain, my essence soared free and lighted upon the nearest weakest essence.' His shoulders moved and his hands swept down his body in a quick, almost shy movement. 'Unfortunately, this was what I ended up with.' And then he laughed, the sound thin and cackling. Wiping tears from his eyes, he continued. 'This body once belonged to the slopman, the servant who cleared the foulness and offal from the camp latrines. And now even the mighty Churon bows his head to it.'

'I bow to the mind, not the body,' Churon said tightly.

'See how he must always have the last word,' Praetens said, shaking his head. 'But enough of this.' He stretched out a wrinkled hand. 'You must surrender to us, lay down your weapons and give us Churon. There has been enough killing this day.'

'I thought there would be more of you,' Buiva said with a sly smile. 'The Torc Allta usually travel in groups, do they not, and someone of your station would not travel these dangerous lands so lightly guarded.'

'I am too weary to decide whether you are mocking me or attempting to rouse my anger. But I warn you that it is not wise to raise me to anger. Even you, a god, would not stand against me.'

'I think if your magic was safe to use you would have used it. But this is the Mire and the laws of Nature and Magic are altered here. Who knows, perhaps you are, like us, bereft of much of your powers and stand before us now as nothing more than an old man.'

Praetens turned away. 'Take them, their flesh is yours.'

'WAIT!'

The voice rang out across the beach, strong enough to set small stones rattling and rippling the surface of the water. A figure stepped on to a tall flattened boulder at the far end of the beach, a tall, thin figure wrapped in a black furred cloak. The figure pointed with a gleaming sickle-hook that took the place of his left hand and again the incredibly powerful voice boomed down the beach.

'Are the Torc Allta ordered to their destruction so easily? Are the fabled were-creatures nothing more than cuine to be slaughtered? You followed the old man today and you lost six of your brothers, truly lost them now, for their flesh has been taken by the scavengers of the Mire and not by their brothers as is their right. He sends you now against a warrior of the Katan, the same warriors whom even the Onelord surrounded himself with, and Buiva, the God of War, a slayer of Nations. What hope have you against them?' The figure dropped to the pebbles and crunched up the beach to stop before Praetens. 'And he sends you against me,' he added very softly.

'And who are you?' the magician asked, attempting to sound defiant but his aged voice trembled and betrayed him.

'I am Paedur, the bard.' From beneath his cloak he pulled a large leaf that had been tied into a makeshift pouch with vine. Slicing through the vine with his hook he dropped the leaf on the ground, where it spilled twelve bloody tusks, all worked with the individual caste-marks of the Torc Allta. 'I killed your brothers today,' he said simply, looking past Praetens to the huge were-creature.

'He lies!' Praetens snapped.

'I do not lie.'

'I believe him,' the Torc Allta said. He looked at the sharp-faced man with the curious hook, then at his two companions and came to a decision. 'We will not fight this day.'

'I order you!' Praetens shouted.

'Six of the Torc Allta were taken from us today because of your orders and they were left without the proper rites because of your orders. I will take no further orders from you this day.' He jerked his short spear at the trio. 'I look at these and I see nothing but destruction. Leave them, master, there will be other times, other places.' The Torc Allta nodded to the two creatures standing before Katani and they stepped back and circled around until they were standing behind their leader and the magician. The huge creature moved up beside Praetens and looked at each of the three faces in turn. 'I will remember you,' he said looking at Katani and Buiva, and then he turned to the bard. 'Your flesh is mine.'

Paedur bowed slightly. 'We will meet again.'

The leader of the Torc Allta stooped carefully, his eyes never leaving the bard's face, and he gathered up the twelve caste tusks from the six slain warriors and dropped them into a pouch on his belt.

'You cannot leave me!' Churon suddenly shouted, realising that they were not going to fight for him.

'You are obviously not worth risking destruction for,' Paedur said, turning away from the Torc Allta and walking down to the chained warrior.

'I once was.'

'That was a long time ago and in a different place.' Paedur turned and watched the Torc Allta shoulder their spears and lumber away, moving almost silently for all their great size and apparent clumsiness. Praetens lingered a moment longer, his eyes on the bard's face, and then he too turned away and hurried inelegantly after the were-creatures.

'Perhaps it would have been better if you had given me to them,' Churon remarked calmly, watching the figures disappear back into the undergrowth.

'We haven't come all this way just to give you back at the last moment,' Katani said, sliding home her sword and smiling with genuine good humour at the bard. 'We thought you were dead.'

'He only killed six of them,' Buiva remarked with a smile. 'Not enough to cause Paedur here too much concern.'

'Their own fear and expectations killed them,' Paedur said. 'They were expecting an army, they were looking for an army, and couldn't cope with the idea of a single killer. The hardest part was removing their tusks,' he added with a rare smile.

'They will come back for you,' Churon said maliciously, 'and I hope I'm there to see it.'

Buiva nodded in agreement. 'They will hunt you, and in force now that they know your capabilities, and you will have to kill them and keep killing them, or be killed. They make bad enemies.'

Paedur ran his fingers through his fine hair. 'I know. I am a bard, remember. I know the legends of the Torc Allta.' He squatted down beside Churon and slipped his hook in under the chains, testing them. He glanced up at the god. 'How long have we before the boatman arrives?'

'He only travels during the twilight hours, before sunrise and after sunset.'

'We have some time then.' He picked up a handful of rough pebbles and tossed them into the blood-black water. 'Listen to me then, and I will tell you of the Torc Allta, the Boar-Folk . . .

In the last days of the Culai before the war with the Humankind, the First Race experimented with the unholy mingling of beast and men, using their magics to delve deep into the bodies of both men and beasts, changing and altering that which differentiates men and beasts, making them unique, and in this way they fashioned the were-folk, that unhappy mingling of beast and man. Of course, there had been creatures that were more beast than man, the true Creatures of the Were, but these were the creations of the gods, and mainly occupied other Planes of Existence to Man.

In the beginning these new were-creatures were merely curiosities, to be looked upon and wondered at and admired, and perhaps that was what caused their downfall, for to possess one of the were-folk became fashionable amongst the Culai, and so their breeding became something of a matter of course rather than a scientific rarity. Soon they became pets and then later, servants, and then of course it became apparent that certain were-creatures, although predominantly human, possessed to a greater degree the attributes of their beast blood, and these talents were seized upon and enhanced, some becoming common labourers, miners, divers and, of course, warriors. The Torc Allta were of the warrior class. Their antecedents were wild boars and their descendants possessed all the savagery of their distant forebears.

And then of course it was discovered that the were-creatures could breed and that their offspring carried tainted were-blood. But the were-folk's breeding cycle was as that of their animal ancestors, and multiple births were commonplace and more than one litter in a season was not unknown. Suddenly, the creatures were no longer a novelty and very quickly became a threat as their numbers increased dramatically.

The Culai response was simple and effective. In their retreat in the City they worked an incredibly complex magic and one by one, race by race, they banished the were-folk from this plane to inhabit the other Planes of Existence, alongside the true Creatures of the Were. And to their credit they did attempt to suit the creatures to the plane.

And they sent the Torc Allta to one of the planes which borders the Mire, which is, I imagine, how they came to be here. Occasionally one appears in the World of Men, but it is usually considered to be a deformed member of the Chopt race.

Paedur finished.

'I will add a piece to your tale, if you will, bard,' Buiva said. Paedur bowed and the god continued. 'I was ... acquainted with the Culai and their elite soldiery, the Storm Warriors. I know they used the Torc Allta as trackers, for they possess one extraordinary attribute which astounded even the Culai who created them. They can track across the Planes of Existence, from one to another. Once they make themselves aware of a person's aura, they can track that aura and there is no way to elude them.'

'Then that is what the Torc Allta was doing when he was staring at you,' Katani said suddenly.

Churon laughed, the sound forced and harsh. 'He knows your aura, now. He will track you. There is no place for you to hide and when he finds you, he will consume your flesh. Bard, you are a dead man!'

Chance is the Demon's Law; with it one might change the world,
against it the Gods themselves are powerless . . .

*Pantheon of the Old Faith*

Libellius, the Lord of Death of the New Religion, differs almost
completely from the traditional image of Death personified in that
he is always depicted as a fat and jolly man, harvesting souls as
another man might harvest fruit . . .

*Balephrenon: the Gods of the New Religion*

Geillard XII, Emperor of the Seven Nations, stood in the top-
most room of the tallest tower of his palace and looked across
his city, out over the walls and into the far distance where the
low line of the mountains was barely visible behind a shifting,
writhing haze. But at this time of morning, the purple peaks
should have been crystal clear, so clear indeed that if he put a
glass to his eye he should have been able to see the snow-caps.

Salier, who was standing behind him, leaned forward and said,
'You see it?'

'A haze . . . a fog?'

'Fire,' the mage said, coming up to stand beside the Emperor.
'Kutor's army are burning the grain fields of Gallowan!'

'Why haven't they been stopped?' Geillard demanded.

'Fodla sent two legions against them yesterday, but there was
no battle. Reports are unclear, but it seems Kutor himself went
out to speak to the assembled Imperial forces, his voice projected
by means of a minor spell, and when he had finished more than
half of our legionaries joined his forces.'

'And the others?'

'Allowed to go free or fight as they wished. Most chose to go
free: some elected to return here; none fought.'

'And where are they now?'

'Some are on the road here.'

'Stop them!'

'My lord?'

The Emperor rounded on the mage. 'They must not reach the capital. Assign them to an outpost and contain them all in one garrison. If they reach here, the effect will be twofold: they'll spread the story like contagion and what will our troops do when they discover their grain ration has been destroyed?' Imperial troops were paid a portion of their wages in grain and salt.

'I bow to your wisdom,' Salier said softly.

'Patronise me and I'll have your head,' Geillard snapped icily. 'One of these days you'll go too far.'

Salier bowed slightly and took a step back. 'I will take care of the returning troops, majesty.' He paused and then said maliciously, 'There is the matter of Prince Kutor.'

'Never give him a title in my presence!' Geillard spat.

'I think I have the man to solve our problems,' Salier said slowly, watching the Emperor's expression. 'He comes from Thome, who recommends him highly.'

'I want to see him!'

'Surely that isn't necessary, majesty. I can deal with him.'

Geillard shook his head. 'No, I want to instruct him personally. My half-brother must suffer before he dies.'

'Perhaps it would be better if he did not see you. There could be talk later.'

'When he has completed his mission, you will have him slain of course.'

The magus bowed and backed from the tower room.

Tien tZo crouched on the broad rose-coloured steps of the Cathedral, still wrapped in his ragged Andam robes, his wooden bowl between his feet on the smooth stone before him. As was customary with the Andam, he did not beg for charity, merely thanked those who gave. However, because he was a priest of the most primitive form of the Old Faith begging on the steps of the Cathedral to the Gods of the New Religion, his bowl had remained empty thus far and all he had collected were curses and spittle.

He looked at the sky, gauging the time, wondering how long he would have to wait. But it was of little consequence; he was in no hurry.

The morning was warm and Tien tZo allowed his mind to drift, snatching a few moments of relaxation, though he was not totally unaware of the movement all around him. He calmed his mind and called upon his own gods and his forefathers, for the Shemmatae honoured their ancestors, worshipping them as minor deities. He called upon the figure of his father and when he could clearly see the man, then called up his grandfather, and then he worked back through his ancestors until he reached the first Tien tZo, the Destroyer of Cities, the Builder of Tombs. He concentrated upon the shadowy figure, building the image in his mind's eye. He always began with the hands; he knew of others who started with the feet or face, but he began with the hands. The first Tien tZo's hands were small, the fingers blunt, the palms and fingers calloused, the wrists thick. There was a ring on the little finger of his left hand, a small, simple band, bright against his weather-darkened flesh. When he was able to clearly see every detail of the ring on the finger, he knew he had achieved his goal – communion with his ancestor's shade. He framed the first question.

'I must kill this man.' He allowed an image of the Hierophant to form in his mind's eye.

'He is deserving of death?' His ancestor's voice was thin and high, not at all what he expected from the squat, bulky warrior-lord.

'He is.'

'Must he die publicly?'

'No. But it would be better if his death were seen not to be an accident and could be blamed on a rival faction within his own people.'

Tien tZo saw the feral smile that drifted across his ancestor's face. 'A ploy I used once.' There was a brief moment of waiting, and Tien knew the image in his mind was reading his memories and absorbing what little he knew of the Hierophant. 'There are guards,' the warlord said finally. 'Is your death called for?'

'I would prefer it otherwise.'

The mage grunted. 'It will not be easy.'

'Killing is easy.'

'Only dying is easy,' the shade said. 'Stealth, I think, is out of the question here; it is expected and must therefore be avoided. Approach the man directly, boldly.'

'I have assumed the guise of a religious group directly opposed to this man and his beliefs.'

'Have you a loyalty to this religion?'

214

'No!' Tien tZo said, surprised.

'Well then, the answer is simplicity itself.' The warlord's laughter echoed through Tien tZo's head. 'Defect. Convert to his faith. Surely that in itself would be enough of a coup for him to see you personally, would it not?'

Unconsciously, the man sitting on the steps of the Cathedral nodded, and broke contact with the memory of his infamous ancestor. The butt end of a spear poked at his cloth-wrapped legs.

'On yer way, beggar. These are the cathedral steps. We don't want them sullied by the likes of you.'

Tien tZo looked up, squinting against the glare of the sun, and found three of the Cathedral guard standing around him. Their surcoats were spotless and the sunlight burned off the white satin cloth. They were armed with blunted spears and clubs – bloodletting within the boundaries of the cathedral being expressly forbidden.

'That's no beggar,' one of the men suddenly said, 'it's Andam.'

The spear came around again and the broad copper head with its flattened tip touched Tien's chin, raising it up. The Shemmat saw their expressions change from dull contempt to open hatred.

'Andam,' the largest guard spat, 'befouling the very air we breath, soiling the steps of the cathedral . . .'

'Praying for forgiveness!' Tien said quickly, seeing the man's knuckles tighten around the staff. The warrior knew he could easily defend himself from these three, but that would mean killing one or possibly all three of them, and the last thing he wanted to do now was to attract attention. 'I was praying to the New Gods for forgiveness.'

The three guards looked at one another. 'What do you mean, "forgiveness"?' the largest, the spokesman, said threateningly.

'I have recognised the error of my ways. I wish to convert to the true way, the way of the New Religion.'

Their expressions changed to disbelief and distrust, but it was obvious that this was a decision beyond them.

'If you're lying, we'll kill you,' the leader threatened.

'I have sat here all morning listening to the voice within, waiting for you to come and take'me to enlightenment.'

Tien saw the look that passed between them – puzzlement,

mingled with a little amusement; they had finally reached the conclusion that he was mad. They herded him off the steps and down an adjoining side street. The alleyway was dark after the sunlight, but remarkably free of the alleyway smells that Tien had grown accustomed too – or perhaps he had just been frequenting the wrong sort of alleyways. He grinned, feeling the rush of exhilaration, suddenly realising that it was going to work. If he got out of this alive, he would sacrifice a whole bothe in his ancestor's memory.

The Cathedral guards stopped outside a door that was guarded by two fully armed Imperial Guards; obviously the edict against spilling blood within the boundaries of the cathedral did not extend to the side streets around it. Their face-shields were down, but Tien could feel their eyes moving across him, and he carefully adjusted his stance, assuming the off-balance, slightly crouching manner of a tired old man. The leader of the Cathedral guards went inside, only to reappear a moment later followed by a second man in the garb of a captain of the Cathedral guard, his rank distinguished by a crimson eye on the shoulder of his satin surcoat.

'You are Andam,' he snapped without preamble.

'I am – I was,' Tien corrected himself.

'Was?'

'I have seen the true way; I wish to convert to the New Religion, the True Religion.'

The man suppressed a quick smile. A converted Andam priest would be quite a coup. 'And how long have you been Andam?'

'Twenty summers.'

'And why this sudden desire to convert.'

'I have spoken with Trialos!'

In the long shocked silence that followed, Tien tZo knew he had them. Only the Hierophant was supposed to have direct communion with Trialos, the Prime Deity of the New Religion.

'Trialos spoke with you?' the captain asked.

Tien nodded.

'And what did he say?' the man asked, now more curious than demanding.

But Tien shook his head. 'I have a message for the Hierophant and it must be for his ears only.'

'It could be a trick,' the captain said doubtfully.

'But to what end? Why should I deliver myself so readily into your hands if I was not telling you the truth. The force of the lord's message has convinced me, an Andam, to convert to the New Religion and the worship of the Lord Trialos. Where is the trickery in that?'

'But why would the Lord Trialos deliver a message to an Andam?' the man asked, more to himself than to Tien.

'Who are we to question the lord's way?' one of the guards said piously.

'It could be a trick.'

'If it's a trick we'll kill him – slowly.'

The captain nodded. 'Take him to the Gate and deliver him to the guards there. He is to be taken directly to the Hierophant.'

In the dim, flickering, candlelit silence of the tiny room, a single figure sat with his back against the chill stone wall. The room was bare and the man was naked; no-one, not even his closest friends or lovers, would have recognised Barthus, the Hierophant. His pale flesh was bathed with chill sweat and the muscles and veins were clearly outlined beneath the taut skin. His usually deep-set eyes seemed to have sunk deeper into his skull and his fine hair was plastered against his head. His breathing was ragged and the pounding of his heart was clearly visible against his chest and at his throat and temples.

There were two candles on the bare flagstones before him and another candle in a niche above his head, but the room was not dark. Tiny traceries of red fire darted along the cracks in the stones briefly outlining them, crackling, hissing, spitting slightly as they moved.

But Barthus was unaware of the darting fire; indeed, he was no longer even aware of the room. His whole consciousness was concentrated inwards on the arcane and complicated ritual for calling on the Lord of the Dead.

But like most of the Gods of the New Religion, he had to be paid to attend, and Barthus was paying with his physical body and immortal soul.

The darting, crackling, sparkling lines of red fire began to coalesce on the bare stones beyond the two candles. Their buzzing had become intense and within the confines of the tiny room they reverberated off the walls so that the naked man felt the sound vibrating deep within his bones, shaking him to his very core. Abruptly, the candle flames began to shiver, and then the candles on the floor trembled and fell over and their flames extinguished, leaving only the tiny light burning on the wall behind the man's head, throwing the room into deep, menacing shadow.

The buzzing stopped and Barthus opened his eyes.

There was a figure sitting opposite him, shadowy and indistinct in the light but Barthus recognised him from his bulk and height: Libellius, Lord of the Dead of the New Religion. His memory supplied the description of the god: a short, stout, jovial man, with a thatch of snow-white hair, deep-set twinkling eyes and a quick and ready smile.

'You called me?' His voice was deep and rich as befitted his appearance.

From a seated position, the Hierophant bowed low, his forehead touching the floor. The God's benign appearance didn't deceive him; he knew how Libellius had become the God of Death of the Religion. 'My lord, a humble servant thanks you for your presence here.'

Libellius waved stubby beringed fingers. 'You called me?' he repeated.

'There is danger, lord. I would not have disturbed you, but the very existence of the Religion is threatened.'

The shadowy figure sat forward and Barthus received the vague impression of his pale, round face. 'Tell me.'

'There is an uprising in the west led by a man called Kutor, half-brother to the present Emperor. He is an ardent follower of the Faith. If he triumphs, and his defeat is by no means certain, then the Religion will be proscribed and the Faith re-established as the official belief in the Nations.'

'If this man Kutor dies, will the rising die with him?'

'If the circumstances of his death are such that he loses all credibility, then I believe so.'

'What steps have you taken.'

'Salier has employed a mercenary from one of the many that are flooding into the city at this moment, listening to the distant drums of war. We intend to have him infiltrate Kutor's camp and then kill him.'

'I can see no fault in that,' Libellius said quickly.

'But I think – no, I know – Kutor is guarded by the forces of the Faith. I have attempted on several occasions to come close to him, but he has, or his guardians have, resisted my best efforts.'

'How do you want me to help?' Libellius asked seriously.

'In any way you can.'

'I can take some from his army,' the fat old man mused. 'I can bring in disease and death; there are those would fall easily to my hand. I could assume the guise of Death, the traditional image of death from the legends, and allow myself to be seen walking the camp.' He looked up at Barthus. 'Well?'

'My lord, any, or indeed all, of these suggestions would be excellent. However, I should add that I do not think you will find the camp unguarded. I have learned that the bard, Paedur, is the prime instigator of this uprising.'

Libellius sat back into the shadows, his breath hissing through his teeth. 'The bard! In that case, we must assume that the rising is being backed by the Gods of the Old Faith. Interesting.' He stopped, shaking his head in puzzlement, 'But that doesn't explain what the bard is doing now.'

'Where is he now?' Barthus demanded. 'I have had my spies watch for him especially.'

'They are wasting their time,' Libellius grinned. 'He is dead at the moment, or more truly, he is within Death's Domain and, saving the Demon's Law of chance, well beyond our sphere of influence for the moment. But we will get him, don't worry. The bard will be ours some day.' The god's eyes closed in dreamy reflection of the tortures it would be his pleasure to inflict on the creature when he was finally captured. His eyes snapped open and he sat forward. 'So, while I create a distraction within Kutor's army, your mercenary will slay Kutor.'

'Will you ensure that Kutor's guards are amongst the first to fall?' Barthus asked.

'I will take as many as I can. And what of Kutor's death itself. How do you wish that to appear?'

The Hierophant shrugged. 'It would be to our advantage to discredit the man as much as possible.'

'Papers could be left implicating him in an Imperial conspiracy to rid the Nations of the last vestiges of the Faith,' Libellius suggested with a chuckle.

'Excellent, lord, excellent!'

'They must appear genuine, mind, for they will be subjected to an intense scrutiny.'

'They will be genuine, lord. Geillard himself will sign them.'

The Lord of Death sat forward, his eyes glittering in the reflected light. 'In the light of this upheaval, this is an auspicious time to further our plans.'

Barthus nodded eagerly. 'That thought had crossed my mind.'

'Then perhaps you should know that the insurgents have infiltrated men into the city.' The God raised his hand, the rings on his fingers taking the light. 'There are but two, so you must not alarm yourself overmuch. However, they are assassins with orders to slay the Emperor, Salier, Fodla and, of course, yourself.'

'I will have them killed!'

Libellius nodded. 'Of course you will, but not immediately.' He paused a moment, allowing the message to sink home, and then Barthus suddenly smiled and nodded in understanding.

'We will let them do our killing for us.'

Libellius nodded.

'Who are these two? How may I recognise them?'

'One is Owen, a Weapon Master. He was one with our brother Kloor, but the bard released him from his vows and shattered the Iron Band and now he guides this uprising. He intends to kill Geillard and Fodla. And of course, by the Demon's Law, he is the very man Salier has employed to kill Kutor!' The God smiled broadly. 'It has a certain comic rationality to it.'

'And the second man?'

'The second is Tien tZo, the slave-companion to Owen. He entered the city disguised as Andam. His task is to kill Salier and you. And even now, he is being escorted into your chambers by the Cathedral guards!'

Barthus surged to his feet, the sudden movement extinguishing the candle above his head, plunging the room into smoky darkness.

'Disguised as Andam, he professes to have seen the true light and wishes to convert to the Religion,' Libellius continued evenly. 'That is why he has been brought to you. However, play along with the scheme. I would suggest you send him on to Salier, perhaps with a request as to how the greatest use might be made of such a man.' He paused and in the darkness, there was the sound of him coming slowly to his feet. 'If you take my meaning?'

Barthus bowed. 'Of course, my lord.' A sudden thought struck him. 'But lord, if this mercenary Salier has employed is already working for Kutor, then surely that invalidates the rest of our plan.'

Libellius chuckled. 'Continue with the plan, but employ a man of your own to do the killing. He will kill Kutor, while Kutor's men will kill Geillard, Salier and Fodla, leaving you in command.'

'It will work out very well,' Barthus murmured.

'It is all up to the Demon's Law,' Libellius said. 'Even the Gods have no say in it now.'

## 21   Churon's Tale

'Death is the last great deceit.'

*Churon the Onelord*

'Welcome back, Churon!' Mannam rubbed clacking hands together and turned from the chained Onelord to Paedur and Katani. 'You have done well. And you too, of course,' he added, looking at Buiva.

The God of War bowed slightly. 'There is nothing to thank me for. As one of the Pantheon, I had my duty to perform.' He jerked his grizzled head towards Paedur and the woman. 'Their task was much more perilous and their reasons their own and they went of their own accord. If there is justice, they should be rewarded.'

'And so they will,' Mannam agreed.

'I want no payment,' Paedur said, suddenly feeling utterly weary, 'merely the life of my two companions who died in the service of the Pantheon. Their deaths were untimely; return them to life in the World of Men, allow them to act out their allotted span of years.'

'Then you are not the paid creature of this, this god?' Churon abruptly demanded, straining forward against his bonds, the wan light from the single window painting his face in a snarl.

'Neither man nor god owns me,' the bard said quietly.

'What tale did he tell you?' the Onelord snapped, glaring at Mannam. 'What lies?'

'Enough! Silence!' Mannam whirled, his leaved cloak rasping, browned and withered leaves scattering across the darkened room. 'Call our brothers,' Mannam said to Buiva. 'Call Destruction and Madness and let us end this thing now.'

The bard stepped up to the Onelord and looked into his sharp blue eyes. 'What do you mean?' he asked softly.

'Leave him be, bard!' Mannam demanded, his claw-like hand reaching for the bard's shoulder . . . only to find itself entrapped within the half circle of his hook. Blue-white fire crackled along

222

the metal and a faint tendril of grey smoke drifted up from between the twisted twigs that served as Mannam's fingers. With an inhuman scream Death fell back, his arm clutched to his body. The bitter odour of scorched wood hung in the air on the still dry air.

'Never touch me!' Paedur said evenly to the fallen figure and then he turned back to the Onelord. 'You attempted to usurp Death's position, is that true?'

'It is true I was plotting to overthrow him.'

'Why?' Paedur asked simply. 'Why did you attempt to destroy him?'

Churon threw back his head and laughed. 'Bard, he is Death, the last great deceit. He has misled you. I never attempted to destroy him; quite the contrary, he has constantly sought my death, my complete and absolute destruction, since I left him. That is why I sought to overthrow him.'

A branch snapped, silencing Churon. 'He lies. Destroy him and be done with it!'

'I want to listen to him,' Paedur said mildly.

'And so do I,' Buiva added surprisingly.

Katani folded her arms and said nothing.

The bard turned back to the chained man and slipped the point of his hook into the hasp of one of the huge locks, and pulled, snapping the lock open. Churon pulled off the chains and then flung them into a corner. He walked to the window-ledge and perched on it, one leg stretched straight out as his stiffened fingers worked on the locked muscles. 'Listen to me, then, and I will tell you my tale – or my version of the Dark Lord's tale,' he amended. 'You may judge for yourselves then.'

Paedur glanced quickly at Buiva and Katani and then nodded to Churon. 'Speak, then.'

The Onelord turned his head slightly, looking out over the silent streets and alleyways of Manach. The light was fading fast and the shadows almost totally consumed him, the darkness swallowing his skin, leaving only his snow-white hair startling against the dusk.

'You must know of my life in the World of Men, you know what I was, what I became,' he said suddenly. 'But whatever you have heard, and I am sure that much of it is true, you cannot know the reasons for what I did. And to understand that, you would have to understand what it was like to grow up a slave,

223

and a slave with my colouring, only hearing the rumours that spoke of the lady of the house whose child I later discovered I was. And then she seduced me, coupled with me when I was a youth, and only when she had conceived by me did she tell me her identity. And yes, I slew her, becase she was a monster, even more depraved than the creatures she used for her pleasure. I ran away, became a slave again, escaped again, and then became a pirate, a bandit, a warrior, a king . . .' He shrugged and smiled wanly. 'But of course, you know all that.'

Churon looked back into the shadowy darkness of Manach, the City of the Dead. 'And then I died. I had never been a very religious man, but when I awoke in the Silent Wood I knew exactly where I was and what to expect. Creatures came for me, the bainte, but they expected me to act as a slave, and that I was not prepared to do. I had been a slave too long in the World of Men; I would not be a slave again in this place. That is how I came to Mannam's attention. I'm not sure what Death expected, or what he was used to with the newly dead, but he certainly never expected resistance.

'Surprisingly, he asked me to return to this place with him; perhaps even more surprisingly I agreed. And that was the start of what I can best describe as a friendship and, if the truth were only known, the first and perhaps the only friendship I had ever experienced in my entire life – or death,' he added with a grim smile. 'You see, we were equals of sorts. He was dead, he was Death; I could not threaten him, I wanted nothing from him. And he posed no threat to me, there was nothing I could give him. Or so I thought.

'Mannam made me his captain, his second-in-command. I patrolled the outskirts of his kingdom, where it borders some of the less ordered Planes of Existence and places like the Mire, keeping out the vermin and the unacceptable intrusions from those places. It was, I must admit, a very enjoyable phase of my . . . existence. Is that the right word?' he asked, looking at Mannam. Receiving no reply, he shrugged and continued.

'And then I discovered the Dark Lord was plotting against me.

'Don't look so surprised or disbelieving, War God. Are the gods so far above deceit and pettiness?' Churon swung around off the window-ledge and looked at the silent group of figures, his gaze coming back to fix on the bard's dark, shadowed eyes.

'Perhaps you know, or then again perhaps not, that this Dark Lord, this Mannam, is not the first to wear the Leaved Cloak of the God of Death.' The Onelord's eyes narrowed and his breath hissed through his teeth. 'I see you know. But do you know that he cannot just pass the responsibility blithely on to his successor? How many do you know, bard, who would so readily accept the position of Death? Look at him!' His arm swept around in Mannam's direction. 'He was a man once – handsome, he told me, strong, proud and handsome – and now look at him, withered, a creature of wood and flesh, of rotting bark and mouldering leaves, of dead foul-smelling sap and decay, like a blasted tree that has rotted and wormed. How many, even though they may be dead, would take on that mantle? How many would take it, even though it promises godhood and immortality? And so the only way he could pass the cloak to me was by trickery and treachery. I would become death and he would assume my body, and who knows, perhaps he would even seek a judgement with Alile, the Judge Impartial, and so legitimately return to the World of Man.

'But at the last moment, I learned of his treachery and fled Manach and made my way into the Mire, where I have – had – successfully avoided the creatures he sent against me.'

Paedur turned to look at Mannam, his eyes narrowing. 'And what of the attacks against him?' he asked Churon.

'Praetens is in the Mire. He no longer wears the body of a Susuru, but his mind is still as foul and evil. He plots with Libellius, the Deathgod of the New Religion, for the overthrow of Mannam.'

'He lies! See how cleverly he weaves his lies!'

'Silence!' Buiva snapped. 'Tell me why the Susuru deals with the impostor,' he demanded.

'When they overthrow Death, Libellius will replace him, but Praetens can control this new god and so, in effect, the Susuru will be the Lord of the Dead. He intends to raise the dead Susuru race to walk the Planes of Life again, to rule the sons of Man.'

'And your place in this?' Buiva demanded coldly.

'I am – was – a figurehead for the living and dead to rally behind.'

'He lies!' Death's voice was high, like wind through a bare branch.

'I believe him,' Katani said quietly.

In the long silence that followed, Paedur eventually nodded. 'So do I.'

Finally Buiva said, 'I don't want to believe him, but I'm afraid I have to; I have no alternative.'

Churon bowed his head and his shoulders sagged. 'Thank you,' he said wearily. 'I didn't think you would believe me. I didn't think any one of you would believe me.'

'Why not?' Buiva asked, sounding surprised.

'Why? Because you and he are Gods of the Pantheon, and this is a bard of the Old Faith and the warrior ... well, she is of the Katan and they have little enough cause to love me.'

'Whatever our beliefs and opinions and even loyalties,' Buiva replied, 'we recognise truth when we hear it. However, there is one thing which still troubles me,' he added, turning to face the Dark Lord. 'Why did you attempt to kill this man? And don't lie to me,' he snapped suddenly, the spiked ball of his mace tapping against the top of his boots.

Mannam had backed up until his cloak was rasping against the chill stone wall and although his face was invisible behind his cowl, his head was turning rapidly from side to side, looking at each figure in turn.

'The Onelord discovered your plan, but surely that is not reason enough for this charade. When he fled Manach,' Buiva persisted, 'why did you attempt to kill him? And why go to such lengths to bring him back here?'

'He must be destroyed, he is dangerous, evil ...'

'How?' the bard hissed. 'Tell me how dangerous this man is. Tell me how he could threaten Death.'

'He knows too much!' Mannam suddenly spat, branches cracking and snapping.

'Ah,' Churon breathed. 'I think I am beginning to understand.'

'Explain,' Buiva said, his eyes never leaving the Lord of the Dead.

The Onelord came and stood between Paedur and Buiva, his hands on his hips, his eyes on Mannam. 'For a long time now, the Dark Lord has been taking souls before their time; he has been bringing the living into the Silent Wood!'

Buiva was first to break the horrified silence that followed. 'Why – in the name of all the Pantheon, why?' His mace flashed out, the ball smashing into the wall by Mannam's head, showering him in chips of stone and sparks. The Dark Lord dropped to the ground in a shivering, rustling bundle. 'WHY?' Buiva screamed, his voice a detonation, and all across the Silent Wood the petrified trees trembled and boulders cracked and split with the terrifying sound.

Mannam spoke, but the sound was a mere sussuration and inaudible.

Buiva's mace flashed out again, the chain entangling itself around the Dark Lord's thin neck, the ball thudding on to his chest. Effortlessly, Buiva hauled Death to his feet and slammed him against the wall, branches snapping and cracking, leaves turning to powder. 'Tell me, god, or I will crush you to punk.'

'For . . . for sport.' Mannam whispered.

'He hunted them like animals,' Churon said quietly.

With a snarl Buiva hurled Death from him, sending him across the room to crash into the wall. He raised the mace again, but the bard's hook captured the chain, staying the blow. The God of War whirled on him, his face contorted, but the bard merely raised his right hand and said, 'Wait.'

The Bard then turned to the Onelord. 'Perhaps it would be better if you were to tell us what you know,' he suggested.

Churon bobbed his head, suddenly nervous, realising he was standing between the grim-faced god and the hard-eyed bard. 'I am as guilty as Death in this respect,' he began.

'Explain yourself,' Buiva said tightly.

'When I came to this place, I thought it was the accepted practice for Death to hunt in the Silent Wood; I thought he hunted the dead, but it wasn't until much later that I discovered that he was bringing the living into the Silent Wood to hunt them.'

'Why the living?' Katani asked, 'why did he not make do with the dead?'

'The dead rise again in the Silent Wood,' Churon said simply, 'and therefore they do not make good quarry; they tend to allow themselves to be killed too easily to end the chase, knowing that they can rise again a little later. No, the living provided far greater sport.'

'How did he hunt?' Katani asked.

'He bred some of the bainte especially for this purpose; the talons with which they usually clutch the essence of man were turned into razor-sharp, incredibly long and strong rending claws. He armoured them, putting spikes on to their wing-tips

227

and heads, and once they had a scent – the vibration of a living human aura amongst all the dead – they were able to follow it tirelessly. He, like I, rode one of the Deathhorses, ugly big-boned, ill-tempered beasts whose stamina and endurance are limitless.'

'You don't seem particularly remorseful,' Katani remarked.

'I knew no better,' Churon said, spreading his hands. 'In my defence I should say that when I discovered and protested – violently – that was when Mannam turned against me and I became one of the hunted.'

'And how did you end up in the Mire in the company of Praetens?' Buiva asked, his eyes still on the unmoving figure of Mannam.

'Death hunted me all across the Silent Wood and on more than one occasion he almost had me. I had some advantages on my side, however. I knew his ways and I was already dead, so his beasts had difficulty tracking me. I cost him dearly too,' he added with a slight smile, 'I slew three of his horses and a score of his favourite bainte.'

Buiva stepped up to Mannam, the mace and chain in his left hand, the spiked ball of the mace dangling just above Death's head. 'Tell me why, Mannam,' he whispered.

'I am a god. I am accountable to no-one!'

'You will account to me!' War suddenly roared, raising his hand, the mace ready to crush.

The point of the bard's hook touched the metal ball, blue fire sparking along it. 'There is another way, Buiva,' he said, his lips moving in a semblance of a smile. He crouched down over the sprawled figure of Death and raised his left arm, his hook glinting balefully in the wan light. 'Although my power is negated in this place,' he said slowly, his eyes on the shadow that mercifully concealed the god's face, 'I have been gifted by C'lte, the Lord of Life, and my hook has burned with the fire of the Lady Dannu.' The bard smiled coldly. 'And you would not want me to touch you with it.'

'Tell me why you did this,' Buiva repeated.

Death looked from Buiva to the bard and then back to Buiva again. 'Because . . . because I was bored,' he said finally.

# 22  The Killing


'In every warrior's life, there is a time of killing, and in every warrior's life there is a time to die.'

*Tien tZo*


'To be brief, then, you will infiltrate the Renegade's army and kill this Kutor,' Salier said quietly as they crossed the small ornamental bridge and went into the Emperor's private gardens. 'The planning and – if you will pardon the word – the execution, will be left entirely up to you. Do you see any problems with that?'

Owen grunted. 'I'd be a fool if I didn't. I'll need a lot more than that before I venture into an enemy camp.' He shrugged. 'But such things can be thrashed out later; now let us discuss payment. How much?'

Salier's eyes closed in momentary satisfaction and he nodded. He had judged the man correctly; he was a hardened killer, a mercenary in the true sense of the word, worshipping only coin. 'The Emperor will reward you well indeed.'

Owen stopped on the gravel path, forcing the mage to stop and turn back. 'If all you can give me now are the promises of an Emperor then I'm off.'

'Name your price,' Salier said softly.

'The Province of Lostrice.'

Salier, who had been expecting demands of coin or jewels, was momentarily dumbfounded. 'Lostrice?'

'I want to be made the Viceroy of Lostrice.'

Salier smiled, a curling of the lips, but it never reached his eyes. 'A high price indeed.'

'I am saving the Emperor's throne,' Owen pointed out.

'Indeed you are. Lostrice it is then. Complete this task and it is yours.' He made to turn away, but stopped when the mercenary remained still.

'You can make that decision?' Owen demanded. 'You have that authority?'

'I am the Emperor's closest friend and adviser. He listens to me.'

'If you're lying, I'll probably kill you too.'

Salier threw back his head and laughed, and then walked on, still laughing.

Owen stood watching him for a few moments, his hands on his hips, absorbing his surroundings. He was all too aware that one of the reasons Salier had agreed to his outrageous demand so easily was that he had no intention of paying. With Kutor dead, his assassin would have to die also. He idly contemplated killing the Emperor now, and Salier also, if the opportunity presented itself, but all his instincts went against it. Although the garden seemed empty, he was uncomfortably aware of the eyes watching him, and he had realised from the first moments Salier had led him across the bridge and into the private garden that the mage was only leading him along selected paths. The garden was trapped, he was sure.

'Warrior?' Salier called.

Owen hitched up his belt and strode down the path after the small, scuttling figure.

The mage led him around a clutch of ornamental trees which had been shaped like warriors locked in battle, and Owen found that the grounds opened out into a perfectly flat lawn that was covered, not with perfectly trimmed grass but rather by ice-smooth sand. In the centre of the lawn was an observatory, a beehive-shaped building of white stone with a long brass looking-tube protruding from a slit and pointing heavenwards.

Salier stopped short of the sand and pointed towards the observatory. 'The Emperor awaits you.' And then he turned and hurried away.

Owen watched the man walk away and then took a deep breath and held it, suddenly feeling as if he was in a dream. It was unbelievable. It was almost as if he were being offered Geillard's head on a plate. Events were moving too fast for him. He knew now what Kutor had meant: he felt like an actor in a play.

He looked across the grey-gold lawn of sand and wondered why Salier hadn't led him out to the observatory. Unless, of course, this was a test. Owen had been more than surprised when Salier had accepted him merely on Thome's recommendation and hadn't even bothered to have his weapons removed before leading him to the Emperor of the Seven Nations.

And now, having led him through the maze of paths, why had he left him here? Accept, then, that everything was not as it seemed; accept, then, that the sand was not merely sand, that the Emperor was now in the observatory and that this was a test, that even now he was being observed and tested. This was a test he needed to pass, and he idly wondered what would happen if he failed.

Owen squatted down and looked closely at the unusual lawn. It certainly looked like sand, except perhaps that the colour was more grey than gold, but that meant little; he had once seen sand the colour of blood. He gripped the hilt of the sword that protruded above his left shoulder with his right hand and pulled, the weapon hissing out of its scabbard, and then he strode back to the ornamental trees and sliced off a long branch that represented a warrior's spear. Cleaning his sword against his leggings he slid it home and returned to the lawn. He probed the sand, almost surprised to find solid ground about a finger-length beneath; he probed again, and was unsurprised when the branch kept going. Returning to his starting point he began probing to determine the width of the path, which was no more than a single pace across, and then he used the length of the branch to determine its direction. It seemed to head straight out towards the observatory, but Owen was too distrustful to depend on that. He snapped the branch across his knee and using the length of wood as a probe took his first tentative steps out on to the lawn. There was a brief moment of panic as he felt himself sinking, but it was only his weight on the sand. Testing every step he proceeded slowly and cautiously across the lawn.

Half way over the path disappeared.

Owen stood in the centre of the lawn, feeling slightly ridiculous. Ahead of him there seemed to be nothing, and even when he described an almost complete circle from where stood with the pole, he struck nothing solid. But if the path ended, he reasoned, it must begin again, and the gap wouldn't be too wide, lest the Emperor himself vanish into whatever terrors lurked beneath the sand. He moved up to the lip of the path he was standing on, and stretching out as far as he could, he continued probing. There was nothing ahead of him. He moved to the left-hand edge of the path and repeated the process, and with similar results. But on the right-hand side he found the path. It was barely a stride away. He stepped cautiously on to it, suddenly fearing that both paths – the one he was on and the one he was about to step on to would disappear, but it remained firm beneath his feet. The path then continued in a straight line to the observatory.

Owen was about to step up off the sand and on to the gravel that surrounded the white stone building when a figure stepped out of the doorway. Owen's reactions were instinctive. He threw himself forward and down, two handleless throwing knives coming to his hands.

'They will probably kill you before you get close.' The voice held just enough amusement in it to infuriate Owen. He came to his feet slowly, looking from the man and back across the sand lawn to the score of crossbowmen who had appeared from the bushes and trees. All the weapons were levelled and pointing at him. He turned back to the tall, thin man and allowed him to see the knife in his left hand. 'I could have this in your throat before they even let off one shot. They would be so shocked at seeing you fall that I'd have a chance to get inside.'

The man smiled. 'And you'll be trapped there, I'm afraid. There is only one way in.'

Owen nodded and returned the knives to his belt. 'You are Geillard.' He made no attempt to bow.

The man nodded, his dark eyes burning deep behind his prominent cheekbones. 'And you are the Warrior. No other name?' he queried.

'None that I wish to use.'

'That is understandable.' He sat down on a slab-like projection of stone that jutted out from the building. Across the lawn the score of crossbowmen kept their positions.

Owen squatted down close enough to the Emperor to use him as a shield if need be. 'You are a trustful man,' he remarked, nodding at the men.

'They are dedicated to me.'

Something in the man's tired voice made Owen look at the crossbowmen again. There was something eerie in their very immobility. 'They are quai?' he asked.

'Of a sort,' Geillard said, smiling, vaguely pleased. The man was intelligent. 'They are not true quai, but Salier makes them for me. They are all volunteers, of course. All thoughts and images are removed from their minds, leaving just one person in their universe, one being for them to look up to, to adore – and to protect.'

'You?'

Geillard nodded. 'They are the finest bodyguards. Fearless, untiring, completely dedicated.'

'And soulless,' Owen spat. He had never been able to overcome his loathing of the quai – the soulless warriors he had encountered in his travels – and his one great, and secret, fear was that he would end up like one of them. However, they also introduced a new element into his plan to kill Geillard. It was unlikely he went anywhere without them; they probably even slept in the same room as him.

'Has Salier explained what is needed of you?' Geillard asked, not looking at the man.

'He has. Has he explained my fee?'

'He has not,' Geillard replied, enjoying the game that was developing. It would be a shame to have to kill this man.

'For payment I want the Lordship of Lostrice.'

'A high price,' the Emperor remarked softly, still watching his quai bodyguards.

'For a difficult task.'

Geillard nodded. 'Agreed. I had intended to offer you a high price and a position here at court . . .'

'Where you could keep an eye on me,' Owen finished.

Geillard shrugged. 'I won't deny it. But on reflection, it might be useful to have you in a position of power. A man of your talents might prove very useful.' Perhaps it would be possible to keep the man alive, Geillard reflected. But no; Salier would insist that he be killed, and he was probably right. A pity.

'Why was it necessary for you to see me? I've done work such as you want for other men and usually they preferred to deal with me through intermediaries.'

The Emperor nodded. 'Usually the instructions for this work would be handled by Salier, but I wanted to have the opportunity to see you, see what sort of man you were, to speak to you, to give you certain instructions, to make certain suggestions.'

'What sort of instructions?' Owen asked bluntly. 'To be honest, I'll take no instructions that place my life in danger.'

Geillard shook his head. 'No, there is nothing of that nature. When you have him – Kutor, I mean – I want him to die slowly. Slow and painful – is that possible?' He turned to look at Owen with such eagerness in his eyes that the hardened warrior was appalled.

To cover his confusion, he looked across at the tireless quai, still covering him with their crossbows. 'That depends on the circumstances,' he said eventually. 'It might be necessary for me to slit his throat quickly and then leave.'

'Well then, you must bring me back something of his to prove that he is indeed dead.'

'What do you want?' Owen asked, although he had already partially guessed.

'His head!'

'No! It's all very well for you to say bring me back his head. But I doubt if you've ever carried a severed head about with you for any length of time. Besides the smell and the flies, they are awkward things to carry and impossible to hide. You can have his ears or his hands or perhaps a strip of flesh if it has some tattoo or birthmark on it. And that's as far as I'm prepared to go.'

'His hands, both of them.'

Owen sighed. 'As you wish.'

'And if you have the opportunity to make him suffer?'

'I'll make sure he knows who's killing him. Will that do? I can tell you what he said or what his expression was like as he died.'

Geillard nodded happily. 'Yes, that will be perfect.'

Salier was standing waiting for Owen when he crossed the sand lawn. The quai had disappeared, although he knew they were still there, still watching him. The mage turned away as Owen came up on to the track and headed back into the forest, leaving the warrior to follow him.

'What now?' Owen called.

The mage strode on, head bent, his hands tucked into the sleeves of his simple dove-grey robe.

'What do you want me to do?' Owen tried again.

Salier continued to ignore him and, indeed, didn't even seem to hear him.

Owen took two long strides and was actually reaching for Salier's arm when the man's head turned slightly, and Owen recoiled at the look on his face, the look of absolute, chilling evil.

'Never touch me, or even attempt to lay a hand on me,' he hissed, his voice scarcely human.

'I was . . .' Owen began, but Salier continued on in the same measured icy tones, 'I tell you this for your own good and not as an idle threat. My art protects me, my aura is charged with power.' He smiled, and it was the look of a snarling animal. 'And that power would shrivel you.'

Unable for the moment to believe or even understand what the magician was saying, Owen contented himself with merely nodding.

'There was a man,' Salier continued, looking away, speaking softly, almost to himself, 'a man who attempted to kill me. He had been a pupil of mine and he should have known better, but he imagined that by slaying me, he would absorb some of my powers; that can happen when a mage is slain by violence.' His steps had slowed and his eyes were almost closed now, mere slits, and his face had settled into a mask of satisfaction; this was clearly a tale he enjoyed. 'He had access to my rooms and so one day he took a shortsword and concealed himself there, waiting for me. From the moment I stepped into the room, I knew he was there, but I was confident of my power and did nothing. It was, and is, my custom to bathe every evening – this is a filthy city – and my former pupil knew this. He waited until I was in my bath and then crept up behind me and drove the sword down into my back. But the force that surrounds me snapped the blade and sprayed molten metal fragments back up into his face. Blind and in agony, I was able to kill him at my leisure,' he whispered. 'He was a long time dying.'

'Why have you told me this?' Owen asked quietly, aware of the pounding of his heart. Did Salier know his true purpose?

'Just to warn you never to touch me.'

'I wouldn't dream of it.'

'Don't.' And the warning was implicit.

The two men walked on in silence. Salier seemed to be meandering aimlessly along the gravelled paths, but Owen knew, once they had passed the same spot twice, that he was merely attempting to confuse. Finally they crossed the small ornamental bridge that led from the private gardens and back into the main palace gardens.

There were two men waiting for them, a servant in white and gold and a guard wearing the blue and black palace livery; both were clearly in awe of the notorious Salier.

Salier ignored the guard and glared at the servant, who was wearing the colours of the Hierophant, Barthus. 'Well?'

235

'Barthus, Hierophant of the Religion, sends you greetings and trust.'

Salier waved his hand impatiently. 'The message!' he demanded.

'The Lord Barthus begs your indulgence and assistance in a matter of import. One of the Andam priesthood has come to the lord protesting loyalty to the Religion and claiming to have spoken with the Lord Trialos. The Lord Barthus is convinced that the man's intentions are genuine and wishes your advice as to how this man may be used to the best advantage.'

Salier was so shocked at the request that he stared at the man for a few long moments. 'And where is this Andam now?' he asked eventually.

The guards spoke up. 'He is contained in the anteroom to your chambers, lord.'

'Guarded?' Salier snapped.

'By four of my most trusted men.'

'That affords me little comfort,' Salier remarked and strode past the man, leaving Owen little choice but to follow him.

The mage allowed the mercenary to catch up with him. 'Would you be willing to undertake an extra task for me, a personal task?'

'You want someone killed?' Owen asked bluntly.

'You are direct.'

'In this profession it is the only honest way.'

'Would you slay the Hierophant for me?'

'How much?'

'My loyalty when you have the Lordship of Lostrice.'

'Is your loyalty worth so much?' Owen asked, and then he quickly answered his own question. 'Do you want him slain before or after I slay Kutor?'

'Before. And I want it to look as if Kutor's men have performed the task.'

'When do you want him killed?'

'Soon,' Salier hissed, 'very soon. You see how bold he grows,' he continued, as they strode into the echoing, slightly chilly corridors. 'He sends this man to me, testing me.'

'Perhaps he lacks your wisdom,' Owen suggested, 'and is unable to make a decision himself.'

Salier's hunched shoulders began to shake and it was a few moments before Owen realised he was laughing. 'Oh, foolish man. We are talking about Barthus, a simple priest who fought and schemed and some even say killed to raise himself to the elevated position of Hierophant. A man whose sole ambition seems to be to spread the New Religion all across the known world, by whatever means possible. He is cunning, infinitely cunning, and everything he does, he does with reason. His ambition is to replace me at Geillard's side, and who knows, perhaps even to replace Geillard himself. Even Fodla, who is opposed to me at many points, is in agreement with me on this. He is dangerous.'

'Tell me when you want his death,' Owen said softly.

They climbed a flight of stairs which led out on to a small landing, which was lined with guards who were standing so rock-still that Owen immediately knew that they must be quai, similar to Geillard's bodyguards. At the end of the landing there was a single iron-studded door and there were another two guards outside it. The mage moved silently down the length of the corridor, his head bent, his hands tucked into his sleeves. As he neared the door it abruptly clicked open. Pushing it, he stepped inside and then immediately turned to the right into a small, dimly lit antechamber. The small room was made even smaller by the presence of four guards, all of them fully human and alert and looking almost comically nervous in the presence of Salier. Dwarfed by the men surrounding him was the Andam.

Salier imperiously dismissed the men and then beckoned the Andam forward with a crooked finger.

Tien tZo stepped forward, fingering the tiny throwing spike the guards had missed when they had searched him earlier. His attention shifted from the mage to the tall warrior standing in the shadows behind him; bodyguard, he assumed, or, knowing the rumours that surrounded Salier, a catamite perhaps.

The mage stepped into the main room, fully expecting the priest to follow him, knowing the warrior would take up the rear. Tien noted that when the warrior came into the large, ornately furnished room, he immediately took up position with his back to the wall beside the door; bodyguard, then, he decided. Salier crossed to a tall, high-backed chair and sank down into it, his hands dangling limply over the edge of the highly polished and ornately worked arms. 'Come here. Stand before me,' he said simply, the command evident in his voice. 'You too,' he added, looking at the warrior.

Tien shuffled over to the mage and stood a respectful distance from him. He could feel the man's eyes boring into him, feel his flesh begin to crawl and his scalp to prickle. The warrior walked around the priest and stood by the chair, his arms folded. Tien looked up at the man, seeing him clearly for the first time.

The shock registered in his eyes – disbelief, amazement, horror. Only his eyes betrayed him, his face remained impassive, but slight as the moment of recognition had been, Salier noticed it.

'You know each other!' It was a statement, not a question.

'No,' Owen began, shaking his head.

Salier turned to look at the warrior standing beside him, and then he casually lifted his hand and moved it through the air, two fingers extended. Immediately, two lines of red fire crackled across the exposed flesh of his neck, searing the skin black, so fast that he didn't even have time to react or cry out.

Salier's face had turned to stone. 'Lie to me and I'll kill you, however useful you think you might be; mercenaries are commonplace. Now, I think an explanation . . .' he hissed, looking from the Andam to the mercenary. He turned back to Owen. 'Tell me!'

'I have never seen this man before in my life. I knew an Andam once, but he was an old man when I was a boy. With the way the light fell, I thought that this was him again.' He shrugged. 'Its nothing; just chance.'

'I do not believe in the Demon's Law,' Salier said icily. He was raising his hand again, a ball of red fire already coalescing in the palm of his hand when he caught a glimpse of movement in front of him and turned in time to see the Andam fling a sliver of silver metal towards his face . . .

'No, Tien!' Owen shouted. The Weapon Master threw himself forward and down, catching Tien across the legs, sending him tumbling across the carpeted floor. They rolled into a polished crystal table, bringing it crashing to the ground, and Owen dragged Tien in behind it.

In the long silence that followed nothing happened.

'I presume you had a reason for that,' Tien said, something close to amusement in his voice.

Owen peered through the thick crystal of the table. 'He is protected by a spell which turns metal to liquid – or something like that.' He could see Salier, warped and twisted by the crystal, still sitting in the chair.

Tien snatched a quick look and then he stood up cautiously, pulling back the cloth hood that covered most of his head. 'I don't think his spell worked,' he remarked.

Owen came to his feet, automatically righting the table. Salier remained in the chair, an expression of absolute surprise etched on his face, the long throwing spike protruding a finger-length from his left eye. The Weapon Master drummed his fingers on the crystal table in frustration.

'Is something wrong?' Tien asked.

Owen shook his head and grinned. 'This was shaping up to be one of the most extraordinary schemes I was ever involved in. I actually thought we might get out of this one easily, but . . .' He shrugged again.

'The Demon's Law,' Tien said. 'Chance . . .'

'Aye,' Owen nodded, 'but what do we do now?'

There was a sudden pounding on the door.

# 23   The Court of the Pantheon

Men are but the playthings of the gods.

*Death's law*

Without the faith of men there are no gods; the faith of men lends
substance to the Pantheon.

*Basic tenet of the Old Faith*

The Gods of the Pantheon were gathering.

With only the bard and Mannam for company in the long
dark library, Buiva had summoned a score of them, calling each
by name, and when the shadowy, shimmering, ghostly figures
had appeared momentarily on the cool musty air of the room in
Manach, he had spoken a single word: 'Trial!'

When he finally turned to Paedur, the bard noticed that the
god's world-weary, lined face seemed to have aged and the shadows beneath his eyes had deepened. 'They will tell the others,'
he said, his voice barely above a whisper.

'What have you done?' Paedur asked quietly, watching the
god intently, although from his lore he had a good idea what
Buiva had just set in motion.

'Trial by peer,' Buiva said, glancing down at Mannam. 'He
has betrayed the race of Man.'

'I had my reasons,' the Dark Lord spat.

'The very race he is oath-bound to protect and serve,' Buiva
continued, ignoring him. 'He seems to have forgotten that without the race of men, the gods themselves cease to exist.'

'Faith lends substance,' Paedur murmured the litany.

'Just so,' Buiva nodded.

'Then he is to be tried by the Gods of the Faith for his crime?'
Paedur asked softly.

'Yes.'

Paedur shook his head in disbelief. 'But he is Death, one of the
most powerful of the gods. Surely he can do what he wishes?'

'He is Death, but in the hierarchy of the Gods he is ranked
lowly indeed.'

Mannam suddenly struggled to his feet and the very air around him crackled with luminous energy. The dry air was suddenly bitter with soured sap and on the shelves behind him books shivered from their places and tumbled to the floor and rolled parchments snapped open. 'I am Death! The gods themselves serve me. You serve me, Buiva, feeding me the carcasses from your many wars. Madness and Destruction both make me offerings. Even the arrogant Lords of Life eventually give me up their subjects. Death is the most powerful of all the gods!'

Buiva's left hand shot out, the spiked pommel of his mace disappearing into the shadows of Mannam's cowl. 'You feed on offal, Mannam, on dead things. You cannot bring anything to life; birth and growth are unknown to you. Those who walk your kingdom are little more than quai.' He turned away in disgust.

'What happens now?' Paedur asked.

'Now we wait for the Gods of the Pantheon to arrive.'

'And then?'

'Trial!'

Katani and Churon had been taken to the library and then locked in, with instructions not to even attempt to break out, no matter what they heard or thought they heard – precautions which, Buiva had assured them both, were for their own safety. Buiva had then taken Paedur to Mannam's huge and sombre throne-room and covered his eyes with layers of thick cloth.

He had waited patiently, only gradually becoming aware of the movement around him, conscious of it at first as the merest disturbance on the chill, dank air.

Paedur's blindfolded head came up suddenly as the Dark Lord began to speak without warning. 'You don't know what it's like. None of you can even possibly comprehend what it is like to be trapped in this body, this existence, with no hope of reprieve, no end in sight.'

The bard turned his head slightly. The Dark Lord was standing off to his right-hand side and all around him Paedur could now distinguish the softly sussurating movements of the myriad Gods of the Pantheon and smell their perfumes. Someone had moved in front of him moments before, and he had known it was the Lady Adur by the deep, earthy odour of fresh greenery and growth. He felt the itchy crawling of power across his skin, the burning of the radiance of the gods on his face and lips, and he could understand why Buiva had blindfolded him. While the Sons of Man could look upon some of the gods, there were others, like the Lady Dannu, the Mother, or the Lady Lussa, the Goddess of the Moon, who were forbidden to him, lest their radiance shrivel him.

'Continue, Death. Explain.' The voice was deep and booming, like rolling thunder on a summer's day. Baistigh, Paedur decided, the Lord of Thunder.

'Acceptance was easy in the beginning, but that was so long ago. I was convinced then that my appearance was nothing more than another part of Death's costume, a means of perpetuating the traditional image of the Dark Lord as somehow being associated with trees and dark forests and the secret places of the woods. It was later, much later, that I discovered that the guise I had adopted from my predecessor had become inseparable from me. And none of you can even begin to understand what it is like to be trapped in the body of a rotting, rotted, foul tree, shunned by both man and god.'

The silence that followed was oppressive and the bard turned his head from side to side, listening, feeling the crawling prickle of power on his skin, tasting the sharpness of it on his lips. He didn't know how many of the gods had arrived but he sensed that the room was crowded with silent listeners.

'Continue,' Baistigh eventually boomed.

'In the beginning I convinced myself that I was performing a necessary function. After all, Death comes to all men, be they great or small, princes or beggars. Death walked the World of Men more frequently in those days and I personally took many of those destined for the Silent Wood. But I could not take them all and my bainte took them for me. Eventually the bainte were taking all the essences of those dead people and I was ... well, I was almost useless.

'To amuse myself I retired here to my City and populated it with examples of peoples from differing times and places. I indulged myself by insisting that all the writers and artists, poets and sculptors who passed through my kingdom should produce one original work or complete the work they had had in hand before their death. The bard has seen my library, but he has not seen the gallery.

'But eventually even this palled.

'And then one day – accidentally, I swear it – the bainte

brought a living soul into the Silent Wood. It was that of a female and she had fallen into a deep sleep in the World of Men, so deep indeed that she was thought to be dead and had been buried with all the ceremony of the Old Faith. As you know, part of that ceremony includes the invocation to Death: "Come, dread spirit, and take this mortal soul". And one of my bainte came and took the soul and brought it here. When she awoke in the Silent Wood, the woman's scream ripped through everything, and indeed, I understand that even in the World of Men, a ghostly echo of her scream was heard.'

Paedur found himself nodding, remembering an obscure piece of lore, and then Buiva spoke from just behind his head, startling him. 'Yes, bard, the Scream from the Void.'

Death continued. 'When I reached her, her suspicions as to her whereabouts were confirmed and she immediately fled from me. And I gave chase.

'And, do you know, it was an exhilarating experience. She was a thinking human-being, clever, terrified, but above all she was alive. And as I chased her, a sudden thought struck me. What would happen if I caught and killed her? Would her body re-appear here in the Silent Wood to continue the chase or . . . or what?

'So I eventually caught her . . . and I killed her. And her body vanished. And it wasn't until later, much later, that I discovered that she had re-appeared in the World of Men, whole and alive but in a strange land, many days travel from her own home. When she finally reached her own home – and I followed her progress carefully – the shock of her arrival sent three people to me.' Mannam's cracking, snapping laughter filled the silent room.

'And so I went on to deliberately take a live body.'

A murmur ran around the room, the sound half-way between a moan and a sigh, and even though his eyes were shielded, Paedur knew the intensity of light in the room had increased. He was aware also that the strength of the myriad odours had increased: they had thickened and he found that his own breathing had become laboured. Fleetingly he remembered that when he had first encountered Death he had been aware of the stench of mould and decay that had hung about him, and later, when he had met C'lte, the Yellow God of Life, he had breathed in the rich odour of spices and herbs the god had exuded.

'And you hunted this Son of Man like an animal.' Buiva made the statement into a condemnation.

'I hunted him for sport,' Death snapped.

'You condemn yourself out of your own mouth,' Buiva said quietly and a quick murmur of assent ran around the room.

'It broke the boredom.'

'How many of the Sons of Man have you hunted?' The voice was female this time, but hard and sharp, imperious and commanding. Dannu, Paedur guessed, and Mannam's deferential reply confirmed that it was the Goddess.

'In truth I do not know.'

'And it does not seem to concern you overmuch.'

'They did not die: they returned to the World of Men again,' Mannam said defensively.

'Ah, but many of them came to me.' The voice was that of the simpering Nameless God of Madness and Delusion. 'The pleasures of your kingdom were just a trifle too much for them. The lucky ones came to me, but the others . . .' The god giggled, the sound high-pitched and totally insane. 'Why, some of them have become killers, bandits, brutes. I know of two that slay only when the Lady Lussa rides the heavens. One has taken to eating human flesh; another has formed a fascination for the myriad forms of fornication with men, women and beasts.' The god giggled again, the sound sending a chill hand creeping up along the bard's spine. 'How many souls have you destroyed with your playing, Death? It would have been better if you had taken them properly, instead of leaving them to rot in human shells.'

'I didn't know.' Mannam whined.

'Your protestations disgust me,' the voice Paedur had decided was Dannu's said coldly. 'You are no longer fit to hold the place of a god in the Pantheon of the Old Faith. You have destroyed good human essences, threatened the very existence of the Pantheon with your foolish and ill-considered games, and you have failed in the prime function of all the gods, no matter what their faith: you have betrayed your charges.'

'They are human!' Mannam spat. 'Little better than beasts, they are the playthings of the gods. The Culai had the right idea: they are cattle and should be treated as such!'

The silence that followed was almost physical and Paedur had to resist the almost unendurable urge to scratch where his exposed flesh burned with the exuded power of the gods. And then, surprisingly, the power began to diminish and the bard had the distinct impression that the gods were silently leaving one by one. The light against his blindfold lessened, which only reinforced the idea.

There was movement beside him and he stiffened as a hand brushed against his head catching the cloth blindfold, and then Buiva spoke from beside his head. 'Don't look at the Goddess; keep your eyes on Mannam or me. But if you value your sanity, you will not look at the Lady.' Paedur nodded and then Buiva twitched the blindfold away. The bard blinked rapidly, his eyes watering – even the dim light was blinding – but kept his head ducked.

'Ah yes, our Champion, the Bard Paedur. What is your part in this foul affair?'

'I am afraid that like Churon the Onelord and indeed the Gods of the Pantheon, I too have been an innocent dupe of Death.'

'What brought you to the Silent Wood?'

Paedur kept his eyes fixed on the smooth, black stone of the bare floor, but from the sound of her voice, he formed the impression of a strong, matronly woman.

'I lost two companions on the Culai Isle when we fought for the Old Faith. I came here to try and claim them back.'

'Death is final.' Mannam interrupted. 'It is a door which opens only one way.'

'And are there not other doors?' Paedur asked, glancing up at Mannam, and then stopped in astonishment at the change that had come over him. The figure of Death had always been tall and thin, covered in a long, dark cloak of seared and withered leaves and with his features hidden beneath the cowl of that cloak. Now he was bent and twisted, like a tree that had been eaten with disease. His cloak was frayed and tattered, the leaves scattered around his feet, and now the face was partially revealed it was not the skeletal face Paedur had once glimpsed, but the face of a tired, incredibly old man, his skin the colour of rotten wood, a web-work of wrinkles lending his face a gnarled bark-like appearance.

'Your companions are dead,' Mannam insisted. 'They are beyond Death's aid.'

'But you are not Death,' the Lady Dannu said coldly.

The bard, whose eyes were on Mannam, saw him look up, saw the agonised expression appear in his eyes, followed by rage and defiance.

'Then who is Death?' he snarled.

'I am!'

Paedur turned, somehow unsurprised when Churon walked up to stand beside Buiva. He bowed deeply to the woman standing behind the bard.

The twisted figure of Mannam turned, his eyes squinting, attempting to focus, but eventually he gave it up. 'And who are you?' he demanded querulously, an old man, squinting, half-blind.

'I am Churon, once Onelord in the World of Men, now Overlord of the Silent Wood.'

'And a God of the Old Faith,' Paedur added softly.

'Why didn't you accept the position when I offered it to you?' Mannam shouted, his voice cracking and breaking.

'You did not offer, you attempted to trick me into taking it. I liked neither your methods nor your terms,' Churon said.

'I hope it twists you as it twisted me,' Mannam said venomously.

'I think not. You forget that I knew what it was to rule in the World of Men; I drank deeply of that cup whilst I lived, and it holds no attraction for me now.'

'And what of Mannam?' Paedur asked into the silence that followed. He kept his eyes low, looking at the shrunken figure of the Dark Lord. He glanced up as Churon turned to the goddess, 'My lady?'

Dannu's voice was hard and cold. 'He returns to the World of Men, as he is,' she added. 'And Death.' Both Mannam and Churon looked up, but she had been addressing the Onelord. 'You will not take him, not now, not ever, not so long as the Gods of the Pantheon rule and the Old Faith holds sway.'

'I don't understand,' Churon said slowly, but the bard understood fully, knew what the once-god had been sentenced to.

'He is not to die,' Dannu insisted. 'You are not to take him. His curse is to wander the Planes of Existence for the rest of eternity . . .'

'Or until the Old Faith dies,' Mannam spat.

Dannu laughed, the sound masculine and totally humourless. 'Our Champion here has ensured a revival of interest in the Old Faith; but I forget, you had a hand in that.'

The venom behind Mannam's eyes was a physical thing, a leaking foulness. 'Then I will work for the downfall of the Gods of the Pantheon and the ending of the Old Faith.' He turned, a twisted, vengeful, embittered old man, and stared hard at the bard. 'And I will have you slain,' he promised. 'For all your god-gifted powers, I will destroy you. You brought me to this, and without you the Faith will wither and die!'

'And will you keep Manach?' Paedur asked the new God of Death.

Churon leaned over the battlements of the City of the Dead and looked down over its wide cobbled streets. 'Probably. I won't keep the occupants in thrall though, as Mannam did; they will be free to come and go as they please.'

'And what of my companions. Did you discover anything about them?'

'I am afraid their essences are beyond me. They both died on the Culai Isle, where, as you know, the laws of the Planes of Existence are negated. And, even if I could discover and re-animate Tuan's existence, the priestess was destroyed when the Chrystallis and the Cords vied for supremacy; her essence was scattered through the void.'

'So my journey here was wasted?'

'Not totally,' Churon grinned. 'Your coming set in motion a train of events that lead to the death of one god and the birthing of another – something not every human can claim.'

They walked slowly along the battlements, no longer even conscious of the blood-stench from the Naman. In another time and another place they might have been two old friends strolling companionably together before retiring for the night. When they reached the stairs they stopped and Paedur turned to Churon. 'Tell me, why did you accept the position of Death?'

Churon rested a coal-black hand on the equally dark stone-work and looked out across his domain towards the shadow that was the Mire, and when he finally turned back to the bard, his blue eyes were sparkling slightly. 'To atone, bard. I'm not sure if that makes any sense to you, or if you even can understand it, but just to atone.'

The bard paused before replying, and then he finally nodded and turned to climb down the steps. 'I understand.'

Katani was waiting at the bottom of the stairs. She was sitting with her back to the cold stones, running an oiled cloth along the length of her longsword blade with a monotonous, almost ritual persistence. She came smoothly and silently to her feet as Paedur and Churon descended.

'What now?' she asked simply.

Paedur looked at Churon.

'A time of parting,' the new god said quietly. 'You, bard, must return to the World of Men; your companions – and the Old Faith – need you and your powers now. And I think you will find your powers enhanced, but use them wisely. Remember the lesson of Mannam: no-one is above retribution. And a word of warning: when Mannam went into the World of Men he promptly disappeared, but be assured he will attempt to slay you, and I would imagine he will side with the enemies of the Faith. Be wary of him.'

'And what of me?' Katani asked, her voice measured and even, but her eyes troubled.

'You are dead,' Churon reminded her.

'Does it have to be so?'

'You are dead,' Churon repeated.

'And you are Death.'

'Would you return to the World of Men?'

Katani remained silent.

'I have need of a companion, someone to protect me from Mannam,' Paedur said, his face expressionless.

The Onelord nodded seriously. 'Of course, and there are no finer warriors on the myriad Planes of Existence than the Katan.' He looked at the woman again, his expression softening. 'It would avail you and I naught if I were to apologise for what I did those many years ago. What's done is done and cannot be undone. I can send you back into the World of Men again, and this time when you die you can at least die with all the dignity and honour of a Katan warrior. That is all I can give you.'

'It is enough.'

Churon bowed. 'Both of you I shall meet again – but not soon I hope,' he added with a smile.

'And I will add a new chapter to my tale of Churon the One-lord,' Paedur promised.

# 24    *The Return of the Bard*

'The first time I met the bard, I was frightened, the second time, I was terrified.'

*Tien tZo*

There was a long crack and the door split down the centre from top to bottom. Guards both human and quai burst into the chamber, squeezing through the shattered doorway. Three died instantly and in the pounding confusion that followed another three went down beneath Owen's sword and Tien tZo's lethal blows.

A gong boomed in the corridor and the guards milling outside the room immediately retreated, giving Owen and Tien a momentary respite. The Shemmat quickly stripped off his Andam robes and began to sift through the armour and weapons of the fallen men, clothing and arming himself, while Owen stood in the doorway, watching the activity in the corridor beyond.

'They're massing for a concerted attack,' he said quietly.

Tien glanced up from a warrior whose throat had been opened. 'Well, they cannot get more than two or three through the door at any one time, and at that rate we hold this room for an eternity.'

Owen smiled tightly. 'Much good it will do us.'

Tien straightened, tightening the buckles on a jerkin of fine link mail. He pulled on greaves that were a little too big for him and cinched the buckles tight. Into his belt he stuck as many knives as he could comfortably carry, and from the swords he had gathered he picked the two best suited to his height and reach. 'I'll check the room; there may be another way out.'

The Weapon Master grunted, his attention on the corridor. Something unusual was happening; the quai and human guards had massed at the end of the long corridor, obviously preparing for an attack, and yet they hadn't moved. From the way they kept looking around, he guessed that they were waiting for a senior officer, and Owen idly wondered who would have enough

249

authority to order an attack on Salier's own chambers. He smiled at a sudden thought: there was only one person . . .

'I am Fodla.' A huge woman in a simple white woollen shift with a massive sword belt strapped around her waist roughly pushed past the guards and boldly strode down the corridor. She stopped exactly in the centre, her hands on her hips, facing the shattered doorway. 'There is no way out of that room. Salier himself designed it that way. The windows are barred and there is a sheer drop to the cobbles below. But to ensure you take no risks, there are archers in the courtyard. The fireplace is barred within the chimney, and even if you manage to bypass that obstacle, there are men on the roof. If you intend to come out, you must come down this corridor.' Abruptly, she turned away and walked back to disappear into the growing numbers of palace guards.

'She's right,' Tien said, taking up position on Owen's right-hand side. 'There are two rooms, this and a bed-chamber which also doubles as a library. All the windows are barred, which, while it keeps us in, also serves to keep them out. There are archers in the courtyard below, but at least the rooms are not overlooked, so we cannot be fired upon. We are trapped,' he added unnecessarily.

'Can we dig our way into one of the adjoining rooms?' Owen wondered idly.

'There are only these two chambers in the corridor . . .' Tien began, and then stopped as a trio of archers took up position at the end of the corridor.

Fodla stepped through the massed ranks again. 'You have a chance now to surrender. Your final chance.' She waited for a reply, but receiving none, stepped back and nodded once to the archers.

The archers were using screamers, broad, triangular-headed arrows with slits cut into the metal which caused them to emit a high-pitched scream as the air whistled through them. The effect was more than psychological; screamers caused massive wounds and the heads were broad and heavy enough to punch through most layered armours as well as chain and link mails.

Two of the arrows embedded themselves into the broken door, punching entirely through the wood, while the third passed directly through the shattered centre and exploded in a shower of sparks and wood against the wall opposite.

Fodla stepped through the archers and spoke again. 'I assume Salier is dead?' Both men instinctively glanced at the still figure in the chair. 'But if he isn't, then I would suggest you send him out.'

Owen looked at the chair again and then nodded to Tien; the Shemmat nodded in understanding. Leaving his swords by the door, he darted across to the huge fireplace and grabbed the mage by the front of his gown and pulled him up out of the chair. Then, half-lifting, half-dragging the incredibly heavy chair, he hauled it over to the broken door.

Three more arrows screamed in through the opening, only to shatter on the wall opposite.

'Come out now!' Fodla demanded.

Owen nodded and Tien heaved the chair out into the opening blocking it. The Weapon Master grabbed the opposite arm and dragged it across the gap. They heard the screaming and then the chair shuddered as two more arrows thudded into the back, the tips of their heads actually pricking through the wooden seat. But the gap was now plugged and the only remaining opening was a head-sized triangular split close to the top of the door.

'They can't get in,' Tien remarked with a wry smile.

'You cannot get out,' Fodla shouted.

'What happens now?' the Shemmat asked, leaning back against the wall, rubbing the flat of the curved swordblade against his sleeve.

'Now we wait.'

'They'll fire the rooms,' Tien said softly, still rubbing the sword.

Owen nodded.

'We could rush them.'

The Weapon Master nodded again.

Tien risked a quick glance out into the corridor. More archers had arrived and two men carrying one of the heavy armour-piercing crossbows were setting up their weapon in the centre of the floor. These crossbows were usually bolted into the ground and used for long-range killing; they were accurate up to a thousand paces, were incredibly powerful and could punch an iron-tipped, brass-bound shaft through three lines of armoured men. At such close range and in the confines of the corridor, the effect of the heavy man-sized bolts could only be guessed at.

'I think we'd better do something,' Tien said dubiously.

There was a creak and a grinding of gears and then the heavy floor-mounted crossbow rocked on its tripod. The enormous bolt punched the heavy chair all the way across the room, literally snapping it in two, splinters and slivers of dark wood hanging in the air like dust. A score of screamers followed, some sinking into the remnants of the door, rocking it on its already torn hinges, others whining around the room to shatter glass and delicate crystal.

Owen readied himself for a suicidal charge down the corridor. 'Well, at least we killed Salier,' he said philosophically. 'Perhaps we might get Fodla also.'

'*Foolish man! Do you think I am so easily slain!*' The voice was a shriek.

Salier was standing by the fire, Tien's throwing spike still protruding from his left eye, a trickle of congealed ichor on his drawn cheeks. His expression was ghastly and the light that burned in this right eye was that of absolute insanity.

Another screamer shattered against the wall, but it was completely ignored. Tien threw a knife underhand, the long, thin, double-edged blade catching the mage low in the throat. The creature – no longer human – staggered, but there was no blood, and Salier plucked it out almost contemptuously from his pale flesh. Turning it in his hand he brought it up to his remaining eye, seemingly captivated by the polished metal, and then he flung it back at the Shemmat. Only Tien's battle-hardened reflexes saved him, the sword coming up automatically, catching and deflecting the thrown knife, sending it ringing against the walls.

Salier raised his left hand and the blood-red glow of fox-fire was already gathering around the fingers when a second heavy crossbow bolt ripped what remained of the door off its hinges. Splinters of wood grazed Tien's cheek and a length of wood almost decapitated Owen, but a flat slab struck Salier flat in the chest, staggering him, sending him toppling backwards. His heels struck the raised marble slabs that surrounded the fire and for a moment he swayed precariously, and then he crashed back into the fire. His robes ignited with a dull explosion.

The scream of the charging guards was drowned by the ghastly ululation from the creature that had once been Salier. A figure, now only vaguely manlike, rose up out of the flames and staggered across the room, its consciousness or dull remembered instinct taking it towards the only exit, the open doorway. Trailing flame and screaming hideously, it staggered out into the corridor, and immediately the guards' shouts changed to screams of terror. Tien and Owen held back undecided, and they watched in horror as the creature staggered down the long corridor, enwrapping everyone it touched in flame. Fodla shouted a command and a score of screamers struck it, sending it staggering, but not knocking it down. The archers on the heavy crossbow were working frantically, cranking the enormous wheel, bending the massive bow.

Owen nodded. 'When they fire that, we'll move. Try and take out Fodla before they get you.'

'You will remain here!'

The voice from behind them was cool and calmly authoritative, and although they had both only heard it on one previous occasion, it was a voice they would never forget.

'*Paedur!*'

The bard, standing in the centre of the room, was as they remembered him, tall, thin, dark-clad and forbidding, radiating power and menace. And behind him stood a figure, a creature out of legend, a fantastical creation that it took them both moments to recognise as a human wearing armour. Tien recognised the archaic style first: 'The skin of the ice-serpents of Thusal – a Katan warrior!'

The Weapon Master nodded, but his eyes were on the bard. 'Where have you been?' he asked softly.

'Later,' Paedur said, a smile curling his lips, lending his hard, sharp features character and a touch of humanity. He strode to the door and stared down the fire-streaked and blackened corridor. The heavy crossbow was now wreathed in flames and the two archers nowhere to be seen, although the smouldering pile of filthy ashes on the floor around it might have been the remains of a human. All the guards, both human and quai, had vanished also, leaving only a single figure facing the flaming creature that had been Salier the Mage. Fodla pulled the broadsword free of its scabbard, undid the buckler and tossed it to one side before advancing towards the creature, dropping into a fighting crouch.

Paedur pulled his furred cloak tighter around his shoulders and stepped out into the corridor, and although he had moved noiselessly, the creature turned, its hideous screaming ceasing abruptly.

Its face was ghastly. The features had been burned away, leaving only gaping holes where the mouth and nose had been, but the eyes remained, dark and alive and in torment. It stared at the bard and something moved behind the eyes and recognition flared. The mouth worked and a sound that was between a hiss and a word escaped the blackened lips. 'Bard!'

Paedur nodded. 'I am surprised you still recognise me, mage,' he said softly. 'It has been a long time.'

'Bard!' The creature spat again and raised a flame-wrapped arm. A long spear of white-hot flame lanced from it, but the bard caught it on his hook, wrapping it around the glowing metal like a thread.

While Salier was distracted, Fodla used the opportunity to lunge at the creature with her broadsword. The metal sank deep into its back and then struck something solid and stuck. The creature screamed and spun around, wrenching the sword from her hand, sending her sprawling. Tiny tongues of flame sparkled in the air around the dazed woman, hissing and crackling like insects, floating down to land on her exposed skin, searing the flesh. And then the broadsword began to melt, the metal running liquid down the creature's body to bubble on the scarred stones.

'Why doesn't it die?' Owen whispered.

'Because it is already dead – long dead,' Paedur said softly, 'and the dead cannot die.'

The Katan warrior reached out and almost touched the edge of the bard's cloak. 'It will kill the woman,' she said evenly, her eyes bright behind the horned demon's mask.

'She is our enemy,' Tien said diffidently.

'She is human, and alive; the creature is unhuman and dead,' Katani said simply.

Tien nodded and bowed slightly. He looked at Owen, 'Master?'

Owen sighed and nodded. He turned to look at the bard. 'Can we kill it?'

'It is already dead,' Paedur said. But he stepped forward and raised his left arm high, the curved hook glinting in the smoky, sooty air. Something like a smile touched his usually impassive features and he spoke a single word, 'Huide!'

The flames rose higher around the creature that had been

human, and the heat was strong enough to force Owen and Tien back. Katani's armour protected her somewhat and the bard seemed impervious to the heat, but Fodla, who was barely paces from the creature and clad in nothing more than a torn shift was badly scorched, her skin turning red and cracking before their eyes. Her red hair began to smoke and crinkle.

Tien touched Owen's arm and pointed.

A fine, pale mist had gathered close to the blackened ceiling. As they watched it thickened and darkened, and then it suddenly began to rain down on the creature.

'Huide,' Owen gasped, remembering the name, 'Huide, the Little God of Summer Rain!'

The creature that had been Salier was now enwrapped in a cloud of hissing steam as the fine mist of rain fell on him. The small flames darting around Fodla were immediately extinguished and slowly, slowly, the raging fire that was burning but not consuming Salier was diminished. There was a dull explosion, as if something had ignited within the mage, and the flames briefly surged again, but the rain intensified and the creature was completely enveloped in a dense cloud of smoke. The fires died and the foul-smelling corridor was suddenly suffused with the fresh odour of damp growth – the smell of a forest after a summer shower.

Without waiting for a command, Owen and Tien ran forward, avoiding the twisting, shifting wreaths of dense white smoke and grabbed Fodla, half lifting, half carrying the huge woman back into what had once been Salier's chambers. Paedur remained, watching the greasy pile of charred ashes, before he too turned away, leaving Katani to take up position beside the door.

Owen and Tien had laid Fodla out on the cold marble flag-stones before the fire. Her shift had been completely consumed by the flames, leaving her naked except for a simple loin cloth, and all of her exposed skin was red-raw and seeping. Her eyebrows had been burned off and her flaming red hair was crisped and seared, leaving only a thin fuzz close to her skull. And yet she still lived, only her strength and stamina having kept her alive so far.

Paedur knelt beside the woman and touched her with the flat of his hook. The chill of the metal sent a shudder through her body and her cracked lips worked, the skin splitting as she moved them, and while Tien hurried to find liquid to moisten them, she uttered two words: 'Kill me.'

Without hesitation, Owen unsheathed his knife and placed the tip beneath the woman's breast, preparing to drive it home.

'No,' Paedur said simply, his hook lifting the knife.

'She is a warrior and in pain, and there is no cure for this. There is nothing left for her but a lingering, painful death, and she deserves better,' Owen said, anger touching his voice. 'She would do the same for me. It is part of the warrior's code.'

The bard nodded. 'And it is also needless.'

Tien returned and knelt by the stricken woman with a goblet of pale amber-coloured wine which he placed down beside her. Tearing a strip of cloth from his borrowed shirt, he soaked it in the wine, moistened her lips and allowed a few drops to trickle down the woman's throat.

'Enough,' Paedur said. 'Now step back.'

Tien looked to Owen and the Weapon Master reluctantly nodded, and both men stood up and moved away from the woman. The bard raised his left arm and allowed his hook to rest barely a hair's breadth above Fodla's body. He moved the hook down to her feet and then bent his head. His lips moved, and abruptly the runes etched into the metal began to sparkle and glow, and then the hook abruptly exuded a pale blue-green light, which seemed to flow from it like liquid and wrap itself around Fodla's burned feet, sinking into the raw flesh. She moaned, shuddering, her eyes opening in shock. The bard slowly moved the hook up the woman's body drawing the blue-green with it, and leaving in its wake clear, pink and unblemished skin.

Later Fodla would describe the sensation as that of being rubbed by damp leaves or moss, but even she could only watch awestruck as the seeping skin dried and the ugly scorched and hard, burned flesh softened and was absorbed back into the bright, pink and clean skin of her body. She watched as Paedur moved his hook upwards, saw it clean and cleanse her skin, removing even old scars and weals that had come from a lifetime of battle. She looked at the man's face, saw the concentration, the intentness, recognised the pain in his eyes. And yet she was a stranger to him; why then should he care?

His hook continued upwards, across her stomach and up over her breasts, and she closed her eyes and allowed the cooling, gentle moistness to soothe her wounds. In those moments Fodla decided that there could be nothing evil in a man who was able to heal like this, and who did so for a total stranger. Fodla had experienced mages and magicians, warlocks and wizards in her mercenary trade, but she had only ever known them to be able to kill or harm; none of them were healers. And the few healers she had known were, without exception, gentle, good people, at peace with their world and themselves – as indeed they must be to be able to heal.

She became aware that the tingling had stopped and there was complete silence in the room. She opened her eyes and looked up into the hard, sharp face of the bard. 'Thank you,' she said simply.

He smiled and the mask fell away, and for a single heartbeat she glimpsed the man beneath the mask. He reached down with his hand and pulled her to her feet with almost casual ease.

Fodla looked past the bard at the two men standing close to the door – with their backs to the wall, she noted with a wry smile. She turned to Owen, recognising him for what he was, a battle-weary, professional soldier, and smiled a little uneasily. 'Thank-you.'

He returned her smile. 'For what?'

'You would have killed me when I was in pain.'

'You would have afforded me the same honour,' he said, something like shyness touching his voice.

'I hope I would have been able to do so,' she said. She looked at Tien. 'And you too, thank you.'

'You are a warrior,' Tien said simply, as if that explained everything.

'And you, what are you?' Fodla asked him.

'I am merely a servant.'

But the Weapon-Master shook his head quickly. 'He is more than a servant; he is a friend,' he said. 'I am Owen, Weapon Master, and he is Tien tZo . . . my companion.'

'I have heard of you both,' Fodla said. 'Indeed, who has not?' She turned to the bard and found he had wandered off and was poking amongst the mage's shelves of scrolls and charts. The Katan warrior was standing by his side as if she were a guard. 'And you, who are you both?' Fodla asked.

The woman pulled off her horned helmet and shook loose her bone-white hair. Her amber eyes sparkled with humour and when she spoke her accent sounded quaint and archaic. 'I am Katani of the Katan, and this is Paedur.'

257

Paedur turned when he heard his name spoken, and Fodla looked with more interest at the tall, dark man. 'Your name is not unfamiliar to me. A fortune awaits the man who kills you.'

Paedur shrugged. 'I am pleased the Imperials hold me in such high esteem.'

'What are you?' Fodla asked quietly.

The bard glanced sidelong at her, something like a smile touching his lips. 'I am a bard,' he said simply.

'The Prince Kutor's forces are unstoppable. It is said the gods themselves are on their side,' Fodla said, lifting the bottle and filling three glasses and then her own; only the bard wasn't drinking.

'When will he enter the city?' Paedur asked, moving away from the shattered door to stand by the table.

'I would imagine there will be one final battle on the plain beyond the gates and that will decide the matter, and that battle will take place within the next three or four days.'

'Then we must ensure that it goes in our favour,' Owen said. He looked at Fodla. 'Are you sure you are with us in this? It will mean betraying everything you have fought for, giving up everything you have achieved, losing what friends, influence and power you have now.'

Fodla bared her teeth in a semblance of a smile. 'Like you, I am a mercenary. For all my apparent wealth, I have little coin. As for everything I have achieved, I could leave it without a qualm, and, like most professional warriors, I have taken care to have few friends. Leaving here will be no great loss.'

Owen nodded; it was an explanation he could accept. He turned to Katani. 'This is not your fight. There is no reason for you to be here.'

The warrior-woman ran her long fingers through her white hair, pushing it back off her face, her pointed teeth giving her face a feral appearance. 'It is a conflict between Good and Evil . . .'

'No conflict is ever so sharply defined,' Paedur murmured, but Katani continued on.

'I will fight this fight because I want to, because I spent all my life fighting for the Faith and what I believed in. And now that I have a second chance, I see no reason to stop.'

'What second chance,' Tien asked, intrigued.

'Now that I am restored to life,' the woman said enigmatically.

Tien shook his head in puzzlement and looked at the bard. He smiled. 'Katani walked the Silent Wood for a long time, before returning to the Planes of Life with me.'

'Do you have the power to restore the dead to life?' Owen asked in astonishment.

Paedur shook his head. 'Only a God can restore the dead to Life.'

'I thought you were a God,' he said.

'Not yet,' Katani said with a smile.

Paedur shook his head and returned to the window, looking down over the courtyard, watching the palace guards filing out carrying the bodies of their slain comrades between them. What looked like a whole legion had arrived moments after he had healed Fodla. Their commander had met them and explained that Salier had gone beserk and attempted a coup, using his occult powers to kill and burn all those around him. She explained that he had only been stopped by the people in the room, who had not only killed the mage but also saved her own life. A squadron of her own personal guard took up position along the corridor, occupying the places so recently vacated by Salier's quai, while the rest of the men cleared up the dead bodies. For the moment, no-one was allowed into the room.

'Where is Barthus the Hierophant?' Paedur asked suddenly.

Fodla shook her head. 'No-one knows. From what I have been able to put together from my scouts' reports, I understand that following his meeting with the Andam,' she smiled at Tien, 'he dressed in simple travelling robes and set off for the palace. Last reports place him with the Emperor, but neither man has been seen for a little while.'

'Will they have been made aware of what happened here?' Katani asked softly.

'Undoubtedly,' Fodla said.

'I would imagine they are attempting to evaluate your position in all this,' Owen said slowly. 'They will be asking if you are attempting a coup: is Salier really dead and if so, did you kill him? And if you did, do you plan to kill them? Will you side with the rebels? What happened to Geillard's and Salier's hired mercenary – namely me – and what happened to the Andam?'

'What numbers do they control?' Katani asked.

Fodla shook her head. 'In this situation it would be difficult to say. The Emperor would control a legion of his personal guard, the Emperor Legion, but they are directly under my command and have all been personally trained by me. They might side with me and they are a highly skilled fighting force. Barthus would theoretically be able to call upon every able-bodied follower of the New Religion to rally to his flag, but I would imagine he will only call on the temple guard and whatever members of the Iron Band of Kloor are in the capital at the moment.'

'We have talked in circles,' Tien said softly. 'We must return to our original question. What do we do now?'

As one, all the heads turned to the tall figure standing by the window. Without turning, Paedur said, 'Fodla will take whatever men she feels will be loyal to our cause and, along with Owen and Tien, return to Prince Kutor and his forces.' His voice was soft, each word carefully considered and delivered. 'Before going you will attempt to destroy as many of the long-range weapons – the ballistae, the oils, the giant bows – as possible.'

'And you?' Owen asked. 'What of you?'

'Katani and I will continue with a portion of the original plan; we will attempt to kill Barthus and Geillard.'

'Will you succeed?'

Paedur turned from the window and looked at each in turn. 'Probably not,' he said with a wry smile.

## 25 Allies

And in his time, Empires rose and fell, and his hand was apparent
in it . . .

*Life of Paedur, the Bard*

As the afternoon turned, Imperial troops marched into the
streets of Karfondal. Although the provinces had seethed in revolution, the capital had remained quiet, with only the additional
numbers of soldiers on the streets and the unusual number of
mercenaries in the taverns giving any indication that there was
in fact a war being fought.

The road to the palace was closed, sealing it off from the rest
of the city, with no-one allowed in, but effectively trapping everyone within. Geillard's palace was situated in the precise geo-
graphical centre of the city, supposedly following some ancient
occult practice, and covered hundreds of thousands of paces in
all directions. However, there was only one main thoroughfare
that led to the palace – the Royal Way – which in turn led out
on to the King Road that bisected the Seven Nations from Thusal
to southernmost Lostrice. A squad of the Emperor Legion, aug-
mented by the Imperial Guard, had taken up position across it,
behind barricades of metal and stone. Heavy ground-mounted
crossbows were bolted into position and behind them sappers
began tearing up the broad marble flags along the tree-lined
avenue that led to the palace. The ugly pockmarks they left in
their wake were designed to trap and snap a mount's hoof or to
render a charge impossible.

Paedur and Katani mingled with the crowd that was growing
to watch the proceedings. Both had thrown dusty travelling
cloaks over their own clothing to enable them to move through
the crowd without attracting undue attention.

Katani nodded at the workmen. 'The sign of defeat,' she murmured.

'A defeat expected is a defeat accepted,' the bard smiled. It
was a Katan saying.

261

There was a sudden commotion and a man wandered out of the crowd, his height and colouring marking him as a mercenary from Thusal, and he was more than a little drunk from his gait. He staggered up to the barricade and demanded to be allowed to pass beyond. The captain of the guard, a slender, dark-skinned woman from Fodla's Emperor Legion, nodded and stepped aside, leaving a space for the leather-clad barbarian to pass through. When he reached the other side he turned to wave at the crowd, and then abruptly disappeared!

'What happened to him?' Katani hissed.

'Someone stuck a knife in his back,' Paedur remarked. 'Come on.' He turned away and made his way through the growing crowd, the people parting almost naturally for the man, although most would have been unaware that they were even doing so.

'Where are we going?' Katani asked.

'There is only one way into the palace,' Paedur murmured, ducking past a deserted fruit stall. 'We'll try some of the side streets.'

There were countless side streets and alleys that led out on to the great open square, but all of these were held by a small group of guards, usually backed up by one of the heavy crossbows.

The sun was dipping in the heavens by the time the bard was forced to admit defeat. All the routes were held. Paedur walked away from the mouth of an alley shaking his head in disgust. It was so insignificant that he had hoped it would have been overlooked, but two bulky figures in black armour filled the end, chatting softly together, their voices echoing off the grimy stones. Katani was waiting for him by a fruit stall, carefully slicing the hard rind from a green-skinned tropical fruit that grew in Lostrice.

'Well?' She looked up from beneath the cowl of the cloak she was wearing over her armour.

He shook his head.

'But there must be some way in,' she insisted, tearing off the last of the skin and turning the pale fruit around and around in her hands, savouring its tart perfume. Since she had returned to the World of Men, she had made a deliberate effort to enjoy every sensation to the utmost, making up for her time spent in Mannam's dark kingdom.

Paedur nodded absently, attempting to recreate the geography of the city from a chart he had seen in Baddalaur's library many years ago and from what he remembered from his stint as Bard to the Imperial Court. There was something at the back of his mind, something from the days of his youth. A smile touched his thin lips, remembering those distant days, the escapades, the pranks, the balls, the women . . . and the smile broadened as he abruptly remembered a way into the palace.

'Come!'

'Where are we going?' Katani asked, breaking the fruit, popping segments into her mouth, wincing at the sharp, bitter juice.

'There is a way into the palace,' Paedur said softly, taking Katani by the arm and leading her through a bewildering maze of mean streets and even meaner alleyways, relying on his visual memory of a single previous visit, of a fog-wrapped night and a wild chase through the backstreets of the capital when he had acted the spy for Geillard.

'How do you know?'

Paedur stopped, hesitating at an intersection. He closed his eyes and then took the street to the right, avoiding a pile of festering refuse. 'I was Bard to the Imperial Court a long time ago,' he said quietly, almost to himself. 'Geillard, who was merely vain and foolish then and not completely insane, suspected his mistress of conducting an affair with a nobleman of the court. He approached me and asked if I would be prepared to follow her when she left the court and report back to him with her eventual destination. The reason why he had chosen me was because, with my infirmity and my unique position at court, I would never be suspected of working for the Emperor. I was a young man then and, like the young, easily flattered, and my expectations and ideals were different. I wanted to be . . . oh, many things,' he smiled almost shyly, 'many things.'

'And so you followed the woman?'

'I followed her.'

'And where did she go?' Katani asked.

'Here!'

The street they had been following had gradually grown meaner, eventually turning into little more than an alleyway, winding down between high-walled foul-smelling tenements. However, it suddenly opened out into a small enclosed courtyard in the centre of which was a well and pump. Paedur stopped in the mouth of the alley and pointed across the square. 'That's where she went.'

Katani looked at the four-storied red-brick building, curiously elegant and completely out of place between its shoddy mouldering neighbours. Although the years had not been kind to it and time and decay had stripped it of much of its grandeur, it still retained enough of the original mouldings and fixtures to give some idea of its former glory. 'It's seen better days,' she remarked.

'It was the town house of a princeling from one of the provinces in the days when the city was smaller, and although you may find it hard to believe now, it once stood in its own grounds. Then the line died out – the last of them assassinated by one of Geillard's ancestors, or so it is said – and the house passed through several hands before it was gambled away in a very famous game that changed the course of the history of the Nations, which I'll tell you about some time. For the past three generations, however, it has served the same purpose.'

'And that is?' Katani asked, although she had already guessed.

'It's a brothel.'

Paedur pulled his cloak higher about his shoulders, and with stooped shoulders he walked slowly and carefully across the cracked cobbles. Katani strode along beside him, assuming the role of son to the bard's old man. 'You never told me what happened to the woman you were following,' she murmured. 'Why did she come here?'

'She was the Madam of the house,' he whispered. 'She disappeared soon afterwards. I suspected Geillard.'

They mounted the worn steps that led to the peeling door. Countless feet had worn the stone smooth and glasslike, and to any observers the old man had great difficulty in mounting the steps, gripping the younger man's arm tightly. In reality the bard was issuing last minute instructions to Katani. 'Kill anyone who stands against us. For the plan to succeed we must hold this house for almost a whole day, and a life or two counts as little when the fate of every man, woman and child in Karfondal is at stake.'

'How many guards?'

'Unknown, but two or more certainly.'

'Women?'

'Again unknown, possibly a dozen or so.'

Katani made a face. 'Do you think two of us will be enough?'

'Individually, we are greater than two; together, we are an army.'

Katani bit down on the inside of her cheeks to suppress a laugh.

The bard raised a hand trembling with age and effort and rapped on the door, twice, and again and then once more. 'I hope they haven't changed the code.'

A panel snapped open and hard, dark eyes regarded them suspiciously. 'Yes?'

'Reports of the excellent entertainment offered by your house has reached even the provinces,' Paedur said, his voice quavering, using the password he had heard all those years ago. He was gambling that it would be unlikely for the brothel to have changed its code or password, if for no other reason than that it would be impossible to acquaint all its customers with the change.

'I don't know you!' the voice said simply, a note of finality in it.

The bard looked up, his eyes catching and holding those of the man behind the door. For a single instant they blazed, burning with an almost visible blue fire, and for a single heartbeat a cold, inhuman creature stared out from behind them. 'You know me, don't you?' Paedur suggested, his voice soft, sibilant, like the hiss of a serpent.

'Yes sir, I know you.' The panel snapped shut, there were the sounds of bolts being drawn back and the door swung open. 'Good to see you again, sir.' A huge man filled the doorway, and even without his heightened senses Paedur would have been able to tell of the man's mixed non-human ancestry. His features were broad, flat and brutish, and there was Chopt blood in his veins certainly.

The bard and Katani moved into the darkness of the hallway, pushed through a heavy leathern curtain that hung behind the door, and stepped into another world.

From without, the building was shabby and peeling, the wood-work rotten, the stonework crumbling, the metalwork twisting and rusting, but within, it was a palace. Paedur had been expecting it, but to Katani it was a revelation. Deep-piled scented rugs covered the polished wooden floors, exuding scents and odours with every step. The decorated walls were hung with tapestries that glittered and sparkled with rare threads and wools. Many of the interior walls had been removed and scores of floor to ceiling mirrors added to the illusion of space.

The doorman ushered them into a room furnished in the style of the Emperor Geillard VIII, natural woods and polished stone richly decorated and embellished with earthen pigments lending it warmth and character.

The hulking doorman stepped back and closed the door, leaving them alone in the room. Paedur looked at Katani and raised a finger to his lips. She nodded briefly and wandered over to the huge open fireplace, standing with her back to it, warming her hands, her hard eyes assessing the room. Paedur meanwhile crossed to a long couch that had been cut from the bole of an ironwood tree and sank back into its naturally smooth curves. He closed his eyes and allowed his heightened senses to come to the fore. He immediately became aware of the tainted life-aura of Katani: although back in the World of Men, she had not truly shaken off Death's hold. He absorbed that into his consciousness, and then felt the burning glow of life from two other watchers in the room, one off behind a false panel behind him and another looking out from behind the scrollwork beside the fire. He reached for a goblet of wine, but stopped when his fingers touched the glass: the wine had been treated with some mind-dulling drug – not enough for the ordinary man to notice, but then, he was no ordinary man. He allowed his fingers to move on to the bowl of fruit and discovered that they too had been bathed in the drug, allowing it to seep into their succulent flesh.

He suddenly became aware of a small group gathering in the corridor outside. He recognised the dulled aura of the doorman walking a step or two behind a red-white glow of a person in command, someone large, seething with anger. Behind these two, three more followed, but their auras were the blank white of professional killers or quai.

Paedur glanced at Katani, briefly touching her mind. She looked up, startled, and he caught and held her gaze, moving his head slightly towards the door. The warrior-maid nodded slowly, casually. He then allowed the image of a person hiding in the panelling behind him and the second man concealed beside her to drift into her mind. She looked at him sharply, unsure if she were actually seeing a true sending or if it was just her imagination. His lips curled in a slight smile and he nodded.

The double doors of the room had been carved and worked with a frieze of rambling, tumbling flowers from all across the Nations, and a tiny rose cut into the wood suddenly dilated. Although he was sitting across the room, the bard's sensitive hearing caught the tiny rasp of the sliding wood and felt the cold gaze of a woman – he had identified the aura as female – move contemptuously across him. The panel closed silently.

Paedur turned his head slightly to catch the murmur of voices. 'I don't know them.' Then, obviously to the doorman. 'They must have bewitched you.' And finally turning to the three cold white auras. 'Kill them!'

'Move!' Paedur shouted.

There was a whisper of steel and, without turning, Katani dropped to one knee and plunged her sword through the scroll-work beside the fire, driving the blade in with both hands locked around the long hilt. There was no sound but when she withdrew the sword it was covered in thick blood.

The bard moved like a shadow, coming up and out of the chair in one fluid motion, spinning, the blade of his hook slicing easily through the thin wooden panelling, taking the hidden observer full across the throat, neatly decapitating him. Paedur shrugged off his cloak, wiping his hook clean in the heavy furred material, and then leapt across the couch for the door – just as it opened!

The three guards rushed in on a figure of death. The first died choking on his own blood as the razor edge ripped out his throat, and the second went down with a hammer blow from the bard's open hand to the centre of his forehead. He was dead before he hit the ground, his skull crushed. The third man's charge carried him past the creature in black – straight on to the blade of an ice-haired demon.

Without pausing Paedur raced down the corridor, pursuing the tall, robust woman in red who had actually been casually walking away from the room when her guards were abruptly slaughtered. She attempted to run, but a razor hook encircled her throat, the point pricking the soft skin beneath her right ear. 'Move, and I'll rip out your throat. You,' he snapped at the doorman, using the Bardic Voice, 'return to the room!' Under the influence of the ancient vocal spell, the man obediently turned and walked back into the room where Katani, thinking him another warrior, promptly killed him.

'Who are you?' the woman demanded, desperately attempting to control her trembling voice. 'What do you want?' In her youth she would have been a great beauty, but time and excess had taken her beauty and charm, leaving her a foul-eyed, hollow-cheeked harridan who had attempted to disguise her age beneath a layer of paints and coloured powders. She was wearing a gown that would have been outrageous on a woman a third her age and which only served to make her look ridiculous, and she carried enough jewellery about her person to feed most of the capital's poor for the major portion of the year.

'Let me say this once to you,' Paedur said, pushing her up against a polished wall, his hand flat against her throat. He raised his left arm, allowed her to see his hook and when he was sure he had her attention, he continued. 'I do not need to keep you alive, in fact, you are probably more trouble than you are worth. Answer me truthfully, however, and you will live to see another sunset, but lie to me – and I will know if you even attempt it – and I will kill you. Understand!'

The woman nodded dumbly.

'Where is the tunnel that leads to the palace?'

The madam's eyes widened in surprise and she shook her head, attempting to disguise her shock. 'I don't know what you mean,' she faltered.

Katani's sword suddenly bit deeply into the wood not a finger's length from her face, severing strands of her grey-brown hair. 'Let me kill her,' Katani hissed, deliberately accentuating her broad accent.

'I told you not to lie to me,' Paedur warned.

'I haven't.'

'I know about the tunnel,' he said simply.

'The tunnel,' she said numbly.

'Let me feed on her,' Katani grinned, baring her pointed teeth.

'The tunnel built in the time of Geillard X, the present Emperor's grandfather, and completed by Geillard XI and used most frequently by the present Emperor and his sometime mistress. Now, I don't have much time. Show me the tunnel!'

Something shifted behind the woman's eyes and they suddenly widened in horror. 'You're the bard!'

'I am.'

'The tunnels are down those stairs, in the second room on the left, behind a pile of disused bedding,' she suddenly gushed, certainly terrified now, whatever her feelings had been earlier.

'Thank you.' Paedur placed the flat of his hook against her powdered cheek and the woman suddenly slumped.

'Is she dead?' Katani wondered.

'Unconscious.'

'What now?'

Paedur looked at the woman, his eyes intense. 'You will have to hold this house; business must seem to be continuing as before. Allow everyone into the house, but no-one must leave. However, if you feel the situation is becoming uncontrollable, fire the house and make good your escape.'

'And you, what of you?'

'I'm going to visit the palace.'


'Imperials coming!'

The rumour moved down the army like wind across a field of wheat, rippling as it went, leaving only stillness in its wake. The rebel army had faced many Imperial assaults over the past days and months and there was nothing new Geillard's forces could throw against them that they hadn't faced already.

When the first sightings occurred, Keshian rode ahead with one of the scouts in an attempt to determine the Imperials' numbers and deployment. And now, from the concealment of a clump of standing stones, he watched the distant shimmer of metal on the horizon. When the army had approached closely enough for the distant rumble of hooves to sound like thunder, the scout climbed one of the rocks and studied the advancing dust cloud with a glass.

'Well man, what do you see?' he demanded.

The young man shook his head. 'I'm not sure. Imperials certainly, but . . .'

'But what?'

'But it looks like Owen and Tien leading them!'

'Let me see.' He stood in his mount's saddle, his fingers hooking into the jagged rock, and he pulled himself up. The scout passed him the metal-banded leathern tube and Keshian put the glass to his eye, following the scout's pointing arm. For a moment he saw nothing but a shifting, swirling blue, but as he turned the tube, the image leapt into focus. There was a small Imperial army riding towards them – he looked for company or legion flags, but curiously found none – but in the lead, armoured and armed, were Owen, the Weapon Master, and Tien tZo, his slave-companion. Between them rode a huge female warrior in the armour of an Imperial commander, and the only woman who fitted that description was Fodla, Geillard's commander and sometime body-guard.

He shifted the glass, attempting to concentrate on their expressions. The image was blurred, but he got the impression that they were all laughing.

He concentrated on the approaching army. There were no flags, no pennants, and while the men and women held to a rough formation, there was none of the rigidity that he would have expected of Imperial troops. Also, their armour and weapons were mismatched, almost as if it were personal choice rather than issue.

'Sir?' the scout asked.

'What do you think?' Keshian asked absently, still watching the riders.

The man's thin face broke into a broad smile. 'There's not enough for an army. I think they're coming to join us, don't you?'

Keshian looked at the man, his face remaining set in the same grim lines it had worn through all the previous battles, and then he suddenly turned away, unwilling to allow the scout to see the moisture that suddenly blurred his eyes. He strode to the edge of the rock and looked down at his mount. He hesitated for a moment and, glancing back over his shoulder, he said quickly, 'I think you're right.' And then he dropped down into the saddle with all the agility of a much younger man and, lying low across his mount's neck, he galloped back to the huge rebel camp. There had always been doubts that they could succeed, but whatever doubts he had entertained had vanished now.

The pickets allowed him through. Amongst the mismatched rebel army, Keshian had become something of a legend, and the tale of his defence of the prince against the assassins had grown out of all proportions, until even Keshian himself was unable to tell what had been the original story they had put out.

The battle-captain found Prince Kutor waiting for him in the centre of the huge camp. The prince had stripped to the waist and was assisting the score of blacksmiths and armourers to forge arrow- and spear-heads. His acceptance by the usually dour smiths and his obvious skill in the task had done more to endear him to the army than any amount of speeches and promises, and it had become customary for people to wander in to assist him, working the bellows or holding the metal, while at the same time seeking his advice or requesting favours. The only reminder of his royal blood were the black-armoured guards standing in the shadows beneath the smith's striped awnings.

As Keshian reined in his mount, Kutor looked up, his face open, expectant. 'Well?'

'You've heard?'

'Rumours.'

Keshian brought his right leg over his mount's head and slid off the sweating beast's back to the ground. A boy hurried over and took the reins from him and another handed him a goblet of warm, thin wine. Keshian strolled under the nearest awning and downed half the goblet in one swallow, while Prince Kutor stood looking at him.

Finally, when he could contain himself no longer, he demanded. 'Well, what's happening out there?'

'There's a small army approaching, a single legion or perhaps two legions strong. There are no pennants, no flags or emblems showing, they're not holding to formation, not wearing issue armour and the weapons are personal. It's being led by both Owen and Tien tZo, and they've another person with them, a woman warrior, a huge creature with flaming red hair.'

'Fodla!'

'My thoughts exactly.'

'What do you think?'

'I think their mission has been successful, or at least partially successful, and they're returning with deserters from the Imperial forces.'

'I can't believe Geillard's dead,' Kutor said firmly.

'Neither can I. But something else struck me as I rode in here.'

'And what was that?'

'I cannot see Owen and Tien leaving the city together, unless they received orders to do so.'

'But who would order?' Kutor asked softly, and then he breathed, 'the bard.'

Keshian nodded. 'I think the bard has returned.'

# 26   The Road to the Throne

'The Road to the Throne is lined with sorrow.'
                    *Geillard I, Emperor of the Seven Unified Nations*

In the chill darkness of the tunnel Paedur the Bard came up against his first obstacle. The brothel tunnel had begun at the bottom of a flight of steps which had brought him some thirty paces below the level of the streets, and had run arrow-straight for over two thousand paces in the general direction of the palace.

In the pitch blackness of the tunnel, the bard's enchanced sight showed everything in stark shades of black, white and grey, and initially he had been wary of traps, but strangely the tunnel didn't seem to possess any. It was a beautiful construction, and there was more than a touch of otherworldly power in its making. He touched the walls with his hook, expecting to feel at least some residue of the power that had created them, but the tunnel was so old that all he could feel were the shadows of the emotions of those who had passed down the long corridor in times past. Shuddering, he broke the contact, feeling faintly soiled by the emotions.

The tunnel was an almost perfect circle, with tall, curved ceilings painted a pale blue and touched with white, fleecy clouds which served to disguise the air ducts. The walls were bellied outward, and thin, deep channels ran along the floor, carrying away the water he could hear gurgling all around him. In niches in the wall, statues in poses both erotic and obscene but with the features of ancient princes and ministers, leered and postured, obviously advertising some of the delights of the house. Further along there were doors, and the bard paused to glance into them. They had been bed-chambers but were now all empty, and they hadn't been used for a long time judging by their general air of decay.

Further on there was another series of doors, but these were barred and locked with heavy, professionally made locks. He idly contemplated ripping them off, but decided against it, and merely contented himself with allowing his enhanced senses to flare as he moved past the wood – only to recoil in horror. Behind the first door were four mouldering skeletons. With enough remnants of clothing for him to distinguish the male and female and the two small pathetic bundles that lay between them. They had been dead a long time. There was a similar bundle of skeletons behind the next door and the next. From the little he could gather without actually breaking down the doors, from the emotional residue that still clung to the cell doors, he thought he was looking at wealthy families who had been incarcerated and then left to starve to death. From the state of the decomposition and the style of dress, he estimated the deaths had occurred in the time of Geillard VI. He sorted through his lore and then nodded grimly. Geillard the Red-handed's rule had been so merciless that a coup had been planned by several of the noble families. But a spy had betrayed them to the Emperor, and in a single bloody night, they had all mysteriously disappeared, their possessions seized, their servants and slaves butchered. No-one knew what had happened to those who had vanished and for a while there had been rumours that they would return, but Paedur fancied he had discovered their whereabouts. As he walked away he vowed that if he survived he would return later and have them buried with all due ceremony.

One hundred paces from the death cells, the corridor curved and he encountered his first obstacle – a dead end.

It was a man-made wall of later construction than the tunnel, rough-hewn square and oblong bricks cemented together to create a crude but effective barrier. It was splashed and streaked with mortar and had all the appearance of hasty work; there was even a space at the top and sides where the mason hadn't allowed for the curvature of the tunnel. Idly wondering why it had been necessary to seal off the tunnel, Paedur placed his hook against the centre of the wall and called upon the Gods of the Pantheon for assistance. There was an immediate sense of disassociation from his body, but he was aware of a growing pressure deep in his skull. Abruptly, his vision doubled and for a moment he saw a constellation of colours shifting and crawling along the walls. He blinked and blinked again, settling the colours into lines and bands that outlined the bricks, and then something hard and bright pulsed through his arm and shimmered along his hook – and the silver-grey metal sank up to his wrist into the wall! He experienced a brief moment of panic and pulled his arm back – and ripped out the whole centre of the wall. He quickly scrambled through the breech, the wall crumbling around him, fist-sized lumps of stone and brick tumbling around his shoulders but leaving him untouched.

And he remembered then that Churon had promised him that the powers he had grown accustomed to before he had entered the Silent Wood would be enhanced. Now the bard wondered to what extent. He had been able to cut stone before he had gone into Death's Domain – and that was what he had just done – but before it usually left him reeling and exhausted. Now he had ripped a wall apart with no effort and no strain. Paedur couldn't help but wonder what the Pantheon had made him.

Immediately beyond the wall, the floor of the tunnel began to slope upwards, and the bard's ghostly sight began to flicker into colour as light seeped in through frequent ventilation ducts, shafting beams of pale yellow-white light down into the darkness. He walked for another thousand or so paces, stopping only when he reached a staircase. He stood at the bottom of the stairs, looking up, allowing his consciousness to move upwards beyond the heavily barred door at the top and out into the room beyond. It was an antechamber off the library, a seemingly innocent storeroom, holding nothing more than duplicated scrolls and badly copied books. He waited, his head tilted to one side, listening with more than human senses, but the room above seemed to be empty. Finally, he mounted the steps silently and then stopped again before the door, listening, probing the room beyond and the library beyond that again, while he examined the locks and bolts. The antechamber was still empty, but there were two readers in the library itself.

The door had been bolted top, middle and bottom with heavy metal bars and there was a lock of the double key variety dead centre – and they were all on the opposite side of the door. However, the door did not sit flush into its frame and the bard merely slid his hook into the gap, slipped the point under the uppermost bar, and pulled. The hook noiselessly sliced through the metal. He repeated the process with the middle and bottom bars, and then simply hit the door with the palm of his hand just below the lock housing. The lock snapped and the door creaked fractionally open.

Now speed was essential. Even he could not defend himself against a palace full of guards and he had no illusions that once it was known that palace security had been breached it would only be a matter of time before he was captured. But a lot could happen before then.

He placed the flat of his hand against the door and pushed. The door moved slightly and then stopped, and the bard's sensitive hearing caught the grinding of hinges. It had been a long time since the door had been opened. Fully realising the consequences, he put his shoulder to the door and pushed. The warped wood protested, scraping off the ground, and unused hinges screamed but suddenly snapped and gave, tumbling the bard into the small room. He recovered his balance as a man pulled open the leathern curtain that separated the antechamber from the library and strolled into the room, an ancient vellum scroll casually tucked under his arm. He was a small, compact man who had seen service in the Imperial Dragoons, a man who had seen much and heard even more and had long thought himself unshockable, but this creature in black with the terrifying eyes and stone face, wielding an evil-looking hook, stopped him cold in his tracks. And then the hook was at his throat and the creature was leering down on him.

'Where is the Emperor now?' The voice was nothing more than a hiss, cold and compelling.

He started to shake his head, but the creature pressed the point of the hook against the wrinkled skin of his neck, drawing blood. 'Don't even think about lying to me now.'

The small man started to shake his head, but stopped when the movement caused the hook to bite more deeply into his flesh.

'Wrong answer.'

And then the curtain parted and a second man stepped through. The man was thin and pale, his eyes deep set and squinting, the patches on his breast identifying him as a professional scholar. 'Is everything . . .' he began, and then his weak eyes registered the tableau and widened in horror. He scrabbled for the knife on his belt, his mouth opening to shout – and died when the bard's hook took out his throat.

'Tell me!' Paedur snarled, turning back to the small, quaking man.

'In his personal library,' the man quavered. He shifted the chart under his arm. 'He sent me down here for this.'

Paedur allowed his senses, his intuition, to assess the truthfulness of the statement, and could find no lie in it. Almost as if he was aware of what was happening, the man twisted his head to look up into the flat, merciless eyes. 'It's the truth, I swear it.'

'How many up there?'

For a single instant the small man thought about defiance, but he was now convinced that the creature was a duaite – an evil one – and with the scholar's blood still wet and warm on the creature's hook, he wasn't prepared to argue. 'The Emperor, Barthus the Hierophant and one other.'

'Who?'

'I've never seen him before. A small, stout man.'

The bard nodded. 'Thank you.' And then he allowed unconsciousness to wash over the man and gently lowered him to the floor. He stooped and lifted the scroll from under the man's arm and carefully unrolled it. It was a standard Deed of Covenant, blank and unfilled. 'Now, why would Geillard want that,' he murmured.


'It is agreed, then?'

Barthus the Hierophant sat forward eagerly, his eyes bright, greedy, fixing themselves on the slender form of Geillard. He glanced quickly at the third man in the room and then turned back to the Emperor. Since the arrival of the renegade army, the tall, thin man had aged almost visibly and now moved with a permanent stoop, and there was a perceptible tremble in his long-fingered hands.

'We must know,' the Hierophant persisted. 'There is no time now.'

'And will this ensure me victory?' the Emperor asked, his voice tired, almost uninterested. Salier's loss had affected him badly: the mage had been more than a counsellor, more than a friend, and Geillard had come to believe him invincible. When he had been told of his loss and then learned of Fodla's treachery, he had begun to suspect that he was not meant to win this battle.

'My lord,' the third man spoke, his voice soft, insinuating, like silk on silk. 'When I have finished, there will be no army left to face you.'

'And in return? What do you want in return?' Geillard demanded, his voice surprisingly bitter. 'Death, I have heard, is a treacherous ally.'

The short, stout man smiled broadly, his eyes twinkling merrily. 'Ah, but Death is also a powerful friend,' Libellius said simply. 'And as you are already a follower of the Religion, we would be asking nothing untoward of you.'

'Then why the Deed of Covenant?' Geillard demanded, turning back to the fire, staring deep into its glowing embers, as if he could read some advice therein.

'Why, merely to ensure that we understand one another,' Libellius said softly, looking at Barthus. Now that the Emperor was no longer looking at him, the broad smile had gone from his face and what remained resembled nothing so much as a fleshy skull.

'And payment?' Geillard said without inflection. 'What would be the payment?'

The Death Lord of the New Religion waved his hand expansively. 'I imagine we would look for certain concessions: the occasional sacrifice, a purge of the followers of the Old Faith, the removal of certain persons in positions of power which we feel might threaten the well-being of the Religion.' He shrugged. 'Nothing you would not approve of.'

'Sacrifices?' Geillard asked tonelessly.

'I think sacrifices might be the wrong word,' Barthus said quickly, 'begging my lord's pardon,' he added quickly to Libellius. 'I think perhaps he meant to say that we would look for certain followers of the Religion to volunteer to allow their bodies to become host to the Gods of the Religion.'

Libellius nodded quickly, the laughter gone from his dark eyes, leaving them like stones. 'That is true. Think of it, Geillard. In your lifetime, during your reign, the Gods of the Religion would assume corporeal form and walk the World of Men. Perhaps even the Lord Trialos himself would walk this Plane again. And what would that make you, eh? What man has yet commanded the gods? What power would you have? Think on that.'

Geillard rounded on the stout man. 'And what will you do if I say no?'

The smile didn't move on Libellius' face, only the fire behind the eyes died. 'Then naturally I would return and leave you to face your enemies.' He shrugged. 'Then I would attempt to deal with your successor.'

'Are you saying I will not survive this battle? Why, don't be preposterous. I have four times the number of men they have; my troops are better armed and we are behind a fortified city.'

The Lord of the Dead made a face. 'Oh, I'm not saying it is a foregone conclusion by any means. They have, however, certain advantages over you.' He leaned forward and began ticking off points on his stubby, beringed fingers. 'All of their troops are there either by choice or because of coin, and I would imagine that even those who are being paid to fight have already thrown in their lot with Kutor. They firmly believe in what they are doing – namely, overthrowing a cruel and heartless despot. Also, Fodla, the captain of your personal guard and your private body-guard, has joined them, along with nearly two legions of your best troops. Salier, your mage, is dead, and finally, and perhaps most importantly, the Gods of the Pantheon and their lacky, the Bard Paedur, fight with them.'

Geillard's shoulders had slumped during the litany of foes, and when he looked at Libellius, the Death Lord knew he had won. 'What will you do?' the Emperor asked wearily.

But it was Barthus who answered. 'My Lord Libellius will assume death's most dreaded form and walk through Kutor's army, taking all those who come within his ken.'

'Including Kutor?' Geillard said, eagerness showing in his voice for the first time in the conversation.

'Especially Kutor,' Barthus continued, 'and as many of those close to him as possible: his advisers, Owen, the Weapon Master, his slave Tien tZo, Keshian, his commander, and Fodla, if she is still with them.'

'Do it, then,' Geillard said, looking at the small, red-clad man, wondering if he indeed had the power to do all he claimed, wondering briefly – but only briefly – if he was indeed, Libellius, Lord of the Dead.

And then the man sitting calmly on the chair facing him began to change, a subtle alteration at first, a smudging of the planes of his face, the features softening, melding, the cheekbones and eye-sockets becoming prominent, the line of his jaw becoming more pronounced, the grin becoming permanent as the lips drew back and the flesh tightened, transforming the jowly face into a skull. Only the eyes remained, and where they had once twinkled with merriment, now they glittered with malice. Libellius stood, and now the short, corpulent body was gone and had been re-placed by a tall, thin, skeletal creature, still wearing the reds that Libellius favoured. He stretched out an arm and a skeleton's claw appeared, the bones clacking together as the fingers opened and closed. 'Such is man's perception of Death, eh?' Libellius asked, and although his soft, cultured voice hadn't changed, coming from those fleshless lips, it sounded obscene.

'Your form is similar to Mannam, the Faith's Lord of the Dead,' Geillard said numbly.

'Confusion,' Libellius hissed, 'confusion.' He folded his arms against his sides and simply winked out of existence . . .

A rebel scout perched in the branches of a tree overlooking the main road into the city was the first to spot the tall figure in red moving slowly and sedately towards them, obviously coming from the city.

'Someone's coming,' he called down to the man on the ground.

'Who? How many?'

'Just one,' the scout said slowly, attempting to focus on the figure, but his eyes kept blurring. He dug the heels of his hands into his eyes and looked again – and found the figure was standing at the foot of the tree! 'Hey you! You!' He struggled to the ground, wondering what had happened to his companion. 'Who . . . who are you?'

The creature in red lifted his head, the white bone of his skull face blotched with red, which dripped from his chin and on to his robe, the blood matching the colour exactly. There was something in the skeletal hand he extended towards the scout. The man looked, drawn against his will, his eyes fixing themselves on the object. For a single pounding heartbeat, his eyes refused to accept what he was seeing, and then he recognised it as a human hand, a bloody hand, bone and tendrils of sinew and flesh still dangling from the stump of the wrist. And then he spotted the small, silver signet ring on the third finger of the shredded hand and recognised it as his friend's. The creature brought the hand to his mouth and bit down on one of the fingers, teeth clacking together over a snapped bone. 'I am Death,' he hissed, bloody froth bubbling between his lips. 'I have come for Kutor's army. Tell him!' And then he turned away.

'What do we do now?' Geillard asked.

'We wait,' Barthus said, crossing to a small side-table and examining the selection of wines and liquors.

The Emperor moved from the fire to the window and stood framed against the grey light, looking down over the courtyard, watching the flurry of palace guards preparing the defences that had never actually been used in the eleven generations of his family history.

Barthus poured two glasses of pale wine from the vineyards of Isle of Forme and carried them across to the Emperor. 'Where is the man with that Deed of Covenant?' he wondered aloud.

'It's here!'

The two men turned towards the sound and somehow Geillard found he was unsurprised at the dark-clad figure with the hook replacing his left hand standing in the doorway. Something like a smile touched his lips. 'Bard?' he breathed.

'I am Paedur, the Bard.'

'So we meet again.' Geillard stepped forward, his hand extended, palm upwards in the grip of greeting. Paedur ignored him; he was watching the Hierophant.

'You see, you're the cause of all this,' Geillard continued, his measured tones beginning to lose something of their calmness. 'You incited Kutor to this uprising; you supplied him with his present commander; you freed the Weapon Master from his bondage and sent him to Kutor; you subverted Fodla. It all comes back to you.'

'This started with you,' Paedur said simply, glancing at the man.

'I remember you from your days here. You could have been great, you could have taken the position Salier or even Barthus here occupied. But you threw it all away.'

The Hierophant had regained his composure. When he had turned and found the bard standing framed in the door, his first instinct had been panic. The bard's reputation was fearsome; why, even the Gods of the Religion held him in respect. But then something cold and cunning settled into the Hierophant's brain. After all, if the bard was the creature of the Faith, was not he, Barthus, the creature of the Religion? Had he not the power to call down the gods themselves to serve him? And did that not make him even greater than the bard, Paedur? This was the Hierophant's territory; he was surrounded by all the symbols of the Religion, in a sanctuary of the Religion. Surely all of these would conspire to weaken the bard?

'Have you come to surrender yourself to the mercy of the

Religion?' he demanded, his voice harsh, overloud. He stepped past Geillard to face the bard. The glow from the firelight took his metallic vestments and turned them liquid, contrasting with the bard's furred cloak, which seemed to absorb the light, surrounding him in a pool of shifting darkness.

'I have come for Geillard, and you too,' Paedur said, matter-of-factly.

'Defeat is upon you and your army,' the Hierophant smirked, 'but surrender to me now, and I will ensure that your life is spared.'

Paedur placed his heel against the door and nudged it shut. 'Kutor's army will destroy you,' he said simply.

Barthus stepped forward and jabbed a finger towards the bard's face. 'Even now, Kutor's army is being destroyed.' Seeing the sudden shifting in the bard's eyes, he hurried on. 'Even now, even as we speak, Libellius, the Lord of the Dead, walks through your prince's army, plucking their essences like ripe fruit. And be assured, bard, your prince, your Weapon Master and his companions will be amongst them.'

Paedur took a calculated risk and, closing his eyes, shifted his consciousness through the Ghost Worlds and the Void to where he guessed the rebel army would be camped. He could only afford to catch a flicker, but it was enough. A tall figure in red strolled through the camp, leaving a trail of bodies in his wake, and it was heading in the direction of Kutor's tent.

Pain brought him back to his body. Barthus had seized on his momentary absence from his physical body to thrust a small poignard into his chest. His leather jerkin had absorbed much of the blow, but the tip of the dagger had still penetrated the skin, enough to hurt but not to harm. He looked from the ornately hilted dagger to the Hierophant's face, and the look in the bard's eyes was enough to send the man scrambling backwards. Paedur plucked the dagger from his chest and touched the cut with the flat blade of his hook, sealing the wound, and then he flung the dagger at the Hierophant. Barthus flung up his hands and created a reddish-blue film between them; the knife struck the magical shield and careered off to bury itself to the hilt in the window-frame not a finger's length from Geillard's face. The Emperor didn't seem to notice.

Something noisome coiled around the bard's scuffed boots and he found a tentacle of congealed filth taking substance in the air before the Hierophant and drifting across the floor towards him. It abruptly tautened, almost pulling him off balance, but the bard stooped and sliced through the tentacle with his hook. The band of filth recoiled and splattered across the room, daubing it in filth and offal, and the room immediately reeked with the odour of faeces and things long dead. The shock sent Barthus reeling back against the wall. Paedur looked around and then picked up a silver goblet in his right hand and threw it with all his might towards the Hierophant, murmuring one word: 'Luid!'

As it spun through the air, the goblet began to alter in shape. It was as if it was being subjected to an intense heat. The metal ran in large silver globules which congealed together, all the while glowing white-hot. Barthus spread his hands and the red-blue film appeared again, but the glowing silver-ball of molten metal passed clean through it, shredding it as it passed. Barthus managed to scream once and then the ball struck. It exploded against his face and the metal immediately ran, covering his flesh beneath a layer of molten silver. Barthus writhed in agony and attempted to peel off the metal mask, but his fingers came away tipped with silver. He crashed backwards into the fire and hungry little flames – Luid the Firegod's creations – began to devour his heavy vestments. There was a sudden burst of intense blue-white fire and the Hierophant's body was rendered into a fine, ash-like powder, leaving only the smouldering garments and the silver horror-struck mask.

The Emperor looked at the bard, his face expressionless, his eyes dead.

'I will return for you,' Paedur promised Geillard, and then he turned and was gone.

## 27 Death

Death was his ally, his companion, his enemy, his bane . . .

*Life of Paedur, the Bard*

Libellius stood in the centre of the field, surrounded on all sides by terrified men wielding pikes and swords. None of them dared approach him. 'I am Death,' he cried, raising his arms and proceeding to take every third man. The remainder of the men scattered in terror. Libellius rubbed his bony hands together and continued on his slow, casual way towards Kutor's camp.

Paedur burst through the opening into the brothel to find Katani cleaning her swords, a score of bodies scattered around the floor. 'Visitors,' she said simply.

'We must get to the rebel's camp,' he snapped, barely registering the carnage, 'Libellius is killing everyone.'

'It's half a morning's ride,' Katani reminded him.

'I know.'

'And there's no way we're even going to get out of the city, even if we could get to them in time.'

There was a sudden knock on the door, startling them both, and then the coded sequence was tapped out. Katani smiled tightly without humour. 'A popular house.' She moved through the leathern curtain and Paedur heard the door open. He didn't need his god-gifted senses to interpret the sounds which followed. Katani reappeared through the curtain and draped the body of the young man across the pile. 'Churon will be busy,' she said, wiping her knife against the dead man's costly silk surcoat.

And Paedur suddenly had the answer.

The bard moved to the warrior and turned her to face him, his hand on her left shoulder, his hook touching her right. 'Do you trust me?' he asked softly, his eyes holding hers.

'You gave me life again,' she said simply, as if that explained everything.

'And if I asked you to kill me?'

'To kill you!'

His hand moved across her mouth, silencing her. 'Would you do it? Would you kill me if I asked you?'

'But what about Libellius, what about Kutor and his army, what about your friends?' she demanded, suddenly angry. 'They are depending on you.'

'I am asking you to do it because of them, for them,' he explained.

'I don't understand,' she said defiantly.

'I need Churon's help to get to the camp.'

'Call him, then. He'll come for you.'

'There are too many dead and dying out there. He will not heed a call from me.'

'So you want me to kill you to send you to him?' she asked.

'Just so.'

Katani started to shake her head – and then she plunged her dagger into Paedur's heart . . .

The archer took careful aim and loosed his arrow. It flew straight and true – and still somehow missed the creature in red. Another fired and then another and then on command the line of archers fired together – and they all missed. There was a shouted command and the archers fell back, but every second man was struck dead.

Kutor, surrounded by Keshian, Owen, Tien and Fodla, watched the steady approach of the figure of Death. Against him they knew there was no escape, no defence.

The bard awoke surrounded by the solidified trees of the Silent Wood, chilled and numb, aching in every muscle – paradoxically human again now that he was dead. He was staggering to his feet when the figure of Katani winked into existence beside him.

The bard attempted to spit the ashes from his mouth, but his mouth was too dry. 'How? What happened?' he mumbled.

'I allowed the next person to call at the house to kill me,' she said, mouthing the words carefully. 'I couldn't let you go alone. But I only hope you know what you're doing.'

'So do I!' Churon, the Lord of Death of the Old Faith, stepped out from behind a tree-like chunk of stone and moved silently over to the pair. His coal-black skin shone with an inner luminescence and his blond hair had been cropped close to his skull. He hadn't affected Mannam's garb of the cloak of seared and withered leaves, but had opted instead for a mantle of stone-grey that blended in with the surroundings almost perfectly. Looking at the cloak, Paedur had the distinct impression that it was actually made of stone.

'It is,' Churon said, answering his unasked question with a smile.

'You know why we're here?' the bard asked.

Churon nodded. 'A desperate measure indeed. No man can ever gainsay your courage,' he said. 'I presume you want me to resurrect you in the rebel camp?'

Paedur nodded.

'You can do it?' Katani asked uncertainly, unwilling to even consider any other possibility.

'No,' Churon whispered sadly. 'I am Death; I cannot give you life.'

'You gave Katani life,' Paedur reminded him.

'That was different.'

'In what way?'

'I killed her; I gifted her,' he said simply.

Paedur straightened and looked Death in the face. 'Libellius is killing the rebel army, and by that action destroying the last chance for the Old Faith to re-establish itself in all its former glory. If you want the Faith to survive, you will think of something. Now think,' he insisted.

'I can shift your corporeal bodies to the battlefield,' Churon said slowly. 'My quai can do that.'

'Not much use to us if we're still dead,' Katani mumbled. 'Can you not breathe some life into us even briefly?'

'I haven't the power.'

'Then who has?' she demanded, her voice cracking.

'C'lte,' Paedur said slowly, a shadow of a smile touching his lips, 'the Yellow God of Life.'

'It will never work,' Churon said. 'The Gods of Life, and the Yellow God in particular, have always been Death's foe.'

'Mannam's enemy,' Paedur corrected, 'but you are now Death. And perhaps he will do it for me, I know C'lte of old, and if not for me, then for the continued existence of the Pantheon.'

Churon shook his head doubtfully. 'I still don't think it will work.'

'It has to,' Paedur snapped.
'And if it doesn't?' Katani asked.
'Then we are dead.'

The figure in red stopped before the small group. It was impossible to ascribe an expression to its skull-face, but his whole attitude was one of overbearing arrogance. Although they knew it was useless, they had drawn weapons, more for the comfort it gave them than anything else.

'I am Death,' Libellius said, his voice sussurating across the distance that separated them, dulling even the screams and panicked shouts from the army beyond. The beasts now had picked up the scent of death and had added their own screams to the general uproar. In contrast, the small area outside Kutor's tent seemed surprisingly quiet and still.

'I have come for you,' the figure hissed, raising his arm, pointing at Kutor.

'You are not Death,' Owen said abruptly. 'Death is dark and wears a cloak of seared and withered leaves.'

The skull-face turned. 'You are Owen, the Weapon Master. I am Libellius.'

'Of the Religion!' Owen gasped.

The creature in red bowed.

Fodla moved a little apart from the group, wondering if she could manage to get around the creature to swing her massive broadsword. The head turned in her direction, 'Tell me how the God of Religion can kill the followers of the Faith,' she shouted angrily.

'You are Fodla, once commander of the Imperial Army,' Libellius said, naming her. 'I am Death,' he continued, answering her question, 'I kill. It is my function. And yet, it is usual for the Death Lords of the various religions to take only their own, but there is no hard and firm law. A balance will be maintained and you may be sure that Mannam will take his quota of the followers of the Religion. At any other time it would mean war, but this suits the Gods of the Religion now, and it is a price we will gladly pay for the defeat of the Faith's army.' He took a step forward and reached out with a skeletal hand . . .

Tien's thrown axe struck the hand and bounced off, leaving it unharmed.

286

'I am Death,' Libellius said simply. 'You cannot kill the dead.' He looked at the small, wiry man. 'You are Tien tZo, the slave-companion to Owen. I will take you too in your turn.' He moved forward. 'And you are Keshian, once Battle-Captain of Count Karfondal, now Commander of this rabble.' The skull turned again. 'And you are Kutor, princeling and pretender to the throne.' Both skeletal hands opened as the creature fixed on Kutor.

'And I am Paedur the Bard.'

Kutor's tent flapped open and Paedur stepped out into the group. There was absolute silence. He moved through them, not acknowledging them, not even looking at them, intent only on the creature in red. And indeed, everyone was so intent on the bard that no-one – except Tien – saw the Katan warrior stagger out of the tent behind him.

Paedur walked up to Death and looked him in the face, much as he had done with Churon earlier, and he found that there was no difference in their eyes; but what was even more disturbing was that their eyes matched his own – they were cold and dead, reflective, like tiny polished mirrors.

'Begone,' he said simply.

'You cannot stand against me,' Libellius said calmly, but some of the confidence had gone from his voice.

'I have stood against the Gods of the Religion for a long time now,' Paedur said with a thin smile. 'I have defeated greater gods than you.'

'I am Death. There is none greater than me!'

'Take what you have slain this day and go; there is nothing left for you here.'

'You are arrogant,' Libellius hissed. He stretched out his right arm, his skeletal hand curling into a claw, his pointed nails touching the bard in the chest just below the heart. And then he drew it back with a hiss. Smoke curled from the blackened tips of his fingers and the stench of burning bone was rotten on the air. For a single moment, the image of the figure in red flickered to be replaced by that of a small, stout man with a pale sweating face.

'And you are weak,' Paedur smiled. 'You have taken many this day; it has left you sated and full – and weak.'

'But I have enough left for you, bard,' Libellius snapped. The air around the bard was suddenly filled with scores of tiny black motes. They circled around his head, snapping and crackling, and it was only when one moved close to his eye that Paedur realised they were tiny human and demonic heads on bloated bodies, their minute mouths opening and closing, buzzing obscenities, tiny teeth clacking. He had heard about them; they were the Stones of Death. If he was wounded, the motes would dart into the wound and continue eating deep into the flesh, killing him in the most exquisite agony. He lifted his hook and described a circle in the air. The image of the circle hung spinning and silver on the air and then coalesced into a tight ball, and then it darted from face to face, the motes crisping as they came into contact with it or attempted to dart through the circle. Libellius' hand shot out, his claw closing on the circle of light and then he crushed it between forefinger and thumb like a flea, silver light spurting like blood.

'This is for you, bard.' He pulled apart his red cloak, and too late the bard realised his mistake as he looked into it – into Nothingness. It was not the soft greyness of the Ghost Worlds, nor the deeper dusky colours of the Void; within Libellius' cloak there was an absence of life, of colour, of sensation. It was more than death; it was desolation and despair. Paedur struggled to escape its dreadful pull. Unconsciously and unwillingly he staggered forward towards Death's clawing grasp. He was blind and deaf, aware only of the need to move deeper into that encompassing blackness. Distantly, dimly, he felt himself moving, something pulling him down, and that part of his mind which remained detached and watching knew that if he fell, then it was all over.

He began to enumerate the Gods of the Pantheon, concentrating all his attention on them. 'Hanor and Hara, the First Great Gods; The Lady Dannu; Mannam ... no, Churon now; the Lord of the Dead. Churon, aid me now!'

And he fell ...

And was caught.

There was a broad black hand in the centre of his chest. It stood out from the blackness of Libellius in that this was a living colour, and as the bard looked, he saw a pair of warm blue eyes staring at him out of the Nothingness ...

It was enough. Paedur was back on the plain before Kutor's flapping tent, facing the red-clad God of Death.

Libellius drew back his arm like a swordsman withdrawing

his weapon from a shoulder sheath, and then brought it swinging forward again, and as it came round a sword formed in it, a long wavy-edged blade of red-black fire. The first blow seared past the bard's chest, tainting the air with foulness and the stench of burning flesh. Paedur caught the second blow on his hook, blue-white and red-blue sparks coruscating, but the force of it was enough to send the man sprawling. Libellius strode over to him, the sword smoking blue-red fire raised high above his head, a smile tightening his skull-face, his eyes bright and victorious. When he was close enough the bard kicked out, catching his knee, sending him staggering, his mouth working. Paedur scrambled to his feet and faced Death once again.

But the Lord of the Dead hung back now, almost as if he was undecided. And then he abruptly raised his hands. 'My children,' he called, and throughout the camp an army of dead arose. All those Libellius had claimed took on a brief semblance of life and began to march towards the centre of the camp. 'You will all fall to my quai,' Libellius boasted as the first appeared.

Owen, Tien, Keshian, Katani and Fodla formed a protective circle around Prince Kutor as the army of the dead approached. Without any evidence of wounds, they were like sleep-walkers, their movements slow and graceful, their eyes wide but unseeing. They advanced steadily on to the group, intent on overwhelming it, but completely ignoring Paedur and Libellius.

'My quai will slay them, and then what will be the point of continuing?' Libellius asked him.

'Even if they all die, even if I die, there will be others; the Religion will never defeat the Faith.'

There was a sudden clash of weapons as the first ranks of the quai reached the small group surrounding Kutor.

'Turn and walk from here, bard. Live out the remainder of your days in peace and solitude. You remember how it was before, before Mannam took you.'

'He didn't take me; I volunteered.'

'He tempted you.'

'This is a fruitless discussion,' Paedur said wearily. 'Only one of us will walk away from here this day.'

'Bard,' Libellius said in astonishment, 'I am a God and you, for all your gifts, are a man. You cannot win this battle, any more than your companions can defend themselves against the quai.'

'But they have succeeded so far,' Paedur remarked lightly, his eyes never leaving the god, his senses telling him how his companions were faring.

'But for how long?' Libellius hissed. 'I took many this day. You cannot hope to defeat them all.'

Behind them the bodies were beginning to mount up around the group. There was little skill required. The quai lacked the imagination to press home the attack or to use any but the most basic cuts and blows, and it was simple butcher's work, lopping off hands and arms, heads, hacking at spines, cutting open veins, lopping off legs. The quai, because they were newly dead, bled and the air stank of blood and offal. The battle was conducted in an eerie silence; there were none of the shouts or cries that had accompanied every conflict since the First Age of Man. The quai were unable to speak and the small group too desperate to even try, but what was even more terrifying was that they were butchering warriors whom they had considered companions, some of whom they had broken their fast with that very morning.

'It is time,' Libellius said softly, looking at Paedur.

'Time?'

'Time to die!'

Death lunged at Paedur with his sword of red fire. The bard threw himself to one side, but the blade sliced through his cloak, searing it, doing what no mortal weapon had been able to do. The bard dropped to the ground and rolled across and to the right of Libellius, hacking out with his hook as he moved past. The metal sank into Libellius' foot, finding something solid, biting deeply, and when the bard rolled to his feet, flames were licking around the wound. Instead of being a skeletal foot, it was now a soft leather shoe encasing an all too human foot. The two images flickered and were briefly superimposed on one another, and then the image of the skeletal foot reaffirmed itself.

'You cannot harm me, bard.'

Paedur cut again, catching the creature low on the arm, just above the wrist, and once again he saw the image of a red-sleeved cloth-covered arm, but this too was only momentary and then it vanished.

There was a sudden cry from behind him and he turned to see that Keshian had gone down, bleeding from a score of wounds, and Kutor had taken his place. Fodla was also bleeding from a bad gash in the thigh and Tien had been slashed across the forehead, the blood seeping into his eyes, blinding him. Even as he watched, the small Shemmat fell back beneath a flurry of blows.

'They cannot hold out much longer,' Libellius hissed, teeth clacking in a grotesque parody of laughter.

Unconsciously Paedur nodded. He knew Death was right this time. There were too many for the small group to stand against, and they were tiring fast. It would end soon. And he was also coming to the realisation that there was no way he could defeat Libellius. Death could not be killed.

'Look, bard, look.' Libellius gestured with his sword, and then the quai who had already fallen, dismembered or disembowelled, rose again to continue the fight, crawling on shattered limbs, dragging themselves on the stumps of arms over their fallen companions to fight again. 'They will fight until they have been hacked to pieces. The battle is ended. You have lost.'

Paedur shook his head, 'No . . . no . . . *NOOOOooooo!*'

His terrifying scream stopped the battle. Even the quai looked towards the source of the eerie sound. Time wound down and the bard moved towards the red-clad figure of Death with infinite slowness. Libellius brought around his flame blade – and the bard plunged on to it. It erupted from his back, still flaming, but the bard's rush carried him down the blade on to Libellius. His left arm rose and his hook found the god's throat, pressed, sliced through bone, almost – but not quite – decapitating it. Locked together the bodies fell, but before they hit the ground, the bard was holding a small, stout, red-clad man in his arm. When they struck the ground, they simply vanished. And the quai fell to the earth, unmoving, truly dead now . . .

Churon, the Death God, dusted off his hands and watched the figure in black appear on the grey, gritty ground. The man stood up and limped towards the Lord of the Dead. 'I thought I had brought you a present,' he whispered.

'He has gone to his own place of the dead. It is something of a curiosity, Death as a member of his own kingdom rather than a ruler.'

'And what of me?'
'You are dead, bard.'
'I have been dead before.'
'And will be again, I promise you.'

# Epilogue

They rode in triumph into the capital and the people lined the streets to hail Kutor, Emperor of the Seven Nations, and his companions, Keshian, his commander, Owen, the Weapon Master, Tien tZo, a Shemmat, Katani, a warrior of the fabled Katan, and Fodla, whom they all knew.

The remnants of their army rode behind them, surprisingly silent for a conquering army, still shocked by what they had witnessed, numb at the loss of so many friends to a foe they couldn't even fight.

Geillard had fled, gone with three trusted guards and as much coin as they could carry. Rumour placed him travelling into the north.

The palace was thrown open for Kutor – there were no attempts at defiance – and he walked the marbled halls in silence, completely numb now that it was actually his, never believing, not even as he rode towards the open city gates, that the seed planted by the bard would flower. His breathing was quick and shallow, and he was almost afraid that he might wake up. But it was no dream, he knew; his wounds and aching muscles reminded him of that.

Fodla and Owen were waiting for him when he reached the throne room. They had gone ahead to ensure there were no traps or assassins lurking in the corridors, while Keshian, Tien and Katani had accompanied him. The huge doors were closed but not locked, and the two warriors put their shoulders to the polished metal and glowing wood to move them. They swung silently inwards. Fodla and Owen stepped inside, weapons drawn, but the room seemed empty, their footsteps echoing in the vastness of the chamber. Geillard had left in such haste that nothing had been disturbed, its treasures untouched.

Kutor walked into the centre of the room, standing in the

pool of coloured light that streamed in through the domed glass roof. The light washed the fatigue from his face, making him seem younger, taller, more of a king, less of a man.

'Was it worth it?' Keshian asked, his voice weak, bitter, his wounds troubling him.

'I'm not sure. Ask me later.'

'You will need to move quickly to consolidate your forces,' Owen reminded him.

'I know.'

'And the people will need to see you,' Fodla said.

Kutor nodded.

'And the dead must be buried,' Katani added softly.

'Yes,' Kutor said, 'that first. We will honour our dead.' The group moved in around him. 'All those who died will be laid to rest with full honours, and then their bodies will be burnt – I don't want the risk of them re-animating as quai again.' He stopped and looked at each in turn. 'And there will be a separate ceremony for the bard, something special – he gave us all this . . .'

'Honour the dead,' Paedur said coldly, stepping out from behind a pillar, 'and leave the living in peace. See to your kingdom, Emperor Kutor. There is much yet to be done!'